EX NIHILO

LEARNING TO LIVE AGAIN

ANA WATERS

To my darling girls who have already made me a grandmother to their babydolls. Yes, I promise to babysit so you can go on dates with your husbands.

For Rhoda. My Bubbe. Matriarch. Friggin Rock Star. Thank you.

"Forget the former things; do not dwell on the past. See, I am doing a new thing! Now it springs up; do you not perceive it? I am making a way in the wilderness and streams in the wasteland."

— ISAIAH 43:19-20 NIV

CONTACT THE AUTHOR

FOR NEW RELEASES, SPECIAL PROMOTIONS AND ANNOUNCEMENTS:

Facebook @ AnaWatersAuthor
Instagram @ anawatersbooks
anawatersauthor@yahoo.com

CHAPTER 1

My comatose heart first showed signs of awakening one warm, March evening. After a particularly hideous day of work at Culver Incorporated, I went downstairs to order a to-go dinner from Chick-A-Yum. Exhausted, I plopped the bag on a table outside of the restaurant and myself in a chair. I knew my job meant filling the legendary shoes of Rebecca Margolin, but I never expected the role to completely change my life.

"Another day, another dinner alone outside of the office," I muttered. "How many more months before they finally hire someone to replace Eric? I'm too young to feel this old."

A burst of noise caught my attention as a group of heavily made up, party girls sauntered by. Once the sun dipped below the horizon in Parkview, our uptown office location transformed from a bustling workplace into an evening hotspot. Peeling off from behind the crowd, an inebriated woman stumbled toward the front entry of the fast food chain I had just vacated. Her exasperated boyfriend trailed behind her.

"Why are we even here?" she whined, groping for the door handle. Her marked resemblance to my former coworker, Rebecca Margolin, left me stunned. Although Rebecca and I worked together at Culver for just a short time, a friendship had bloomed due to shared suffering and faith in Jesus. Trying to make sense of the situation, I realized I would never see Mrs. Margolin publicly intoxicated let alone with a man other than her husband.

The woman's boyfriend seemed familiar, but I couldn't quite place him. Our eyes met and his narrowed, confirming my sense of déjà vu. Unsettled by my reaction to his intense blue gaze, I quickly averted my attention back to my plastic dinner container.

"Do I know you?" I heard him say, suddenly standing above me.

I gulped before responding. A litany of food allergies meant I had to choke down a dry salad. I took a sip of water before meeting those powder blue eyes again.

He lowered his voice and asked, "We haven't dated or anything, have we?"

Eyes wide, I turned my attention to his inebriated lady friend. We both watched as she finally managed to open the restaurant door and step inside. Mincing toward the order counter in sky-high heels, she attempted some sort of seductive walk. Instead, she careened into a garbage can and upended several dirty trays sitting on top of it. I shook my head in disgust and looked away.

"So, have we dated?" he asked again.

Stunned at his coldness toward his girlfriend, I responded with equal ice in my tone. "I wouldn't let you touch me with a ten-foot pole."

I expected the familiar stranger to take offense at my impertinence. Instead, he smiled. Dozens of overheard conversations from my coworkers, Deondre, MacKenzie, and Lexie finally clicked into place. Bearded, blue-eyed, mystery man no longer remained a mystery.

Armed with far too much personal information to find him attractive, I managed to defy the odds anyway. My open Bible on the table caught his attention, and I watched him read the page before sharply returning his gaze to me.

"I *know* I've met you somewhere," he said, his eyes searching my face.

I shrugged and raised my eyebrows in innocence. If I didn't open my mouth, I wouldn't have to lie.

Blue Eyes lifted a dark eyebrow in return, determined to discover my identity. Unfortunately for Kyle Goldstein, I found nothing attractive about cheating boyfriends, especially after my one and only failed relationship. Moreover, if even half of MacKenzie's tales about Kyle held true, I'd be better served hiding the source of our mutual acquaintance.

"Five minutes for fresh chicken fingers," Rebecca-clone announced from the door with a giggle, "but I can't open the sauce packet. Stupid sauce!" She let the door slam shut as she staggered back inside.

"Seems like she's had enough sauce already," I muttered.

Kyle surprised me with humor in his eyes and a triumphant gleam.

"Taylor," he said, emphasizing my name, "how is everyone at Culver these days? I'm sure they keep you buried and over-worked in the marketing department."

I responded with an artificial smile. "We've had some turnover lately, but nothing I can't handle. Our top producer and his wife just had a baby, so as you can imagine, we've had lots to celebrate."

I watched to see how my news landed, but Kyle's expression remained smug. "Turnover, hmm? Is that why you have a bowl of rabbit food for dinner at nine o'clock at night?"

I took a large bite of my salad. "Mm, well that's just divine!" I said with panache. "Utterly delicious." I wiped the side of my mouth with regal dignity.

The smile on Kyle's face grew until it reached his eyes. "There's some pretty good-looking shrubbery in the planters behind you if that salad doesn't do it for you."

I glared at him.

"So, how are things *really* going at Culver?" he asked.

I ignored him and stabbed at my salad so I wouldn't stab at Kyle instead.

Amused, he kept pushing. "I heard Phil fired the snowflake they hired when they replaced Rebecca. How long have you been handling things on your own?"

"I thought *you* were the expert on replacing Rebecca," I clipped.

"Hit a nerve, Taylor?"

Despite the edge in Kyle's voice, his eyes flicked over me appreciatively. Most men dismissed my petite frame and mousy hair and eyes as too childlike, and the reminder was a cold splash of water to keep my ego in check. This was perverse amusement and nothing more.

"I'm shocked you even know my name, Goldstein. Congratulations."

"Obviously, you remembered mine. I must have made quite an impression on you."

I smirked. "Oh, people still talk about you at Culver."

"Ah," he said, "and you enjoy all of the juicy gossip just like the rest of them, right?"

"You tell me," I shot back. "How did you know about Eric

getting fired? You left Culver over a year ago. Nobody even called him a snowflake until he got that stupid haircut and a series of unfortunate tattoos."

He grinned. "Like you said, people talk. Curious to hear what they say about you, Taylor?"

I stood up from my chair, not very intimidating as I barely squeaked over five feet tall, but my temper compensated for my lack of stature. "I've put up with a lifetime of manipulators trying to screw with my head, so don't delude yourself into thinking you have an easy win here. If you have something to say, Goldstein, then go ahead and say it. Otherwise, let me enjoy my dinner in peace."

"It's Kyle," he said.

I raised an eyebrow.

"I hate being called Goldstein. I don't work at Culver anymore, and I want nothing to do with that place."

"Yet, you still keep tabs on everything going on in the office. You knew about Rebecca and Ted's baby, and you knew about me working alone in the marketing department. You seem to have at least one foot firmly planted there."

"Like you said, people talk."

"Apparently, they talk to *you*," I said, looking him over with disdain. "Quite a conundrum for the man who claims he wants nothing to do with the place."

Powder blue eyes assessed me again, and I shifted uncomfortably. With his drunk girlfriend pitifully attempting to shove napkins and ketchup packets into her to-go bag, Kyle Goldstein's seeming interest in me turned my stomach. No matter what I thought of the woman teetering on stiletto heels at the restaurant condiment bar, I would never wish the pain of an affair on anyone.

The outside door opened and closed with a decided thud as

Kyle's girlfriend rejoined him. She looped her arm through his possessively.

"Kyle," she whined, "stop talking to the librarian and let's go! I can't get the lid off my coffee."

Kyle inclined his head and offered me a wry smile. Evidently, he found Rebecca-clone equally as cringeworthy, but he turned his attention to her anyway.

"Nice talking to you, Taylor," he said.

I rolled my eyes and sat down. I dared a glance back up once I felt sure they'd departed. Kyle aided his swaying, mess of a girlfriend down the street, and I jerked in surprise at his soothing tones. The enigmatic behavior stirred feelings in me I didn't care to identify.

"Librarian?" I finally said, touching my chin length bob. Rebecca-clone's passing remark cut deep.

Throwing away my trash, I located Clara, my favorite Chick-A-Yum employee. Hers was the familiar face whose work shifts often coincided with the nights I just didn't want to make another bowl of gluten free pasta.

"Clara, can I ask you something?"

"Sure, *mija*."

"Do I look like a librarian?"

"No," she said in heavily accented English, "you look like the girl from the cartoon doggy show. The one always losing her glasses when they solve mysteries. *Scoopy Dog*, right?"

Disheartened to hear I gave off the bookworm, nerd vibe even to people who actually liked me, I mumbled out a "thank you" and excused myself.

I trudged my way back to the parking deck lost in thought and not expecting to encounter Kyle Goldstein a second time in one night.

"Heading home?" he said, coming along beside me.

"Are you stalking me?"

"No. Well, maybe."

"Where's your Rebecca-clone?" I said with saccharine sweetness.

Kyle's face pinched, clearly not enjoying the reference. "Sent her home. The vomiting usually commences in a few hours, and I didn't feel like hanging around for that."

"Nice."

"You don't like me," he said, brushing past me to blockade any forward progress.

I glared at him. "Very perceptive. Now, why don't you leave me alone?"

Kyle held my gaze, and I silently cursed my weakness for blue eyes. Smirking, he said, "Don't pretend you didn't enjoy our little banter outside of the restaurant."

"I don't flirt with other people's boyfriends," I snapped. "Get out of my way, Goldstein."

"It's Kyle," he said, "and are you planning to beat me up, Taylor? I'd like to see you try."

"What information can I possibly supply for you about Rebecca that you don't already know? She's happy, she's in love, and she's a mother. Are we done here?"

"What did she tell you about me?"

"Why do you care?" I asked, exasperated. "Look, it's been a long day, and all I want to do is go home. I have pepper spray in my purse, and so help me, if you don't move, I will not hesitate to use it."

Though not overly tall by male standards, Kyle still towered over me. "You haven't told me why you don't like me."

I looked up into his eyes, again annoyed with the surge of attraction I felt. I vowed to start another fast from my movie queue of Joan Austin remakes and romantic comedies. Kyle's lazy smile indicated he noticed my reaction to him.

"You're cute, Taylor."

"You're gross, Kyle."

"You don't look at me like you think I'm gross."

"You have nice eyes, okay? Also, you're a selfish pig, at least to hear your former coworkers tell it. I can't believe you're hitting on me after sending your drunk girlfriend home. I want no part in whatever sick game you have going on here."

"Her name is Heather," he said, "and I didn't send her home just to talk to you, so don't flatter yourself."

I pursed my lips and raised an eyebrow. "Not buying a word of it."

"Not that it's any of your business, but Heather and I broke up more than a year ago. I found her completely wasted after happy hour today, and I brought her to Chick-A-Yum to get food and coffee. End of story."

"Things didn't look broken up with the way she hung all over you."

"She could barely walk in those shoes. Of course, she held onto me! Do you believe everything you see, Taylor, or do you bother to ask questions? You seemed smarter than that."

"Don't insult my intelligence by literally *insulting my intelligence*," I fired back.

"I'm not the villain you seem to think I am, no matter what rumors you've heard," he said.

My eyes glanced over the vacated parking garage and Kyle's annoying presence still in it. "Like I said, don't insult my intelligence."

"You don't believe me?" he asked.

I held his gaze, no longer shaken or ashamed by my initial

attraction to him. Confessing it somehow made it easier to overcome. "Not a word."

Kyle said, "MacKenzie Pascale is a gossip and loves inventing Lifeline movie drama. Whatever she doesn't embellish, she'll flat out lie about. Sometimes, she provides useful information, but mostly you learn to take it with a grain of salt." He handed me a business card. "Call me sometime if you ever want to find out the truth."

"And what about the things Rebecca's told me?" I asked, unable to help myself.

CHAPTER 2

KYLE TOOK A STEP TOWARD ME, HIS EYES HOLDING mine captive. "And what exactly did Mrs. Margolin have to say about me?"

I gulped. If this was me intimidating Kyle into leaving, I was failing miserably. Weary from the battle of wills, weary from the past few months of overtime, I sighed and dropped my shoulders.

"Nevermind," I said, breaking eye contact. "I don't have the time or energy for this. I'm tired, and I want to go home."

"Giving up so easily?" Kyle asked. When his hand came under my chin to lift my face, instinct kicked in. I slapped his hand away with enough force to surprise us both. I didn't appreciate the gesture coming from a stranger any more than I did from the woman who routinely made a habit of grabbing my face to get her point across.

I glared up at Kyle, seeing *her* face, rather than his. "Leave me alone," I growled.

Eyes wide, he said, "You're different."

"Excuse me?"

"No offense, but I thought I'd have you eating out of the palm of my hand. All alone with salad for dinner? You looked like you'd gone a while without some male attention."

I scoffed. "And you thought I'd enjoy some from you, is that it?"

"You haven't pepper sprayed me yet."

"Don't tempt me."

Kyle's smile widened into a full-fledged grin. "You're definitely different."

"I believe the words you're looking for are *not desperate*," I retorted.

His blue eyes twinkled mischievously. "Why is my business card in your purse?"

"Because I might need to blow my nose later, and I'm fresh out of tissues."

Kyle laughed. "It makes sense why they hired you. Are you responsible for Joe Trautweig's RFP for Tricity Corp? Rebecca's been gone from Culver too long, and there's no way Trautweig writes that well."

"How did you know about it?" I said, too surprised to deny the truth.

"Heather works for Tricity."

"As what? Entertainment?"

Regrettably, Kyle wasn't wrong about my need for attention. It seemed like centuries since I had last picked up my verbal sword and participated in a genuine duel. Though I'd been asked out on dates over the years, most notably by Ian Horner in the AV booth at church, none of them had piqued my interest or my intellect quite like Kyle Goldstein.

"Go out with me," he said, blue eyes searching my face. "You know you want to."

"Go to church with me," I heard myself reply, "You know you need to."

"Done. Where will I be dragging myself Sunday morning while I think about plans for Sunday night?"

"You're disgusting."

"No, I'm not," he said, "or you wouldn't have offered."

"I didn't offer what you're insinuating," I spat.

Kyle rolled his eyes. "Don't you go on dates at night, Taylor? Or maybe you're the one who had something else in mind."

"Don't flatter yourself."

"Aren't you the one who said I had 'nice eyes'?" he asked with a note of teasing.

"Yes, and I'm regretting it more and more by the second."

"If you weren't interested, you wouldn't be standing here flirting with me. You're not fooling anyone other than yourself, Taylor."

Annoyed, I said, "Chalk it up to a long day. One you're making even longer." I pulled my keychain from my purse, pepper spray very clearly attached to the key ring. "Consider the date rescinded. We're done talking, Kyle."

"I'm sure I'll see you around."

"Let's hope not."

"Ever been kissed in a parking garage?" He eyed my mouth with an intensity that indicated more than just a flirtatious bluff.

Whenever Rebecca described Kyle, she had always mentioned how he hid behind hideously large glasses. Lucky for me, someone must have told him to start wearing contact lenses instead. It made my pepper spray infinitely more effective. With the string of profanity unleashed at my non-idle threat, I had a feeling old Blue Eyes might reconsider his quest to turn me into Rebecca's replacement. I had enough of that to deal with at Culver.

I shared the story with my younger brother, Gabriel, the following Sunday morning when he offered to drive me to church.

"What a creep!" he said, weaving in and out of traffic. "Did you just leave him there in the parking garage?"

"No, I found one of the security guards to let them know what happened. I assumed Leonard took care of it from there."

"It's nice to see my feisty sister back. Does this mean you'll go out with Ian Horner now?"

"How did we get from Kyle to Ian?" I asked incredulously.

"Taylor, you haven't flirted with anyone since you and Mitch broke up. Maybe God's giving you a sign."

"What does this have to do with the AV guy at church?"

"Look, I'm sure Ian probably owns every *Cyclone Shark* movie ever made, but at least it gets you back in the game. You need the practice, Taylor, and at least it's a free meal, right?"

I rolled my eyes. "That sounds all well and good for *me*, Gabe, but it hardly seems fair to Ian. I have zero interest, and it already makes me uncomfortable feeling him watch me at church. I'm there to worship God, not impress anybody in the sound booth."

My brother side-eyed me with a smirk.

"What, Gabe? You don't believe me?"

"Sorry, Sis, but you mention your biological clock every other conversation we have. Unless you plan to adopt or drop by a sperm bank, you're eventually going to need a man to fulfill the dream. At least Ian is a live one."

"Leave it to my baby brother to tell it as bluntly as possible."

"We both get that from Mom."

"Request to change the subject," I said tightly.

Gabe exhaled in disgust as we turned into the church parking lot. "Seriously, Taylor? Are you ever going to move on? You need to let go of all this stuff with Mom."

"Don't start with me," I said, pointing my finger at him. "I don't appreciate the interference no matter how well intended you think it is."

"There are two sides to every story, and you always focus on your own. Maybe you should stop talking to your friend, Rebecca, because you're distorting things to make our family sound like hers. How long was her dad's prison sentence anyway?"

"Not long enough," I deadpanned.

Gabe raised an eyebrow. "What, so now you're going to tell me you know more than the district attorney?"

"Pastor Bernard Ivy pled guilty to nine different crimes for a reason. No matter how many years he sits in prison, nothing short of a miraculous encounter with God will change anything. Rebecca said when they uncovered the will for his elder, Bud Riley, he'd left a thirty-page, notarized confession implicating both of her parents in God only knows what. They officially shut the doors of First United of Hillcrest after a 'Free Pastor Ivy' campaign fizzled outside of the brainwashed, inner circle. So, yeah, I'd say I know what I'm talking about."

"Look, Taylor," Gabe said, assuming the tone of omniscient father figure, "trying to equate the Ivy family with Mom is totally unfair. It wasn't easy for her being a single parent raising two kids. You need to stop judging every little mistake she's made."

I bit my tongue at the Sarah Meyers fantasy version of events now parroted by my brother. I appealed to Gabe's logical side instead. "Has it ever occurred to you that Mom doesn't treat us the same way? That she tells you stuff behind my back to manipulate you into lobbying on her behalf?"

My brother scoffed. "You both say the exact same things about each other, so there's got to be a happy medium somewhere."

"Or," I said before my brother could start another sanctimonious lecture, "one of us is a proven liar, drama queen, and attention seeker. I'm going to go out on a limb here and say it's probably the person with a fourteen-foot mugshot all over the city."

"Mom has those billboards up for business, Taylor. Besides, you helped design them!"

"Terri Dominic sells twice as much real estate as Mom, and she doesn't have an outdated Glamorama Pic plastered along three different interstates."

My brother exhaled a long suffering sigh. "At least you got that job at Culver so you guys aren't constantly at each other's throats anymore at StarRealty. Not that you two don't have enough to fight about already."

"Look, can we just drop it for now? I'd like to actually enjoy church today, and talking about Mom doesn't help."

Gabe frowned but acquiesced. "Maybe you'd rather talk about Ian Horner instead. Should I tell him where to pick you up this Friday?"

I smirked. "Not unless you want to be responsible for disappointing him again. I've lost track of how many times Ian's asked me out or tried talking Bible theology with me. I wish he'd find somebody else."

As it turned out, God had granted my request. I overheard the children's ministry director, Genevieve, talking with Gabe about an upcoming date with Ian. I felt a momentary pang of jealousy then scoffed at my own vanity. When I walked past the sound booth, I offered a genuine smile to Ian. I finally felt safe that the friendly gesture wouldn't be perceived as something more. Through his fluff of overgrown hair, Ian nodded and turned his focus back to the sound board.

As the service began with a lively song, I raised my hands in praise and my voice to harmonize with the worship team. I didn't struggle with the dread of Ian's eyes tracking my every move. I felt completely free...right up until my mother arrived and sat in the back row of our tiny, rented church space.

I had joined Freedom Church two years earlier and shocked my family by attending a congregation led by my former brother-in-law, Brian, and his wife, Chloe. God used Brian to help pick up the pieces when Mitchell Ross lost his mind and ran off with StarRealty's leggy receptionist. My mother claimed she saw the affair coming a mile away and launched a blitzkrieg of passive-aggression at me with relationship blogs like, "Spice up your love life so your man won't cheat."

Conversations regarding boundaries and personal space served no purpose other than raising my blood pressure. As anyone who negotiated a home sale with my mother could attest, you didn't go into an argument with Sarah Meyers expecting to escape unscathed.

"What good did saving your virginity do?" my mother had said with a sneer. "It's obvious you need a little help in that department, Taylor, or you would have kept your husband satisfied. You've looked down your holier-than-thou nose at me for years, but I've never had trouble getting a man. It certainly would have served you better instead of all that 'love is patient' baloney you used to preach at me."

Insulted and infuriated, I said, "If by 'getting a man' you mean sleeping with anything male that walks into the doors of StarRealty, you can save your breath, Mom. I don't see any member of your legion of boyfriends stepping up to pledge a lifetime of love and fidelity."

Her collagen filled lips pursed into a red pout. "Maybe if you weren't such a prude, Taylor Marie, I'd still have my top buyers' agent instead of having to deal with all of Mitch's whiny clients. You have no idea what a toll your divorce took on me."

"Are you kidding?" I gaped. "I can't believe you're standing there acting like my divorce was somehow more painful for *you* than it was for me! Mitch was my husband, Mom, not just some business partner."

"Obviously, I wasn't married to the man—"

"That's right. You weren't," I interrupted, "and this isn't a contest. Even if it was, I'd still win."

Sulking, she glanced down at her perfectly manicured nails. "Mitch skipping town with that little bimbo really screwed me over too, by the way. Not everything has to be all about you right now."

My mouth fell open in disbelief.

She continued, "I was just about to book a cruise when I got stuck trying to pull listings out of an imaginary hat for Mitch's clients. I had to cancel my vacation plans, and the stupid travel agent still sent me a bill anyway! Taylor, you know how much I've always wanted to go to the Bahamas, and Mitch ruined it. Why can't you show me some compassion when I've sat and listened to you complain over and over for the last year?"

I inhaled a taut breath, fiercely clinging to my last shred of self-control. "Are you serious right now?"

"What?" she asked, wide-eyed.

"How on earth did you manage to turn my divorce into some ridiculous pity party for yourself? Am I supposed to feel sorry for you because you missed out on yet another lavish vacation?"

"I'm just trying to get you to see my side," she whined.

The pressure cooker lid on my temper finally exploded. "For once in my entire life, could you *not* make everything all about you?!"

My mother grabbed my chin with her acrylic nailed hand. "How dare you speak to me that way! I'm your mother!"

February 12, 2015 became the last time I ever allowed Sarah Meyers to lay a finger on me. I didn't break her hand when I slapped it off my face, but I easily took out three acrylic nails.

I wished it had been all five.

CHAPTER 3

OVER A YEAR HAD PASSED SINCE THE HAND SLAPPING incident, and my mother looked exactly the same. She sat in my church with sunglasses, heavy makeup, and a large, blonde bouffant hairdo. Surrounded by a room full of young families and jean-clad millennials, my mother easily stood out. Either she'd just finished hosting an open house, or she'd found a way to feed her obsessive need to be the center of attention. Knowing my mother, probably a bit of both.

"Why is she here?" I hissed to my brother.

"You guys need to talk," Gabe whispered back.

"This is why you offered to drive me, isn't it? Because, you know best, don't you, Gabriel Alexander Meyers?"

At the use of his full name, my brother's eyes went wide. "Taylor, don't you think you're being—"

"Ridiculous?" I said loudly enough to disrupt the entire service. "I'll tell you what's ridiculous," I shrilled, pointing directly to the botoxed woman in the back row.

"Taylor," Brian said from the podium microphone. "Not the time or place."

My head snapped to my former brother-in-law and then back at my mother. I felt stifled and strangled, as if "Freedom Church" had suddenly become a prison holding me hostage.

From the corner of my eye, I caught Brian's nod to Chloe in the front row. She rose angrily from her seat, and I shoved past my brother toward the exit. I felt the eyes of the room upon me even with Brian's best efforts to refocus attention back to his sermon. Ian Horner glanced over from the sound booth, and his expression seemed pained. Shrugging off his concern, I stormed through the sanctuary double doors. My Amazonian, former sister-in-law would catch up soon enough.

Steeling myself for the onslaught yet to come, I focused my gaze on the sprawling campus of First Baptist of Parkview. Freedom rented their worship space from the monolithic church, and borrowing the children's chapel from FBP's day school hardly interfered with their stadium-sized crowds. I took a few deep breaths and looked beyond the enormous steeple of the main worship center into the midtown city skyline.

"That couldn't have waited thirty more minutes?" Chloe demanded from behind me.

I turned to face the 5'10" fashion model masquerading as a lowly pastor's wife. "Thanks for the compassion, Chloe. As always."

Her face tightened, neither of us forgetting the worst day of my life. Chloe's grim expression gave way to a self-righteous sneer. "You could at least celebrate your mother hearing the gospel, Taylor. Instead, you threw a public tantrum because she won't meet your silly demands for reconciliation."

"Since when is being treated with respect a 'silly precondi-tion,' Chloe?"

With a long suffering sigh, she said, "You always have to make things so dramatic, Taylor. If you keep sitting on your high horse waiting for people to do things exactly how *you* think they should, you're going to wind up all alone."

"Chloe, I have no idea what you're talking about."

She rolled her eyes. "How about your thirtieth birthday party? You had a complete meltdown because of your mother."

"Wow," I said in disgust. "Why don't you tell me how any sane person would react to being publicly humiliated in a room full of family and friends on their birthday?"

My former sister-in-law pursed her lips.

"Oh, and let's not forget how Sarah Meyers was a single mother, thus making her divorce infinitely more traumatic than mine," I said bitterly. "Why would I want to maintain a relationship with someone who trivializes my pain and suffering because she acts like it's a competition over who's suffered more?"

Chloe flicked her wrist in annoyance. "Taylor, how many times are you going to rehash the same old garbage? We get it already. We got it the first nine hundred times! Stop the 'woe is me' drama and just get on with your life."

Unfazed by Chloe's accusation, I said, "I'm tired of being brushed off by all of you. When do *my* feelings actually start to matter? My brother's constantly on my case to indulge that woman's fragile ego, but she gets a free pass to mock my faith for the last twenty years and counting. I'm sick of the double standard."

I instantly recalled how my relationship with Jesus had created wedges between my mother and me. In the summer before sixth grade, she had pawned me off on a friend's family for a week of Vacation Bible School. It had never occurred to Sarah Meyers that Jesus would change my life at eleven years-old. From then on, I soaked up every youth group sermon about "dating is outdated" and purity rings. Meanwhile, my mother gleefully shook loose the shackles of matrimony to pursue whatever pleasures she had felt entitled to partake.

"Look," Chloe said tersely, "Brian and I have been there for you, and we even let you join Freedom. You've repaid us by telling everyone your sad life story. Taylor, you need to move on from your past and probably from Freedom too. I know this is tough love, but someone has to finally tell you the truth."

Stunned, I inhaled a harsh breath at Chloe's sucker punch.

She continued, "We all hear you belting harmony from the pews, Taylor, and it's just obnoxious. Everyone can see your desperate need for attention. We invited you to sing on the worship team, but you said you were too busy with your job to commit the time."

"That's because I *am* too busy," I argued. "I'm lucky if I get home before seven most nights."

Ignoring me, Chloe said, "You just didn't want to sing back up on stage, so you play lead singer in the pews instead."

Coolly, I replied, "I am not singing for the benefit of anybody other than Jesus."

"You may not want to hear this, Taylor, but you're a lot more like your mother than you realize."

"Excuse me?" I hissed.

Chloe folded her arms across her perfectly draped, tunic blouse. "Sarah sat in the back of the church. You're the one who disrupted the service with your selfish little outburst. I've been telling Brian for two and a half years that you need to stop playing the victim, but he feels guilty because his brother broke your heart. Taylor, you need to stop pushing away the people who want to be a part of your life because you're forcing yourself on people who don't."

Inhaling an angry breath through my nostrils, I entertained the thought of smacking the condescension right off of Chloe's perfectly contoured face. Unfortunately, I knew I would have to repent to Jesus for it later. I also would never be able to reach that high wearing my ballet flats.

I remembered the business card in my purse, that "emergency tissue" I vowed to get rid of days earlier. Feeling both angry and rebellious, I threw caution to the wind and began texting Kyle Goldstein while Chloe slung more accusations.

"Taylor, did you hear what I said?" Chloe demanded. I had a feeling she would have been more than happy to repeat herself had my phone not chimed with a text from Kyle.

Scanning over the message, I chuckled softly. God had provided an unexpected escape, and I intended to take it. Not bothering to dignify Chloe's newest remark with a response, I smirked at her, turned, and walked away. The church doors slammed behind me with a flourish.

The two mile march to *Los Bravos Cantina* allowed me time to work off steam from my confrontation with my former sister-in-law. Rather than indulging in various scenarios of verbally vaporizing Chloe, I instead pondered over Kyle Goldstein's willingness to meet me after I had pepper sprayed him three days earlier.

I spared little concern over the state of my appearance when I finally greeted Kyle, but he looked me up and down in wonder. I could only hope my eyes were brightened by the exercise.

"Did you walk here?" he asked. His eyes rested on my windblown coiffure. "All the way from Five Flags over Jesus?"

I smirked. "I don't actually attend the mega church. I guess I'm no longer a member of the mini church that meets in the kids' chapel either."

"Was the sermon that bad?" Kyle asked, reaching over to pick an errant leaf from my hair.

I stopped short at the tender gesture, strangely affected. I stared up at the man who increasingly became more enigma than stigma.

Not missing a beat, Kyle said, "I'm not a monster, no matter what Mac or anybody else has told you. I have a hard time believing Rebecca even said that. We used to be close, you know."

"She's said as much."

"So, why do I feel like you're judging me based on the opinions of other people?"

"Explain the parking deck."

"You first," he retorted. "As I seem to recall, the night security guard wasn't flushing out your eyes with milk after getting pepper sprayed."

"I assume it worked," I said, picking up my verbal sword again with relish. "Your eyes seem fine, and you look no worse for the wear."

"That's only because you didn't see me crying on the inside," Kyle said with a playful pout.

"I've done a lot worse to men threatening to take advantage of me in parking garages. Consider yourself lucky."

He grinned. "Are you secretly a ninja or something? Because that would be pretty cool if you were."

I winked and let Kyle surmise whatever he wanted.

His laughing blue eyes seared into mine. The current of attraction reminded me of the long drought since I had last felt pretty, witty, or desirable.

Kyle picked up his sword for another verbal sparring round. "Thanks for passing along that tip to Leonard, by the way. It's obvious you're not completely heartless, Taylor, or you would have just left me there to suffer. If there's a silver lining here, it's that I didn't give my contact information to a complete psycho."

"What else was I supposed to do?" I said in my own defense. "You threatened to kiss me, and you wouldn't let me go."

Kyle looked at me for a long minute, my words suddenly taking on new meaning. I didn't think I still had it in me, but I blushed.

"You're even cuter in the daylight," he said.

I raised an eyebrow. "You saw me in the daylight for a week before you left Culver."

"I was, um, a little distracted at the time. I'm not anymore."

"What does that mean?"

"Exactly what I said. I don't know what people have told you about me, but I'm pretty sure there's an old saying about not believing everything you hear."

"Rebecca never said anything unkind about you, Kyle. Other than your old glasses anyway."

"Good to know," he said with a wry smile.

"Look, I know I owe you an apology. Not about the pepper spray—because you earned that—but for the assumption about Heather. I assumed you were still hung up on Rebecca and that you hit on me with your intoxicated female friend just a few feet away. It doesn't excuse your behavior in the parking garage, but I do feel like a jerk for jumping to conclusions. I hope you can forgive me for that, at least, and I appreciate you meeting me here today."

Although I'd be loath to admit it to anyone at Culver, I savored the charming sparkle in Kyle's eyes. After the tongue lashing from Gabe and Chloe, I eagerly welcomed a friendly face and some witty banter.

"What do you say we take the *schmoozing* inside?" Kyle said, opening the door for me.

I followed him into the cantina, already familiar with the restaurant. My favorite server, Carlos, sat us in a small booth.

"The usual, *señorita*?" he asked.

I offered a large grin, not bothering to open the menu.

"You're here with him?" Carlos said, gesturing toward Kyle. "*¿Es tu novio?*"

I blushed at the idea of anybody being my boyfriend...in Spanish or in English.

"*Solo somos amigos,*" Kyle interrupted before placing his entire order in perfect Spanish.

With a wink and a cheeky grin, Carlos turned to Kyle and said, "*Si no son novios, deberían ser.* Make it a good date for her, okay?"

Kyle responded with a large smile for me. "I guess we'll see. Right, Taylor?"

"Family or study abroad?" I asked once Carlos disappeared into the kitchen.

Kyle took a scoop of salsa with his chip before answering. "What do you mean?"

"Most Americans don't speak Spanish that well without being Hispanic themselves or having some kind of cultural immersion experience. All the Spanish I learned in high school consisted of some girl named Maria locating books in the library. Carlos teaches me little bits of conversational Spanish when I come in."

Kyle laughed. "I did a semester abroad at Oxford, but my grandmother was Argentinian. That's where the semi decent accent comes from. If you've never had a four and a half foot woman yell, '¡*Sinvergüenza che!*' at you, I'm not sure you've lived at all."

I barely recognized the tinkling little giggle I emitted. Had I ever made a sound like that even when dating Mitchell Ross in college? Before I could censor myself, I blurted out, "Is this how you impress women? You bust out the romance language card, and they swoon at the sound of your non-American accent?"

"Heather doesn't speak Spanish."

"She could barely master English."

Kyle gave me a tolerant smile. "She was drunk, okay? You act like you've never made a mistake in your life."

My mirth immediately died. The old wound still bled, and Kyle's remark hit far too close to home.

I swallowed back the tears stinging my eyes. "What was I thinking? It was a mistake meeting up with you. I'll never live it down at work if they find out."

CHAPTER 4

I STOOD UP TO LEAVE, BUT KYLE PLACED HIS HAND over mine. "I have a medical condition."

I glanced down at his hand hoping it didn't transmit via skin to skin contact. I looked back up at him in revulsion.

"Ever heard of foot in mouth disease?" he asked.

"Do you mean *hand*, foot, and mouth disease, like what kids get from school?"

"No, I mean the kind where someone has a knack for saying the wrong thing at the wrong time. Metaphorical foot in mouth."

"Oh."

"We got off to a really bad start, Taylor. Can we hit the refresh button and try again? No history, no friends in common, just two people who met outside of a Chick-A-Yum one night and wound up eating Mexican food together in Parkview."

I sat back down wanting to get to brass tacks. "What expectations do you have here, Kyle? We can't escape the fact we have you-know-who in common, and she and I share very similar religious beliefs."

"So I gathered when I saw you reading one of her favorite Bible passages."

That surprised me. "Is that why you looked like you saw a ghost the other day?"

Kyle nodded. "It took me a second, but then I remembered how I knew you. And I agree, this would definitely be less awkward without *her* in the middle. Then again," he said with a smile, "I might not have met you otherwise."

"You're laying on the charm pretty thick there, pal."

Guileless blue eyes met mine. "You think this is all for show? That there's no possible way I might be interested in you outside of your connection to Rebecca?"

I wore my skepticism on my face. "For the sake of argument, let's assume I'm not some convenient distraction to help mend your broken heart. I'm acquainted enough with the Jewish stance on Jesus to take any of this seriously."

"First of all," he said, finishing up another tortilla chip, "the state of my heart is just fine—not that it's any of your business. I moved on a while ago. Dating Heather was pretty desperate and stupid, but seeing what happened to my sister was enough of a wakeup call."

"Your sister?" I asked.

"I'm sure Rebecca has mentioned my twin sister, Jessica."

"Only that they're not as close as they used to be. She didn't say why, just that Jessica broke off an engagement about the same time Rebecca got married. It seemed to cause distance in their friendship."

Kyle met my gaze full on, and I could look nowhere else. "My sister had her heart broken by this self-righteous, fake-Jew pervert who went out and married the first girl he could trick into covering up his porn addiction. My family lost a small fortune on nonrefundable deposits for the wedding. The final blow was Jessica's old fiancé getting help for his issues even though he refused to do that for my sister. It sent Jessica down the self-destructive spiral she's on right now. I think the new wife is barely out of college."

"That's awful, I'm so sorry."

Kyle exhaled a weary sigh. "Jessica's dating some married guy at her office like she's trying to get back at all cheaters by being one herself. It gave me a real hard look at what I did to Heather by leading her on."

"Is that why you found her drunk? Trying to get over you?"

Kyle let out a mirthless laugh. "No, public intoxication is an unfortunate habit of Heather's, and thankfully, now part of my past. My sister and I have both made some pretty dumb decisions because of alcohol, and it seemed time to stop pretending like I'm still twenty-one. I saw some college kid with the same pair of glasses I used to wear, and I realized I looked like an idiot."

I laughed. "Rebecca's mentioned those plastic frames a time or two."

"You mean that I looked like the 'before' picture of a nerd makeover?"

I didn't expect to laugh so hard. I also didn't expect water to come shooting out of my nose. Kyle laughed while helping me clean up. I didn't expect that to happen either.

"So what's your story?" he said, already halfway through our bowl of chips. "Are you one of those girls who thinks men find it attractive when you eat two bites of food and then pretend you're full?"

"Food allergies," I replied after swallowing a sip of water. "I get horrible eczema and fatigue if I eat certain foods. Avoiding them helps with inflammation in general."

"Inflammation? How old are you, sixty-five? I figured you're in your mid-twenties."

"According to Heather, I should be inhaling library dust and telling young hooligans to shush."

"You dress like an old lady, but since that seems to be the new fad, I thought I'd guess younger than older."

"Thanks," I said dryly, "because my self-esteem didn't take enough of a blow today at church. I don't think old ladies wear jeans and cardigans to church."

"I believe your sensible work pants and blouse did that for you the other day."

"And yet you still hit on me. Do you have some sort of librarian fetish?"

Kyle's grin turned my stomach into a mess of girlish knots. I couldn't remember having this much fun since the early days of my relationship with Mitch. My thoughts soured as I wondered how my ex-husband transformed from charming Christian into narcissistic adulterer.

"You do have more in common with Rebecca than I thought," Kyle said, studying me.

I swatted the light brown fringe at my forehead self-consciously. "What do you mean?"

"She used to do that too."

"Do what?"

"Get lost in thought, sort of drift out of one reality into another. You're not related to the psycho Ivy family too, are you?"

"No, I've got my own psychos to deal with."

"Like ones from the church?" Kyle asked.

I took another sip of water. "No, my ex-husband, my larger

than life mother, and my enabling little brother. I think that's enough for me."

Kyle took a few seconds to process all of the information. "Ex-husband? You barely look old enough to be married. How long were you guys together?"

"We dated for a year, were engaged for another, and technically married for six. Officially, we've been divorced for three years."

I watched Kyle mentally trying to figure out the math.

"I'll be thirty-two in August," I said, wondering how he would react to the news.

Kyle grinned. "Does that mean I can reference movies from the late eighties and early nineties and you won't look at me like I've sprouted a second head?"

"I suppose there's definitely an advantage to hanging around people your own age. Less drinking, more talking," I said with a pointed look.

"*Touché*," he said good naturedly. "I don't remember the last time I had this much fun on a date."

"Is that what this is?"

"*Sí*, the whole kitchen is watching you two like a ping pong match," Carlos said, apparently overhearing far too much and placing our entrees before us.

Kyle glanced at my plate. "So your 'usual' is a fajita without any of the fun? How do you enjoy it without a tortilla, cheese, or sour cream?"

"What about you? Are you expecting, or do you normally eat enough for two?"

Kyle's eyes lingered on my face for a moment. "She answers a question by asking her own question. Do you and Rebecca share hidden Jewish parents as well?"

The smile faded from my face.

And subsequently Kyle's.

"Long story," I finally said, "and not one suitable for a first date. Or whatever this is."

Kyle nodded in understanding. "Are you going to do the whole thanks to God for the food thing?"

The side of my mouth lifted. "Care to join me?"

"Not really, but I'll enjoy watching you."

Chuckling, I closed my eyes and prayed silently. I thanked God for the blessing of allergen free food, and I asked for His blessing on our conversation. I also asked Him to guard my heart and help me make sense of why I felt so comfortable with a man whose reputation screamed nothing but trouble.

"Are you and Jesus discussing the meaning of life, or can I start eating?" Kyle deadpanned.

I cracked open one eye and startled, my attraction to Kyle stronger than I cared to admit. When he grinned at me, my returned smile came of its own accord. I certainly didn't subscribe to the world's notion of every relationship needing some sort of "spark" to ever stand a chance, but none of Ian Horner's attempts to woo me with pious sounding homilies had ever caused this kind of a reaction. Going toe-to-toe with Kyle Goldstein about my parking deck ninja skills kindled something in me that had fallen dormant during the halfway point of my marriage.

"So, how are things at Cooper & Jaye?" I asked. I enjoyed a bite of charred onion and steak while awaiting his answer.

Kyle shrugged. "Fine, I guess. At least it's not the gossip fest Culver likes to pretend it isn't."

I sighed. "I won't argue with you there. Phil and Miss Belle do their best to discourage it, at least."

"Miss Belle," Kyle said with a sarcastic laugh. "How is the old battle axe?"

"Battle axe?" I repeated. "I don't think I'd go that far."

"She didn't do me any favors in the romance department, that's for sure."

"Ah," I said.

Kyle stopped, fork in midair. "You think I'm talking about Rebecca again, don't you?"

"You weren't?"

"No, actually. Believe it or not, my world does not revolve around Rebecca Ivy." He held up a hand before I could correct him. "Still getting used to it, but believe me, I've moved on."

"Fine, I'll bite. How did Miss Belle mess up your love life?"

"I dated the receptionist at Culver," he said.

Immediately, my hand balled around my napkin into a fist.

"Things were going great, and I was totally cool with her being a single mother."

I met Kyle's eyes to make sure I'd heard that correctly.

"You okay?" he asked, glancing down at the mangled napkin in my hand.

"I, um, don't have good associations with the words *romance* and *receptionist*," I said.

Kyle raised an eyebrow at my cryptic response but pressed onward. "I really thought I might be falling for Morgan, but Miss Belle encouraged her to get back together with her ex. I guess he wanted to work things out because of their son, and hey, Miss Belle knows what's best for everyone, right?"

"Were you planning on marrying Morgan and becoming a stepfather?"

Kyle looked appalled. "No, why?"

"I'm trying to understand why you'd be upset that your ex-girlfriend wants to give her child a loving home with two parents, especially with his biological father. Obviously, you weren't willing to step up to the plate."

"Hey, just a second there! We only dated for three months. It was way too soon to talk about 'til death do us part.'"

"Kyle! She was a single mother. Didn't it occur to you she was a package deal? That she wanted a potential father for her son as well?"

"You really do remind me of her. It's starting to scare me a little bit, actually."

"Her who? Morgan?"

"Rebecca."

"You know what," I said, pushing away my half eaten plate of food, "I am my own person, and I wish people would stop comparing me to her."

"Who else is comparing you to Rebecca?"

"Everybody!" I said, throwing my hands up in the air. "Every stupid document I design at Culver they compare to Rebecca's. If we get some new branding guidelines from corporate, I get push back like, 'Well, that's not how Rebecca did it.' Look, I think she's an incredible woman, but she's not a freaking saint, she's not perfect, and I'm tired of being in her shadow. I'm never going to live up to the expectation. All I can be is myself, and I'm tired of that not being good enough for people."

Cautiously, Kyle asked, "Can I explain what I meant, or do you still think I agreed to meet with you to get my Rebecca fix for the day?"

"Surprise me."

"Rebecca and I went to visit some crazy, Messianic synagogue a while ago. My sister's ex is a member there, and I dragged Rebecca with me because I wanted to make sure the place wasn't a cult. I figured she'd know better than anybody what one looks like."

"True," I said.

"So after all of that *mishigas*, we went out to eat, and she and

I had almost the exact same conversation about Morgan. Rebecca asked about my intentions, was I ready to be a father, and so on. That's all I meant by my comment, Taylor. You and Rebecca say a lot of the same things, probably because you're both Christians, but I definitely don't see you as her clone."

"Is that so?"

"Physical differences aside, you have a lot more fire. Rebecca was so beat down and depressed because of her family. After Jason abandoned her, she walked around like a zombie for years. I don't know the story with you and your ex-husband, but I have a feeling you'd be the type to light his clothes on fire while belting out a country song."

The dark cloud lifted, and I laughed until tears streamed down my cheeks.

Kyle's expression held awe and amusement. "I'm right, aren't I?"

Finally gaining control of myself, I replied, "About the country song, no. About the clothes, you better believe it."

CHAPTER 5

BEING A FIRST DATE OF SORTS, I DIDN'T GO INTO great detail regarding the rise and fall of my marriage. No matter Chloe's accusations that I deliberately looked for sob story sympathizers, there were many things better left unsaid. Our lunch date grew into a dinner date, and Kyle single handedly consumed three baskets of chips, his combo plate, and another two tacos.

"You know your metabolism will finally catch up with you one day, right?"

Kyle shrugged. "Guess I'll have to enjoy it while it lasts then, won't I?"

I smiled, taking a second to enjoy that blue gaze again. "I, um, really didn't think today would end up quite like it did."

"The part where you finally got free of your praying mantis, former sister-in-law, or the part where you spent the day staring dreamily into my eyes and wishing you had kissed me instead of pepper spraying me in the garage?"

"Staring dreamily? You wish."

Kyle's mischievous grin said otherwise.

"How much of this bravado is actually Kyle the person, and how much is Kyle the womanizer?"

"Womanizer?" he choked.

"Come on, Kyle. Santa's list of naughty girls is probably shorter than yours."

He had the decency to look embarrassed. "Well played," he said, saluting me with a beer he'd ordered thirty minutes prior. "Sure you don't want something?"

"I thought you said you weren't drinking alcohol anymore."

"I said I wasn't getting falling down drunk anymore. Are you one of those teetotalers who thinks that alcohol is the devil?"

"Considering my mother is a borderline alcoholic, I probably should. Unfortunately, I have issues with gluten, yeast, sugar, and sulfites, so that doesn't leave me a lot of options in terms of fermented beverages. I guess kombucha would fall into that category, but I don't think that's what you were talking about."

Kyle's expression of abject horror made me laugh.

"You're looking at me like I'm some kind of a freak," I said.

Recovering quickly, he said, "So, do you need an epi-pen or something? Does it bother you that I'm drinking in front of you?"

"It bothers me that I'm going to have to ask you for a ride home eventually, and I want to be sure you're totally sober."

"What do you mean you need a ride home? Why didn't that come up in the past five hours we've been sitting here?"

"I guess I was too busy staring dreamily into your perfect blue eyes," I retorted, sticking out my tongue.

"Wow, so now they're dreamy *and* perfect too? I must be doing something right."

"As long as I don't have to go crawling back to my brother

for a ride home, I'll supply you with whatever adjective you'd like."

Kyle laughed then exhaled a contented sigh. "It's been a long time since a woman actually kept me on my toes. I'm not sure why I agreed to meet up with you, Taylor, but I'm glad I did."

"Perhaps my text message saying, 'Life sized praying mantis attacked me at church,' piqued your interest."

"No, I'm pretty sure it was just you."

My blush came naturally. Rebecca had not exaggerated Kyle's wooing skills. How he failed to effectively use them on her remained a mystery.

"What do you say we get out of here?" Kyle asked. "Your buddy, Carlos, has been eyeing this table, and my rear end has been numb for an hour."

"How about a walk?"

"Didn't you get enough of that on your trek over here? Is your next stop to Middle Earth to get rid of a ring?"

It felt so good to laugh and to do it with my entire body. I couldn't remember the last time my cheeks actually hurt from laughing and smiling so much. Glancing down to cool my blush, I rose from the table to gain some distance from Kyle and the feelings he stirred in me. He stood up a moment later and laid down an extra twenty dollar tip for Carlos. My favorite server had bussed our table the entire time and worked hard to keep our tortilla basket truly bottomless.

"That was nice," I said, noting the bill stuck under Kyle's beer bottle.

He smiled down at me. "Carlos is a good guy. I'm probably in here at least once a week anyway."

I smiled back and followed Kyle toward the exit. I ducked under his arm as he opened the door to the busy sidewalk outside.

"I'm not much of a cook," he said, falling in stride next to me. "I'd probably save a small fortune if I actually learned."

I nodded. "I'm decent, I guess, but probably not much you'd enjoy eating."

Kyle grimaced. "So, tell me again what you can't eat."

"Dairy, shellfish, gluten, corn, sugar, yeast, nuts, and any kind of food additives, preservatives, or dyes."

Kyle whistled. "If I buy you a piece of cardboard, are you good for a month? No wonder you're so tiny."

I slapped his arm playfully. "Believe me, I eat. I just can't eat junk, no matter how much I want to sometimes. I used to be a sour gummy addict."

"Seriously?" Kyle said, walking me back to the parking deck of infamy.

"Absolutely true," I said. I turned and waved hello to Leonard in the security booth.

"Looks like you two worked things out," Leonard said with a knowing smile.

"She forgave me," Kyle replied. He pulled me tight against him and planted a kiss on the top of my head.

I smiled uneasily, but not because I found Kyle's touch unwelcome.

Quite the contrary.

We walked up the winding ramp to the first tier of parking spaces, and Kyle stopped in front of a black sedan.

"Nice," I said. "Leather seats, sunroof..." I continued cataloguing the features as I saw them.

Kyle looked amused. "Do you sell cars on the side or something? I've never seen anyone do that."

"I worked in real estate marketing for eight years before I took the job at Culver. It's almost impossible for me to walk into a house without immediately making a list of feature bullets in my head."

"Such as?"

Thinking of my own home, I said, "Soaring, two-story entry way with cherry hardwood floors. Beveled, glass front door flanked by transom windows."

Kyle motioned for me to keep going, clearly enjoying himself.

"Light and bright kitchen with white cabinets, stainless steel appliances, and gorgeous granite counters."

"And you just come up with all of this stuff on the fly?" he asked, pushing a button on his fob to open the car.

I leaned in to pull my door handle, but Kyle's hand rested on mine. I twisted to look up at him, nervous energy pulsating as I stared in his eyes.

"You should let me do that," he said softly.

I turned my face away before I practically begged Kyle to kiss me. The shame of that realization cooled the longing in my gut. I slipped my hand out from under his as he pulled the door open. Kyle gestured for me to sit inside, and I offered a tight smile of thanks and slid into my seat. Kyle closed the door and walked to the driver's side.

Once he sat down, he shut the door but left his keys sitting on his lap. "Taylor, do you find the thought of me touching you revolting, or is it the stories you've been fed by other people?"

I jerked back in surprise. "Why do you think I find you revolting?"

"Well, you did pepper spray me."

"I did."

"And just now. I mean, obviously you've been married, but you act like you've never been touched."

Embarrassed, I looked away. "You're not totally wrong, Kyle, as far as me being inexperienced. Mitch was my first boyfriend and the only man I've ever been with."

"But you've been out since you got divorced, right?"

"Maybe less than you think."

"I see," he said slowly. He put the keys into the ignition and started the car.

"You're my first date since the divorce, Kyle."

Arresting blue eyes found mine, searching for any hint of a lie.

"Me?" he said, stunned. "The first man you've been on a date with since your divorce is me? Womanizing, disgusting, still hung up on a married woman, Culver pariah, me?"

I winced as he listed off every way I'd misjudged him. Kyle was right that I had turned him into a villain without actually knowing him. Though part of me wondered if he simply wanted to get my guard down, I saw nothing but sincerity on his face. Opting for the straightforward approach, I simply said, "Yes."

As he held my eyes with his, I both feared and secretly hoped Kyle might take advantage of the opportunity to right the wrong done against him in that very same parking garage. Instead, he surprised me by nodding and asking me to guide him to my home.

I lived just outside of the city, technically the suburbs, but only by about a half a mile. Mitch and I had sold our massive, suburban home and split the proceeds to pay for our divorce. It ensured we'd never have to see one another again. I reinvested my money into a cute enclave of brick row houses that reminded me of a school trip to Philadelphia. With a realtor for a mother, I knew the hidden pitfalls of purchasing new construction, but there was still something cathartic in watching my future home start as nothing more than a lump of dirt. It seemed like the perfect metaphor for my life after the divorce.

Not comfortable giving Kyle my punch code for the gate entry box, I hopped out of the car to tap in the five digits and stood aside as he pulled his car through the receding gate. I trailed shortly behind, letting myself back in the car once he stopped.

"Thank you for understanding," I said, buckling my seatbelt.

"First man to see your house too?"

"Other than family, that would be correct. My house is the end unit over on the left. There's an extra spot you can use without angering Mrs. Wolitsky."

"Ah, and why would we want to avoid the wrath of Mrs. Wolitsky?"

"Because she's a busybody and enjoys playing HOA police. I think she gets a thrill from turning people in. Maybe too many spy movies, I don't know."

Kyle turned and smiled at me for the first time since we'd entered the car. "Just so you know, this isn't how I expected the day to go either. I'm totally fine if you'd like to exit the car without inviting me in."

I searched his eyes. "This isn't some backhanded way to boldly go where no man has gone before, is it?"

Kyle's wince told me just how badly I'd botched the end of our date.

"Good night, Taylor," he said, jaw rigid.

I sighed. "I'm a hypocrite. A total hypocrite. Here I am going on about how my family judges me based on my past, and I'm doing the exact same thing to you, aren't I?"

"Yeah," he said. "Yeah, you are."

"You are everything and nothing I thought you'd be, Kyle

Goldstein. I'm trying to figure out what's real, what's exaggeration, and what's misunderstanding."

I watched Kyle expectantly, not sure whether he would cry, kiss me, or force me to use the pepper spray attached to the keys in my hand.

"You know, you're not what I expected either," he finally said.

"Let me guess. You had me pegged as some uptight, serial spinster who was going to club you with the Bible for any little infraction, right?"

Kyle met my eyes along with a sheepish grin on his face. "I appreciate the honesty. And you're not wrong."

We shared a quick laugh.

"How about a real date?" Kyle asked. "Maybe lunch sometime this week?"

The faces of countless Culver coworkers flashed before me. They'd all be full of warnings about the lazy, lovesick lothario known as Kyle Goldstein. There was one person I trusted to be completely honest with me, and moreover, who would pray before speaking.

I told Kyle I would think about it and asked for some time and space. Since he had my phone number, he said he would text me later in the week.

He waited for me to unlock my front door before pulling away, and I felt both sadness and relief that the evening did not end the way it could have. Part of me longed for a kiss not given, and part of me quaked in fear of making myself vulnerable again. I also knew exactly what the world would have to say about me dating Kyle Goldstein.

At that moment, I had very little interest in the opinion of the world, but in the longtime object of Kyle's affection.

I needed to talk to Mrs. Ted Margolin, formerly Rebecca Ivy.

CHAPTER 6

"So I saw your email," Rebecca said as we sat in The Soaring Scone, Parkview's renowned brunch eatery. "What's going on?"

"Where's Tabby?" I asked. "I don't remember the last time I've seen you without mini-me and the baby stroller."

Rebecca's smile illuminated the entire room. "Ted's mother offered to babysit, and I wasn't about to say no. We finally got Tabby to take a bottle, and I jumped at the chance for a few hours alone. I absolutely detest pumping, but it's worth it."

Most of the Mommy-speak went over my head, so I just listened and nodded. "You look great, by the way," I said, changing the subject. "Do you have a hair stylist you can recommend? I had some drunk girl recently call me a librarian, so I'm thinking it might be time to change things up a little."

"Really?" Rebecca asked with a laugh. "I hope you took it with a grain of salt, Taylor. Drunk people are known for their honesty but not necessarily their accuracy."

"Part of me wants to try a cute, pixie cut, but another part says I'll wind up looking like a Lost Boy in a stage production of *Peter's Pen*. Ultimately, I just do nothing and suffer insults from alcoholics instead."

Rebecca raised an eyebrow at me as she took a sip of water. We got our usual meals, me because of my allergies and Rebecca because she refused to eat pork anymore. We chatted about work and motherhood before Rebecca got to the matter at hand.

"So...what's his name?" she drawled.

"What do you mean?"

Rebecca pulled a face. "I know this look. That petrified, 'is this really happening, but I can't wipe the stupid grin off my face' look."

I took a deep breath. "It's um, complicated."

I didn't mistake that eye roll. Rebecca was not giving an inch. She stared me down, waiting for the rest of the story.

"Not Jessica Goldstein complicated," I finally said. "More like Kyle Goldstein."

That certainly got Rebecca's attention. It got everyone's attention because she choked on her water and coughed profusely.

"Are you okay?" I asked.

Hoarsely, she replied, "Are *you* okay? Is Kyle harassing you or anything? Looking for dirt on me?"

I eyed my former mentor for a moment. "No, he's not harassing me," I said.

Rebecca took another sip of water then cleared her throat. "But you brought him up, so I'm wondering what's going on. The last thing I heard about Kyle came from his sister. She said he found some girl who looks exactly like me but not necessarily the sharpest knife in the drawer."

"Yeah, about her..." my voice trailed off.

Rebecca cocked her head in question.

"She's the one who thinks I look like a librarian. I was working late last week, eating dinner outside of Chick-A-Yum, and she showed up with Kyle."

"I see."

"She could barely walk in those massive heels, but Kyle was sober and trying to figure out where he knew me."

"So you talked to him?"

I blushed.

"What else happened, Taylor?"

"I pepper sprayed him in the parking garage."

Rebecca's jaw hit the table about the same time our meals did. I said a quick, silent blessing then opened my eyes to see her still staring at me.

"Did you just say—?"

"Yup," I answered, enjoying my vegetable and egg scramble. "I thought Kyle was going to make a move on me, and I threatened to pepper spray him. He thought I was kidding, and so yeah, I sprayed him."

Rebecca studied my face for a moment. "You're still blushing, so there's more to the story here. You wouldn't have asked me out for a '911 lunch' if that was the end of it."

If I could expect compassion from one person on the planet, it would be Rebecca Margolin. She had already survived a lifetime of her father, Bernard Ivy, plus her old church leader known only as "Pastor Sociopath." Any aid from my own family had fallen by the wayside. My former in-laws blocked me on social media following the Sunday morning blow up, and my brother ignored my text messages and phone calls.

"Nothing really happened until yesterday," I said, taking the last bite from my fruit cup. I gave a full play-by-play of the day's events.

Rebecca sat back in her chair and processed the information. Finally, she said, "So, Kyle actually agreed to meet up with you? Even after the pepper spray?"

"He did."

"And you sat in the restaurant for almost five hours?"

"We did."

"And in that time, other than the awkward side hug thing, he didn't attempt to lay a finger on you, seduce you, or anything remotely inappropriate?"

"Correct."

"Hmm," she said, resting her hands on her belly. When she noticed my surprised stare, Rebecca laughed and said, "No, no, no. Not pregnant again. Just an old habit from Tabby being in there. That, and I ate too much, but those potatoes are so good! If you're ever making roasted potatoes, just add some rosemary like they do here. A little goes a long way, and it will blow your mind!"

"Good to know," I said absently.

"Taylor?"

"Yeah?"

"You're destroying your napkin."

I looked down to see I'd ripped apart another innocent, mouth wiping aid.

"I feel like you're waiting on me to say something, Taylor."

My brow wrinkled in confusion.

"Are you looking for my approval?" she asked. "Or are you looking for some kind of horror story about Kyle?"

"I honestly don't know. I thought you might have some insight to share."

"What did God say when you asked Him? I'm assuming you did."

I sighed heavily. "That's just it. My mind ping pongs from

one end of the spectrum to the other. I think I hear one thing, but then another voice comes in saying the opposite. Rebecca, I am scared to death of how I feel when I'm around him."

She frowned. "Are you picking up on similarities to your ex-husband or your mother, or is this a different kind of fear?"

"Based on everything MacKenzie and Deondre have said, I have a picture of Kyle that completely contradicts the man with me on Sunday."

"So, you're wondering if he put on a good show, or if we, and I include myself here, have misjudged Kyle?"

"Exactly!" I said, extending my hand with a flourish.

"I hate to be the bearer of bad news, Taylor, but I'm not the Holy Spirit, and I can't tell you what to do. I don't know Kyle's heart, only where it was more than two years ago. Based on what you've shared, it seems like he's grown up in a few areas."

"I know you said he always had tons of girlfriends, but how was he as your friend?"

"He was wonderful, Taylor. Very compassionate, concerned, thoughtful, and always willing to help. He and Jessica didn't understand the extent of the abuse coming from my family, but that's also because his parents are pretty normal. I did see some character flaws, but it's not like any member of the human race is exempt from that. There were times I felt Kyle could be manipulative and sneaky, but not necessarily out of malignant narcissism so much as conflict avoidance. He would rather someone else take the impact instead of facing the rejection himself, if that makes sense."

I nodded. "Yeah, I get that. You've taught me so much about *triangulation,* and my mother does it to me and my brother all the time. She works him up with her sob stories, and he wants to go charging on a white horse to defend her honor. When he inevitably gets shot down, Gabe's the one feeling the sting of rejection rather than my mother. She uses that to prove how horrible I am, commiserating with him because they now share a common suffering."

"Sounds about right. My parents did that to me and my sister, Ada, especially."

"Speaking of, is she going to jail as an accomplice to your parents?"

Rebecca shook her head. "My sister has plenty of issues and misplaced loyalty, but she had no idea how badly my parents manipulated and used her. She gave the DA plenty of ammunition for trial, but I can't say it was entirely unselfish. Ada has a vindictive streak most people know better than to cross. Part of me knows my parents are reaping what they've sown, but it still hurts watching my mother and sister rip each other apart to avoid punishment."

I shook my head in awe. "You're such an inspiration, Rebecca. I'm not sure I've fully forgiven Mitch for what he did to me. Mostly, I just avoid thinking about it. Then something happens, like Sunday, and I'm reminded of just how much pain I've buried."

"Taylor, everyone processes grief differently. I wasn't able to work through a lot of this stuff until I had a legitimate support system with people who understood the kind of trauma I'd endured. I left Culver because I couldn't handle the stress of it all anymore. I had a breakdown."

My eyes widened in shock. My hero had feet of clay after all.

"Ted finally convinced me to go to counseling, and I still see my therapist. I love my husband, but it's not all riding off into the sunset when you survive this kind of abuse. I have my good days and bad days too. I see my beautiful girl, and I can't believe how my parents looked at me with anything other than the love

I feel for that precious child. I can't wrap my brain around that level of sickness."

"Thank you for sharing that with me, Rebecca. I know I've had you up on a pedestal."

"I know you did," she said gently, "and you don't need my approval, Taylor. Kyle was devastated when he found out about me and Ted. I'm not saying he hasn't made some really stupid choices because of his pain, but I do know he's a good person and a loyal friend. Obviously, we're not close like we used to be, but I sincerely wish him every happiness in the world. The last conversation he and I had, he asked if there was anyone else out there like me. He said he'd been looking, but he couldn't find her."

"Well, he found your clone," I said morosely, never more aware of my own plainness seated across from the dark eyed beauty who radiated the kind of joy I hoped to one day obtain.

"Taylor, what made me different from all the other girls Kyle dated was Jesus. You have to know that. It's not curly hair or brown eyes but your testimony of overcoming suffering because of your relationship with God. There's a warrior in you the world has tried to beat down into submission. Kyle talks big about being Jewish and looks down on Messianics for not being 'real Jews,' but I also know he admires the changes he saw in me once I got free from my family and Pastor Sociopath. He saw the work of the Holy Spirit healing and delivering me. What he admires in me is the Messiah, *his* Messiah if he'd ever let go of his pride long enough to see it."

"Oh," I murmured.

"Taylor, if I felt I had any warning from God that this was a bad idea, I would tell you. Ted considered himself agnostic at best when we got married, and he's still coming to understand things about Jesus bit by bit. We're trying to preserve who we are as Jews by researching and practicing the feasts of the Old Testament. At the same time, we don't want it to become an idol where we worship 'being Jewish' rather than Jesus. It's a tightrope, and one we're still navigating."

"Wow," I said. "I know Ted is a new believer, but I had no idea he wasn't a Christian when you married him."

"I don't think he really considers himself a 'Christian' now either. He's not interested in Messianic Judaism, and we're both tired of looking for the right label to describe us. At this point, we just tell people we're Jewish believers in Jesus and leave it at that."

"I'm glad God turned things around for Ted, but what about light having no fellowship with darkness? I can't really entertain the thought of a serious relationship with someone who isn't a Christian."

"When Ted asked me to marry him, I knew God wanted me to do it. It didn't make any sense to me, and I've heard all the same Christian dating lessons you have. If I had been in a place to counsel myself eighteen months ago, I would have called the idea of marrying someone I barely dated for a month totally insane. One second, I'm meeting his parents for Thanksgiving dinner, and four days later, we're married."

"Wow," I said.

Rebecca smiled. "The wonderful thing about God is that He's not required to fit inside the boxes we make for Him, even the ones that sound super holy from the outside. Sometimes we're so busy trying to look and act like perfect Christians, we suck all the life and adventure out of following God. It becomes about performance rather than walking out our faith daily."

Capping an end to our conversation, the alarm on my phone buzzed, letting me know I needed to go back to work. When I mentioned the latest Request for Proposal from Culver's top, east coast producer, Rebecca warned me not to expect much support from her husband with regards to Kyle. She warned me, in fact, to seek God above all else. She also advised me to protect my privacy as long as possible.

After hugging my old friend goodbye and heading toward my office high rise, I prayed anew, encouraged by Rebecca's testimony and her parting admonition. By the time I returned to my desk, Kyle had an answer to his text message from earlier that morning.

For the first time in a long time, I had a date for Friday night

CHAPTER 7

"So tell me about your big date," my college roommate, Stephanie Donato, said. "It's so nice to be getting ready together for a night out. You need a social life, girl!"

I giggled, gliding my flat iron through a section of hair. "Oh Steph, it was just like a movie. Things like this don't ever happen to me."

"Details! You said you saw him across the circle at Bible study and he just eyed you the whole time, right?"

"Yes!" I squealed. I moved the iron to smooth out my overgrown bangs. "I'm so glad I switched to the Monday night small group."

"Tell me again what he looks like because I'm trying to picture this," Stephanie said. She took a liberal dose of aerosol hairspray to her hot roller curls. While jealous that my junior year roommate could cajole such beautiful body into her hair, my ceramic flat iron gave my shoulder length bob an "edgy" feel. At least that's what I told myself anyway. Unsure how *edgy* one could look in a purple baby doll dress, black tights, and mary janes, I commended myself for going all out for my first, real date since senior prom. Finished with my hair, I grabbed a cotton swab to touch up my attempt at "smoky" makeup. My eyes that had always seemed a lackluster, greenish brown suddenly popped against the black eyeliner and plum eyeshadow.

"What do you think?" I said, twirling around for approval.

"I think Mitchell Ross will be eating out of the palm of your hand, that's what I think," Stephanie said. "Oh, but you need some bling! You can borrow my silver necklace." She pulled off a pendant from her jewelry rack. "You are too cute!"

I fought against my overly sticky lip gloss to part my lips. "You don't think the makeup is too much?"

Stephanie clucked her tongue. "Girl, it's 2006! What's the point of putting on all that makeup if it doesn't look like you're wearing any? Let Mr. Sapphire Eyes know you made a little extra effort for him."

I blushed. "He really does have the most gorgeous blue eyes I've ever seen, Steph. Every time I looked up during Bible study, he was just staring at me. I could barely concentrate!"

"But you said he's bald?"

I shrugged, adjusting my dress by the floor length mirror attached to our door. "Mitch shaves it really close since it looks like his hairline is receding anyway, but I think it works for him. Kind of like that guy from all the *Transponder* movies. It definitely makes those eyes stand out even more. I can't believe he's even interested in someone like me."

"What do you mean, someone like you? Taylor, you're smart, you're cute, and you're as wholesome as a loaf of multigrain bread. Besides that, you have something most girls on this campus—even the ones in your little Bible study—can't say they do. I know these hardcore Christian guys are really into the v-card."

"Ugh, Steph, do you have to put it like that?"

"Sorry, I call it like I see it. That's why you love me even though I'm a heathen."

"You're not a heathen," I said, sticking my tongue out at her. "Obviously, we have a difference of opinion on a few issues, but you've met my mother. To say I'm a little jaded at this point is probably an understatement."

"You said that she up and decided to start smoking? At forty-five years old?"

I exhaled in disgust. "According to Sarah Meyers, 'Sometimes you just want a cigarette after sex.'"

"Gross! Why does your mother think you want to know about all the skeevy guys she goes out with?"

"Your guess is as good as mine. Half the time, I think she just enjoys rubbing it in my face to get a reaction."

"A reaction? Like what, nausea?"

I rolled my eyes, tugging on my tights for maybe the thousandth time before glancing at my bedside clock. The phone rang from the front desk of our all-female dorm announcing that Mitchell Ross was downstairs to see me.

I squealed one last time with Stephanie before heading down six floors to reach the lobby. As I searched for my sapphire eyed suitor, I collided with someone else's Friday night date. He offered a smile of apology beneath emo styled hair sweeping over his face. Awkwardly, we both attempted to avert one another before he brushed past me into the awaiting arms of a girl from my hall.

"Taylor!" a deep baritone voice called from across the room.

I turned and smiled at Mitchell Ross, glad that my four inch heels closed the distance between his six feet and my five feet and two inches.

"You look really pretty," he said, his eyes traveling over my iridescent eyelids and glossy lips. As his gaze went no further than my neck, I beamed, thankful this date might prove far different than some of the lecherous stares I received while helping Stephanie during her weekend benders.

"Is there anything special you wanted to do tonight?" Mitch said, guiding me outside.

"I really enjoy walking," I said, "and I love the gardens around the library."

"In those shoes?" he asked.

So, he did manage to sneak a peek below the neck.

"I don't really have a preference," I said, smiling up at him. "Are you hungry? Would you rather go get something to eat?"

"A walk around campus sounds nice. Usually, I'm in such a rush to get to class that I don't stop and enjoy the gardens or the fountain."

We traveled in companionable silence until I began humming a favorite tune of mine.

Mitch looked at me, pleasantly surprised. "That was beautiful. Will you sing for me?"

I gulped. "Here?"

"Sure," he said. "It might even catch the interest of some of the drunks on this campus. Have you ever done any outreach or mission work?"

I shook my head. "Have you?"

"I've gone on a few mission trips to Mexico and El Salvador. I've always thought about living in a foreign country one day, sharing the Gospel, and bringing Christ to the world."

"Wow."

Mitch smiled down at me. "Well, it's the dream anyway. My older brother, Brian, is in seminary studying to be a pastor."

"Wow," I repeated, impressed by the Ross brothers' spiritual ambition.

"So how about it, little lady? Will you sing that song for me?"

I blushed.

But I sang.

I garnered the attention of several couples milling around the library fountain, some who even applauded and told me I ought to pursue singing professionally. Mitch placed an arm around me and proudly showed off his "little songbird." I felt like a precious jewel whose worth had finally been discovered. When Mitch proposed one year later in that exact spot, I thought my girlhood dreams had finally come true.

Four years later, the nightmare began and so did the sudden changes in the man I thought I knew. Though Mitch was never overweight, he suddenly became obsessed with his physical appearance. Along with seven days a week at the gym and hundreds of dollars in supplements came backhanded comments about me being *scrawny*. Next, came the hair plugs. Mitch claimed that clients trusted a man with a head full of hair rather than his old buzz cut.

When his church attendance dwindled, my anxiety skyrocketed. When our sex life became nonexistent, I started asking questions.

As I got dressed for my date with Kyle, I was reminded of how many times God used that worship song from long ago as a milestone marker in my life. I sang it on my first date with Mitchell Ross. It played as I marched down the aisle of our small, summer wedding following college graduation. I sang it again for Mitch on our first anniversary. I sang it with grief stricken tears on our fifth anniversary when I simultaneously discovered Mitch's infidelity and the baby I had miscarried. I sang it leaving the courthouse after signing my name on the divorce decree. It was the tune that began and ended all ties to Mitchell Benjamin Ross, the man who had promised me a lifetime of love and faithfulness but broke his vows in the most humiliating way possible.

Sitting on a bench outside the restaurant where I knew Kyle Goldstein awaited me, I hummed the chorus to that same song. I closed my eyes to worship my Lord and Savior and dedicate the evening to Him. I thanked God that no matter what transpired that night or any night thereafter, I would still praise Him. It wasn't glittery purple eyeshadow intermingling with the tears on my cheeks, but I couldn't help but be reminded of that other first date that had so completely changed my life.

I felt Kyle's presence without opening my eyes.

"Normally, I'd say 'penny for your thoughts,' but I have a pretty good idea of what you're doing."

Although probably a puffy eyed mess, I found I didn't much care. At least I didn't have any foliage in my hair this time.

"You're beautiful," Kyle said, and I knew he meant it.

"Thanks."

"What was the song you were humming?"

"Oh. It's an old favorite of mine. It's gotten me through a lot."

"Did you sing it at your old church?"

"Just in the pews. I used to sing on the worship team when I was married, but I haven't really wanted to since the divorce."

Kyle raised an eyebrow. "Any particular reason why?"

"I don't know. I guess I felt like a fraud. When you're expected to be some beacon of Christian perfection but your private life is falling apart, it's hard to lead people from the stage."

Kyle studied me for a moment. "That sounds like it would suck. Big time."

I laughed, wiping the earlier tears from my cheeks. "That it did. The praying mantis tried to get me back on stage, but I'm not sure if that was for Brian's benefit or if she hoped to look good by association."

"The little bit I heard was amazing. I get why they wanted you up there."

"Maybe we'll do karaoke one of these days," I teased.

Kyle's eyes brightened. "I'm game."

"Really?"

"Sure. I mean, I guess I can carry a tune. My sister hates singing in public, but I think it's fun. It's always easier when you don't take yourself too seriously."

"Or the reaction of other people too seriously."

Kyle inclined his head. "Yeah, that too. What do you say? Dinner and singing?"

I smiled, seeing my life come full circle. I wasn't sure what to make of this new beginning, but I was willing to take the next step forward. The Lord spoke to my heart with verses from the book of *Joel* about restoring double what the locusts had eaten, and I knew I'd abandoned my desire to sing long enough. Kyle extended a hand to help me off the bench, and I enjoyed his warm hand holding mine.

Once on my feet, Kyle pulled me gently toward him.

"Hi," he said, smiling and staring into my eyes.

"What are we doing?" I whispered.

"I have absolutely no idea."

"That makes two of us."

Kyle sighed in relief. He finally released my hand, though I almost wished he hadn't.

"This doesn't make any sense," he said.

"Agreed."

"But here we are."

"Yes," I said, mesmerized by powder blue eyes.

"Are you one of those crazy, Christian fangirls who think I'm part of God's chosen people?" he blurted out.

I laughed, thankful for a break in the current of electricity crackling between us. "You know these people mean well, right?"

"Everybody says they mean well after they get caught doing something stupid."

I chuckled. "Ain't that the truth!"

Kyle raised an eyebrow. "Are you thinking about your ex, or did you have someone else in mind?"

"A few people actually. My brother thinks he's doing good by trying to force me and my mother into having a relationship."

"Is she anything like Deborah Ivy? I promise I'm not trying to drag Rebecca into this. I just want to understand where you're coming from."

I nodded, willing to give Kyle the benefit of the doubt. "Selfishness comes in a lot of different flavors. You start with innately selfish, like little kids who haven't learned the world doesn't revolve around them yet. Theoretically, you grow up, remove yourself from the center of the universe, and then gain some insight into the feelings of others and how your behavior affects them."

"Did your mother miss the memo?"

"I'm pretty sure she burned the memo. Have you ever seen those billboards that say, 'Sell it with Sarah'?"

Kyle's eyes grew large. "*That's* your mother?"

"Yup."

"Are you sure I'm thinking of the right billboard, Taylor? Huge blonde hair, hand under the chin, enough cleavage to make you think she's selling something other than real estate?"

Seeing my mother through Kyle's eyes made the shame even worse. "And here you thought the possibility of me preaching at you might be your biggest worry, huh?"

"What does your mom have to do with you?"

I shrugged. "Tainted by association?"

"This is a date, not a marriage proposal, Taylor. Oh," he said, taking note of my stunned expression. "Were you...? Is that what you were hoping...?"

"No!" I exclaimed, cutting him off. "I mean, yeah, it's something I would like to try with a non-fraud someday, but I don't have any grand ideas that we..." my voice trailed off as I gestured between the two of us.

Overly bright, Kyle said, "Doesn't it feel like there's this insane pressure to make everything so all-or-nothing in your thirties? Like tick-tock, the whole biological clock and all of that?"

I winced, unable to hide how Kyle inadvertently trampled on such an old, deep wound. Worse, I felt like more of a fool than that overly made up, twenty-one year-old from eleven years earlier. After a perfectly benign dinner, I claimed sudden fatigue as my excuse to skip karaoke.

Whether Kyle believed me or not, the flirty text messages came to a screeching halt. They grew nonexistent after a week or so. Though the rejection stung, knowing I had survived far worse than an unexpected attraction and two dates made it much easier to overcome.

CHAPTER 8

DAYS AND MONTHS ROLLED TOGETHER AS I MOVED forward and welcomed my new coworker, Julie Easton, into the marketing department. I received the "Culver Super Star" award also given to my former mentor, and ironically, the nomination came from her husband, Ted. I used my $250 cash prize toward a professional haircut at one of the upscale Parkview salons and hardly recognized myself once the highlights and wispy layers were cut into my hair. Nobody was going to confuse me for a Lost Boy anymore, certainly not with the confident spring in my step, brand new riding boots, and YouTV makeup tutorial videos.

I barely recognized the woman formerly hidden underneath shapeless clothes and "old lady wear," as Kyle had so eloquently put it. Although part of me hoped to see him on those Chick-A-Yum nights, it never happened again. I did spot Heather one other time, and she looked fairly cozy with a guy much more suited to her party girl lifestyle.

Sitting on an outdoor bench by the Culver office high rise,

savoring the sounds, smells, and crispness of fall, I closed my eyes in worship of God. I was reminded of the Scriptures saying all creation declares His glory as a popular Christian radio tune found its way just behind my lips. The peace of God washed over me as my heart cried out in praise and my lips hummed along.

When I opened my eyes, I discovered I had an audience.

The three Margolins broke into happy applause including baby Tabitha. The little cherub sported two impossibly cute pigtails on her head and a gummy smile.

I stood up and embraced Rebecca, eagerly taking Tabitha in my arms for a friendly squeeze. The baby eyed her mother, unsure if she would stay with me willingly.

"How old is she now?" I asked.

"She'll be one in a month and a half," Rebecca said as she made silly faces at her daughter.

"Taylor, I had no idea you could sing like that," Ted said. "The look on your face gave me goosebumps"

I blushed, embarrassed by the attention. "Thank you."

"That is high praise coming from this man, and you know he won't just blow smoke up your rear end," Rebecca said, taking a squirming Tabitha back in her arms.

Ted added, "I was planning to treat the Cheesecake Confections team for lunch later this week to celebrate the win. I hope you don't have any other plans on the calendar, Taylor, because you're also included. Can you eat French food?"

"I'd have to look at a menu. I hate being a pain because of all the food allergies, but dairy does not like me one bit. The French cook everything in butter, right?"

At Ted's open mouthed expression, I quickly amended, "Not that it really matters. I mean, I can always bring something from home and then just sit with you guys. I don't want to be a bother."

"It's no bother at all," Ted said easily. "Taylor, where do you normally go for lunch when you eat out? You know, other than this place over here with Rebecca?" He gestured backward toward The Soaring Scone.

Meekly, I said, "I like Los Bravos. I know it's not as fancy as your usual lunch spots, so please don't feel obligated to make any special considerations just for me."

"I love that place. Sounds great!" Ted said. He planted a kiss on his wife and daughter as he said his farewells. "Honey, I'll see you at home. Taylor, I'll see you in an hour after my Triple J conference call. I've got a presentation with one of those all organic, turkey bacon companies, and I have a feeling you're going to have your usual fun researching stock photos."

I grinned. "Always."

As Ted turned toward the office, Rebecca grabbed my arm. "You have a gift, Taylor."

"For what? Finding random pictures of food?" I quipped.

Rebecca's expression held no humor. "You are a worship leader, my friend, and I don't just mean you sing well. I saw God's presence all over you, and it ministered to me by the way you praised Him."

"But I wasn't singing full voice," I said.

"Exactly! Taylor, what you have is a calling from God. You do graphic design for a living, but don't forget to use this gift God has given you, okay? Have you found a new church yet?"

"Obviously, I won't be going back to Freedom, but I've just been enjoying my Sunday mornings. It's been a while since I stayed consistent about my epsom salt baths, and it's really been helping with my lower back. Too many hours sitting in that computer chair at Culver is not so *bueno* for me."

Rebecca raised an eyebrow. "What about this Ian character?"

"What about him?"

"You said he tracked you down on FaceSpace and asked you out for what, the third or fourth time? Sounds like he doesn't want to take no for an answer."

"He has the personality of a wet mop, Rebecca, and hair to match."

"If he's willing to keep pursuing you, you might want to reconsider your opinion of him, Taylor. You said Ian read the riot act to your former in-laws for running you out of the church, didn't he?"

I shrugged. "Yeah, I guess."

Rebecca pursed her lips and stared at me. "Look, it can't be any worse than going out with my former best friend's brother, okay? Kyle might have given lots of lip service about romancing you, but he totally chickened out."

"I scared him off, Rebecca. He wanted burgers, and I practically begged him to marry me."

Mrs. Margolin rolled her eyes. "Whatever. It sounds like Ian knows what he wants. Kyle doesn't seem to have a clue. You told me the Lord convicted you for prejudging Kyle based on what everyone else has told you. What if you made the same mistake with Ian?"

"In this case, I'm judging Ian based on what I've personally seen and experienced, Rebecca. The guy is about as exciting as watching paint dry."

"It's your life, sweetie, but maybe there's more to him than what you see on the surface. I know I had a lot of ideas about my own husband before he showed any interest in me, and I wasn't necessarily wrong at the time either. Don't close yourself off to the possibility of a blessing just because it doesn't come packaged the way you thought it would," she said, bouncing a now fussy Tabitha on her hip. "Just think about what I'm saying, okay? Even though things didn't work out with Kyle, you found someone worth knowing underneath all of the rumors. You were willing to take that leap of faith and get out of your comfort zone. Your new haircut and everything about you screams 'ready to do something different with my life.' So do it already!"

The advice Rebecca offered sounded similar to the counsel my mother gave three years earlier, except Sarah Meyers's timing couldn't have been any worse.

"What do you say we go to that new karaoke club downtown, Taylor?" my mother had suggested. "Singing always seems to cheer you up."

"I just got divorced today," I said, plopping down on a kitchen barstool. "'Til death do us part' lasted six years, and the last year we spent fighting over every dime Mitch tried to cheat me out of."

"Which is exactly why we should celebrate, honey. You're free! You can live it up and meet some men with *real* hair instead of that dead dog Mitch plugged in up there."

I looked up at my mother, not sure whether she was attempting to make a joke or actually serious. Sighing, I realized it was the latter.

"I just don't understand what happened, Mom."

My mother sat on the stool next to me. "He never liked you singing up on stage at church, honey. He said the bass player made eyes at you. Mitch complained about it all the time at the office."

"Well, isn't that rich?" I spat. "I didn't really care for the way Mitch used our bed to impregnate both me and our receptionist."

"Apparently, bald men are more virile," my mother said,

absently picking at one of her nails. "I swear I just read something about that in a magazine last week."

I stared at the woman in disbelief.

"What?" she said.

"Mom, I know you think you're helping, but you're not."

"Look, if all you want is a baby, Taylor, there are plenty of other fish in the sea. You're young, and you have plenty of time. No need to get tied down with a kid before you're thirty. If there's one thing I regret more than anything, it's having kids so soon with your father. It just ruined everything."

I closed my eyes and silently counted to ten before responding. My mother's legitimate cluelessness was both astounding and horrifying. "Mom, do you really think this was just about having a baby? I wanted to start a family with the man I pledged to spend the rest of my life with. The man who told me we'd grow old together as missionaries somewhere. He was supposed to have a family with *me*, not some twenty-year-old secretary."

"Well, your father went off and had two kids with that woman he married, but you don't see me crying about it, do you, Taylor? Dwelling on all of this negativity isn't good for you. Mitch moved out more than a year ago. You need to get on with your life and stop living in the past. I tell you that all the time."

Stunned into silence, I removed myself from the room before I forcibly shut my mother's mouth. The last time I'd felt so irate was when I'd discovered another woman asleep in my bed and my showering husband rinsing the adultery from his body.

"Don't you turn your back on me, Taylor Marie!" my mother shrilled from the kitchen.

"We're done, Mom," I said. "Go clubbing, go out with your boyfriend *du jour*. Do whatever you want. Just get out of my house." I plopped down on my family room sofa, emotionally drained.

"You little ingrate!" she fumed, stomping over and towering above me in four-inch stiletto heels.

I massaged the growing headache in my temples. "I don't have the time or the energy for this, Mom. This has been one of the worst days of my life and one of the worst years of my life other than your divorce from Dad."

"I rescheduled my entire day to rush over here and comfort my daughter in her hour of need," my mother said, patting her hair dramatically. The crocodile tears emerged next. "I may as well have stayed in the office if you were going to abuse me like this."

Flipping the manipulation right back on Sarah Meyers, I said, "You probably *should* get back to work, Mom. You were StarRealty's top associate this year, and we both know how much your clients are counting on you now that Mitch is gone."

My mother's tears miraculously vanished as surprise manifested on her face instead. "Well, that's very thoughtful of you, Taylor Marie. I appreciate you thinking of someone else's needs right now." Feeling charitable, she added, "I understand why you might be more sensitive than usual today. I was devastated when your father abandoned me with two small children to go live with that Elaine woman. Of course, you're not a single mother like I was, but I'm sure this is hard in its own way. Why don't you give me a call later this week, and I can take you to that new singles bar I found last month? It should keep your mind off of Mitch for a couple of hours."

I responded with a tight smile. My mother would forget about me as soon as she left the room. She pressed her cheek to mine with an air kiss, satisfied she had completed her motherly obligations. Her platform pumps clacked quickly through my front door.

Performing a much better job of comforting me, Brian stopped by later with his then-fiancée Chloe to offer sympathy and a shoulder to cry on. The Ross brothers shared the same sapphire blue eyes, though Brian sported a head full of golden curls rather than Mitch's receding hairline.

I happily welcomed Brian's embrace as Chloe stood off to the side. Her jade eyes narrowed as she surveyed our McMansion.

"Thanks for coming over," I sniffled, wiping my nose on my sweater sleeve.

Chloe rolled her eyes and looked away.

Oblivious, Brian took in my appearance and frowned. "I just don't understand what happened, Taylor. I've tried talking to Mitch, but I'd probably have better luck with a brick wall."

"None of it makes sense, Brian. Three years ago, we were happy. We were talking about starting a family. They finally let me sing lead on the worship team at church—and not just the pittance song for the female vocalist either. Mitch called it a travesty they had me singing backup. He told me he would say something to Pastor Mark."

"And did he?" Brian asked.

I shrugged. "I thought he had when they finally had me leading the worship set, but Mitch copped this horrible attitude when I told him. It just didn't make any sense, Brian."

"That does seem weird," he admitted.

"Meanwhile, Mitch taught early morning Bible study for three years, and I never complained about us going to church in separate cars every Sunday. Mitch said he didn't like me going to music practice on Thursday nights, but half the time, he was showing houses and wasn't home until late anyway. I don't understand why he suddenly changed his mind."

"I remember," Brian said with a grimace. He followed me into the kitchen as Chloe trailed behind him. I caught her eyeing my possessions with an awed look on her face.

I offered them both a drink. Chloe declined, but Brian joined me in a glass of sparkling water. Smiling, I remembered how much Brian and I both enjoyed a twist of lime in what he called our "mutual, non-alcoholic beverage of choice." He grinned as I produced a lime wedge for each glass.

The green citrus paled in comparison to Chloe's sour expression.

Brian studied me over the rim of his glass. "He didn't deserve you, Taylor. I know Mitch is my brother, but he never treated you right."

Chloe's mouth gaped open, as did mine.

"Brian, why didn't you ever say anything?" I asked.

"It wasn't my business, Taylor. I tried dropping a few hints to Mitch, especially when he made all of those nasty comments to you about your weight. You're small. So what? It's not like he didn't know that when he first asked you out or when he married you."

I watched Chloe run her fingers down her own, svelte frame. I shook my head at the ridiculous notion that Brian's glamazon fiancée seemed jealous of me. However, once Chloe and Brian exchanged vows two months later, her frosty treatment persisted into chronic excuses to avoid my company. It intensified when I felt God led me to join Freedom Church.

The other Mrs. Ross didn't like that one bit.

CHAPTER 9

A YEAR AFTER MY DIVORCE, I STEPPED INTO FREEDOM
Church for the first time. Brian greeted me with a huge grin and
a grappling bear hug.

"Isn't it great?" he said, his hand sweeping over the tiny
church chapel. "FBP gave us an amazing deal on the rent. They
also let us borrow the sound and projection equipment here so
we don't have to worry about storage or weekly setup."

Inserting himself into our conversation, a tall stranger said,
"In my last church, we had to set up and break down the equipment twice a week. We did it once for music rehearsal and
again for services." After eyeing me up and down, he turned to
Brian and said, "Aren't you going to introduce me to your
friend?"

Brian's smile faded. "Ian Horner, this is Taylor Ross, my
sister...er um, well Taylor."

Ian didn't miss the slip. "I thought you just had one
brother."

Brian cleared his throat, squirming. "That's correct. Taylor is...um *was*, my brother's wife. She's not my sister-in-law anymore, but she'll always be my sister in Christ."

Throwing Brian a lifeline, I did my best to muster a smile for the shaggy haired interloper. "Ian, you said you work AV, right?"

"Sound too," he said, jerking his head to shift the flop of hair from his eyes.

"Oh, well that's really impressive. I've had to work the soundboard in some extreme circumstances, but I usually just leave that for the professionals."

The last comment piqued Ian's interest. "Care to share about some of these extreme circumstances?"

Brian glanced between the two of us and then across the room at his wife and newly pregnant, mother-to-be. He headed toward Chloe before getting waylaid by some other church members. I swallowed convulsively, reminded that my ex-husband had welcomed a healthy baby boy with his mistress. Meanwhile, my womb and arms lay barren. I fought at the tears in my eyes.

"You okay?" Ian asked. "I assume your ex-husband is a complete idiot. He'd have to be to leave someone as pretty as you."

A genuine smile finally made it to my lips. "Yes, he's an absolute idiot. Textbook idiot. You may, in fact, find his hair plugged mugshot next to the very word in the dictionary. I assume this incredible bouffant is all your own?" I said, gesturing to Ian's overgrown mane.

"I don't think anyone has ever called my hair *incredible* before."

"Well, there's always a first for everything, right?"

"If it's not too personal to ask, how long have you been...uh, not married?"

Flattered, but not interested, I dodged the question. I made small talk for a few more minutes and then found an excuse to leave. I located a spot in a back pew and opened my Bible to *Psalms*.

"I saw you talking to the new sound guy," Chloe said as she sat down next to me. "He's not my cup of tea, but you could always do worse, right?"

"How are you feeling?" I asked, remembering Brian's mention of Chloe's morning sickness. "Did the peppermint tea help?"

"Yeah, how did you...oh," she said, pursing her lips. "So, Brian's brilliant idea was yours?"

"I was pregnant at one time too, remember?"

Compassion briefly flickered in Chloe's eyes. "Yeah. I forgot about that."

I took a deep breath and slowly exhaled. "Obviously, I wasn't pregnant for as long as I wanted to be, but I did find some helpful morning sickness remedies. I could email them if you want."

"That might be nice," she said. "I feel nauseous all day long, not just in the morning. Brian made chili for dinner the other night, and I couldn't stop gagging."

"Was it the onions or stewed tomatoes? Brian swears they enhance the flavor, but I can't really stand either one of them."

The smile disappeared from Chloe's face. "So Brian made chili a lot for you...and Mitch, I'm guessing?"

"Sure. He came over to our house all the time for Sunday dinner. Well, until you guys started dating."

Chloe's tight expression grew even more strained. "Brian used to ramble on about his amazing sister-in-law, how much she loves Jesus and this incredible singing voice she has. I almost wondered if something ever happened between the two of you." She searched my face for any sign of guilt.

Answering her easily, I said, "Chloe, I was already engaged to Mitch by the time I met Brian. I look at him as a big brother, and I'm sure he gushes on about me the way I do about Gabe. I was head over heels in love with my husband until I discovered x-rated text messages to that tramp and the woman herself in my bed."

"Yes, well, we don't need to bring all of the disgusting details into the house of the Lord," Chloe said primly. "We've all heard this part of the story, Taylor. More than once."

I arched a brow at Chloe's increasingly bizarre behavior.

As if snapping out of a daze, she brightened and said, "What do you think about going back to your maiden name? After all, it's a little awkward with both of us having the last name Ross, don't you think? People might assume you're the pastor's wife instead of me."

"Is something wrong, Chloe?"

"What do you mean?"

"You obviously don't like the fact that Brian and I are close. I've only ever seen him as a brother, and I can assure you, he sees me the same way."

Chloe scoffed. "Well, of course I know that, Taylor. I just don't think you're aware that this *closeness* comes off as extremely inappropriate. As someone who knows what it's like to be cheated on, I'm sure you can understand how awful that feels. You said God told you to join our church, but I have to wonder if you're not trying to replace Mitch with Brian."

The idea of this statuesque beauty being threatened by me seemed laughably absurd. However, the green eyed monster sat before me glaring with unveiled resentment.

"Why are you really here, Taylor?" Chloe said through gritted teeth.

"I'm here because God told me to come. I can't go back to my old church, and I believe the Lord wants me here."

"What Bible verses did you use to confirm this?" she asked.

"The book of *Ruth*. Naomi went back to the land she fled and to the place that reminded her of what she'd lost. God used it to bring healing and restoration."

Chloe's lips pressed into a thin line. "I see."

"If the Lord tells me to go someplace else, then I'll go. Truly, my only motivation in being here is obeying the Lord. My mother and my brother think it's absolutely nuts if it makes you feel any better, Chloe."

"So, none of this had to do with Brian standing up for you at your thirtieth birthday party a few weeks ago? About some kind of hero worship because one of the Ross brothers finally protected you from Sarah Meyers?"

"No!" I insisted. "Where would you even get that idea?"

Chloe shifted uncomfortably. "Brian may have mentioned something about it."

"Brian actually said that? Those were his exact words?"

Chloe rolled her eyes. "Okay, well maybe not word for word, but he kept going on about how your mother tried to upstage you at your own party. He said somebody needed to defend you."

"And you think I'm here because of *that*? That I would actually take God's Name in vain just to make cow eyes at my ex-husband's brother? Chloe, I've been through hell and back with Mitch's lying and adultery. I would never wish that experience on anybody, least of all Brian or you. I hope you can believe me on this."

Chloe's expression said, "I totally misjudged you." Her body language said, "But you'll never get me to admit it." Instead, she cleared her throat and glanced over to the sound booth. "With a decent haircut, the AV guy might even be cute. Any chance you'd go out with him?"

"Eh, I don't know. I just met him. He's okay, I guess."

"Beggars can't be choosers, you know. Brian said you turned down two StarRealty agents."

I rolled my eyes. "They only asked me out to get back at Mitch for screwing them over on deals. Honestly, I'm ready to start looking for another job. I feel suffocated in that office."

"I imagine anybody feels that way working with Sarah Meyers," Chloe said. "It must be hard when everyone knows the office drama queen is your mother. People naturally assume you're just like her."

While certainly not blind to my mother's mountain of faults, Chloe's remark stung. At my prolonged silence, Chloe stood up and beelined toward her husband. She wrapped a possessive arm around him and leaned her head against his shoulder. Brian seemed surprised by the sudden display of public affection but glad to receive it. He smiled down at her and placed his hand on her belly. I closed my eyes against the grief and asked the Lord why on earth He had brought me to Freedom Church.

The answer came in Brian's impactful sermon about trusting God's goodness no matter the circumstances. Heedless of Chloe's disapproval, I greeted my former brother-in-law after the service with tear-laden words of gratitude. I ignored Chloe's upturned nose at the streaked mascara on my cheeks, and Brian told me I glowed with the presence of God. The other Mrs. Ross didn't appreciate that observation.

Reliving the old pain as though experiencing it anew, I attempted to shake off the memories and focus back on the present. I stood up shakily from a bench outside of the Culver high rise. As I tried to regain my physical and emotional equilibrium, I bumped right into Miss Belle coming back from her lunch break.

"Ooh, child, you near scared me to death!" she said, grabbing onto my arm.

Tears welled in my eyes, so desperately in need of human warmth.

"Taylor, baby, what's wrong?" she asked, concern on her face.

"How much time do you have, Miss Belle?"

She glanced down at her watch. "I've got fifteen more minutes before I have to clock back in, but I can always spare a few extra. What's going on?"

I summed up as briefly as I could, my eyes watering here and there as I tried to state the history of events as quickly as possible.

"Mmhmm," Miss Belle said, clicking her tongue. "That man stole your dreams, your innocence, and then went and had *your* baby with that floozy. Your sister-in-law sounds like a real piece of work too. I can't imagine what I'd do if Mr. Vickers had ever pulled some kind of chicanery like that."

"I heard Taylor burned his clothes," a male said from just beyond us.

I glanced over at Kyle Goldstein in horror.

"This is a private conversation!" Miss Belle scolded. "Didn't your mama teach you any manners?"

Kyle didn't budge, but his eyebrows raised over my changed appearance. His blue eyes searched for something in mine.

"Is there something going on here I should know about?" Miss Belle said, looking back and forth between the two of us.

I stood up and pulled my new confidante along with me.

"Miss Belle, we better get back to work. Bonnie is really cracking down on associates abusing their lunch hour."

"Good to see you too," Kyle said dryly, his eyes never leaving my face.

I didn't bother with a forced smile before breaking into a near sprint toward our office. Though unsure how much of our conversation Kyle had overheard, I knew he learned far more than what I'd shared on our measly two dates.

"Well, you could certainly cut that tension with a knife," Miss Belle said as the elevator doors closed. "I forgot that Cooper & Jaye just relocated their office to the building next door."

"Swell."

Culver's mother hen raised a penciled brow. "Are you fixing to tell me what's really going on now that he's gone? And does Rebecca know?"

"Nothing is going on, Miss Belle. And yes, Rebecca already knows."

"That boy is nothing but trouble, you hear?"

"I've heard."

The elevator doors dinged open to the eighth floor, and we stepped out. Miss Belle grabbed my arm and stared into my eyes for a solid thirty seconds.

"Mark my words, Taylor Ross. That young man can con the skin off a snake, but don't trust him as far as you can throw him. He's got his mind on one thing, and it ain't living happily ever after with a nice girl like you."

I nodded, not surprised by Miss Belle's counsel. I struggled between unwillingness to accept her warning and the sinking suspicion that denial would finally give way to reality.

"I'll be praying the Lord brings somebody real special,

Taylor. You deserve it after all of the shenanigans you've been through."

"Thank you," I said simply.

Miss Belle walked through the double glass doors of our office suite while I stood outside of the elevators trying to collect myself.

When the doors dinged behind me, I didn't think much of it. Not until I saw my purse extended over my shoulder and realized I'd forgotten it outside. In my rush to get away from Kyle, I had inadvertently given him the perfect opportunity to come and find me.

CHAPTER 10

"NEVER THOUGHT I'D STEP FOOT BACK IN THIS place," he said.

I turned to face Kyle Goldstein and secretly thrilled to stare into his powder blue gaze again. My inner warning bells flared as I melted in his eyes.

The man was not safe for my heart.

Clearing my throat, I said, "Ted is in the office today, and I really don't think it's a good idea for you to hang around."

"I'm not afraid of the mighty Margolin."

"Look, we both know how much Culver associates love their gossip. Seeing you here is going to cause trouble for me, especially after the lecture I just got from Miss Belle."

"Oh really?" he sneered. "And what did Culver's self-appointed, moral compass have to say about me?"

"Take a wild guess, Kyle. What were you doing downstairs anyway? You had no right to eavesdrop on our conversation."

"I haven't seen you in months, Taylor, and I just wanted to

stop by and say hello. I didn't want to interrupt while you were talking with Miss Belle."

"How about just walking away? You had no problem doing that six months ago."

Kyle looked stunned. "I was under the impression you wanted nothing to do with *me*."

"Goldstein! What brings you back to our neck of the woods?" my CEO, Phil Robbins, called as he approached us. His saccharine tone belied his set jaw and narrowed gaze.

"Taylor left her purse downstairs," Kyle said, meeting Phil's stare without flinching.

Phil's chin rose in the air, sizing up Kyle as if meeting him for the first time. "Margolin's in the office today, Goldstein. Did you want to stop by and say hello? I'm not sure if you've heard, but he and Rebecca had a baby. Hard to believe that little princess is going to be one already. Time sure flies, doesn't it?"

Faking a cough I said, "You know what Phil, I suddenly don't feel very well. I think I'm coming down with something. I probably better just go home before I infect the entire office."

Phil glanced between the two of us. "Yeah, I hear there's a lot of that going around this time of year." Turning to Kyle he said, "Goldstein, always nice to see you again. Hope all stays well over at Cooper & Jaye."

"Likewise," Kyle said coolly.

"Take care of that cough," Phil said, clapping me on the back. Close to my ear, he added, "I hope you know what you're doing here, Taylor."

I met Phil's eyes and nodded. His expression grim, Phil looked at the two of us before walking through the front doors and badly pantomiming a conversation with the receptionist.

"Get me out of here. Please," I begged.

Kyle nodded, pushing the elevator button. The doors immediately opened, Kyle's chariot already awaiting us. I stepped inside and watched the doors close on a slack jawed MacKenzie who happened to catch sight of us on her way to the ladies' room.

"I'm doomed," I said, burying my face in my palms. "It's going to be all over the office before we even make it to the lobby. I think I might legitimately be coming down with something now."

I felt Kyle's gaze on me, but I lacked the strength to subdue its effect anymore. Instead, I chose to flee temptation altogether and study the elevator buttons.

"Are you going to look at me, Taylor, or just keep pretending you've never been inside of an elevator before?"

The doors opened downstairs, and I was never more grateful to step out of a confined space in my life. Feeling Kyle reach for my arm, I pulled away and marched diligently toward the parking deck. Rather than suffering through another claustrophobic elevator ride to my car on the fourth floor, I took the stairs and hoped to lose Kyle somewhere along the way.

He followed me wordlessly, and I simply pretended he was an unwanted shadow until we arrived at my red hatchback. As if replaying the events of our first date all over again, Kyle's hand fell on mine when I reached for the door handle.

This time, however, Kyle didn't hesitate in making his move. With one hand still laid on top of mine, he used the other to cup the side of my face and pull my lips against his. Shock and surprise gave way to feelings long suppressed and ignored since our last meeting that spring.

Kyle finally ended the kiss, both hands cradling my face. He rested his forehead against mine. "That was unexpected."

"Yes," I whispered.

"Thank you for withholding the pepper spray."

I chuckled softly.

Kyle pulled back to look into my eyes. "I've been waiting six months to do that."

"So why didn't you call me? Text me? Anything?"

"I didn't think you wanted me to. You couldn't wait to leave the restaurant."

I closed my eyes, closing myself off to Kyle and to the feelings I didn't want to feel. I wanted to pretend that one kiss didn't completely erase six months of self-imposed indifference to Kyle Goldstein.

"Why are you hiding from me?" he asked.

My eyes flew open. "Why did you hide from me for half a year?" I said, angry at him and at myself. I jerked my face away from his hands and took a step backward. "Why are you kissing me now? I was just about to tell Ian Horner I'd finally go on a date with him. He asked me out two years ago."

"And you weren't interested, Taylor, or you would have already done it. He's not the one you want."

"How do you know? I was moving on with my life and with a man I know is a Christian." Thinking back to my last date with Kyle, I added, "Ian isn't going to break my heart by telling me he's not ready to have kids."

"That's not what I meant!" Kyle said.

"Yeah, right," I scoffed. "You don't want kids with *me*, but then you'll go and impregnate the first skanky receptionist who looks your way."

Kyle's eyes widened. "Okay, we're obviously not just talking about me anymore. Taylor, you didn't share much about your ex-husband, and until today, I had no idea you lost a baby."

"Like I told you, it's not exactly first date material. More like the kind of stuff you learn when you overhear a conversation never meant for your ears."

"I did it again, didn't I?" he asked.

"Did what?"

"That night at Burger Palace," he said, replaying that night and piecing together the missing information. "I was trying to make a joke about babies and the biological clock. I ruined the entire evening without even realizing it."

I shook my head. "It doesn't matter, Kyle. We want different things. You're not looking for anything serious, and I realized I'm finally ready to go down that road again. My biological clock *is* ticking, and I *do* want a family of my own sooner rather than later."

Quietly, he asked, "Did you see all of that happening with me?"

My mouth opened and shut. "I never said that."

"But you were leaning in that direction, weren't you? At least considering the possibility until I opened my big mouth and inserted both feet?"

"Kyle, I—"

He cut me off with another kiss that left me staggering backward against my car. I ducked away from him, locating my keys and my pepper spray.

"You have to stop!" I said, catching my breath. "You can't keep doing this to me, Kyle. Stop playing with my head!"

"I'm not playing with anything, Taylor! I want all of those things, and I want them with you!"

My keys promptly collided with the cement floor. "What did you just say?"

Kyle took a tentative step toward me. "Do you think I wanted to scare you off by telling you I think you're the one I've been searching for the past fifteen years? Disgusting, Rebecca-obsessed, non-Christian Kyle Goldstein? The one who has the nerve to think he'd be good enough for the singing choir angel?

Wasn't I just a pleasant distraction until you found some pure-as-the-driven-snow Christian? Like this Ian guy you apparently can't wait to marry?"

"I didn't say anything about marrying Ian. Rebecca told me to go out with him."

Voice thick with sarcasm, he said, "Why am I not surprised?"

"Look, she's the one who encouraged me to go out with you too, okay? She told me you chickened out six months ago, and that if Ian was still pursuing me—unlike you I might add—I may as well give it a shot."

"Rebecca told you to go out with me?" he asked, stunned.

"She told me to pray about it and trust what the Lord said. She told me if God had given her any kind of a warning about you that she would have said something, but it was still my decision to make. By the way, she just wants you to be happy."

Kyle surprised me when tears filled his eyes. "I wasn't expecting that. I wasn't expecting any of this, actually."

"You and me both."

"You're going to keep talking to me about Jesus, aren't you? This isn't going to be one of those agree to disagree things, right? It's your way or the highway?"

"I told Rebecca I would never consider dating a non-Christian. The Bible is clear about light having no fellowship with darkness."

Kyle's shoulders sank in immediate dejection. "Obviously, I'm the darkness in this scenario, and God says you should have nothing to do with me. You'd have to compromise your religion."

"Rebecca also told me that God doesn't always work the way we expect. She said we can suck the adventure out of our own lives by trying to be 'perfect' rather than trusting when God asks to do things that don't make sense."

"So, now you're saying you think God wants us to be together? I'm confused."

I prayed briefly before answering, wanting to be sure I didn't misspeak after so many months lost to assumption and fear of rejection. "Kyle, the honest answer is I don't know. I can't make another mistake like I did with Mitch. I was so ready to get married that I ignored the warning signs I'm only now seeing three and a half years after the divorce. I can't go through that heartbreak again. I can't handle another 'I told you so' victory dance from my mother as she sleeps her way through the over-fifty singles crowd in Hillcrest."

"She did that to you?" he gaped.

"More than once. She resented my faith in Jesus. She resented my contentment being single while she filled her own emptiness with any man who showed her attention. Beyond all that, my mother has to be the star of the show. Her highs are always higher than yours. Her lows are always lower than yours. She projects herself and her own emotions onto you. Whatever she would feel in a situation is exactly how you must be feeling. You have no right to think or feel anything other than what Sarah deems acceptable."

Kyle looked horrified. "You know, when Rebecca talked about this stuff with her family, I never really got it. I mean, conceptually, I understood what she was saying, but I just couldn't believe people actually behaved this way."

"Believe me, they exist. My father is no cake walk either."

"Oh yeah? What's his story?"

I took a deep breath willing to go for broke. "He and mother divorced when I was eleven. Although he's Jewish, we didn't grow up practicing anything and certainly not after my parents split. I'm not sure how much he was even around when my parents were together. My father remarried less than a year after the divorce. My mother said he had two other kids, but I never met them. He abandoned me and my younger brother, Gabe, and we haven't heard a peep in over twenty years. My mother went to work for a real estate agency and eventually got her license. She was gone most of the time, and she used me as free housekeeping and childcare for my brother."

"Free childcare? You were just a kid yourself. What the heck was she out doing?"

"She claimed she did it all for us and wined and dined her clients to sell houses. Of course, she also liked to wine and dine with her million boyfriends too. We had the school bus to take us to and from school, so she didn't need to bother with any of that. I would stay home alone with my brother, babysitting, cooking dinner out of a box, and doing laundry. As soon as I got my driver's license, my mother bought me a car so I could do the food shopping too. She liked to remind me about that car when I dared to complain about anything."

I took comfort in Kyle's look of revulsion. "I don't even have words, Taylor. It sounds like child abuse. At the very least, it was neglect."

"She took care of us financially. We always had food and clothes," I said, not quite ready to turn Sarah Meyers into another Bernard Ivy.

"But she dumped all of her responsibility as a parent on you! It's just so unbelievably selfish." After a brief pause, he said, "Do you think she ever messed around with your ex?"

"They worked together, believe it or not. My mother prefers to list houses, since it's less effort for her, and Mitch worked as her buyers' agent." Ruefully, I said, "She was more upset about having to deal with his clients than with him abandoning her daughter."

Kyle exhaled in disgust. "And you really think nothing ever happened between them? Based on everything you've told me and that tacky billboard, I wouldn't be surprised."

"I can't let myself go there, Kyle. There's enough water under the bridge as is. I haven't actually spoken to my mother in eighteen months. The last time I saw her was the day I met you at Los Bravos. My brother tried to stage an intervention and tricked me into going to church without a car. He thought he could force us to talk."

Kyle picked up my keys from the floor. He eyed the pepper spray on my keychain like an old frenemy. "Do you believe in third chances? Maybe a do over now that everything is out on the table?"

"What do you say to being the first man I've invited over to my new house? I'm not much of a cook, but I can handle scrambled eggs and turkey bacon. For dinner, not breakfast, just so we're crystal clear about that."

Kyle grinned, his blue eyes sparkling. "I don't want this to start like every other relationship I've had."

"Me neither."

CHAPTER 11

"NICE," KYLE SAID, RUNNING HIS HAND ALONG THE banister in my foyer. "You have a good eye for design."

"Thanks. Staring at pictures of everybody's else's houses for close to a decade gave me a good idea of what I wanted in my own home one day."

"So, is this the dream?" he asked, looking at me intently.

I smiled and shrugged. "No, not necessarily. But it's all me, my taste, instead of letting Mitch dictate everything."

"The more you talk about this guy, the more I want to punch him."

A full-fledged grin appeared on my face. "I certainly wouldn't stop you."

I led Kyle past the front entryway and dining room into the kitchen and living area. His eyes traveled over gold flecked, granite counters, white display cabinets, and a large window over my apron style sink. Turning to me, he said, "When I asked you to make me flyer bullets, you described your own house, didn't you?

"Guilty as charged."

"How can you live with a kitchen like this and not actually cook?"

"Well, what does your kitchen look like?" I asked.

"Old and outdated. Hence, I eat out."

Moving on from the kitchen to my family room, I gestured for Kyle to join me on the brown leather sectional.

"How can you afford all of this on the salary they pay you at Culver?"

"I own the house outright. Mitch and I had a lot of equity in the gaudy monstrosity out in Winthrope—plus some later discovered funds he squirreled away. After paying off my divorce attorney, I took the remainder and invested it in the townhouse to avoid capital gains tax. My mother listed these townhouses for the builder, and she cut her commission to help me out. A lot of the furniture I inherited from her when she decided to update her own home for the five millionth time, or she gave me a heads up about an estate sale. My mother is selfish, but she's not all bad."

Kyle smiled appreciatively. "That's quite a connection you've got. And you never wanted to go into real estate yourself?"

"Like I could compete with my mother's billboards," I deadpanned.

"You seem to know a lot about the industry, Taylor. I'm surprised you didn't go for more money."

"Did you get a raise when you switched to Cooper & Jaye?"

"Substantially."

"Were you happier with more money?"

Kyle conceded the point with a quick shrug of the shoulders. "So marketing is what you love to do then? Even if the compensation is better in sales or account management?"

I folded my legs underneath me on the sofa. "What I love to

do is sing, but I have no delusions of making some sort of music career out of it."

Kyle spotted my guitar case in the corner of the family room. "You play?"

"Eh, well enough so I don't need my own accompanist if I'm leading worship."

"What exactly does that mean?"

I raised an eyebrow. "You don't have worship in synagogue?"

"We worship God, if that's what you're talking about."

"Do you guys sing songs? You know, a band on stage or maybe just a piano or something?"

"The cantor sings some songs, and I think Rabbi Epstein mentioned getting a piano, but mostly it's just chanting. That Messianic place Rebecca and I went to had a small band. Definitely a new experience, but the music wasn't that great. The main guy sang offkey, and you could barely hear the girl at all."

I rolled my eyes and laughed. "Typical. I don't think there's much difference between that synagogue and half the churches I've visited. Mitch and I attended a non-denominational church that felt exactly like my college campus ministry experiences. Same dimmed lights and rock concert feel, except the members all had jobs to go to on Monday morning instead of classes."

"Sounds like you were a Christian rock star at your church. That must have been fun."

"Being on the worship team is an interesting experience, especially if you're the only female in a group full of guys."

"Why, do they hit on you or something?" he said with a wink.

"Total opposite. They ignore you. I remember begging the guys to rekey songs so I could sing lead, and they looked at me like I had three heads. I finally picked up the guitar and taught myself how to play. I made new lead sheets to fit my voice instead of having to screech out notes meant for tenors to sing. The guys didn't have much respect for vocalists, especially if you were 'just a singer.' Occasionally, they threw me a bone during the service, maybe one slow song before they relegated me to my usual, background vocals."

"You do not have a 'background' kind of voice, Taylor, and I'm not just saying that either. There's something about how you sing that just grabs you in the gut. I won't ask you to sing for me if you don't want to, but I really enjoyed listening to you outside of the restaurant. You were in your own little world."

Smiling, I replied, "I was. And I am when I sing to Jesus. Prayer is one way we connect with God, and I know from personal experience that worship is another."

Kyle looked thoughtful for a moment. "When I say 'worship,' I think of bowing down on the floor. When you say it, you're talking about singing or music. Am I right?"

I nodded. "Rebecca and I have talked a lot about the similarities and differences between Jewish and Christian congregational worship. The older Christian denominations borrow pretty heavily from the Jewish service order."

"Like the pope wearing a *yarmulke*?" Kyle said, gesturing toward his head at my look of confusion.

"I always wondered what you call those little beanies."

Kyle grinned at me. "You're cute."

"So you've said."

We stared at each other for a moment, wide grins on both of our faces. Kyle's expression shifted from humor to desire as his blue eyes stared into mine with a hunger I had never experienced before. Even in the heyday of my relationship with Mitch, he had never looked at me like that. I found it to be equal parts thrilling and absolutely terrifying.

Unable to hold his gaze, I looked away.

"You're scared, aren't you?" he asked.

I nodded.

"Of me?"

"Of myself," I confessed, daring a quick glance back up.

"Look, I was around Rebecca long enough to know where you're coming from with all of the no sex before marriage stuff. I heard all the lectures about *soul ties* and how sex connects us to people in ways God only designed for marriage."

My fear melted into genuine surprise. "She said that to you?"

Kyle's wry smile confirmed the answer. "Unless you and Rebecca have radically different views of this stuff—and I'm guessing you don't—I've already been forewarned about what to expect."

"Remind me to thank her," I said, "and I don't mean that as a joke, either. I really had no idea how to broach the subject. Even though I'm obviously not a virgin, I still feel like one in some ways. Does that sound weird?"

"You said that Mitch is the only boyfriend you've ever had, right?"

"Right."

"I don't want to get too personal here..." his voice trailed off.

I sighed and shrugged. "We may as well rip the bandage off. You're not just messing around here, are you?"

The intensity of Kyle's gaze answered before his mouth did. "No."

I nodded. "Just checking. What do you want to know?"

"Seriously?"

"Yeah, seriously."

"You're right that you act like a virgin, and I'm trying to understand why."

"You're wondering if I'm frigid and that's why my husband went looking to get his needs met elsewhere, right? My mother certainly felt that way. She sent me every spice up your sex life article in existence."

"Taylor, you didn't kiss me like you're frigid, but you react like you've barely been touched. Sort of like throwing something in the microwave. It starts off cold, but it gets hot really fast."

Hot on my cheeks was a blush born from just how keenly Kyle saw my inner struggle. Pressing onward with blunt honesty, I said, "My relationship with Mitch wasn't a very passionate one. It was more transactional than anything else."

Kyle frowned. "And you said your marriage fell apart when Mitchy-boy realized he wasn't the only show in town?"

"Wow," I murmured. "You know, I could never put my finger on what triggered the collapse until you just said that. I don't think Mitch ever saw me as my own person. Everything was all about Mitch. My job as his wife was making him look and feel good while having no needs of my own. Intimacy was never about him wanting *me,* just using me to meet his own needs. Anything he ever did for me, he called, 'helping you out,' like he was doing me some kind of favor. Then, it was all back to Mitch and whatever he wanted."

Kyle's lips pressed into a line. He raked a hand over closely cropped curls before answering. "I'm not exactly innocent in that area either. I know how I treated Heather. I look back and see how selfish I've been my entire life, and it makes me sick to my stomach. Rebecca was so different from anybody else I had ever known."

"Different how?"

Kyle held my gaze. "She gave. She gave even though I knew she dragged herself by her fingernails just to make it through each day. If my sister needed something, Rebecca was there. If her brother went back to jail or rehab, Rebecca had to calm her mother down. Every time her sister had some relationship crisis, Rebecca sat on the phone for hours just letting Ada suck the little bit of life she had left in her."

"Were you wanting Rebecca to do that for you?" I asked, searching his eyes. "I can see why that kind of codependent relationship might be appealing. Rebecca tried to show the love of Jesus to her friends and family, but even she will admit she got stuck actually trying to *be* Jesus instead of being *like* Him."

Kyle's forehead wrinkled for a moment. "I don't know if Rebecca felt like she couldn't say 'no' because she wasn't allowed to or because she didn't want to."

"Maybe a little bit of both," I said with a shrug. "Rebecca told me that when you're dealing with narcissistic people, they just drain the life and energy out of you. They bleed you dry like a vampire. When you complain or try to leave, they use shame, guilt, or even some pretty ridiculous stunts to ensure they don't lose their ego supply."

"That's probably what happened with Mitch," Kyle said. "He got mad you weren't around to fawn all over him and his amazing Bible teaching skills. He didn't like you getting attention by singing on stage or that your world didn't revolve around him anymore."

"You're right," I said, the weight of Kyle's words washing over me. "I think that's also the reason Mitch put off having children."

"What do you mean?"

"He knew I'd do the exact opposite of Sarah Meyers and be a very hands-on mother. It meant there'd be less attention for him. For years, I asked Mitch when we could start trying for a baby. The one we did conceive was by accident. That being said,

I'm almost positive that tramp's pregnancy was a deliberate set up."

"Does she have a name?" Kyle prodded gently.

"The same one as Pastor Sociopath, I guess."

His eyes widened. "Do you think she purposefully set out to ruin your life? The way that monster did to Rebecca?"

"I know she never liked me, not even from her first day working at StarRealty. I caught her making eyes at Mitch, and I talked to both of them privately about it. Mitch insisted she was totally harmless and that he wasn't interested. When I talked to her, she said if our *Christian* marriage was so wonderful, then I had nothing to worry about."

"So, she went after your husband deliberately?"

"Not a doubt in my mind. Mitch just ate up the attention. I honestly don't know what he thought he could get from her that he wasn't getting from me."

"Herpes?" Kyle deadpanned.

I burst into a fit of high pitched hysterics that had Kyle laughing along with me.

When I finally got myself under control, I replied, "Herpes, huh? Is that what they call 'experience' nowadays? Maybe Mitch liked the thrill of forbidden fruit. At this point, it doesn't really matter. The longer Mitchell Ross is out of my life, the more I realize how much he stifled me. I will never admit this to my mother, but she was right about him. She never liked Mitch."

"But she worked with him," Kyle said, confused.

"My mother knew Mitch was good at putting on appearances, charming clients, and making the sale. As a son-in-law, she found him to be rude and condescending, but she ultimately blamed *me* for the divorce."

"Are you kidding?! What kind of mother would do that?"

I shook my head sadly. "I got saved at eleven years-old. I

preached to my mother about fornication while she went out of her way to flaunt her sex life in my face. To blame Mitch's adultery on my inexperience made her feel vindicated for all of the abuse she claims I put her through with my religious beliefs."

Kyle looked incredulous. "So, she excused your husband's adultery because she wanted revenge for how you behaved in middle school? That's insane!"

I rolled my eyes. "Welcome to the Meyers family version of crazy."

CHAPTER 12

TAKING A BREAK FROM THE HEAVIER TOPICS OF Mitch or my mother, Kyle and I engaged in a scandalous series of Mad Gab, fill in the blank stories. And by scandalous, I mean that I laughed so hard I almost wet myself.

"How do you do that?" I wheezed before dissolving into another fit of giggles. "Kyle, you pick the most out of left field words that work perfectly! I can't even read this!" I threw the pad down so I could wipe the tears off of my cheeks.

Kyle beamed at me, and I realized that I liked the slight crinkles around his eyes when he did. Holding back a laugh, he said, "Did you think you're the only person who knows what 'pulchritudinous' means?"

At the mention of *that word* again, I fell off the couch. Not figuratively. Literally.

Distressed, Kyle jumped from his chair and bent down to make sure I was okay. His beautiful blue eyes were all concern for me. "Are you sure you didn't hurt anything?"

I smirked. "Other than my pride?"

The smile returned easily to Kyle's mouth as did those delightful little lines beside his eyes. He reached out a hand and cupped the side of my face.

"I like the haircut," he said. "It suits you, Taylor. And no, you don't look like a Lost Boy."

"At least it's a step up from a librarian."

"Not in those boots," Kyle said, his eyes glancing toward my discarded footwear in the corner.

I placed my hand over his. "Thanks for the laughs and thanks for listening. It means a lot. Compassion and sympathy are in short supply these days."

"So I gathered. And your sister-in-law sounds like a real peach. I went out with a girl like that once. She was gorgeous, but she was also insanely jealous and insecure. All she really had going for her was her looks, and she was afraid people would find out there was nothing below the surface. Of course, some guys like beautiful, stupid women."

"And you prefer dowdy, intelligent librarians, right?"

"Beautiful librarians," he corrected, staring into my eyes and raising the hairs on my arms. "You don't look like a librarian anymore, Taylor. Not in those jeans, and definitely not with that haircut. Those Parkview stylists know what they're doing."

"You make me feel beautiful," I said, "and not just because you're so fond of the adjective. No wonder all the ladies find you irresistible."

The lines beside Kyle's eyes migrated to the sides of his mouth in a frown, and he dropped his hand from my face. He closed his eyes and exhaled wearily. "The 'naughty list' isn't as long as you think, Taylor. Half of it was for Rebecca's benefit, and not every date ended up in my apartment...or my bed."

Remorseful, I said, "It was a totally stupid thing to say, Kyle, and I'm sorry."

"It's an ice bucket to the face and probably the best thing that could have happened. I had no idea how I was going to force myself to leave you alone here."

My eyebrows raised in question.

Kyle continued, "We barely know each other, Taylor, but I feel like I've known you my entire life. I guess this is what people mean when they say you just know when it's the right person."

Afraid of the answer, I still asked the question anyway. "The right person? I'm not misunderstanding your meaning here, am I?"

"I'm not stupid enough to rush into an engagement like my sister did. I mean, I'm glad that Rebecca is happy, but I think her story has to be the exception, not the rule."

"Kyle, I'm still trying to figure out how we went from two dates six months ago to potentially talking about a whole lot more."

He chuckled. "Me too. I know what I want, but I also know that if I rush this, I'm going to ruin it. Sort of like a cake. Or at least what I've been forced to watch when my sister puts on that British baking competition at her house."

I grinned. "I'd like to meet your sister if that doesn't seem too forward. She sounds really cool, actually."

"Even though she's playing the role of the 'other woman'? Doesn't that hit a little too close to home for you, Taylor?"

"Kyle, you know your sister better than anybody, right?"

He nodded.

"Do you think it's more likely that your sister went after this coworker of hers, or that he went after your sister knowing she had just broken off her engagement? I know for a fact that Mitch's little tramp went after him, but nothing you've told me about your sister makes me think she went looking for an affair.

She sounds like she's in a lot of pain and that she's being taken advantage of."

"And you want to help, right? Are you going to talk to her about Jesus? Rebecca tried already, and it didn't go so well."

"Do you think that all Christians do is just preach Jesus at people? That we're not real people with real pain, just like everybody else?"

Kyle exhaled a short burst of laughter. "Honestly? Yeah, I do. Most of the ones I've met act like they have it all figured out."

"My heart goes out to your sister, Kyle, and I'd like to just try being a friend. Believe me, I know firsthand how so-called 'Christian' comfort can be nothing more than self-righteous condemnation. Chloe told me that my lack of faith kept God from saving my baby's life."

Kyle held up his hands. "Back up a minute. Chloe actually told you that it was your fault your baby died?"

I seamed my lips, not wanting to unearth the old memories.

"There's another story here," Kyle said, searching my eyes.

I sighed. "Chloe did eventually apologize...well, sort of. She said she was sorry I misunderstood her. She backpedaled like crazy when Brian caught wind of what she'd done."

Kyle had a few of his own comments regarding Chloe's unrepentant behavior. I blushed at his vehemence.

"Haven't we had enough of my poor, pathetic stories for one day?" I said, eager to change the subject. "Besides, my leg is starting to fall asleep sitting like this."

Kyle stood up, then helped me to my feet. He didn't release my hands. "Whoever told you that your stories are pathetic was a selfish, heartless sadist."

"Well, then I guess that makes me all of the above."

Kyle's brows raised. "Why would you tell yourself that, Taylor?"

"Because it's ancient history, and I don't like talking about it."

"If it's so ancient, then you shouldn't look like you're ready to cry. You're barely holding back tears in those beautiful eyes of yours. I'm still trying to figure out what color they are, by the way."

"Muddy. That's what my mother always called them. Nothing special."

"And you believed her?"

I shrugged.

"Taylor," Kyle said, grabbing my shoulders, "I thought you'd be the one preaching at me about how God loves you and all of that, but I think you're the one who needs to hear it. What your sister-in-law did was absolutely disgusting. I don't care if you're Jewish, Christian, or whatever. You don't go around saying stuff like that. When did she tell you that garbage?"

"The day I found out I lost the baby," I said quietly. "I came home early from work because I started bleeding. I hadn't even told Mitch I was pregnant yet, but I told Chloe, thinking she'd be happy to have a future niece or nephew. I had an OB appointment that morning and found out the baby had no heartbeat. I don't know why I even bothered going to work afterwards—maybe to get my mind off of things—but I came home once I started cramping."

"Was Chloe in the house?"

"No, I called her on my way. She told me to 'speak life' and that I needed to have faith that God could raise the baby from the dead."

"That's just sick!" Kyle said angrily. "How did you even talk to the woman after that?"

"Because losing the baby wasn't the only horrific trauma that day."

Kyle closed his eyes and took a deep breath. "This was the part I overheard with Miss Belle. You came home to grieve, and there they were."

"The homewrecker was asleep in my bed as if it was *her* bed, *her* house, *her* fifth wedding anniversary! I was planning to surprise Mitch with the pregnancy once I confirmed everything was okay with the OB. The surprise was all on me apparently," I said, dissolving into tears.

Kyle pulled me into an embrace, and I took full advantage of the opportunity to sob against his chest. With so many tears to shed, I found it difficult to determine which to mourn first. I had made peace with the baby lost years earlier, thankful my child would never know the abandonment from its father like I had suffered from Jonathan Meyers. I rejoiced that my child played in heaven free from the pain of this world.

I realized I had never formally forgiven Chloe, only that I chose to move on for the sake of my relationship with Brian. Chloe had never taken responsibility for her lapse in judgment, and she funneled anger at herself into resentment toward me instead. She was livid when Brian read her the riot act rather than agreeing with her callous words. He had forced her into an apology she didn't want to give, and she hated me for that too. I prayed and asked God to help let go of the injustice done to me.

I mourned for my own innocence lost, the near shipwreck of my faith when I railed at God for bringing me a lying adulterer posing as a godly, devoted husband. I wanted to know why things went so abysmally wrong when I'd done everything "the right way." Mitch's infidelity made a liar out of me and a source of mockery for my mother.

Kyle released me to retrieve a box of tissues from my breakfast bar. He presented the box to me as he looked at me with pitying blue eyes.

"Don't feel sorry for me," I said after blowing my nose.

"How am I supposed to feel, Taylor?"

"Just no pity, okay? My mother uses tears and guilt to get what she wants, and I refuse to be anything like her."

"It's not guilt or pity keeping me here, Taylor. My heart physically aches for you. Calling it 'wrong' feels like such an understatement to the hell you've been put through."

I sniffled and blew my nose. "Chloe told me I just play the victim and share my 'woe is me' story to get sympathy."

"Chloe is an entitled, self-righteous hypocrite whose opinion means less than nothing as far as I'm concerned. I can't imagine your brother-in-law being happily married to her anyway."

That surprised me, and my tears dried up. "Why would you think Brian's unhappy? I've seen the two of them publicly and privately, and Brian genuinely loves his wife. It's why I don't understand this crazy jealousy Chloe has for me."

"Why did Brian marry Chloe? Beyond the fact she's apparently some gorgeous amazon?"

I thought for a moment, trying to remember the Sunday dinner when Brian first mentioned Chloe. "He said he asked out a girl working in the coffee shop. He called her stunning even with the uniform, visor, and ponytail. Brian said when he told her, 'God bless you' as he was leaving that she started to cry. It was actually a really sweet story. Brian said he couldn't believe someone so beautiful would ever go for somebody like him."

"Does Brian look like he belongs in a belltower at Notre Dame?"

I chuckled. "No, he's not ugly at all. Mitch is definitely the better looking of the brothers, even with the receding hairline. Brian's kindness draws people to him."

Kyle studied me for a moment. "And nothing ever happened

with you two? You never felt anything for Brian even after the divorce?"

"Absolutely not! I saw Brian as a big brother, and he referred to me as his little sister all the time. Brian never looked at me with adoring eyes or ever did anything inappropriate. *Ever,*" I added, seeing Kyle's look of skepticism. "Chloe invented this nonsense in her head."

"Maybe she saw what you two tried to deny."

"Are you saying that Brian has feelings for me that I don't know about, that he doesn't even know about, but the praying mantis can see them clear as day?"

Kyle shrugged. "You told me you're tired of everyone at Culver measuring you to Rebecca's golden standard. What if Chloe feels the same way about you? She said Brian talked you up all the time with your love for God and how you sing. Does *Chloe* talk about Jesus as easily as you do? Does *Chloe* sound like a choir of angels should be singing backup?"

I blushed at Kyle's compliment but also gave thought to his words. Simply, I replied, "No."

"Okay, so what does Chloe offer outside of looking good next to Brian and making beautiful children? Is she Saint Teresa feeding the poor and taking care of orphans?"

"Not really. Most people find Chloe pretty aloof. She uses her kids as an excuse to leave early while Brian talks or prays with people."

"I rest my case."

I sat dumbfounded. "I'm her Rebecca Ivy, aren't I?"

"Concerning Brian Ross, it sure sounds like it."

"What about as far as you're concerned?" I asked boldly. "Am I being held to a Rebecca Ivy checkbox of traits?"

"I told Rebecca I wanted somebody *like* her. Obviously, if she and I were meant to be together, we would be. If I had arrived fifteen minutes earlier to my sister's condo, it would have been me pouring my heart out to Rebecca instead of Ted Margolin."

"She did mention that you discovered their relationship pretty painfully."

Kyle's expression looked haunted as I watched him conjure the memory. "Not quite like Mitch and his mistress, but I walked in on Rebecca in her pajamas with Margolin at my sister's breakfast table."

"Why was Rebecca in her pajamas? And why was she at your sister's house?"

"Rebecca had a PTSD blackout, and she spent the night at Jessica's place. Margolin asked Rebecca out on a date a day or two earlier, but my sister took it upon herself to call the mighty Margolin to let him know what happened. He blew off meetings with Triple J and Guildcorp to rush over there."

My eyes grew large. "That's pretty serious. I bet Deondre hit the roof."

Kyle scoffed. "Deondre hopes to eventually join the producer, good ole boy club, so he took it with relish. He also dumped his work on me and MacKenzie."

"The benefits of being an Account Executive, I guess."

"Deondre never really liked me anyway. He said I spent too much time pining for Rebecca."

"Was he right?"

CHAPTER 13

KYLE SHRUGGED. "YES AND NO. I DID SPEND A LOT OF time at Rebecca's desk, but she was also one of my best friends. I knew she went through a lot with her family and the secrets with her old church."

"Pastor Sociopath," I said. "Now, we hear about him almost nightly on the news."

"The guy deserves to fry. I can't believe it's taking this long for things to go to trial."

"They charged him with multiple counts of lewd conduct and sexual assault of minors. I heard they also opened an investigation into tax evasion and other fraudulent activity after they gave his ex-wives the option to testify or face prosecution themselves. It takes a while to sort through that much evidence."

"Makes your head spin, doesn't it?"

I nodded. "My life has certainly been filled with its share of heartache, but I would not trade places with Rebecca for a minute."

"Especially since you'd be stuck with boring old Ted Margolin instead of here with me," Kyle said with a cheeky grin.

I laughed and returned his smile. "You're pretty cute too, you know that?"

"She finally admits it!" he said with a triumphant clap of the hands. "I believe this calls for a celebration. Apparently, you're allergic to anything that isn't water, but hopefully, you have some food I can eat."

Taking the hint, I stuck my tongue out at Kyle before heading into the kitchen to forage for sustenance. I opened my fridge and located a carton of brown eggs and nitrate free, turkey bacon.

I felt Kyle just behind me taking in the contents of my healthy food supply. "I see you like shopping at Joey's Real Food."

I chuckled and ducked under his arm with the eggs and bacon. I pulled a skillet out from a lower cabinet and my trusty bottle of olive oil from the spice cabinet to the right of the stove.

"Where are the plates and silverware?" he asked. "My mother didn't teach me much about cooking, but she certainly showed me how to set a table."

I smiled. "So we're suddenly going formal with our breakfast for dinner?"

Kyle shrugged. "Eh, it's the least I can do."

"How about I teach you a little bit of cooking so we start breaking millennial stereotypes?"

"I'm game."

Kyle and I thoroughly enjoyed the cooking tutorial. We laughed at eggshells that fell into my mixing bowl and Kyle's simultaneous fascination and disgust with turkey bacon. He asked why I needed so much olive oil to cook it since he just threw his traditional bacon in the pan. Bacon was, in fact, one of the few items Kyle Goldstein knew how to cook at all.

For one so proud of his Jewish heritage, I found Kyle's familiarity with pork products rather shocking. It seemed like such an odd dichotomy, this deep love for Israel and desire to preserve his ethnic identity, yet Kyle only seemed to understand it superficially. He accepted cultural norms as "that's just how we do it," yet never stopped to question why. When I brought this to Kyle's attention during our breakfast-for-dinner, he seemed perplexed.

"What do you mean, do I check the Bible with what Rabbi Epstein says?"

I raised an eyebrow. "Exactly what I said. Do you go home, pick up your Bible, and read the passages for yourself?"

"Why would I do that?"

"Why wouldn't you? Don't you want to be sure what he teaches lines up with what God says? Why do you think so many kool-juice drinkers supported Bernard Ivy for all of those years?"

Kyle scoffed. "We don't have all of that weird, hyper spiritual lingo you Christians do. Besides, the Torah is really, really complicated. Not even the rabbis understand it."

"Who told you that horse manure?" I blurted out.

"Rabbi Epstein," Kyle said, all humor gone from his face.

"Your rabbi actually told you not to bother reading God's Word?"

"The Torah is totally different than your Christian Bible."

"Was it this same rabbi who taught you that too?"

"What are you saying?"

"Kyle!" I said, exasperated. "Don't you understand who you are?"

"I know who I am," he said defensively. "Most persecuted

people group on the planet. Hated the world over. Blamed for everything that goes wrong. If it's not anti-Semitism, then it's anti-Israel, anti-Zionist garbage spewed from the left, the right, and pretty much anybody in between. What's your point, Taylor? What does that have to do with the Bible?"

"Kyle, you talk about the Torah, but do you know what it is?"

He looked at me like I was a complete moron.

I exhaled in frustration and prayed silently for patience. "Let me rephrase. You know the Torah is a physical scroll inside the ark in your synagogue. I totally get that. But do you know what the Torah says? Do you want to know? Do you know that the books of the Torah, those books you believe Moses wrote, are the exact same books in my Christian Bible?"

A light bulb finally flickered. "Wait, what?"

I jumped up excitedly from the table. I pulled three Bibles down from my family room wall unit: my own NIV study Bible, *The Complete Jewish Bible* Rebecca had given me a few months earlier, and a 1960's JPS *Tanakh*, the only artifact I possessed proving my connection to Jonathan Meyers.

I opened all three books to *Genesis 1*, inviting Kyle to join me on the couch.

"See, it's all the same. 'In the beginning, God created the heavens and the earth,'" I said, pointing from one Bible to another. "The translation will be different, but it's all the same source material. One is a Christian translation, one is Messianic Jewish, and one is traditional Jewish. The Messianic and Christian Bibles have the Old and New Testaments. The Messianic and Jewish Bibles have the books ordered differently, but it's all the same books."

"This looks too big to fit onto the Torah they have in synagogue," Kyle said, more pensive than I had ever seen him.

"The Torah is the first five books of the Bible, Jewish or Christian. I don't want to talk to you like you're ignorant, Kyle, but since your rabbi doesn't seem to think you need to actually read what it says, would you like me to explain?"

Kyle nodded, but his expression remained inscrutable.

"The Bible starts off with the book of Genesis. You can see that the JPS Bible has the Hebrew name over here—which I can't read—but the Messianic one has an English transliteration. Genesis starts with God's creation of the cosmos and then tells the narrative of the Jewish patriarchs from Adam to Noah, Abraham, Isaac, Jacob, all the way to Joseph." Seeing Kyle's flustered state, I said, "Am I losing you, Kyle? You look confused."

"How...I mean...how do you know all of this? And why don't I know anything about it?"

"You went to Hebrew school, right?"

"Yeah."

"Did you have a *bar mitzvah*?"

"It was a *b'nei mitzvah* with my sister, but yeah. We did ours together."

"What did they teach you being Jewish means? Is it just about celebrating holidays, eating certain foods, and making sure you don't believe in Jesus?" I held up the JPS Tanakh, figuring Kyle might be the least intimidated by that translation. "Kyle, the people in this book are your ancestors. You are related by blood to the men and women on the page. This is why those fangirl Christians get so excited when they meet you. Your existence proves that God exists. He even says so in *Deuteronomy 7*."

"You've totally lost me, Taylor, and I'm honestly overwhelmed right now." He handed the Tanakh back to me as if lightning might strike him for touching it.

I laid the book gently on my lap. "This is the only link I have to my father. My mother trashed every photo and every memento we had. I found this buried in a box when I moved out of her house and into my first apartment with Mitch."

"So, it means a lot to you, then?"

I smiled sadly. "You can see the inscription on the first page. Given to Jonathan Meyers by my long lost grandparents, Irving and Sylvia Meyers."

"I hear there's a boon on Jewish grandparents coming out of the woodwork these days. You and Rebecca are starting a trend."

Ignoring his droll remark, I continued, "I like to read out of the JPS, especially when I'm studying in the Old Testament. The Messianic translation follows pretty closely to the JPS, and the transliteration is a fun challenge. My semester of linguistics gets put to good use when I try to pronounce everything. Mitch taught a series about the history of Bible translation. He talked about how these Hebrew names and places wound up with j's and w's when neither letter exists in the Hebrew alphabet. I found it fascinating."

"Sounds like Mitch was quite a scholar," Kyle deadpanned. "I don't know how you can take anything he said seriously considering his holier-than-thou routine was all a scam."

I met Kyle's gaze head on. "You sound jealous."

"Do I?"

"Yeah, you do. There are plenty of people who study the Bible from an academic or historical perspective. They can tell you the ins and outs of Biblical history, culture, and translations, yet they know nothing about the God they read about on the page. It's all very clinical and detached, like a museum curator describing a painting and reciting facts about the artist. That's not the same thing as knowing the painter personally.

Mitch could talk circles around people with his knowledge of the Bible. He could win almost any argument or debate. But if you asked him about his relationship with Jesus, what God was doing in his life, all he could offer was some generic answer he probably stole from his brother."

Kyle's expression turned sardonic. "Is this the part where you talk to me about having a 'relationship' with God rather than a 'religion'? It's sweet, Taylor, but Rebecca and a hundred other Christians have tried the same conversion tactics. I'm Jewish. I don't need Jesus."

"Well, what do you need?" I asked.

Kyle looked at me for a long minute. I did not imagine the sudden pounding of my heart or the lack of moisture in my mouth.

"I'm a package deal, Kyle. You know that."

He sighed and closed his eyes wearily. "I know."

"I am not going to preach at you, hit you over the head with fire and brimstone, or trick you into coming to church with me. That's not my style. Manipulating takes time, effort, and strategy, and I tend to be more of a go-getter and ask questions later type. I do want to talk to you about God, but I want to share what He's done in my life."

"You mean like sacrificing your virginity on the altar for a total pig? What about losing a baby or walking in on your husband's mistress? Let's not forget smug Saint Chloe looking down her nose at you. Taylor, if you're trying to sell me on Jesus based on all of that, you're going to have to do better."

Kyle's words cut deeply, and I flinched in pain. "I've yelled and screamed at God about the state of my life. I never doubted He sent Jesus to die for my sins, only that He seemed pleased to watch me suffer. It was a line of thinking Rebecca rebuked not long after we met. She reminded me that Jesus also promises us joy, peace, and comfort, not just suffering for His sake." I glanced over at Kyle, watching him watch me with regret clear on his face.

"This isn't just religion for you, is it?" he said. "This whole Jesus *shtick* is your entire life. And I just took a huge du—"

I cut him off. "As I'm sure you can imagine, nobody overcomes the things I've been through overnight. I've also been ignoring it for a long time hoping it will disappear on its own or fade into distant memory."

"And then I came along," Kyle said ruefully, "and stirred it all up again."

"Kyle, I haven't really been living. I've been existing, getting by each day. All of the old wounds came alive once blood started flowing there again. I'm not at peace with everything that's happened, and I need to be before our relationship can go anywhere. It's probably going to get a lot uglier before it gets better. If you want to cut loose and run, I would totally understand."

"I told you I wanted this relationship to be different than any other I've had, and I meant that," Kyle said. "I just had no idea it would be so hard."

"What do you think marriage is, Kyle? Even if you're married to the right person, there's still challenges and heartache. There's the unforeseen incidences of life. Chloe and Brian have a toddler and a new baby with more energy than I've ever seen. Chloe's unfriendliness may also come from being completely exhausted while Brian spends more time with the Freedom members than he does with his own kids. It's not an uncommon thing for couples in ministry and one that our mutual friend can certainly attest to."

"So you're saying Ted and Rebecca aren't living life happily ever after? That it's all a facade of family togetherness?

Everyone sure seemed cozy with those Thanksgiving photos she emailed my parents."

I reached over to hold Kyle's hands. "It's not a facade, Kyle. The Margolins are happy. It doesn't mean life is problem free. Rebecca still gets harassed from former church members, but she's not fighting these battles all alone anymore. I'm not at liberty to share any of Ted's story, but he hasn't exactly lived a charmed life either."

Kyle looked down at my hands and slowly stroked my palms with his thumbs. His piercing blue gaze sought something in the muddy waters of mine.

"Taylor, I haven't been through a tenth of the garbage you have, but you have more hope and insight into life than I think I'd have in a hundred lifetimes."

I glanced down at the Bible still sitting in my lap. "It all starts there, Kyle."

His thumbs stilled.

"I know it sounds corny, but I would have probably killed myself from grief if not for Jesus. There's a verse in *Psalm 27* that says, 'even though my father and mother forsake me, the Lord will lift me up.' When I found that Bible verse, I clung to it with everything I had in me. Is my life perfect? No. Did everything work out like a fairytale because I believe in Jesus? No. But the Lord reminded me that He's not finished with my story yet."

"So, you think God sent me as your knight in shining armor?"

"I already have a savior, Kyle. I don't need another one."

My response caught him off guard. "That's a funny word, isn't it? People always talk about Jesus as their 'Lord and Savior,' but I've never really understood why. Savior from what?"

I smiled gently. "The easy answer is 'from our sins,' which is true. He also saved us from responding to things the way the world does. Sin is not just in the things we do but also how we react to life's curveballs. People wonder why I still praise God and sing to Him even though He seems to be refitting my broken heart one small piece at a time."

"Yes," Kyle said, blue eyes full of compassion and wonder.

"Christians talk so much about the death of Jesus, but we often forget about His resurrection. The Bible says the power that raised Jesus back to life is the same Holy Spirit of God living in all who profess Jesus as Lord. The Living Word of God, Jesus Christ, is the creative power that spoke the universe into existence out of absolutely nothing. The Latin is *ex nihilo*. He is the same creative power who can take the rubble and destruction from my marriage and transform it into something more beautiful than I could ever imagine. The hope I have in Jesus goes far beyond the cross."

We stared at one another silently before tears found their way down Kyle's cheeks and into his beard. He never explained the cause, only assured me that everything was fine and he needed to get going. He held me in a long embrace before exiting the front door. I sighed and leaned back against the wall in my foyer, wondering what God had in store for us next.

CHAPTER 14

BASED ON ALL OF THE SCRIPTURES I READ THE following morning, the Lord seemed to be warning me of a backlash to my unexpected day off of work. I knew I could trust Miss Belle and Phil to keep things with Kyle under wraps, but the wildcards remained MacKenzie and our temp-to-perm receptionist, Brooklyn.

"Feeling better?" the recent college grad asked from behind the front desk.

I offered a small smile, not two seconds in the office and already on the defensive. "Much better, thanks."

"Who was the guy?" Brooklyn said mischievously. "I don't normally like facial hair, but it totally works for your mystery man. Oh, and the way he looked at you! It was totally a *Prideful Prejudice* moment. You know when Dancy stares at Annabeth playing the piano at Pemberton," she said, fanning herself dramatically.

No longer annoyed but curiosity piqued, I reassessed our

newest Culver hire. "I take it you're a fan of the six hour version of *Prideful Prejudice*?"

"Collier Firthe. Best Dancy ever. Sorry, not sorry," she said as if speaking in hashtags.

"Agreed. He's my favorite Dancy too."

Brooklyn batted her lashes. "Speaking of favorite men, anything you want to share about your mystery guy? Is that your boyfriend or something?"

While my mind scurried to craft a veiled response, I heard Ted Margolin's trademark sound of squeaky loafers and jangling keys heralding his arrival to the office.

"Good morning, Brooklyn," he said with a quick lift of the chin. "Taylor, can I speak with you in the conference room, please?"

I nodded and followed the mighty Margolin into one of our smaller meeting rooms. He choose one more secluded from the main office thoroughfare.

Once Ted closed the door, I decided to go on a pre-emptive strike. "Look, I already know what you're going to say. I got an earful from Phil and Miss Belle yesterday."

Shockingly, bits of gold glittered in Ted's eyes instead. "Good thing I don't take my cues from either of them, hmm?"

My head cocked to the side. "Come again?"

"Did you actually pepper spray Goldstein in the parking garage?"

I blushed then laughed. "Yes."

"And he still agreed to meet with you after that?"

"Yes."

"And six months later, he shows up at Culver—which couldn't have been easy for him—and it's all to see you? Do I have my facts right, Taylor? Phil thought he could get me to run interference when he filled me in yesterday. Quite a shock for

the old man when I called him out for humiliating you and
Goldstein."

"Why does everybody call him Goldstein instead of Kyle?"

Ted shrugged. "We just do."

"I don't know him as 'Goldstein' like the rest of you. To me,
he's just Kyle, and he's nothing like the way any of you have
described him. Well, other than his knack for sticking his foot
in his mouth. He's done that a few times already."

"I get the impression you thought I would offer some kind
of dire warning against dating Goldstein. My wife certainly
thought so," Ted said.

"You started the conversation with 'Taylor, I need to speak
with you,' so I braced myself for the worst."

One side of Ted's mouth lifted. "I can't fault Goldstein for
being drawn to the same qualities in you that he saw in
Rebecca. You both share an unwavering faith in God that's hard
to resist. Likewise, both you and Rebecca went unnoticed and
unappreciated in this office for a long time. After the Cheesecake Corp RFP, my wife asked if I had recommended you for
Culver Super Star."

I smiled. "Figures she'd be behind that somehow."

Ted's lopsided grin spread into a full smile. "My wife cares
about you a lot, Taylor. I think she sees you as the little sister
she wishes she had in Ada. I want you to know we've both
prayed for you, specifically about this situation with Goldstein.
You have our full support no matter what you decide to do. Not
that you need our blessing or approval, but Rebecca thought
you could use some moral support right now."

Tears pricked my eyes at the thoughtfulness of both
Margolins. Aware of Ted and I being alone in an office together
even with glass windows making us visible to the rest of the

Culver associates, I refrained from the hug I wanted to give him. Instead, I beamed at the mighty Margolin.

"Thank you so much, Ted. I didn't realize how much I needed to hear that. MacKenzie saw us going into the elevator yesterday, and I've been dreading coming back to work."

"She stopped by my office fishing for information yesterday."

I rolled my eyes. "Doesn't MacKenzie already have a note in her file for gossiping? She gripes about it all the time."

"I reminded Ms. Pascale of that note when she made her thinly veiled inquiries. I hope she leaves you alone, Taylor, but there's only so much I can do. Regardless of what happens with Goldstein, I highly recommend keeping things low profile. My wife and I were not so fortunate in that area, and it caused some unnecessary trouble for us."

"Speaking of, Deondre has walked past the conference room three times. Either he's looking for you, or he's looking for intel."

Ted gave a resigned sigh. "Wouldn't it be wonderful if grownups actually behaved like grownups?"

"I'd have nothing for my memoirs if that was the case," I said dryly, pulling open the door.

"Are you writing too?" Ted asked.

I glanced up at him. "Too?"

"My wife said she wanted to put some things to paper, share her story, and see if she can reach out to others with similar experiences."

"Ted, I was mostly kidding, but you should definitely tell Rebecca to write a book. I know I'd read it!"

That golden twinkle found its way back to the mighty Margolin's eyes. His face lit up any time someone mentioned his wife.

I smiled all the way to my office thinking about my friends

and their happy marriage. Unfortunately, Julie misinterpreted my grin as a night well spent with Culver's former bad boy.

"You know me a lot better than that," I said coolly, offended at the assumption.

Julie pressed on, unfazed. "Brooklyn said it was like watching a soap opera. Whoever this Culver baddie is, apparently it's he who shall not be named. Phil sent out a memo yesterday about respecting the privacy of current and former employees."

Just another thank you I owed to Ted Margolin. Kyle might find himself surprised to learn about that.

"Anything you care to share?" she coaxed.

"Why? So I can be everyone's source of entertainment for the day?" I snapped. "Thanks, but no thanks."

Hurt brown eyes met mine, and I sighed.

"I'm not trying to be mean, Julie, but please consider how'd you feel in my position."

"You mean having some blue eyed hottie sweep me out of here and put a goofy smile on my face the next morning? Where do I sign up?"

I rolled my eyes at the sensationalized series of events. "This is exactly why Phil sent an email about office gossip."

This time, Julie wore the sour expression. "Deondre said this guy's totally hung up on Ted's wife, and he up and quit Culver because of it."

"Sounds like everyone enjoyed their big info swap," I said before plopping into my chair. I matched a revised document draft on my desk with the electronic version on file and began editing. I could feel Julie staring at me.

"You already got your fill of gossip, yesterday, Julie. I'm done talking about it."

"It wasn't like that," she insisted. She stood in front of my workstation so I faced both her and my computer monitor.

I clicked on a textbox to make several edits before meeting Julie's gaze again. "Look, we have a ton of work requests to get done before EOB today and tomorrow. I'm not discussing my love life with you, and I'm annoyed you went behind my back. If you have a question, then ask. Otherwise, can we just focus on work, please?"

Julie's lips bent into a sharp frown. "Did it ever occur to you that we might be happy for you, Taylor? Instead, you're acting all self-righteous just because we're curious."

I stood up to my full five feet and a whopping, two extra inches. "I don't appreciate being labelled as self-righteous by the same people hypocritically dissecting my life."

"It becomes our business when you bring it to the office," Julie said, arms crossed petulantly over her chest.

"Working together does not entitle you to know what goes on in my life after hours or even during business hours, Julie. Unless I choose to share something regarding my personal life, please consider it off limits. Let's just stick to a healthy working relationship, okay?"

My brand new coworker tendered her resignation shortly thereafter. Julie also spread unflattering tidbits about me around the office by painting me as controlling, holier-than-thou, and possessive of our work documents.

By Friday, Phil informed Julie Easton that Culver Incorporated no longer required her presence. He also called me into his office to discuss the situation.

"Seems like we just can't keep anybody here," he said from behind his desk. "Your job position has not been an easy one to fill, Taylor. We either find the graphic designer with no real copy editing skills or the worker bee who does what they're told with zero initiative. You and Mrs. Margolin are a rare breed, Taylor Ross, and I want you to know Bonnie and I are working hard to find a better fit this time. Sometimes, it feels like searching for a unicorn."

I swallowed, relieved to still be employed.

Phil chuckled softly to himself. "I remember being in a similar situation with Rebecca, of her sitting there just like you are, deer in headlights, absolutely convinced she was going to lose her job over office gossip."

"Phil, I—"

He cut me off with an upheld hand. "Your personal life is none of my business, Taylor, and I had no right to interfere. The mighty Margolin finally got one on the old man over here, and he put me in my place. I'd like to extend an apology to you and Goldstein for how I behaved. Ted corrected several assumptions, and I'm glad to hear everybody has moved on."

I nodded, not sure what to say.

"Your work here is exceptional, Taylor, and we hope you will continue on with us at Culver. No company is perfect—as I'm sure you know—but I will not tolerate needless gossip in a professional environment."

"Thank you," I finally managed to get out.

"As I told the Margolin lovebirds almost two years ago, keep the extracurricular activities extracurricular, and I will do my best to stop any office murmurings."

I smiled, glad to see the Phil Robbins I remembered and respected rather than the man who displayed some of his warts during the horrible elevator fiasco.

"You make all of us look a lot better and brighter on paper, Taylor. Joe Trautweig can't shut up about what you did to his Tricity RFP."

My tentative smile transformed into a full grin. "I heard a

little something about that," I said, recalling Kyle's mention of it before I'd promptly pepper sprayed him.

"Does this mean you can put me back on the wedding guest list?" Phil asked, his usual humor back in effect.

I laughed. "We're not quite there yet."

"I saw the way Goldstein looked at you, Taylor. Brooklyn was practically salivating at the front desk! Even when he dated one of our former employees, I never saw that expression on his face."

My smile fell at the mention of Morgan. I knew the pain and resentment Kyle still carried because of how the situation unfolded.

"Goldstein's not still mooning over her, is he?" Phil asked. Immediately realizing his *faux pas*, he added, "None of my business, sorry. I assumed you knew Goldstein has a bit of a past at Culver."

I nodded. "We all have a past, Phil. He may be 'Goldstein' to all of you, but he's 'Kyle' to me. Whoever he was before is not the man he is now."

"For your sake, Taylor, I certainly hope so."

CHAPTER 15

"SOUNDS LIKE YOU'VE HAD AN EVENTFUL WEEK," KYLE said as he dipped a chip into a Los Bravos salsa bowl.

I twisted my straw in my water glass. "At least I'm getting a bonus for all of my troubles."

"I assume this means you're backlogged like crazy," he said.

"Things are slow for right now. Everybody's gearing up for Christmas in a few weeks."

"What about you?" he asked.

"What about me?"

"'Tis the season for family togetherness and all of that. My family usually hosts a big Chanukah party. We do a white elephant gift exchange with my aunts, uncles, and cousins. Sort of a Goldstein family tradition."

I brightened. "Sounds like a lot of fun and good memories."

Kyle grinned. "It is. You should come."

"You want to introduce me to the family already?"

"Since your former in-laws left you in the dust and your brother sided with Mother Dearest, it sounds like a lonely time of year for you. You shouldn't be alone, Taylor. You're too much fun."

I smiled, warmed through by his honest compliment. "Thank you."

"Goldstein?" MacKenzie called with faux innocence. "What are you doing here?" She stood over the edge of our table accompanied by Lexie Arterton, Kyle's replacement at Culver.

Not missing a beat, Kyle replied, "Having lunch at Los Bravos like I do practically every Tuesday. Taylor's off the clock, and we're in the middle of a private conversation here. Do you have something earth shattering to share, Mac, or are you just looking for buzz to bring back to the hive?"

MacKenzie pursed her lips, eyes narrowing. "It wasn't that long ago you drowned your sorrows in tequila while mourning the loss of a certain Culver employee, Goldstein. Maybe you'll have better luck trying to score with her replacement."

If looks could kill, Kyle would have filleted MacKenzie with his tortilla chip. As the idea came to me, I stifled my giggle while reaching for my pepper spray.

"What the...?" MacKenzie's question abruptly ended.

"Kyle, I just love a little extra spice on my food, don't you? But I tell you what, I always have the darndest trouble with this little spray can." I pushed down on the sprayer deliberately toward the gaping magpies. "It's just I can never figure out how to hold the sprayer properly. See?" I stood up and pointed the can directly into both of their faces.

They looked at me with wide eyes. From my periphery, Kyle's beaming grin and twinkling blue eyes nearly caused me to break character. Instead I turned to my coworkers and said low, "I know why you're here, and it's beyond petty. Go live your own lives instead of meddling and commenting on mine."

Turning my back to them, I sat down next to Kyle, held his

face with my hands, and planted a firm kiss on his lips. He responded by pulling the back of my head toward him and returning the kiss with equal measure.

"You guys are disgusting!" MacKenzie screeched from behind us.

Ignoring her, I found myself rather distracted by the man whose kiss caught fire of something inside of me.

"*Que bueno, mis amigos. ¡Felicidades!*" Carlos announced, placing our entrees on the table.

Kyle broke the kiss and leaned his forehead against mine. "That was amazing," he said, tracing his fingers along the side of my face. "I don't know if I could have stayed as calm as you did. MacKenzie really just twisted the knife in, didn't she?"

"I see what you mean about Culver and the gossip problem."

Kyle pulled away with a pained expression. "I wish I'd never let Mac talk me into going out after my last day at Culver. I knew exactly what she wanted, and I went along with it anyway. One of the worst mistakes I've ever made."

I offered a comforting smile. "A very wise person once told me that if you learn from a mistake rather than repeat it, then it stops being a mistake and becomes a life lesson instead."

Kyle's eyes took on a knowing glint. "Rebecca said that to me too. More than once, so apparently, they're not *life lessons* quite yet."

"Stay away from tequila and busybodies. Seems pretty straightforward," I quipped.

Kyle stared into my eyes and then frowned. "What are you doing here with me, Taylor? You don't deserve all of the..." he struggled to find a non-curse word, "*bovine feces* MacKenzie and her ilk are going to shovel on you."

"First, thank you for the Mad Gab worthy substitute," I said with a chuckle. "Second, I've been through a lot worse than this as far as office dramas go. Stupidly, I stayed at StarRealty for more than two years after I first discovered Mitch's cheating."

"Are you a masochist?" Kyle said. "Why would you do that to yourself?"

"Moral support. At least it seemed that way when the office rallied around me after Mitch and that tramp took off. But when your coworkers eventually tell you they all knew about the affair, it's hard to take their sympathy very seriously."

"No kidding."

The emotion welled up as I relived those horrific conversations. "What kind of...*bovine feces*...excuse for friends is that? Freaking cowards is more like it!"

"We seem to have a fire sale on cow droppings today," Kyle deadpanned.

The rage slowly subsided as I pulled myself back to the present. "Better than dropping the words I'd like to use, I suppose. Although, I did have a bit of a potty mouth as all of Mitch's lies came to light during the divorce."

Rather than surprise, the blue gaze meeting mine held a fair amount of mischief. "Miss Prim and Proper engaged in sailor speak? I do declare, I am quite scandalized," he said, affecting a southern accent.

I physically felt the sparkle in my eyes. Those old parts of Taylor Meyers breathed life into the emotional husk known as Taylor Ross. To experience joy and laughter caused from real life rather than living vicariously through a movie or television character encouraged me to the depths of my soul. Until that moment, I hadn't realized just how long I'd lived under a dull, gray cloud of depression. I wanted to start living, not just existing.

"You did it again," Kyle said.

"Did what?"

"That thing where you disappear into your own head. Also, our food is getting cold, and we both have to get back to work soon."

I smiled, really smiled, and Kyle's expression warmed in response. "Wow," he breathed.

I raised an eyebrow.

He shook his head, unwilling to share his thoughts. Instead, he pulled my "no-fun fajitas" toward me so we could eat side by side rather than across from one another.

"Can you feel them staring into your back?" Kyle asked around a mouthful of burrito.

I rolled my eyes. "If by *them*, you mean Carlos and the rest of the waitstaff, I think I've already gotten used to it. If you're talking about the two little vultures waiting to pounce on me the second you leave my side, I plan to walk with my pepper spray in plain sight."

"I know Kung Fu," Kyle said, his Keenan Rivers impression spot on.

"You weren't kidding about the movie references, were you?"

Kyle took another bite before answering. "I'll have to introduce you to my on-again off-again girlfriend, Arizona Prime. She's my favorite streaming service."

"Ah, I've been in a long term relationship with her brother, Señor Filmflix, for a while."

"Is this her brother from another mother? I thought for sure she was French," Kyle said, verbal sword clearly in hand.

"We'll call them 'European,' and then we can both feel fancy without the lingering questions of parentage," I said, more than ready to do battle.

Kyle paused, apparently finding some sort of treasure in the mud of my eyes. "They're green, Taylor. Green and brown with a pop of yellow. When you laugh, they become something different altogether. I don't have a word for it, but I'm determined to find it."

"Spoken like the king of Mad Gabs," I said, taking a bite of food.

"I wish you could see yourself the way you really are," he said.

"Likewise."

We shared a sweet moment before Carlos refilled our water glasses sporting a cheeky grin on his face.

"*Ay, mira a los novios enamorados,*" he crooned before disappearing to another table.

I shook my head and chuckled. "He is so shameless. And he thinks I don't understand what he's saying, which is even funnier."

Kyle glanced over my shoulder, and I turned to see Carlos laughing and pointing at us along with a few other servers. I blushed, and the laughter grew.

"I'm pretty sure he knows you know, Taylor, and he seems to take a great deal of pleasure in watching both of us squirm."

"I'd kiss you again if it would shut him up," I said.

"Well, he did just say we're in loooove," Kyle teased, dragging out the word. "Why don't you kiss me again just for the fun of it?"

"Tempting."

"Is it now? If it's the burrito aroma you love so much, I can see if they make it in a toothpaste flavor. I'll be sure to always have that burrito breath whenever you feel the need to lock lips. In fact, it might just make me irresistible. Have you thought about that, Taylor? Are you sure you're ready to handle that much burrito goodness?"

My verbal sword lay abandoned on the ground. I was laughing too hard to pick it up.

Kyle merely smiled, polished off his lunch and then finished the remains of mine. He walked me back to our office plaza before taking my hands in his and planting a kiss to my forehead. Things seemed happy and bright, a new future shaping into focus beyond the Ross or Meyers families.

"Well, well, well," a smug voice said, approaching us. I didn't recognize the woman, but she clearly knew Kyle and vice versa. Her hard expression read "up to no good."

"Don't do this," Kyle begged her.

My brows drew together in confusion, shocked by Kyle's transformation to complete invertebrate.

"Can I help you?" I asked, not liking the way Kyle's acquaintance eyed me up and down.

The dark haired stranger rolled her eyes dismissively. "She looks a little young, don't you think?"

I turned to Kyle, waiting for him to stand up to this bully the same way he had put MacKenzie in her place thirty minutes earlier. If nothing else, I figured he'd hold his ground like he did with Phil and Miss Belle. After the brilliant way I'd rushed to his aid at Los Bravos, I naturally assumed Kyle would return the favor.

Instead, his gaze darted back and forth between me and our latest verbal assailant in panic. A weary sigh filled my lungs. Regardless of Kyle's excuse for standing there like some sort of shrinking violet, Mitchell Ross taught me how to defend myself a long time ago. I didn't have a choice.

Squaring my shoulders and squelching the disappointment of Kyle's inaction, I took matters into my own hands. "*She* is standing right here, and I'm not hard of hearing. Your attempt to shame me into silence isn't going to work either. Frankly, it just screams of insecurity and jealousy."

Kyle and his lady friend both wore the same stunned expression. Initially taken aback by the resemblance, I brushed off the warnings in my gut and continued on with a full head of steam. "I don't know who you are or who you think you are to Kyle, but why don't you go slither back to whatever hole you came from? I've dealt with vipers a lot nastier than you, sweetie, and I've just about hit my limit for the day."

Of all the things I wasn't expecting in that moment, the saucy stranger dissolving into genuine tears was probably at the bottom of my list. Even more surprising was Kyle's abandonment in order to wrap a comforting arm around this woman rather than me. The first man I had trusted since my break up from Mitch turned out to be no better than the same coward who had also deserted me for another woman.

"Kyle?" I asked weakly. As I stared at him and his sobbing counterpart, dread began to fill me. Though Kyle kept his hair short, the woman beside him sported long, glossy curls the exact same color. She was shorter and wider in stature, but there was no mistaking the same, deep set eyes. His were powder blue. Hers were honey brown.

My hand came up slowly to cover my mouth while Kyle looked at me like a wounded puppy. His protective stance next to his sister heralded the death knell of our brief courtship.

Jessica Goldstein's tears subsided as she glanced back and forth between the two of us. "She is nothing like Rebecca," Jessica spat, glaring at her brother, "and I think you're absolutely insane dating a Christian. They're all a bunch of hypocrites, just like this one and her ex-husband," she said, attacking me with a knife wound of her own. "Kyle told me all about you, hon. Nice try, reeling him in with the jilted wife *shtick.* Of course, it's supposed to make you look like a saint compared to me, right?"

Mouth agape, I stared at Kyle. "How could you!"

Kyle looked back and forth between the two of us, clearly unwilling to get in the middle. He may not have been the casanova villain as portrayed at Culver, but self-preservation clearly won out over self-sacrifice.

Summoning my last bit of dignity, I stared down Kyle's twin sister and said, "This is the face of 'the other woman,' Jessica. What might be nothing more than a meaningless fling to you is absolutely devastating to the wife who was promised a lifetime of commitment."

Turning to her brother I said, "Kyle, I don't know if I'll ever hear from you again, but in the event I don't, thank you for helping me laugh again and reminding me that I need to start living. I told you I don't need you to be my savior, and you more than proved that today. I'll be just fine without you."

Not giving either one of them a chance to respond and hoping to restrain my sobs until I could muffle them in a private bathroom stall, I marched with false bravura back into my office high rise.

Kyle did not follow me into the Culver lion's den.

CHAPTER 16

Taylor, I haven't heard from you in a while. My offer still stands. That Christian concert I told you about is happening at the pavilion tonight. If you're not busy, I hope you'll pray and consider going with me, Ian sent me via FaceSpace messenger.

After two weeks of silence from Kyle and the prospect of my first Christmas completely alone, I swallowed my pride and finally agreed to a date with Ian Horner. Though hurt by Kyle's inaction, I at least understood it. Understanding it, however, didn't mean I liked it.

I had already experienced the pain of family conflict with Mitch. My ex-husband knew where his bread was buttered, and he always sided with my mother. Privately, he might admit she could have handled a situation better, but it paid to ally himself with Sarah Meyers.

After a blistering work day at StarRealty, my patience wore thinner than usual after my mother's inebriated antics during a realtor award banquet later that evening. I lit into my husband after we sat in frosty silence on the drive home.

"Mitch, she was practically falling out of her top! I don't care if she's your boss, she's also your mother-in-law! Why didn't you say something?"

"Why would I?" he said, yanking at his tie and discarding it on the bathroom floor. "You did more than enough to humiliate the family."

"Me?" I said shrilly. "How could I have possibly humiliated our family more than my mother's drunken karaoke and burlesque show?"

"You didn't have to snatch the microphone from her and apologize to the room, Taylor. Everyone seemed to be having a good time."

"At her expense, Mitch! I'm sure they just wanted to see if her surgically enhanced bust would fly out and give herself a black eye!"

"Stop being melodramatic, Taylor. Everybody was drinking."

"Not everybody," I said, annoyed. A recent trip to an allergist finally uncovered the source of painful eczema that rendered my hands a cracked, itchy, and bloody mess. My inability to drink alcohol also meant my husband had a built-in, designated driver, and I resented it. "You certainly had more than enough to drink tonight."

"Prude," he muttered under his breath.

My irritation grew. "All of the boozing makes you a big hit at office parties, but it's not pleasing to God. You look like a hypocrite sermonizing to your clients about sin in the world while completely ignoring your own."

My husband turned to glare at me as if his displeasure would cow me into submission. "Do you think God would be pleased with how you publicly dishonored your mother, Taylor? Pull the log out of your own eye first."

The contempt dripping in Mitch's tone took me aback.

Before me stood a complete stranger who just happened to look like my husband with hair plugs. Frustrated and infuriated by his transformation, I gave vent to my anger.

"My mother dishonored herself!" I yelled. "And don't you dare lecture me about *what would Jesus do* while you had our spindly legged receptionist hanging all over you tonight!"

A momentary flicker of guilt caused Mitch to shift his gaze away. "I've told you a thousand times I'm not interested, Taylor. I'm married to *you*, remember?"

He said "you" as if our marriage was some sort of punishment. When we exchanged wedding vows nearly five years earlier, Mitch had called me "the greatest gift God has ever given me." Tears stung my eyes as I struggled to understand why our marriage felt so hollow. Our promising beginning had grown into a barren tundra lacking any warmth.

Glancing up, I saw Mitch had returned his gaze to the mirror, inspecting his enhanced hairline to be sure everything appeared natural. Emblematic of the man before me, too much of Mitch centered around the appearance of things rather than genuine substance. I missed the close buzz cut that made Mitch look like a real person rather than a life sized, fashion doll. I studied my husband studying himself, still so handsome even though I was furious with him.

"Mitch...we...I don't even remember the last time we..." my voice caught on a sob.

He met my eyes in the mirror, as if truly seeing me for the first time that evening. I prayed silently, begging God to do something with my marriage. I knew we were both miserable.

"You look really pretty tonight," Mitch said quietly, olive branch extended. "I don't think I got a chance to tell you earlier."

Like a parched bloom finally tasting water, my head lifted.

Mitch walked toward me, holding me with the tenderness in his sapphire eyes. He stood before me with a soft smile that felt like the promise of answered prayer. I sighed as he tugged the bobby pins from my tight chignon and ran his fingers through my hair.

"Things haven't been the same since you started singing on the worship team," he whispered against my temple. "I think we were a lot happier before you wasted your time doing that. Now, we're both too busy for each other."

Not wanting to start another fight, especially at the first display of genuine affection I'd experienced from my husband in well over a year, I ignored the temptation to correct him. I wrapped my arms around his waist and leaned my head against his chest. I knew Mitch took delight in how strong he felt compared to my diminutive size.

"There's the girl I fell in love with," he crooned. "Will you sing for me, my little songbird?"

Seeking to escape the agonizing loneliness of my marriage, I sang Mitch the song we danced to as newly pronounced husband and wife. I hummed as we reconnected for the first time in six months. I sang with all I had in me as I held a positive pregnancy test three weeks later.

Blinking back tears that returned me to the present, I stared at my office computer screen. Ian was already replying to my FaceSpace message with an extensive array of emojis.

I'll meet you there at 6. They have all kinds of food at the park, so don't worry about eating beforehand.

Before I could address my allergy issues, Ian fired off another message.

I checked with the facilities manager, and he said a couple of vendors have gluten free options and all natural hot dogs. My niece has a bunch of allergies, so I'm used to the dietary restrictions. I hope that puts your mind at ease a little bit.

Touched, I smiled at my screen. A moment later, the sound of Ted Margolin's imminent arrival caused me to close the message window. I pulled up the recent presentation Ted had sent over for updates.

The squeak of his loafers stopped as he rapped on my office door frame. "How are you holding up?"

I shrugged. "I took your wife's advice during Tabby's birthday party and finally agreed to a date with Ian. Rebecca is amazing, by the way. Thank you for making food I could eat."

Ted grinned at my lavish praise for his wife. "She enjoyed the challenge, and I enjoyed making the cake."

"So I heard," I replied, memories of the pink, elephant shaped confection forever etched in my brain. Tabby's party epitomized every mom blog post of, "this is how you celebrate your baby girl's first birthday." I frowned as I wondered for the thousandth time if I'd completely blown my chance at happiness by retaliating against Kyle's sister two weeks earlier.

Reading my thoughts, Ted said, "Don't do it, Taylor. This is all on Goldstein, not you. He's the one who should regret not standing up for you. Rebecca's sister pulled a similar stunt when we first got together."

"Not everybody is like you, Ted," I replied. "You go into multi-million dollar corporations and sell them on how awesome you are. That takes confidence. Kyle doesn't have that."

Ted looked tempted to spit out a pithy one liner at Kyle's expense. Instead, he said, "Taylor, any man worth his salt will defend his woman. If he's too attached to his family, his ego, or a fear of being rejected, he'll hide behind her. He'll just stand there and watch her get bludgeoned by an abuser. Then, he'll turn around and blame her for getting angry at the attacker. He'll nitpick how she defended herself so he can take the focus off of his complete failure to protect her. If she calls out his behavior, he'll find some way to shame her for exposing his own weakness of character. My wife describes it as a covert form of narcissism."

"I can't imagine you were talking about yourself," I said, unable to reconcile Ted's personality with the perfectly detailed description he'd provided.

Ted's expression became pained. "It happened to someone pretty close to me and my wife."

Not wanting to pry, I changed the subject. "I didn't expect Rebecca to rip into Jessica, especially since the two of them haven't talked in over a year. I told Rebecca I wish she'd just left it alone."

"Taylor, I can only tell you about my experiences with Goldstein from a few years ago. The cowardice you saw is no different than what I observed when he worked here."

"Is that so?" the man himself said from my doorway.

"Kyle, what are you doing here?" I demanded.

"My thoughts exactly," Ted said, staring down Kyle like an old foe.

Kyle closed my office door behind him. "You wanna talk about cowardly, Margolin, when you have your wife call up my sister and read her the riot act? Don't you think Taylor did enough by humiliating Jessica in front of the entire office park?"

Kyle's skewed version of the facts reminded me of countless times Mitchell Ross treated my mother's abuse as normal, but then he shamed me for any anger at her antics. The same bait now sat before me, tempting me to explode at the ridiculous distortion of reality. I was reminded of my words regarding

Jesus saving us from our human response to things, and I knew I had to show Kyle different. For his sake and for mine.

"I was wrong to attack your sister the way I did," I said contritely. "Jessica surprised me, and she hurt me. I should have listened to the Lord telling me to slow down, especially when I noted the physical similarities between you two. For that, I sincerely apologize. I also have to thank you, Kyle."

"For what?" he said, confused.

"For reminding me of the pain I experienced every time Mitch refused to stand up for me. For reminding me just how badly it hurt when the man I loved refused to defend me from people attacking me. I told myself I would never let any man get away with treating me like that again—present company included."

Kyle looked troubled and pained. "You *loved*?"

"Figure of speech, Kyle. Don't read into it."

"Margolin, can you give us a minute alone, please?" he said tersely. "I'm sure Phil already has security on their way to haul me out."

"I don't think so," Ted replied, standing directly in between me and Kyle.

Noting Ted's protectiveness of me, Kyle's expression hardened. "Unless, of course, Taylor is an even bigger hypocrite than her ex-husband."

Whatever pity I felt for Kyle Goldstein died instantly. I fought back tears at the worst possible accusation he could have thrown at me.

Seeing my expression, Ted said, "You know, Goldstein, you're probably your own worst enemy. If my sisters ever pulled a stunt like what Jessica did to Taylor, they'd be roadkill. A woman isn't such a delicate creature she can't protect or defend herself, but when the man who claims to care for her feeds her to the wolves, don't expect her to hang around for more abuse."

Unmoved, Kyle said, "They don't pay me to listen to your sanctimonious lectures anymore, Margolin. Are you done?"

Taking a steadying breath, I sidestepped the testosterone fueled stare down and opened my office door. "Thanks for your interest in Culver's marketing department, Mr. Goldstein, but I'm not going to Cooper & Jaye. Hope you have a pleasant rest of your afternoon."

Kyle stared at me in disbelief. "Just like that, Taylor? I'm dismissed from your life just like that?"

From behind us, Ted exhaled in disgust.

"Good afternoon, Mr. Goldstein," I repeated as several heads poked up from their cubicle workstations.

Kyle stood in front of me and searched for any shred of vulnerability in my eyes. Closing off his access to my inner turmoil, I whispered, "Please just go."

"Andalusite," he said.

I looked up at him, not understanding his meaning at all. He took the opportunity to dive deep into muddy waters. "The color of your eyes is andalusite, Taylor. Just thought you should know that."

At my open jaw, he smiled sadly before taking his leave.

The squeak and jangle of the mighty Margolin approached as Kyle exited Culver's office through a side door.

"I'm sorry, Taylor," Ted said. "You did a great job holding it together, though."

My shoulders shook while my seamed lips worked to hold in the sob aching for release. Ted squeezed my arm briefly and said he'd call Rebecca and pray for me.

I returned to my desk and took measured breaths to help to calm my nerves. Going against my better judgment, I searched for images of "andalusite" online and discovered a much better adjective for my eye color than my mother's favorite put-down. The gemstones blurred as moisture filled my eyes bearing the same brown and greenish hue.

I cancelled my date with Ian, citing an emergency, but I promised to reschedule. I offered the first Friday after New Year's as proof I wasn't brushing him off. When Ian asked about my Christmas plans, I avoided an answer. When he asked about New Year's Eve, I told him I had to get back to work.

I gave myself permission to cry the second I entered my front door. I remembered every place Kyle stood and every place where I welcomed him into my home and into my heart. I sobbed through a bowl of gluten free cereal and coconut milk, burying my cries into countless hours of movie reenactments of two hundred year old tales. It was a time when men seemed to know what they wanted.

CHAPTER 17

BEFORE I COULD CONTEMPLATE WHAT TO DO WITH the remaining work week, Rebecca sent me a text message asking if I was okay. She followed up by saying she would do for me what was once done for her. Although cryptic, I soon discovered she meant call in sick to the office on my behalf. I knew it would also light a fire under Phil to get a second person in the marketing department to help me. Because of the winter holidays, one with many of our office members either already on vacation or home with kids out of school, I didn't feel too guilty about taking the necessary time off.

After being relegated to Rebecca Margolin's shadow for over two years at Culver Incorporated, I resented how she played such a central role in the demise of any potential relationship with Kyle. It was the comparison that launched Jessica Goldstein's remarks. Her jealousy and bitterness toward Rebecca found a convenient scapegoat in me. Yet, as much as I wanted to blame Rebecca, I had to lay the blame where it belonged.

I told Kyle I'd vowed to never be thrown under the bus

again, and the perfidy of Mitchell Ross lingered as a cautionary tale. Mitch's version of our tragic marriage included a brief admission of guilt, yet he cited his infidelity as an "isolated incident" since he'd only been *caught* one time. He easily retold the way I hurled shampoo bottles at his head like a deranged madwoman. He conveniently omitted the part where I discovered his post-coital shower while his mistress slept on my pillow.

During the divorce, Mitch's flying monkeys came after me with hate filled texts and emails. When my lawyer confronted the issue, they claimed Mitch had no control over the behavior of others. I felt even more powerless to stop the emotional abuse than when I still shared a roof with Mitchell Benjamin Ross. To my surprise, my mother stepped up to support me.

"I've always told you that religious folks are nothing but hypocrites," my mother said as she helped box up the Ross family china. "And I can't believe Cindy asked for the dishes back considering what her son did to you."

I bit off a piece of packing tape with my teeth. "She can have it. I never liked the pattern anyway. Mitch didn't particularly care for it either."

"Do you know how many of my boyfriends had wives and kids and then raised their hands up on Sunday mornings, Taylor? None of that holy talk is real," she said.

Though not surprised my mother played the role of "the other woman," her inability to see how her careless words affected me sent a surge of moisture to my eyes. Sniffling and wiping the tears away, I found some extra newspaper and hoped the crinkling noises would mask my grief.

Her china blue eyes lasered in on me instead. "Does Mitch know about the baby, Taylor?"

I shook my head. "What's the point, Mom? He said he

didn't want one anyway. It would just be one more way to tell the world what a failure I was as a wife."

"Forget what stick woman said about the miscarriage, okay? I tell you, I can't stand these church ladies with all of their hyper spiritual talk. They pretend like Jesus sits up there and applauds them for how they judge and criticize the suffering of others."

"Not everybody is like Chloe," I said, wrapping a tea cup. "Did I tell you Brian almost called off the wedding because of what she said to me?"

"You told me," she replied, wrapping a plate. "I always wondered why you didn't dump Baldy and go for the older brother. It seemed like you and Brian had more in common anyway. He certainly treats you better than Mitch ever did."

I looked sharply at my mother. "So, it's wrong for Mitch to cheat on me, but it would have been perfectly fine for me to marry his brother instead?"

My mother flicked a hand of acrylic nails in my direction. "It's not wrong for my daughter to be happy, which is all I ever want for you, Taylor."

"Even at someone else's expense?" I asked pointedly. How my mother missed her own hypocrisy always astounded me.

"Look, I'm not saying I haven't made mistakes, Taylor, but I don't regret doing what makes me happy after wasting fourteen years being married to your father."

"What about the wives of those husbands you slept with, Mom? How are they any different than me?"

Not missing a beat, she said, "Because, I would never disrespect another woman's home by sleeping in her bed. There's just certain rules about these things. You don't get involved with a married man and then try to replace the wife. Not unless you're some kind of a psycho like Mitch's tramp. The men I dated were married for eons, bored, had problem teenagers, or their wives had lovers too. I don't know if anybody buys into this whole 'til death do us part' mumbo jumbo anymore. When you get to be my age, most men are just in it because they don't want to pay alimony or they need to maintain appearances."

I exhaled in disgust. "If that's really true, Mom, why would anybody bother getting married? Why do little girls dream about their wedding day if it's nothing but misery and partner swapping?"

"Exactly my point!" she said, already moving onto her third plate while the same teacup lay motionless in my hands.

I shook my head, refusing to believe my mother's theory held any validity.

"Look, you can sit there and judge me all you want, Taylor Marie, but I'm just laying out the facts for you, honey. People aren't much better than animals. We all have needs. If I help a woman out because she's too much of a prude to do what her husband likes, but she's the one with the big, fancy house and the designer clothes, then it's a win for everybody, right?"

"If the goal of your life is sexual gratification and money, then yeah, it definitely sounds like you'd be getting everything you wanted, Mom. I can't argue with you there."

My mother tsked at me. "You make it sound dirty, Taylor."

I met her eyes letting her know she had not mistaken my meaning.

"Well, at least you don't have any kids stuck in the middle of all of this mess," my mother said as an aside. "When your father walked out on me, I had two little mouths to feed. I had to take him to court to get any kind of child support."

"No, we don't have any kids stuck in the middle," I repeated, the ache of my empty womb nearly toppling me over in grief.

I sobbed silently while my mother rambled on about divorce attorneys and child support laws. Her voice eventually became white noise while I robotically packed up meaningless items into boxes. Art pieces and vases I once prized served as painful reminders of Mitch's duplicity.

"I used to date a guy who runs an auction house," my mother said, breaking through my fog. "Taylor Marie, even though you never take my advice, if I can get you to do one thing, please get yourself a good attorney. I'm almost positive Mitch has more money than he's letting on. The bank statement you showed me doesn't reflect even half of the closings I know he's had in the past six months."

Confused, I said, "I didn't show you any bank statements."

"You left your mail on the island. I was doing my job as your mother to make sure you're being taken care of."

Too tired to reprimand her for invading my privacy, I nodded.

"Promise me, Taylor," she said urgently. "Mitchell Ross is the lowest kind of snake, and if he thinks he's going to screw my daughter out of money after bringing that hussy into your bed, he's got another thing coming. You don't mess with Sarah Meyers's daughter and get away with it!"

My mother proved to be both a help and a hindrance during the year of litigation leading up to my eventual divorce. For that one year, our relationship was the best it had ever been. I certainly didn't approve of my mother's conversation topics or life choices, but we united against a common enemy: Mitchell Ross. My brother claimed it was an answer to his prayers, and God allowed my divorce to bring the reconciliation he desperately longed to see between mother and sister.

While a sweet notion on the surface, Gabe's assertion ignored my mother's culpability in our historically strained relationship. He blithely trivialized my pain and devastation as a means to an end. In the Meyers's household, that "end" would always be keeping Sarah Meyers happy. My unwillingness to enable it eventually brought cracks to the happy veneer.

"How can you be so ungrateful after all that I've done for you, Taylor Marie!" my mother demanded as she stormed into my brand new home. "Who hired that private investigator and found more than half a million dollars your ex-husband had hidden in Caribbean bank accounts? Me! Who helped get you into this townhouse for a fraction of what we charged all of your fancy pants neighbors? Me!" She reached for my chin, but I managed to duck away in time. "Taylor Marie, you look at me when I'm talking to you!"

I threw my keys down on a side table and turned to glare at my mother from a safe distance. "You invited me for a mother-daughter dinner. Instead, you subjected me to a voyeuristic make out session with your married boyfriend. Meanwhile, his wingman ogled me all night as if I was just as easy as you are!"

"Don't you dare take that tone with me, Taylor Marie Meyers! Just when I think my daughter and I might finally have a real, grown up relationship, you start acting like that self-righteous twelve year-old all over again! And by the way, you're welcome for the two closing checks I gave you to help furnish your dollie dreamhouse. I would appreciate a little more gratitude, young lady."

"Stop throwing this house in my face, Mom! I never asked for your commission on either sale. You don't get to control me just because you *chose* to give me money. Not unless you seriously think you can bribe me into having a relationship with you."

Ignoring me, she continued with her martyred monologue. "Do you remember what I went through getting Triple J to hire me as the listing agent for this enclave? I lost lifelong friends in the industry fighting over this nothing little neighborhood, Taylor Marie. My accountant had the brilliant idea to use my commission and buy store credit at the furniture outlet rather than hand you a check that Mitch could try to claim half of in litigation. You have a brand new bedroom suite upstairs because of me. Is it so wrong if I just want to help you break it in and remove all traces of Mitchell Ross from your life?"

I sighed wearily. "Mom, I get that you're trying to help. I just need you to listen to me instead of assuming that whatever you would want in this situation is exactly what I want too. We're different people, and we have different values."

"Have you ever considered an overhaul of these holier-than-thou values of yours, Taylor? Is abstinence some sort of way to punish yourself to be good enough for God? How do you plan to keep a man if you don't know what you're doing in bed?"

"Mom!" I said, aghast. "You referred to me as, 'my daughter, the lifelong virgin.' Then, you asked that disgusting lech if he'd be willing to teach me a few things. On what planet is that appropriate behavior? You knew exactly how I would react!"

"I just think getting you a little action will help loosen you up, Taylor. You're wound up tighter than a mattress coil."

"You would know," I snapped.

My mother pursed her lips. "Are we really back to that again, Taylor? You sit at home in your pajamas, moping and watching all of your stupid Joan Austin movies, but I'm actually out having a life and enjoying myself. You tell me which option sounds more appealing."

"Mom, you told me it took you years to get over the divorce from Dad. I need more than two months before I can think about another man in my life. I thought you would understand."

I could have predicted the petulant tone that followed.

"Can't a mother just want her daughter to be happy?"

Grief and anger loosened my lips. "This has nothing to do with me being happy, Mom. You just don't want me to be upset anymore because it steals the spotlight off of you and your rehashed tales of woe."

My mother looked as though I'd slapped her. Expectedly, Sarah Meyers turned on the water works. I was less certain whether they were real or staged since I'd never been so brutally honest with my mother before.

"Is that really what you think of me?" she said, hurt.

"Sometimes," I admitted. "Please, try to remember I just had my entire life ripped out from under me, Mom. It's not something I'm going to recover from overnight."

"Well, when your father—"

I cut her off. "Mom, this is about *me*, right now, okay?"

"What, so now I can't even try to relate to my own daughter?"

I sighed. "Mom, I just want you to listen."

"I've listened for hours, Taylor Marie! I sat with you while you cried, and I've been there helping you pick up the pieces and move on with your life."

"And I appreciate that, Mom, but—"

Ignoring me, she continued, "You're so focused on yourself, Taylor Marie, that you can't even give your poor mother a shred of compassion. I suffered through a divorce too, you know! Do you even care about *my* pain?"

Frustrated, I said, "Mom, I've been listening to your pain since I was eleven years-old. What are you possibly going to tell me that I haven't heard a thousand times?"

My mother sniffed indignantly. "Well, since I'm obviously not welcome here, I'll just leave you to your fantasy life of movie men. Unlike you, I'm smart enough to go out and enjoy the real thing."

With a flourish, Sarah Meyers stormed out of my front door. She sent several texts and pictures to remind me how much fun she had without me. The jabs were petty, mean spirited, and all the proof I needed that nothing had really changed in my relationship with my mother.

No matter what Gabe insisted, I had expected nothing different.

CHAPTER 18

MERRY CHRISTMAS, TAYLOR! I HOPE YOU'RE HAVING A HAPPY HOLIDAY, Ian sent over FaceSpace messenger.

"Bah humbug," I said to my laptop. I couldn't think about any man but Kyle, and that came accompanied by pain and regret. I typed up a response to feed into my self-destructive pity party and sure to get Ian Horner interested elsewhere.

Not feeling very festive, sorry. Beginning to hate this time of year. Never so glad to see the end of a December in my life.

"All right, Mr. Horner, let's watch you scurry off in the face of real human emotion," I said bitterly. My mind conjured up images of blue eyed rats fleeing a sinking ship. All of them were named Kyle, of course.

I watched as ellipses showed Ian typing, deleting, then retyping a response.

Sorry to hear that. Mine hasn't been so great either. Brunch with my parents came with a heaping side of guilt. Indigestion always available for dessert.

I chuckled in surprise at Ian's reply, though not undeterred in my quest to be left alone from the entire male species.

Santa didn't even bother with coal. Silent treatment from family and a guy I'd just as soon forget.

"Yes, you have competition, Ian. I'm not the woeful, lost puppy you're going to scoop up and get to adore you," I haughtily declared.

After a long pause, Ian finally began typing.

I always wondered if there was somebody else in the picture. Guess I was right. Why did you agree to go out with me?

Your persistence.

Ah. So, you took pity on the AV nerd to help mend your broken heart. I never took you as that kind of girl, Taylor. Seemed more like Chloe's department.

I inhaled sharply at the rebuke and the truth behind it. Mortified at my own selfish behavior, I sat in silence. Ian began to type again.

Look, I get I'm not some movie star here, but I've liked you for a long time, Taylor. Probably since I knocked into you a million years ago in the Bromwell dorm lobby. I heard you singing at the fountain, and I recognized you the first time I saw you walk into Freedom. Since your ex was some kind of Bible scholar, I tried to impress you with devotionals I memorized...

My hand flew to my mouth in shock as Ian continued. Memories of the emo haired stranger I bumped into on my first date with Mitchell Ross fused together with my encounter of shaggy haired Ian Horner ten years later. I realized how horribly I'd misjudged him—and treated him.

Apologizing profusely, I asked Ian if he liked Chinese food. He said yes followed by a request to meet up "just as friends." I agreed wholeheartedly, desperate to make amends for my atrocious behavior.

We met around four o'clock, joined by many of Parkview's Jewish citizenry also enjoying Chinese food on Christmas. I did a double take when Ian entered the restaurant, barely recognizing him beyond the khaki pants and navy fleece hoodie I'd seen him sport several times at church. With his overgrown hair now cut into a relaxed fauxhawk, I remembered Chloe's offhand remark that Ian might be cute with a better haircut.

Understatement of the century.

I noticed Ian about to self-consciously run a hand through hair that no longer existed. With a sheepish grin, he said, "I'm still getting used to it. The look on your face was worth it, though."

"I wasn't sure it was really you," I said, finally able to see Ian had eyes. Not blue, but dark brown with thick lashes.

"That's a pretty sweet haircut you got too," he said, gesturing toward my coiffure. "I don't usually like short hair on women, but you make it look cool." At the strained smile on my face, he tacked on, "Not that my opinion of short hair on women really matters since this isn't a date anyway. Ian, shut up."

I laughed. "It's okay. I was ready for something different."

"Because of the idiot?"

I raised a brow. "Why did you call him that? You know, you said the same thing about Mitch the first time I met you."

Ian's eyes freely roamed my face, but no lower. "Two guys stupid enough to lose you? That definitely qualifies as an idiot in my book."

"What if I'm not as wonderful as you seem to think I am? I believe that was proven earlier today."

"I watched you put up with Chloe for almost two years, Taylor. You'd smile even when she cut you down or snubbed you. She'd glare at you while you sang during worship. She spread slander about you to people in the church so they'd deliberately shun you. But you didn't leave, Taylor. Not until she got your brother to bring your mother to church."

"How...?" I couldn't even finish my question.

"I overheard Chloe talking to Gabe about it after you left. She said they were better off without you, and Gabe and your mother took off in a huff. Chloe wore this sick smile. It looked like a demon."

I shuddered involuntarily.

"My thoughts exactly," he said. "I tried talking to Pastor Brian, but he didn't want to be interrupted. He and the elders were having some hush hush meeting about the offering. So, I gave Chloe a piece of my mind since I knew nobody else would do it."

Glancing up at the man towering over me by at least a foot, I imagined his ability to intimidate the other Mrs. Ross far outweighed mine. "I presume that didn't go very well."

"She told me there wasn't a chance in...well, you know where, you'd ever go out with me."

"Sounds like something Chloe would say."

Ian's grin produced dimples. "I told Chloe you wore the title of Mrs. Ross with a lot more class than she ever would. She slapped me, but it was totally worth it. I left Freedom and haven't looked back."

Too stunned to formulate a response, I stared up at Ian with his new haircut and stubbled jaw. Without the abundance of hair covering his oval face, I could easily make out a strong chin, straight nose, and hooded eyes. My mother would call them "bedroom eyes." I held no such aspirations of finding out.

"If I knew you were going to look at me like that, I would have cut my hair a long time ago," he said with a teasing smile.

I blushed but recovered quickly. "What prompted the change?"

"My sister is a hair stylist. She told me to stop moping around after things didn't work out with Genevieve. She also told me I was thirty-three years old, not a member of a boy band, and it was time to look like an adult."

I laughed again, surprised that this incarnation of Ian Horner possessed such a good sense of humor. "Well, it definitely works for you. I can actually see your face. Why have you been hiding it for so long?"

I didn't mistake the slight reddening of Ian's face or the growing smile on mine.

After a brief pause, Ian said, "When you've been taller than everyone since ten years-old, you look for ways to hide. I'm more of a behind the scenes kind of guy anyway. Hard to do when you're six foot four."

I glanced up at him, glad I wore my heeled boots. "You seemed tall from down here, but then again, everybody does when you're barely over five feet."

Ian crouched down, meeting me at eye level. "Better?" he asked.

I nodded, shocked and amazed at my own reaction to Ian Horner. The surge of unexpected attraction left me feeling off balance. From just beyond us, the hostess announced our table was ready, and I inhaled a sigh of relief.

After placing our orders, Ian offered to pour me a cup of hot tea. Our fingers brushed as he handed me the cup, and my teacup rattled as I placed it back down on the saucer. When I glanced up, I found Ian watching me.

"Does it feel a little sacrilegious to be here on Christmas?" he said, looking around. "Of course, a lot of scholars think Jesus was born during the Feast of Tabernacles in the fall, so hey, maybe not," he said, editing his own statement.

"Did you research this, or are you trying to impress me again?" After an awkward pause, I quickly added, "Since this is a just friends, non-date, I can ask a blunt question, right?"

"Nice try," Ian said, not letting me off the hook, "but since this *is* a just friends, non-date, I'm not trying to impress you whatsoever. It was a genuine statement."

I grinned. "Good to know."

"Do you do a lot of extra-Biblical studies?" he asked before pulling a handful of fried noodles onto a plate. I watched him scoop some duck sauce and a healthy dose of Chinese mustard next to it. Apparently, Ian Horner liked a bit of spice in his life.

I blushed at where my thoughts went next. As much as I wanted to blame my mother for all of those "spice up your love life" articles, something about this man felt more like winning the jackpot rather than settling for a consolation prize.

Ian noted my flushed expression, but didn't comment on it. Instead, he gestured toward the food and said, "Do you want to pray?"

"Excellent idea," I said.

And I meant it.

Ian held out his hand across the table, and I took it tentatively. Following a simple grace, Ian stared at my tiny palm encased in his, and my heartbeat accelerated. Ian glanced up, his dark eyes holding a knowing sparkle.

Closing my eyes again, I silently offered a quick prayer of repentance for my horrible attitude that morning and just held on for the ride. Whatever God intended for this just friends, not a real date, I felt as though I stared down the top of a roller coaster about to begin its descent.

"Do you do that often?" Ian asked, having relinquished my hand at some point during my musings.

"Do what?" I said.

"Get lost in thought. Do you daydream, or is your brain churning through millions of lines of code?"

"Spoken like a web developer," I said, verbal sword hopeful for a worthy opponent.

"Guilty as charged," came the reply of steel against my blade. "We can't all have the glamorous Parkview jobs."

I chuckled. "I create glamorous looking and sounding documents but nothing quite as exciting as some of the other Parkview folks who roam the streets."

"Well, I can't say Winthrope is all that exciting, at least not the industrial part where I work, but there's some good restaurants. Do you normally come out into the burbs?"

"I, um, used to live in Winthrope," I said. "The non-industrial, new money part."

Taking in my expression, Ian deduced the rather obvious. "Well, that explains Chloe complaining about your *extravagant lifestyle* to Genevieve. I overheard a lot of those conversations after church. If envy had a picture in the dictionary, I think Chloe's face would be next to it. I know we're not supposed to speak ill of our leaders, but I just don't get it, Taylor. Did you guys have some kind of fight or something, or has she always been so nasty to you?"

"Both," I replied. "It was recently brought to my attention how much Chloe may have resented my relationship with Brian. He and I were pretty close before they met."

"I saw that when he introduced me to you. Pastor Brian didn't want to share."

"As I recall, you weren't exactly subtle with how you butted into our conversation, Ian. Kind of high-handed, actually."

He shrugged. "I didn't like the way he looked at you."

"What do you mean?"

"Like Christmas morning, no pun intended. I had already been at Freedom for nine months, just sort of watching things from the back of the room in the sound booth. I don't know if Brian ever looked at Chloe the way he looked at you. His whole face lit up."

"That's only because I surprised him by showing up at church," I said. "There never was any interest on his part or mine, I assure you."

"If you say so, Taylor."

"Ian, you can't tell me that the brother-in-law who treated me like a kid sister, who was in love with Chloe from the second he laid eyes on her, was secretly in love with me too. No offense, but it sounds like the kind of soap opera melodrama the women in my office like to dream up."

Ian shrugged again, willing to let the dispute remain unresolved. I had enough confusing thoughts and emotions roiling around in my heart and head.

The raging fire did not require another log.

CHAPTER 19

AFTER OUR JUST FRIENDS, NOT A REAL DATE EVENING, Ian Horner asked me out for another non date. He invited me to a New Year's Eve party at his sister's house. He said it would be a low key evening of wine, board games, and fellowship.

No pressure for a kiss or anything at midnight, Ian added over FaceSpace messenger.

That's good, because I don't think I could reach up there anyway.

I could bend down, or I could pick you up. Do you have a preference?

Blushing, I typed back, *I didn't think "just friends" did those sorts of things. Especially on non-dates.*

True. But it gives me something to look forward to.

I giggled for maybe the first time since college, then startled when I noticed Phil standing in front of me.

"Are we engaged in a little extracurricular flirting during office hours?" he purred.

Having learned Phil's sense of humor a while ago, I offered a sassy grin and a sing-songy, "Maybe."

"Have you patched things up with Goldstein, or is this

someone who will refrain from adding extra dramatics to our work day?"

My online flirtation with Ian forgotten, my mirth transitioned quickly into embarrassment. "I had no idea Kyle was going to show up like that."

Phil rolled his eyes. "There are some people who claim they hate drama, yet we always find them in the center of it. Often self-created. I'm glad the mighty Margolin was around to protect you from whatever shenanigans Goldstein had in mind."

"Phil, I think Kyle stopped by to see Ted, not me. Apparently, Rebecca ripped his sister a new one."

Phil's expression said otherwise. "He came here to see you, Taylor. That's what he told Brooklyn when she tried to stop him on his way in."

"Oh."

"What about this new fellow you've already got? Looks like you didn't waste any time picking up the pieces."

"I am not that kind of girl," I said defensively.

My CEO grimaced. "I'm meddling again, and I apologize. I'm acting like some overprotective father type instead of your boss."

I smiled. "I don't mind the fatherly advice, Phil. Mine went AWOL a long time ago. I wish I had listened to everybody's warnings about Kyle."

"Do you think Goldstein used you to replace Rebecca?"

I exhaled slowly, giving myself a few seconds to review my brief time with Kyle. "No, I don't think I was ever meant to be a replacement for anybody. I'm not sure Kyle knows what he wants. If he does, he's still so tied to his family, he'll never be able to leave and cleave."

"Leave and cleave?" Phil asked.

"The Bible says a husband is supposed to leave his father

and mother when he gets married and cleave to his wife." At Phil's bewildered expression, I further explained, "Basically, a separation has to occur physically, emotionally, and spiritually. There's plenty of horror stories about the overbearing mother-in-law who can't cut the cord to her son. She refuses to relinquish her role as top female in her son's life, so she makes things miserable for the daughter-in-law. Of course, that can be true of any family member who thinks they supersede the spouse. If there aren't healthy boundaries with the old nuclear family, there will always be strife and resentment in the marriage."

"Spoken from experience?" Phil asked, surprised. "You look a little young to have already been married, Taylor."

"Yes, I was married before, but I don't have any monster-in-law stories to share. My mother-in-law certainly spoiled my ex-husband, but she was pretty hands off up until the divorce. Then, she just wanted all of her stuff back."

"Sounds like a delightful woman," Phil deadpanned.

"But I did have a merry Christmas this year after all," I said, eager to change the subject. "Very pleasant surprise actually."

"So...what's his name?" Phil coaxed, reminding me of a middle school girlfriend wanting to know which boy I liked in P.E. class.

I laughed. "Not telling. If I've learned anything from the whole Kyle Goldstein disaster, it's to keep all of that business hush hush."

"It's nice to see you smile with your eyes, Taylor. I hope this new guy sticks around for a while. Just make sure you're not too goo-goo eyed to focus on my RFP. Margolin's not the only producer around here bringing in the bacon. Speaking of, we have interviews lined up after New Year's for potential marketing department hires. We've been less than satisfied with the recruits from our usual staffing agency, so we asked Mrs. Margolin if we could borrow her expertise and have her look over a few of the resumes that get past Bonnie."

"Isn't Rebecca in full time Mommy mode right now?"

"Mrs. M says she can work on it while the baby sleeps, and she really wants to make sure we get it right this time. She's concerned you might try to find work elsewhere due to unneeded stress from current and former employees."

"We're not looking at more turnover, are we?" I asked.

Phil sighed. "Unfortunately, I'm just the CEO, not some all seeing eye. I'll admit Culver can be a bit slow to handle trouble-some employees, and I've probably been too passive in thinking they'll just weed themselves out naturally. As usually occurs, the squeaky wheel gets the oil. In this case, my top producer and my favorite, former employee spent an entire dinner going to bat for you. Margolin even pointed out client complaints regarding one particular unit group who seems to spend more time gossiping than actually working. Frankly, I had no idea Miss Belle covered for all of them for so long—or how shoddy our client support has been. It was eye opening and humiliating to say the least, but it's also why I keep Ted on the executive board to give me honest feedback."

"They did all that for me?" I asked. "Why? I'm nobody. I'm just the girl who replaced the irreplaceable Rebecca Ivy. Half the people here still call me, 'the Rebecca girl,' and I've been at Culver for almost three years."

Phil shook his head sadly. "People are people. You have good ones, you have not so good ones, and then you have the folks somewhere in between. Taylor, you're definitely one of the good ones, and whether the associates here can appreciate that or not, believe me when I tell you we are willing to do quite a bit to keep you."

"It's not about the money, Phil."

He waved me off. "Well aware, Taylor. If you were in it for the money, you would have found a better paying job. There's a personal level of dedication to your craft, pride of ownership that is rare in your job position, and if I may say so, frequently missing from your generation."

I frowned. "Not every millennial got a participation trophy growing up, and not all of us are lazy. Don't forget that many of us were raised by *Generation Me* aka all of you hippie, free love, baby boomers who had everything handed to you by your parents so that you wouldn't have to struggle like they did during the Great Depression."

Phil raised an eyebrow. "Are you blaming the selfishness of *your* generation on the selfishness of *my* generation? Seems like more of that responsibility shirking you snowflakes have perfected."

Sitting back in my office chair, I sized up my CEO to see whether he meant this conversation seriously or in jest. Nothing about Phil's posture or facial expression displayed humor, nor was that infamous, naughty twinkle found in his blue eyes.

With mild accusation, he said, "Do you really believe it's all our fault?"

I met the challenge in his tone head on. "The level of boomer self-obsession is off the charts, Phil. I have my parents to attest to that. It's your generation who willingly inject dead parasites into their faces lest they have a wrinkle. Muscle cars, ED pills, collagen, constant dieting, yuppie materialism...that's all you guys and your quest for wealth, sex, and eternal youth. Are you telling me the apple fell so far from the tree?"

"Meanwhile, your generation covers themselves in tattoos and piercings, demands crazy wages with zero skill or education, and then wonders why they can't find work. They sponge off their so-called 'selfish' parents while wasting their days as social justice warriors from the convenience of their keyboard or cell phone. Paid for, yet again, by mom and dad."

"Then we have the chicken and the egg, don't we Phil? I won't argue my generation has plenty to answer for, but has anyone asked why these kids get away with it? If you want to act indignant about snowflake millennials on their electronics all day, why aren't you addressing the parents who are enabling the behavior? There's a reason why the kids feel entitled to behave the way they do. I'm just suggesting we put proper focus on the people responsible for shaping the worldview of *my* generation. It doesn't mitigate our responsibility, but it certainly helps explain it."

Phil crossed his arms over his chest. "There's more to you than meets the eye, Taylor Ross. As quiet as you seem to be in the office, I have a feeling a spitfire lurks somewhere underneath. People would be wise not to double cross you."

"Well, I did pepper spray Kyle Goldstein in the parking garage the night we officially got acquainted."

The sparkle returned to Phil's eyes. "A little birdie named Leonard mentioned something about that, but I didn't know Goldstein was the unlucky recipient. Too bad you didn't spray him while he was in the office. Would have put a nice finish to things. Not that I'm meddling, of course."

"Of course," I grinned.

"Interesting chat," Phil said, tapping on the back of my desktop monitor. "You've given me some food for thought, and it's nice to see someone who knows her own mind instead of parroting social media talking points. I'm sorry Goldstein wasn't smart enough to seize the opportunity when he had it."

My grin dimmed into a tight smile. "For every millennial

who grew up coddled, spoiled, or raised in the image of their narcissistic parents, there's also the kid who was forced to grow up and be the adult in the family. We were taught about self-sacrifice from a very early age because it was demanded of us over and again. Rebecca went through that with her own family, and so did I."

Phil nodded for me to continue.

"You called me and Rebecca unicorns, Phil, and there are those of us determined to do and be better than our parents. We know firsthand how ugly selfishness can be, how destructive it is. We do everything in our power to become the exact opposite, almost to a fault. Jesus tells us the one who truly loves is the one willing to lay down his life for his friends. I don't doubt Kyle cared about me, but he just cared about himself a lot more."

"So he sacrificed you instead of himself? Is that what you're saying?"

"That's exactly what I'm saying, and I won't settle for that again. I can't. I have to believe there's better out there for me."

Phil smiled. "What about this mystery man who put a smile on your face when I walked in here? Do you think he's another unicorn like you, Taylor?"

I shrugged. "Could be. For now, I'm just making a new friend and getting over the disappointment of what could have been. I feel so stupid for not listening to all of you."

"Goldstein sold you a bill of goods and failed to deliver. It doesn't make you stupid for trusting him, Taylor. It makes him stupid for not being trustworthy. Meanwhile, spend time with people who make you smile, and don't give a second thought to those who don't. It's not selfish to take care of yourself. Mrs. Margolin reminded me of that when she told me you were going to burn out if we didn't get you some help *pronto*."

"I guess we unicorns have to look out for one another, don't we?"

"God willing, He'll send you a partner in life to do that too. You'll probably go off, marry your mystery man, start repopulating the earth like the Margolins, and I'll be right back to where I was two years ago."

I laughed. "Repopulating the earth?"

The familiar twinkle returned to Phil's eye. "Just invite me to the wedding. And if he's Jewish, the *bris* too."

Not totally sure what Phil meant, I researched the word "bris" once he exited my office. My hand covered my mouth in shock, and I sent Ian a quick message.

Ever heard of a bris?

After a brief pause, Ian wrote back, *Never been to one, but I've heard of them. Why?*

Just something silly my boss said.

Um...ok? Why is your boss talking to you about Jewish circumcision practices?

He wanted to know who made me smile while I was sitting at my desk. We followed that with a rather lengthy discussion about whose generation was more selfish. The bris came up later.

After a pause, Ian wrote back, *Still not seeing the connection, but I'm also up to my eyeballs in code. I can't replicate this bug customers are complaining about on the commerce site. Proverbial needle in haystack.*

I don't want to keep you from work, Ian. We can talk later.

I'm not sure I can concentrate while wondering how you segued from generational selfishness to circumcision. Would you be interested in sharing the details with me before New Year's? Say, this evening, perhaps?

Is this a date, or another 'just friends' thing? I wrote, feeling the lines blur between what I said I wanted and what might actually be true.

After a long pause, little ellipses showing Ian typing, deleting, retyping, and then repeating the process several times over, I finally got a reply.

What do you want it to be, Taylor?

I just want to spend time with someone who makes me smile.

After inserting several happy faced emojis, Ian wrote, *Hypothetically speaking, if I kiss you, and it puts a smile on your face, would that be acceptable? Hypothetically, of course.*

I grinned. *Hypothetically?*

I could almost feel Ian's smile through the other end of the computer. *Hypothetically, the best kiss you've ever had in your entire life.*

Hypothetically, that's a pretty tall order.

Well, I am 6'4" and that's not hypothetical.

I chuckled. *Hypothetically, are you driving down to Parkview, or am I meeting you somewhere near Winthrope?*

Hypothetically, let's meet halfway in Hillcrest, and dinner's on me. It's a real date, and God willing, I will make you smile until your cheeks hurt. Anything beyond that, we'll leave in His hands. Sound fair?

I responded with some smiling face emojis of my own.

CHAPTER 20

"YOU LOOK BEAUTIFUL, AND THAT'S NOT hypothetical," Ian said as he greeted me outside of Sylvia's Bar & Grille in Hillcrest.

I bestowed Ian with my first smile of the evening. "I had someone tell me that I look and dress like a librarian. I'm glad to hear that's not the case anymore."

"What's wrong with looking like a librarian?" he asked.

I paused, not having given much thought to that before. All I knew was the instant shame from Rebecca-clone's dismissive comment and Kyle's agreement with it. Troubled, I wondered why those words still haunted me seven months after the incident.

"Taylor? You still there?"

I glanced up at Ian, at the concern in his dark eyes. "Sorry. I guess there really isn't anything wrong with looking like a librarian. The person who said it just reinforced a lot of things my mother likes to criticize about my appearance." Ruefully, I added, "How's that for an overshare?"

Ian raised a brow, studying my face.

"What?" I asked.

"I don't know who made the comment to you, but it's obvious it got under your skin. Was the person who said it as close to you as your mother?"

I scoffed. "Hardly. She was also intoxicated at the time."

"Why do you care what some random drunk had to say about you?"

"That's what I was just trying to figure out. There was a second person who agreed with her, and he approved of my recent wardrobe and hairstyle changes."

"Ah," Ian said. "And this would be the idiot who almost ruined your Christmas?"

I nodded. "That would be him."

"Why was his opinion so important to you?"

"Kyle was the first man I went out with after the divorce. It was the first time I felt anything after Mitch."

"What's so different about this guy?" Ian asked. "I asked you out all of those other times, but you always had an excuse."

I grimaced, not wanting to start off my first real date with Ian this way. I also didn't want to lie to him. "Kyle just caught my attention like nobody else had up until then."

Ian's jaw clenched and unclenched. "I see."

"I'm sorry, Ian. I don't want to hurt you, but you deserve an honest answer. Can we just drop it and talk about something else? Please?"

He hesitated for a moment, then went for broke. "Would you have been flirting with me on text and messenger if I had cut my hair two-and-a-half years ago? Is that all I needed to do this whole time?"

"Ian, I had already agreed to go out with you before you cut your hair, remember? I had no idea you'd done anything different until I saw you at Christmas. Our first meeting at Freedom was definitely off putting, but I wasn't in a place to go out with anybody back then either. It wasn't just you, Ian."

"Are you sure you really want to go out with me now, Taylor? I mean, before we go on this supposed date, I'd like to find out if I'm just some rebound guy. I want to spare both of us the pain and embarrassment if that's all this is to you."

"Can we sit?" I asked. "I promise I'll answer your question, Ian, but I'm going to wind up with a neck cramp staring up at you."

Ian looked around, noting a complete lack of outdoor seating. He gestured toward the curb, and I followed. I sat with my knees pulled up to my chest while he stretched his long legs out into the pavement. Seeing Ian almost at eye level afforded me a better view of his face and several days' worth of scruff on his cheeks. I also noted tufts of chest hair visible from his v-neck sweater. A surge of attraction pulsed through me, and I swallowed convulsively. When I could trust myself to look up again, I found Ian staring out into the parking lot.

I took a deep breath and said, "Ian, this is a first date, but I feel like we're heading into deep waters awfully quickly here. I was hoping to get to know you, not jump right into each other's backstories right away."

Ian looked me square in the eyes, unsettling me with the potency of his gaze. "Are you still in love with him?"

I exhaled a mirthless laugh. "We were never in love, Ian. Kyle and I went on a grand total of maybe four dates. The first date was sort of an accident. The next one was a disaster. The third one followed right after a disaster. The last date was so disastrous, it ended any chance of a real relationship."

Half of Ian's mouth picked up into a smile. "You've used the word *disaster* three times, but you still seem hung up on this guy, Taylor. You said as much on Christmas. Are you saying one dinner with me erased all of that? I'd like to think so, but my ego's not quite big enough to believe it."

I offered a small grin in return. "Everything that happened on Christmas caught me by surprise, Ian. You really shocked me, and I'm not even talking about your hair. I had a lot of preconceived ideas about you, some from misunderstanding, some from my own blindness. I don't think I've said this yet, but thank you for standing up for me against Chloe. It means a lot. More than I can say, actually."

Ian acknowledged my last statement with a nod. "You're welcome, Taylor."

"It actually highlights the biggest difference between you and Kyle."

"How so? How did things eventually end with him?"

"Kyle shared private details about me with his sister, and she used that to publicly humiliate me. Kyle just stood there watching the whole thing happen. I think a mannequin would have been more lifelike."

Incredulous, Ian said, "He didn't defend you or even apologize?"

"Nope."

"I can't believe he just let his sister tear you apart! What was her problem with you anyway?"

"Because I'm a Christian. Because they're not. Because of my history with a cheating husband and her history of playing the mistress."

Ian whistled. "Wow."

I sighed wearily. "Tell me about it."

"How did you get mixed up with someone like this in the first place? Is he Mr. Universe or something?"

I chuckled softly. "Kyle's good looking, but not anything out of a magazine ad. I just felt alive when I was around him. He has a very quick wit, and I forgot how much I missed the give and take of really good verbal banter. I always imagine it as some kind of a sword fight."

"And then there's me," Ian said with a grimace, "always making a complete fool of myself whenever I'm around you. I've also been told I'm pretty intense."

I met Ian's dark gaze. "You did just fine on Christmas."

"That was a non-date."

I smiled. "You're doing all right so far tonight."

"Other than grilling you about some guy you've already told me you don't want to talk about."

"Other than that," I said good naturedly.

"Taylor, if there's any chance this guy's going to swoop back into your life, I don't want to be around for that."

My brow wrinkled. "I'm not sure I'm following you, Ian. I've seen you around for a few years, but it's not like we're planning to get..." my voice trailed off as Ian's face revealed his intentions. "So, this wasn't just a 'first date' for you, was it?"

"How long have I been trying to get you to go out with me, Taylor?"

I gulped. He wasn't kidding about intense.

He pressed on self-deprecatingly. "And I'm apparently doing everything I can to sabotage myself with the woman of my dreams."

I gagged and then coughed on my own saliva.

"I wasn't supposed to say that out loud," Ian said. "Less than ideal response from dream woman."

"Do you narrate a lot?" I asked once I'd recovered.

"Only when I'm nervous. Super annoying, I know."

I laid my head against my knees to take in Ian's profile from a different angle. "Not annoying. Different. I might even go so far as to say charming in its own unique way, especially since you just called me your dream woman."

"Which caused you to choke."

I laughed. "All of this wooing is very new for me, Ian. It's hard to tell what's flowery sentiment and what's real these days."

He nodded in understanding. "So, we're back to the idiot who betrayed your trust, can't admit he did anything wrong, and is probably blaming you for the whole thing anyway. I'll tell you what, Taylor, you really can pick 'em."

My stomach dropped as did the smile from my face.

Ian looked genuinely dismayed. "I know I just said something really stupid, Taylor, and I feel even worse for needing to ask how I screwed up."

I closed my eyes and took a deep breath. I prayed for patience as a burst of tears simmered just below the surface. "What did you mean when you said I can really pick 'em?"

In a pained voice, Ian said, "Taylor, can you open your eyes and look at me? Please?"

Reluctantly, I obeyed his request.

"Taylor, I just meant you have a lot of lousy people in your life, not that you deliberately choose for them to be there. I was thinking about Brian and Chloe, your mom and your brother, and all of these selfish people who seem to go out of their way to hurt you. I didn't mean for that to sound the way it came out. Will you forgive me?"

"I forgive you," I said quietly. "Can we go inside? I'm starving."

Ian nodded, holding out a hand so we could stand up together. I waved him off, still tender after his unexpected blunder.

"I ruined our first real date, didn't I?" Ian said, trying to run a hand through nonexistent hair.

"You didn't ruin it," I said gently. "You caught me off guard a few times, but I've still got a lot of healing I need to do. Honestly, I feel like you're getting the short end of the stick here, Ian. I don't know if I'm ready for anything more than just friends right now."

"With me?"

"With anybody," I said truthfully. "I don't want to waste your time or get your hopes up."

"What about all of the back and forth over text? Is that you actually flirting with me or just the verbal banter you said you like so much?"

"A little of both. You make me nervous too, you know."

"Why? Because I look like King Kong next to you?"

Tired of hearing Ian demean himself, I reached up to pull his face level with mine. Instantly, I melted into bottomless, brown eyes. Ian's gaze lowered to my mouth then back up to my eyes in silent question. The sound of my heart thudded loudly in my ears.

"I was wrong," I whispered. "I can't be just friends with you after all."

Ian leaned in, and my eyelids closed as our lips met. His kiss held a tentative sweetness, but it didn't take long for me to explore his scruffy beard beneath my palms.

Ian groaned and pulled away. He held onto my hands as he stretched back to his full height.

"I...I...didn't expect you to..." he stammered.

I squeezed the large hands dwarfing mine, wondering if Ian even felt it. He returned the squeeze.

Almost laughing at the irony of the words coming out of my mouth, I said, "This isn't a marriage proposal, Ian. It's a date. I don't have any expectations here outside of having a pleasant evening with you. Hopefully, with lots of smiling and good conversation. I'm done trying to figure any of this out anymore."

Unexpectedly, Ian leaned back down and kissed me with a passionate fire that left me breathless. When he pulled me into his arms, he rendered Kyle Goldstein a distant memory. My comatose heart was now fully awake and hungry. If not for Ian cradling my face when he pulled away, I would have crumbled onto the pavement in a jelly-kneed heap.

Still bent low so he could look directly in my eyes, Ian said, "This is more than just a date for me, Taylor. I can't pretend it isn't."

"Can you wait for me to catch up?" I asked, breathless.

"I've waited for more than two years, Taylor. I've got patience in spades. Persistence too, in case you haven't noticed," he said with a grin.

Those dimples might just have been the undoing of me.

I had no doubt Ian Horner fully meant what he said. I remembered my brother's admonition to me months earlier when he told me Ian fit the bill as a potential match for my clanging, biological clock. I could only smile at God's sense of irony and the absolute peace flooding my heart, mind, and soul.

Ian looked entranced. "I don't mean this as any kind of a line here, Taylor, but you are seriously the most beautiful woman I have ever met."

I scoffed. "I think you need to get out more."

Ian kissed me one last time before we entered the restaurant. By the time we walked in, I certainly felt like the most beautiful woman in the room.

And there was nothing hypothetical about it.

CHAPTER 21

"Kate, this is Taylor. Taylor, this is my sister, Kate," Ian said, introducing me to the woman six years his senior and host of our New Year's Eve festivities.

"I like your cut," she said, gesturing toward my hair. "Definitely suits your face. It takes a lot of confidence to go that short," she said, glancing back and forth between Ian and me.

Taking in Kate's asymmetrical, purple tipped bob, I could probably say the same about her. She stood somewhere in the middle of the fourteen inch gap between me and Ian, probably closer to Ian's height with her boots on.

"How long is Fiona staying with Mom and Dad?" Ian asked his sister.

"Just until tomorrow night. Her dad's picking her up after that."

"How old is your daughter?" I asked.

"Twelve," Kate said with a twinkle in her dark eyes. "My relationship with her father ended a lot more amicably than some of my friends. You wouldn't believe the divorce horror stories I've heard."

I glanced sharply at Ian whose expression seemed as pained as mine. Initial panic subsiding, I realized Ian had not followed in Kyle Goldstein's footsteps. My shoulders relaxed about the same time Ian's hand lay gently on the small of my back.

"Did I say something wrong?" Kate asked, noting the tension between the two of us.

I tried to offer a bright smile. "Just a bit of a misunderstanding."

Kate's own smile dimmed, but she didn't push the issue. Instead, she introduced me to some other guests. Most of them already knew Ian, and they eyed me as if trying to rate my compatibility with the brother of their hostess.

"Maybe this was a bad idea," Ian whispered close to my ear.

I glanced up into his eyes, warmed by the compassion and concern found there. "I feel like a prized pig being inspected before auction."

"I'll outbid anyone here. You're coming home with me tonight."

Ian's impassioned decree raised my eyebrows along with the temperature in the room.

"That sounded a lot better in my head," he said. "I was following your metaphor and accidentally stepped into another one."

"I don't think I'd call yours a metaphor," I managed to reply. "More like an idiom. Unless you were being literal, in which case, it's just a simple, declarative sentence."

Ian grinned at me, dimples proving an even greater weakness than blue eyes. "If I had known grammar could be so exciting, I would have paid better attention in eighth grade."

My turtleneck sweater suddenly felt stifling. I pulled at the collar to allow some cooler air inside. "Seems like you're doing just fine with your in-person swordplay, Mr. Horner."

He leaned down, lips parted, and I wondered if he intended to stake his claim in the middle of his sister's apartment. Instead, Ian lifted a wayward eyelash from my cheek. I couldn't recall ever feeling so aware of every nerve ending in my body.

Kate cleared her throat in front of us. "Sorry to break the mood...well not really, since everyone is watching you guys like it's *Days of Our Children,* but we're going to pray and get started."

I chuckled softly while Ian flushed.

Lacing her arm through mine, Kate pulled me toward the rest of the group. "My brother has talked about you incessantly for close to three years, Taylor. I'm glad to know you really exist."

"Incessantly?"

She shrugged sheepishly. "Okay, well a lot. I'm not trying to scare you, which I probably just did. I just mean my brother has liked you for a long time, and I'm glad you're giving him a chance."

I met her eyes, searching for hidden warning. I saw only kindness and curiosity instead.

"He's definitely persistent," I said cautiously, not sure how much I wanted to reveal or how much Ian might want revealed.

Kate grinned. "That too. He's also the kindest, sweetest, and best brother I could possibly ask for. He's an incredible uncle to Fiona, and she adores him like a second dad."

I glanced across the room at Ian who watched me and his sister with a bit of a frown on his face.

"Your brother doesn't seem too happy right now," I said.

"That's because he thinks I'm warning you not to break his

heart and all the other stuff big sisters like to do when they're looking out for their little brothers."

I smiled. "I can relate. My brother is five years younger than me, and I practically raised him. Unfortunately, we're not as close as we used to be."

"Ian never mentioned you have a brother."

Thankful for Mr. Horner's discretion, I caught his eye again and gave him a quick nod that I faced no danger talking to his sister. Nevertheless, he made his way to my side.

"Can I have my date back, please?" Ian said, though his tone sounded more like a command than a request.

Kate's eyes widened as her gaze traveled between the two of us. "I've never really seen this alpha male side of my brother before, Taylor. It's kind of nice." She gave a saucy wink to Ian and then left to mingle with the rest of her guests.

Ian stood protectively next to me. "Kate means well, but sometimes she likes to meddle—especially in my love life. I don't think I've introduced her to any girl I've gone out with since college."

"That's a long time, Ian."

"I didn't have anyone I wanted to bring home. For ten years, I didn't have anyone at all."

"Seriously?"

"My sister thinks I hid underneath my hair."

"What prompted the change?" I asked.

"When you agreed to go out with me. Kate told me she would disown me as her brother if I didn't come over and finally let her cut my hair."

I glanced over at Ian's sister happily engaged in conversation with a small group of women. "Remind me to thank her," I said, more to myself than Ian.

"Why's that?" he asked.

I held his gaze, relieved and secretly thrilled to know I affected him with my eyes as much as he did to me. "I finally got to see you."

If not for the raucous laughter bursting forth from the other side of the room, I probably would have leapt into Ian's arms for another hypothetical kiss.

"This is why Paul says it's better to marry than to burn with passion," Ian said low.

I stepped away from him as the reality of our situation sunk in.

"I scared you, didn't I?"

I nodded.

"Hmm," he murmured.

"Anything else?" I asked.

Ian tugged gently on my arm, grabbed our coats off the coat rack, and then told his sister we'd be back in a few minutes. He placed my wool peacoat around my shoulders as he shut the door behind us.

"Ian, what's all this about?"

"Taylor, we're playing with fire. I can't pretend that I don't want to do more than just kiss you, but we're both on the same page regarding sex before marriage, right?"

"We are," I said, shame over my impassioned responses washing over me. "I promise, I've never acted this way before in my life. Not even with Mitch. Maybe I'm more like my mother than I realized."

Ian delved deep into my eyes. "You're a beautiful, desirable, wonderful woman who deserves to be treated that way, Taylor. But, I also see the way you look at me. The problem is, we're not married."

"Slow down!" I said, holding up my hands. "This is only our second date!"

"I agree," Ian said. "We definitely need to slow things down. The Bible says not to stir up or awaken love until it wants to arise, and the kissing has to stop."

"You kissed me!" I said. "Three times I might add."

"You started it," he said with a smile. "I'm only taking credit for the other two."

"Well, what do we do, Ian? I like you. A lot. Am I ready to marry you? No. Am I ready to marry anybody right now? No."

"I've never been married or engaged, but I came close right after college. The girl I dated when I bumped into you in the dorm lobby is the only serious relationship I've ever had."

Surprised, I asked, "Ian, are you a virgin?"

He blushed. "I know it's shocking to admit for this day and age, but I am. Which is why I'm begging you to slow things down, cut me loose, or let me know there's a happy ending so I don't lose sight of the prize."

"The prize being me or just sex with me?" I asked bluntly.

Ian didn't flinch. "Taylor, it's always been you. If I only wanted sex, I could have done that years ago. I had the opportunity, but I chose to wait. You kiss me like you have a lot more experience than I do."

"I was married, Ian. Of course, I have more experience than you."

"That's what I need you to understand, Taylor. None of this is meaningless or harmless kissing for me. It probably means more than it should, but I've also been in love with you since I met you, and I never thought you'd feel the same way about me."

"Not that it stopped you from trying," I said quietly, my own insides a roiling mess of confusion, hope, and all out panic.

"Jesus said we don't have because we don't ask. So I asked. I even tried dating Genevieve after I told myself it would never happen with you, but that was a bust. She just talked about Freedom and Pastor Brian the entire night. She seemed more interested in him than in me."

"You don't think they're...you know?" I asked. After seeing my own, phony Christian husband deceive the world, I could no longer put any sin past anyone.

Ian shrugged. "I don't think Chloe makes it easy on him, but Brian doesn't seem like the kind of guy to copy his brother's sins."

"That's how the affair started with Mitch. This leggy receptionist got hired at our office, and she made it obvious how much she admired my husband."

"Did you confront them about it?" Ian asked.

"Of course! Mitch told me I had nothing to worry about."

"What about the girl?"

I inhaled and exhaled slowly, the shock and pain of that moment forever burned in my brain. "She told me that if we had such a perfect Christian marriage, I shouldn't have anything to worry about."

"So, this was no accident?"

I shook my head. "She knew exactly what she wanted, and it was my husband."

"We don't have to talk about this, Taylor. It's obviously upsetting to you."

I smiled through a sheen of tears. "I promise I'm okay. I just don't want to lead you on, Ian, and I certainly don't want to cause either of us to stumble."

"You and Kyle?" he asked hesitantly.

"Did we sleep together?" I finished for him.

"I don't want to offend you, Taylor. I just can't imagine you kissing him the way you kiss me and things not going from one place to another. You said he's not a Christian, so I'm guessing he feels differently about sex before marriage. I'm not judging you if you did, by the way."

"You're right about Kyle," I said. "His views on sex differ vastly from yours or mine."

Ian's mouth became a thin line, apparently bracing himself for the worst.

"But we never slept together. We never came close. Also, Kyle never kissed me like you did the other night, Ian. I'm not immune to what you do to me either. Believe me, I'm just as human."

He released a slow sigh. "So what do we do, Taylor? I know what I want, so I guess the better question is what do *you* want?"

Pulling a page out of Ian Horner's book, I raked a hand through the little bit of hair I had left on my head. "This has been the craziest week of my life, Ian. And that's just it. It's only been a week. Everything always seems amazing at the beginning of a relationship. I made the mistake eleven years ago of rushing ahead and marrying someone who became a completely different person after we got married."

"You know I'm not Mitch, don't you? I'm not this Kyle guy either. I want a wife, a mother for any future children, and a life partner. The day I officially met you at Freedom, God showed me *Proverbs 18:22*."

Before he could recite the Scripture, all the color drained from my face. Ian reached out to steady me. "I'm guessing you already know what it says," he said warily.

"Mitch quoted it the night he proposed to me."

"Oh."

The tears threatening to burst forth finally escaped down my cheeks. "I just don't understand why God let Mitch use that verse knowing what he would eventually do. I don't understand why He gave that same verse to you, Ian. It's like He's mocking how I was deceived and manipulated. Like my mother does."

"Or," Ian said gently, "God's taking what the locusts have eaten and restoring double what you had before. He's redeeming what was used for evil, and He's using it for something good. *Romans 8:28* and all that," he said.

At that moment, I knew.

I absolutely with every fiber of my being completely, totally, and utterly knew.

I was going to marry Ian Horner.

CHAPTER 22

"Here I thought dating Kyle Goldstein would be the craziest thing you'd ever tell me," Rebecca said the following weekend in my family room.

"No more crazy than my mother reaching out to me two days later saying I'm in danger from Mitch. Oh, and she misses me. What do you think? Just another Sarah Meyers stunt?"

Rebecca paused before she answered. "She's your mother, Taylor. You know the whole history with mine, but I truly believe your mother loves you in her own, warped way. Maybe she had a come-to-Jesus, or maybe she realized treating you the way she has isn't acceptable anymore. Obviously, she wants to protect you from your ex-husband regardless of anything else."

"Or she wants something," I said. "I don't mean to sound cynical, but I know Sarah Meyers."

Rebecca smiled at me. "God is bringing a lot of new things in your life, Taylor. It's possible He wants to do something new with your mother too. He loves her just as much as He loves you."

I shrugged. "I can quote you Bible verses about all things being possible with God, but I also know we still have the free will to choose Him or reject Him. My mother will tell you she believes in God, even in Jesus as God's son. She also wants to be in control of her life and doesn't want anyone telling her she can't do whatever she wants."

"Sounds like a toddler."

"I guess you'll be finding out soon enough."

Rebecca's face lit up at the mention of her daughter. "That little girl is getting into everything! Ted finally kid proofed the kitchen cabinets, and we bought one of those plastic octagons to keep Tabby corralled in the family room. When my husband gutted the house years ago, I don't think he realized a wide open floor plan makes it impossible to put kiddie gates anywhere other than on the bedroom doors."

"Speaking of, how are you feeling?" I asked.

Mrs. Margolin burst into what Ted called her "megawatt" smile. The beautiful display illuminated the entire room. Rebecca rubbed her stomach absently as she replied, "Still in shock, to be honest. I tested negative right before Tabby's party, but on a whim, I decided to try one more time a week later. Lo and behold, we got Tabby a little brother or sister for her birthday."

I grinned, so happy for my friend and thrilled to see her living the dream she deserved. "Does the rest of the family know yet? Do you want another gender reveal shower?"

Rebecca laughed. "No, no, we were blessed with so much stuff for Tabby. I think we'll probably do things a lot more low key this go round."

"Even if it's a boy?" I asked. "Ironically enough, Phil asked for invitations to my child's bris. And my wedding too, of course."

Rebecca looked initially shocked before she burst into laughter. "I can't put anything past Phil, can I? You scared me for a minute there, Taylor."

"My metaphorical purity ring is still on my finger," I quipped.

"Have you talked to Ian about what you shared with me? Do you guys have a time frame? Since neither of you are attending a church right now, where would you consider going for counseling, let alone getting married? I didn't think anybody would break my record for a quick engagement."

"Slow down, preggo! You're the only person I've told, and that's because I'm looking for accountability. I need to make sure I haven't taken complete leave of my senses just because Ian gave me the best kiss of my entire life. There's nothing hypothetical about that."

"Ah, you told me about that conversation," she said with a chuckle.

"Everything's happening so fast, Rebecca. I sat here in limbo for forever, and now I can't even keep track of how quickly things are moving."

Mrs. Margolin's face took on a faraway look. "That's exactly how I would describe my relationship with Ted. It's funny how you feel like you were in a coma for three years, because Ted suddenly appeared in my life about three years after Jason left me."

"But Ted was always around. You told me he watched you for years."

"Not unlike Mr. Horner," she said wryly.

"You know, I've complained so much about being in your shadow, Rebecca, and here I go, basically following in your footsteps again. Well, except Ian is taller than Ted."

"Really? Ted is six foot two."

"Ian is six-four, and he's got a leaner frame. Not gangly or anything, just more like a swimmer, I guess."

"But other than that, they're exactly the same, right? Is Ian also a Jewish, gourmet chef who negotiates commercial insurance coverages and renovates houses in his spare time?" Rebecca asked playfully.

I rolled my eyes. "Fine, they're not identical. Thank you for the reminder. Ian ran the sound and visuals at Freedom, and he did a really good job on the board. I always knew when someone else filled in on sound because the mix would be off. The instruments would be too hot, and they always overpowered the vocals."

"That's all over my head, Taylor. I can barely carry a tune, so there you go. You've got one up on me."

On cue, my cell phone buzzed with a text from Ian. Rebecca gave me a sassy wink while I scanned through the message.

Hope you're having a good time with your friend. Just wanted to let you know I was thinking about you and praying for you.

I held it up for Rebecca to see. Appropriately, she cooed and grinned.

"This one's a keeper, Taylor. I'm so glad I kept pushing you to give him a chance."

"Well, you did mention unexpected packages, and Ian was definitely unexpected. Anything I say using the word 'package' is going to sound completely inappropriate, so I'm not even going to try."

Exchanging a quick look, Mrs. Margolin and I fell into a fit of giggles. It reminded me of the excitement I felt with my college roommate before my first date with Mitch. As if replacing old memories with new ones, Rebecca even pored through my closet to help find the perfect dress for a double date with Ian's sister and her boyfriend.

"We want you to look classy, age appropriate, and like a million bucks," Rebecca said, flipping through several hangers. "How did one person accumulate so many cute, little cocktail dresses?" she asked.

"Networking mixers with Mitch. My options were to stay home and worry about him driving drunk or endure tedious evenings in uncomfortable shoes but at least know my husband got home alive."

"Sounds fabulous," she said dryly before stopping to assess a beaded, purple sheath. "Va va va voom, Taylor! When are you wearing this one again? Ian would need a drool bucket!"

I laughed. "Probably when I won't be thinking how much I want him to appreciate how good I look wearing it." After a brief pause, I said, "Rebecca, can I ask you something?"

Taking note of my tone, she glanced up from a faux wrap dress to meet my gaze. "What's up?"

"Normally, I'd just come right out and ask, but I don't want to force you to divulge anything you might not be comfortable sharing."

Rebecca released the dress to face me from inside of my walk-in closet. "Sounds pretty serious."

I sighed. "I just keep coming back to that verse from *Song of Solomon*, the one about not stirring up love until it's ready."

"Let me guess. The problem is you're ready?"

"Yes!" I squeaked. "Even before Mitch and I got married, I never fought so hard to keep my thoughts clean! Not that sex is dirty in the proper context, but I find myself constantly battling to keep my thoughts in check."

"Sounds about right, Taylor. You had to know your relationship would be attacked spiritually. God brought Ian into your life as a lot more than just a soft landing from Kyle."

"And that's the other thing! God gave me those verses when I was semi-dating Kyle and after. I keep coming back to them."

"Why are you reading *Song of Solomon* if it's causing so much confusion and turmoil for you, Taylor?"

"Take it up with Him," I said, pointing upward. "I know God wants me to get something I'm just not seeing yet, but I have no idea what."

Matter-of-factly, Rebecca said, "Then why are you asking me instead of God?"

"Prophetic gifting?" I said weakly.

Rebecca pulled a face. "Taylor, whatever you're afraid of facing with Jesus, you're going to have to deal with eventually. As your friend, I will support you, encourage you, and if need be, tell you something you don't want to hear. But you can't keep coming to me like I'm the Holy Spirit. The answers need to come from Jesus, not me. You've told me a hundred times you're tired of living in my shadow, but then you keep running to me and hiding behind whatever advice I give you. Sometimes I feel more like your mother than your friend."

Stung by the accusation, I said, "Aren't you the one who decided to call Phil on my behalf over Christmas? What about offering to look at resumes for new marketing department hires? Don't act like this is all on me, Rebecca."

"We're not talking about me right now," she said.

"No, but we need to. I didn't say anything because I sincerely appreciate the help and concern you have for me, but it seems like some lines got blurred on both sides. You tell me to stop running to you instead of God, but then you jump in and act like my savior. You did it with Phil, and you even did it with Jessica Goldstein. I never asked you to call either of them."

Rebecca inclined her head to concede the point. "My old tendencies to mother everyone combined with your need for a parental figure work in a wonderfully codependent way, don't they?"

"Up until the resentment creeps in. I start feeling stuck under your thumb, and you start feeling used. No win situation for anybody."

Rebecca sighed. "All right, so why don't we try this *Song of Solomon* situation from the top? You said God gave you these verses while dating both Kyle and Ian, but you don't know why."

"Correct."

"What ideas have you come up with so far? Even if they seem contradictory, at least it gives us a starting point."

I paused to collect my thoughts. "There's the obvious message about not jumping into any kind of a physical relationship. I've kissed Ian three times, and it's sent me into a deluge of thoughts and dreams going well beyond PG-13."

"You didn't tell me you dreamed about Ian," Rebecca said.

"It's embarrassing to admit."

"Why? You're an adult, Taylor. You've been married before. All of this stuff is being stirred up, and it's the exact reason why Paul told us to marry rather than to burn with sexual desire. What you're feeling is natural. What you choose to do with it is trickier."

"Ian said the same thing on New Year's Eve. My mother would also agree that everything I'm feeling is normal. Her advice beyond that is obviously very different from yours."

"Not much of a surprise. I did finally see one of her billboards," Rebecca said.

I groaned and covered my face. "They're awful, aren't they?"

Rebecca let out a throaty chuckle. "Yeah, I can't lie, Taylor. Although it's an impressive amount of cleavage for a women's business suit."

I rolled my eyes. "I remember going with her to the mall and buying that outfit. The jacket originally came with a built-in camisole. My mother cut it out at some point and then had the brilliant idea to stick a bustier underneath it instead."

I watched Rebecca cringe on my behalf. "I'm sorry, Taylor."

"I can't imagine what would happen if I looked like my mother and people thought that was me up there."

"Well, there's that at least. Your mother also looks um, very surprised."

"Botox," I said, "and whatever else she can use to wind back the hands of Father Time. My mother was an absolute knockout in her early twenties, and she feels like she wasted all of her youth and beauty being married to my father."

"So she's trying to reclaim time lost?" Rebecca asked.

"Except she's fifty-six, not twenty-six, and my mother's been reclaiming her youth for the past twenty years. Also, you can't live like that and not expect the drinking and debauchery to show up on your face eventually."

"Do you think she resents you for being prettier than her?" Rebecca asked, rummaging through my litany of party dresses again.

I nearly choked on her words. "Prettier than my mother? Are you kidding?"

Not even looking up, Rebecca said, "I didn't stutter."

"You're one of my closest friends, and I love you, Rebecca, but I think your bias is affecting your judgment."

"Taylor, your mother is a very attractive woman, plastic face aside, but your features are unique. For every Marilyn Morrow, there's a Holly Hepburn. If you try convincing me Holly wasn't a gorgeous little pixie just like you, I'm going to start calling your own bias into question."

"There is no way I look like Holly Hepburn!"

"Look in the mirror, Taylor. I'm not saying you're identical, but look at yourself. Ian called you the most beautiful woman he's ever seen."

"I could wear a burlap sack, and Ian would say that."

Rebecca shot me a look saying I'd just ended my own argument. Point taken, I walked over to the mirror situated above my wide dresser and inspected my features. I wanted to see them through Ian's eyes rather than my mother's put downs or Mitch's rejection.

I no longer referred to my eye color as muddy, but I could never call them andalusite after the way things ended with Kyle. I settled on hazel-green, hoping to be accurate rather than vacillating too far between my mother's pejorative or Kyle's poetry. The rest of my features I labeled as gamine, all of them being petite, well formed, and in balance with my heart shaped face.

"I'm beautiful," I mouthed, gingerly touching my cheek in the mirror.

I felt Rebecca watching me. "Taylor, God made you fearfully and wonderfully. This is the woman Ian sees, and you need to own it."

Thinking of Ian and his unapologetic admiration of me, I slowly began to understand God's insistence on *Song of Solomon*. The Shulamite felt shame over her appearance. Solomon emphatically praised her beauty instead. My hazel-green eyes began to see things very differently.

CHAPTER 23

"I LIKE YOUR HAIR," MY MOTHER SAID, GESTURING toward my pixie cut. "I think women look better with longer hair, but this style suits you."

"You're not the first person to say that," I said, immediately thinking of Ian and the four weeks we'd been inseparable since Christmas.

"I didn't know if you'd meet with me after that mess at Freedom," my mother said as she sipped on her nonfat latte. "Showing up at the church wasn't a good idea, and I told your brother the same thing. He said Chloe cooked it all up—probably just to get you out of there. She was always jealous of you, Taylor."

Knowing Ian's testimony confirmed the story, I studied my mother. She had recently undergone another round of facial injections because her eyebrows looked painfully arched. In general, her face seemed more rubber mask than mother. As much as I wanted to stay angry at Sarah Meyers, compassion and pity moved me instead. My mother's plastic surgery began to reflect and expose her flaws rather than hide them.

"You're awfully quiet, Taylor Marie," she said, taking another opportunity to glance over my skinny jeans, sweater, and leather jacket. The slight lean of her head indicated her approval.

"What do you want me to say, Mom? There's a lot of water under the bridge, and I'm not totally convinced you aren't playing one of your games."

"Why can't we just forget the past, start over, and try again?" she pleaded.

"Because you hurt me, Mom. Repeatedly, deliberately, and without so much as a thought for how your behavior affected me. And before you try to flip the script and accuse me of doing the same thing to you," I said, as she opened her mouth to interrupt me, "you can't expect me to care about your feelings when you dismiss mine out of hand."

"Well, what do we do, Taylor? You just described exactly how I feel."

"Do you care that you hurt me, Mom? Do you even understand how?"

"Do you?" she shot back.

Clearing my throat, I replied, "Oh, I perfectly understand why you're mad at me, Mom. You're mad because I don't take your advice and because I won't do what you think I should do. You're also mad because I won't support or validate the lifestyle you want to live. You're hurt because you can't control me."

"I just want what's best for you," she said with feigned hurt.

"And that is how you always justify invalidating my feelings."

My mother scoffed. "Have you been reading psychology books or something, Taylor? Stop trying to analyze me."

"This is my point, Mom," I said, gesturing between the two of us. "Whenever I bring up how you've hurt me, you either shame me or play the victim. You don't take responsibility for anything, and then you act like I'm the monster for being upset with your behavior."

"Taylor Marie, you love to tell me all the ways I've failed you as a mother, but you never stop and look at all the ways you've judged and mistreated me. I'm your mother, and you're supposed to honor me. Isn't that what your Bible teaches?"

Irritated, I said, "You don't get to cherry pick Bible verses to attack me and then dismiss what it has to say about your own behavior, Mom. We're not playing this game anymore. I'm not a little kid, and either you stop treating me like one, or I will walk out of here and never look back. Are we clear on that?"

"What's his name, Taylor?" my mother said after a long pause.

"Excuse me?"

"I saw you on Christmas. You were at Lotus Garden. I was there with Barry."

"I have no idea who Barry is, Mom."

"My boyfriend. He's a serious boyfriend, so no need to make that face at me, Taylor Marie. He's actually the first man I've enjoyed having around in a while."

"What's his story? Married? Has a son you think I should be sleeping with too?"

My mother looked mortally wounded. "This is really what you think of me, isn't it?"

"Of course it is!" I exclaimed. "What else have you paraded in front of me for the past two decades?"

"Lower your voice!" she hissed. "We're in a public place, and there might be clients here."

"You're suddenly embarrassed people might find out what

you're really like, Mom? Because the cleavage filled billboards around the city aren't enough of an advertisement?"

"What happened to the sweet, little girl who used to think I hung the moon?"

"I grew up," I said plainly. "I saw how you manipulated and used me to raise my brother, then turned him against me when I no longer complied. You can hide behind your hurt all you want, Mom, but you deliberately ran to Gabe with your sob stories. Mitch did the same thing during the divorce, recruiting people to attack me so I would roll over and let him do whatever he wanted."

Unfazed, my mother glanced down to inspect her nails. "Speaking of Mitch, apparently things aren't working out between the two of them."

My full head of steam instantly derailed. "What? What are you talking about?"

"Either Mitchell Ross came back to his senses and realized what he's lost, or finding out he's not the biological father of the son he's been raising opened his eyes."

My anger toward my mother dissipated as shock filled me instead. "How do you know all of this? Is this why you wanted to talk to me?"

My mother nodded. "I felt you had the right to know. Mitch's latest scandal with that hussy became the talk of the national realtor convention three weeks ago. They presented him with some kind of sales award. Either he got rid of those awful hair plugs, or he decided he'd get more attention going completely bald."

"Bald?" I croaked, not able to picture my ex-husband completely devoid of hair.

"As a cueball," my mother said, taking another sip of her latte. "I tell you, I almost didn't recognize him. He had a gaggle of women fawning all over him, and he gave this drawn out, sob story about what's-her-face. Of course, he was the innocent victim,"

"Of course," I said, saddened and disgusted that nothing had changed in Mitch's behavior.

"I thought you'd be proud of me, Taylor Marie, because I told everybody what a lying, cheating weasel he is. He actually came up and talked to me, asking all sorts of questions about you. He told me he's still in love with you."

I was almost positive my face matched the color of my white sweater. Oblivious, my mother continued on with her tale, eager to have a cessation of hostilities between us.

"He thought you were still heartbroken and mooning over him, Taylor. I'm not sure what Brian told him about you since the divorce, but Mitch assumed you hung around Freedom to stay close to him vicariously."

Regaining my composure, disbelief quickly turned to anger. "No doubt. Chloe certainly felt that way.

"So, after we made some chit-chat—Mitch trying to butter me up with how great I look—he finally cut to the chase and asked if you're dating anyone. He said he misses you and hopes he might still have a chance."

Not wanting to take her support for granted, I said, "Did you tell him there's not a snowball's chance in Arizona it'll ever happen?"

My mother grinned, but the painful stretching of her skin caused me to wince. "I didn't use the word 'Arizona,' but the idea was the same. I also mentioned you and your new boyfriend looked very cozy on Christmas. Of course, the guy could be the janitor at Culver for all I know, but it seemed better to make sure Mitch knows you've moved on."

"Are you fishing for details, Mom, or just letting me know what happened?"

She winked at me. "Maybe a little of both."

"Why didn't you try to interrupt or introduce yourself?" I asked, genuinely surprised.

"Taylor Marie, in the entire time you spent married to that hair plugged jackass, I never saw you look at him or laugh like you did with your mystery man. I also never saw Mitch look at you the way this guy did. Is he taller than Mitch? It looked like it."

"By six inches. His name is Ian, Mom. You may have seen him in the sound booth at Freedom."

My mother's jaw fell open. "The AV guy with the big, bushy hair is the fashion model you had dinner with on Christmas? I almost wondered if you hired a male escort because he's so good looking!"

I cleared my throat, and miraculously, my mother took the hint.

"I just got very excited, Taylor Marie. You can't fault me for that. You know that I only—"

"Want me to be happy," I said, cutting her off. "I know, Mom. And I am. It sounds like you are too. You said your boyfriend's name is Barry, right?"

My mother's eyes sparkled. "He just gets me, Taylor. He doesn't judge me. He hasn't even tried to sleep with me—not for a lack of trying on my part. He said he wants to take his time. I didn't think men like that still existed."

Reminded of how much Ian and I struggled with our own physical desires, I felt like my mother and I had switched roles. I smiled.

"This is good," my mother said. "Mother-daughter bonding. I know you said we need to talk through a lot of things, Taylor, but I'd rather just move on. I can't handle the sarcastic comments anymore. They hurt."

Noting the sadness in my mother's eyes, I bit back the caustic remark that would have proven her point. Instead, I replied, "When you felt rejected by me, Mom, you acted petty and spiteful. You said incredibly hurtful or demeaning things to get back at me."

My mother took a sip of her coffee, swallowed, then nodded. "You're not wrong, Taylor. It pains me to admit it, but you're not wrong. I probably relied on you too much when you were younger too."

"There's no probably about it, Mom. I had to grow up so you could act like a teenager. I'm not minimizing all the things you've done for me, like the financial generosity, but it doesn't erase the pain I have either. It also hurt when you threw your gifts in my face like it made up for all the other things I didn't get from you."

"Like what?" she said, offense beginning to stiffen her posture.

"I needed the freedom to do and be something other than what you thought I should. I needed you to let me have a life outside of how it could directly benefit you. Any time you disapproved, you whipped out the mother card or pulled some ridiculous stunt. I won't even talk about my thirtieth birthday party, or we're going to have a huge fight."

"Probably best to leave that alone," she agreed.

"So, now what, Mom? You're happy. I'm happy. Can I get back to my life, and you get back to yours?"

Though unable to wrinkle her brow, I could still see hurt on her face. "You don't want me in your life, Taylor? Who's going to be there if things don't work out with your fashion model?"

I sighed heavily. "I have a good feeling of where things are heading with Ian, but I don't know what label best describes our relationship right now."

"I was hoping for better news, Taylor."

"What? Why?"

"Because Mitch said he's determined to win you back. He thinks this Ian guy has what belongs to him."

"I do not belong to Mitchell Ross! We signed divorce papers to make sure of that."

"Just know he's lurking around town, and he took a job with some boutique brokerage in Parkview."

"What about his baby momma?" I said mockingly.

My mother waved a dismissive, acrylic nailed hand. "From what I understand, her parents now have custody of the boy, and it's probably best for everyone that way."

"That's so sad. I lost my baby, but they chose to abandon theirs."

My mother shrugged. "You can't pick who your parents are."

"Ready to go?" Ian asked from behind me. "You said fifteen minutes, right?"

My mother glanced all the way up and all the way down. "He's even better looking up close," came her external monologue that should have been delivered internally.

Ian looked at me questioningly.

"Apparently, my mother saw us together on Christmas. She was on a date with her boyfriend, Barry."

"Ah," Ian said, inching even closer to me.

My mother took notice of Ian's protectiveness, even smiling as she saw his hand on my shoulder. "This is good, Taylor. Really good. Just don't forget about what I told you. That sociopath has access to property tax records, including yours, and I hope you're still using your security system. I wouldn't put it past Baldy to pull a drive by."

"What sociopath?" Ian demanded.

Before I could answer, my mother said, "Taylor's ex-husband has delusions of winning her back. Oh, did I let the cat out of the bag there, honey? He knows about Mitch, right?"

I rolled my eyes, but on the inside. Despite the headway Sarah Meyers and I made in our relationship that day, some things would never change. I hoped Ian didn't scare easily.

"He knows," Ian said, referring to himself in the third person. "If I ever meet the scumbag face to face, he's getting the black eye he deserves for what he did to Taylor."

Straining against the new botox injections, my mother grinned as much as physically possible. Gesturing to Ian she said, "Hang onto this one, Taylor Marie. I already like him a million times better than Baldy. You'll have a lot more fun running your fingers through his hair anyway."

Ian and I both had the decency to turn red while my mother excused herself. She immediately jumped onto her cell phone to get back to her 24/7 realtor gig.

"That was..." Ian's voice trailed off.

"Painful?" I suggested.

"That too."

I turned to face Ian. "My mother said she saw Mitch at some realtor convention three weeks ago. He broke up with the receptionist and thinks he can win me back. Apparently, he's even more determined since my mother saw us on Christmas and told him I have a boyfriend."

"Is that what I am?" Ian asked playfully, the subject of my ex-husband temporarily on the backburner.

"You're more than that, and you know it," I said, smiling up at him. "That's the other thing I wanted to tell you, Ian Horner. It's not an 'if' for me. It's a 'when.' I've known since New Year's."

Ian released a whoop of joy that got the attention of everyone in the room. He pulled me into his arms and spun me around. I hung around his neck for dear life while Ian laughed. He sealed the deal with another, non-hypothetical kiss. It was the kind of kiss that had me calling Rebecca Margolin later that day asking which justice of the peace she and Ted used when they got married.

CHAPTER 24

Bogged down in interviews over the next few weeks on top of my already heavy workload, I didn't see much of Ian through the end of February and into early March. We communicated throughout the day via text and messenger, but the face-to-face time suffered. The Culver associates certainly noticed the pep in my step, but they refrained from asking questions. MacKenzie submitted her resignation from Culver as Account Administrator to take a promotion as Account Manager at Cooper & Jaye. Phil presented the situation as MacKenzie seeking an opportunity for career advancement. Rumbles from Deondre's unit group suggested other reasons.

"She's not working with Goldstein's group, is she?" Lexie Arterton asked, stirring creamer into her morning coffee.

"Opposite sides of the building as far as I know," Deondre said. He quickly shut his mouth once he saw I'd entered the break room area.

"Morning, guys," I said blandly.

Lying through his perfectly white teeth, Deondre said, "We

were just saying how happy we are for Mac and her promotion to AM."

My insincere smile matched his. "Sure you were."

"There's nothing new with you and Goldstein, right?" Lexie asked. Deondre gave her a scathing look that made her physically recoil.

I frowned. "Is there something you guys want to tell me? Or is there something you hope I'm going to tell *you* instead?"

"I just wanted to make sure things wouldn't be weird if MacKenzie comes back to visit," Lexie said, nervously pushing a red tendril behind her ear.

"I knew it!" Deondre shouted.

Lexie shifted her gaze away.

"Deondre, do you mind if I talk to Lexie alone, please?" I asked.

Deondre sped out of the break room, no doubt eager to relay the latest drama—real or manufactured—with the rest of the office. I rolled my eyes and sighed.

"What's going on, Lexie?"

She visibly gulped, apparently scared to death. I raised an eyebrow.

"Mac is going to kill me," she whispered.

"Let me guess. She took the job because she's sleeping with Kyle? Or wants to?"

Lexie's jaw dropped. "I...how...how did you...yes," she finally admitted.

I shook my head in disgust. "I'm not an idiot, Lexie. Thank God, I was never in love with Kyle Goldstein."

"I'm pretty sure he's just using her to get back at you," Lexie said, apparently needing to unburden herself from MacKenzie's secrets. "You have to know how much she hates you after what happened at Los Bravos, Taylor. It was all Mac would ever talk about. She and Julie go out to lunch together, and I stopped going with them because they just gripe about you the entire time."

"Wow, so all of this animosity is because I won't let them make me the subject of their office gossip? Sounds like they take care of that all on their own."

Lexie bit her lower lip. "For the record, Mac believes Goldstein was really in love with you. She thinks she's stealing him from you somehow."

I gave a resigned sigh. "He was never mine to steal."

"But at the restaurant!" Lexie protested. "You guys looked so in love. Even the waitstaff made comments about you guys."

"You speak Spanish?" I asked, surprised.

"Enough to understand what they were saying," she hedged, "but then you looked so sad right after that. We all just assumed you broke up. When Goldstein showed up before Christmas, nobody knew what to think."

"Can I ask you something, Lexie?"

She looked up from the styrofoam coffee cup she'd been studying throughout our conversation.

"Why does my love life matter to any of you? We're coworkers. We do a job together. We earn a paycheck, and then we all go home. I'd hate to think your own lives are so boring that you have nothing better to do than use mine as some kind of reality TV entertainment."

Lexie now seemed mesmerized by the linoleum floor pattern.

"Look," I said, "I'm not angry even though I should be. I can't control what anybody does in the situation other than myself. I think Mac and Kyle will ultimately just hurt themselves by trying to get revenge on me, but I'm doing just fine, Lexie."

"Really?" she asked, finally making eye contact.

I nodded.

Lexie offered a tentative smile. "I always appreciated how Mac and Deondre took me under their wing when I first started at Culver. From the way Mac trashed Goldstein, I expected his work to be really shoddy. Instead, I found out how much work Deondre dumped on Goldstein but always took credit for in business meetings."

Thinking about all I'd observed from Deondre himself, it lined up with Kyle's version of events. "Goldstein has a knack for playing the role of walking contradiction. It makes him impossible to hate, but he can also be frustratingly selfish. I don't loathe the man, but I hope he gets some things figured out."

"Do you have a new boyfriend or something?" Lexie asked. "You just seem really happy and zen, you know?"

I gave her an impassive smile. "I'm doing well, Lexie. Moving forward with my life in a lot of ways."

Shoulder-length, red curls bobbed in response. "I get it, Taylor. I wouldn't trust me either."

"Have you tried talking to Phil or Miss Belle?" I suggested. "You know how much they both detest all of the office gossip."

Lexie shook her head emphatically. "No way! Phil scares me to death, and if Deondre finds out, he'll make life miserable for me. I really need this job, and Deondre has been here a lot longer than me. I doubt they'd take my word over his anyway." Her gaze quickly darted around the room as if the walls had ears. "Please don't say anything, Taylor, even if you think you're trying to help, okay?"

I wanted to do the exact opposite, but I acquiesced with a nod. Despite initial appearances, I knew Lexie was different than most of my blabbering coworkers. There seemed to be a hidden story behind the mousy behavior, as if she had the back-bone beaten out of her a long time ago.

"What?" Lexie said, pushing the same wayward curl behind her ear.

"Nothing," I replied. "You just reminded me of someone."

Content with my answer, she scurried out of the break room, and I took a moment to collect my thoughts about all of Lexie's revelations. Inhaling a deep breath, I fired off a text to Ian asking if he could meet me in Parkview for a late dinner. I missed seeing his face.

"Good morning," Ted said, walking into the room with a cup of coffee from *Vincenzo's*. He opened the refrigerator to place a plastic container inside. "Leftovers," he grinned. "Nesting hormones and the Food Station make for some pretty incredible dinners from my wife."

Feeling my face genuinely smile for the first time that morning, I glanced up at Ted. I was happy for a distraction from my morose musings about Kyle Goldstein.

Perceptive as always, Ted asked, "Everything okay with you and Ian?"

I nodded. "Yeah, just got a bit of strange news from Lexie."

"Goldstein and Mac?"

"How did you know?"

"Rebecca and I had lunch at Los Bravos last Tuesday. Witnessing the two of them maul each other turned my stomach."

I pursed my lips.

"I'm sorry, Taylor. I should have realized this would bother you."

"I'm not still hung up on Kyle," I said quickly. "I'm just sad at the self-destructive behavior. Maybe God will use the situation to bring healing to whatever issues they both have, but I can't imagine any relationship based on revenge possibly ending well."

Ted's expression turned grim. "Goldstein stopped by our table thinking he would hurt Rebecca or you by pawing on MacKenzie. Pretty pathetic spectacle, so we got up and left. I'm glad to hear you're not heartbroken about it."

"Ted, I'm in love with Ian. The feelings are mutual. I'll always be thankful to Kyle for waking me up from my divorce coma, but that's as far as it goes. Kyle has his own journey, and who knows if God won't take the situation with me to awaken some things in him too? We did have a really good conversation about the Bible and what it means to be Jewish beyond just a cultural identity. If for no other reason, maybe God brought us together for that."

Ted shrugged. "Anything's possible, I guess. Either way, I'm glad you're handling it well, Taylor, and I'm even happier for you as regards to Ian. He's a good guy."

"The best," I corrected. "I can't believe what an idiot I was for not seeing it sooner."

"God's timing," Ted said. "It helps you appreciate and hold onto the blessing even tighter when you realize how close you came to missing it."

"Spoken from experience?" I asked, already knowing the answer.

Mr. Margolin's twinkling eyes and grin were exactly as Rebecca always described. Ted walked with me back to my office before heading toward his own executive suite. Thankful for a respite in candidate interviews, I put my shoulders down and barreled through more projects than I initially thought possible for the day. Miss Belle stopped by with deli leftovers from a Lunch & Learn meeting.

"You need to eat, child," she said, depositing the wrap, olive oil kettle chips, and a green apple on my desk. "You're already a tiny little thing anyway, and they'll work you to death here if you let 'em. I made sure to ask for gluten free too."

"Thank you, Miss Belle," I said, touched by her thoughtfulness.

She studied my face for a moment. "There's some office wildfire going around about some former employees. I must have talked to Deondre a hundred times about keeping his big mouth shut and letting a body get their work done in peace."

"I heard, Miss Belle, and I'm fine. I promise."

She nodded. "Good. That boy ain't worth your time or your tears, you hear?"

Sage advice.

Ian and I met up for a quick dinner, and then we decided to enjoy the unseasonably warm weather with a stroll through Parkview. I looped my arm through his and leaned my head against him.

"Thanks for meeting me," I said.

He glanced down in surprise. "You're kidding, right? I haven't seen you in almost three weeks. Wild horses couldn't keep me away."

I laughed. "I appreciate not being smothered or getting a workaholic guilt trip about it. As much as I love my job, it's been so much drama of late. I'm halfway tempted to start looking elsewhere."

"What about further into the suburbs?" Ian asked. "I don't know how much you know about air purifiers, but my company always needs help in the marketing department."

"Your marketing is web-based, and all of my experience is with collateral design. I'm not sure if this old dog wants to learn any new tricks."

"Old dog?" Ian repeated with a teasing smile.

I rolled my eyes, but grinned. "Eh, maybe. We haven't really discussed the job situation, but I guess now's as good a time as any." I followed Ian as we dodged a gaggle of clubgoers. "What are your thoughts about stay-at-home mothers? I don't want to pry into your salary, but can we even afford to do that?"

"Have I mentioned how much I love your practicality?"

"It's served me well," I said, verbal sword in hand.

"What kind of a lifestyle did you have in mind?" Ian asked, placing his arm around me and shielding me from another group of passersby. "Your house is pretty fancy, Taylor, but you filled me in on the backstory behind it."

"It's definitely my childhood dream house."

"Do you want to stay there, or would you rather start someplace fresh?"

"It's crossed my mind, Ian. Of course, we can always sell it with Sarah," I said, quoting my mother's catchphrase.

"Are you two officially on speaking terms now?"

"I think so. My brother still ignores me, but my mother says she's working on it. For now, we're allied against a common enemy, and in that at least, I know she'll do what she can to help. The hard part is always the clash of personalities."

"We must be saving a fortune on premarital counseling talking about all of this now," Ian said, guiding me toward a series of benches overlooking a busy intersection.

"Tired already?"

"Long day. Long drive," he said, gesturing for me to join him on a bench.

Ian tucked me into his side, arm around my shoulders, and I leaned in toward him. "I wish marriage was as simple as all of this, Ian. Sitting on a bench, not thinking about bills, potential kids, in-laws, or work. Just enjoying each other's company and forgetting the rest of the world exists."

Ian squeezed me against him and planted a kiss on the top of my head. "Well, why can't it be all of that? We just have to be intentional about making time for each other."

I reached over to cup the side of his face. "This is why I love you, Ian Horner. Well, one of many reasons."

"I will never get tired of hearing you say that," he said, captivating me with dark eyes and dimples.

After a lingering kiss, we sat and watched traffic go by. We put talk of the future on hold, instead letting tomorrow worry about itself as we enjoyed the last few hours of today.

CHAPTER 25

"BUT THIS IS YOUR DREAM HOUSE!" MY MOTHER protested as she bustled through my front door. "I worked so hard to get you here, Taylor! You can't just throw it all away on a five month relationship. Ian hasn't put a ring on your finger yet, honey. Before you start making plans for the future, you should have a little insurance that he's really in it for the long haul."

"Mom, I would marry him tomorrow if I could."

"Which is what concerns me," she said, throwing her purse on my kitchen counter. "How much do you really know about Ian Horner? Does he have a past? An illegitimate kid somewhere? Sociopathic tendencies like Baldy?"

"Ian's a virgin, Mom, so no worries on the baby momma front."

Sarah Meyers evidenced her shock with a sudden, dead calm following her tornado of mothering. "Did I just hear you right?" she gasped.

I nodded. "Yeah, Mom. He's been waiting his whole life.

Apparently, for me. There's not a ring on my finger yet, but believe me, marriage has always been Ian's intention toward me."

"Give me just a second to process this, Taylor Marie."

I grinned. "Take all the time you need. You want anything to drink?"

"Water. Ice. It's too early for a real drink."

Perhaps this was Barry's influence on my mother. Hiding my surprise, I grabbed a glass for my mother and filled her drink order on the refrigerator door.

"Are you thinking of another church wedding like you did with Baldy?"

"Probably not."

Again, the unmistakable look of surprise registered on my mother's face. "Am I hallucinating? My daughter, queen of the purity ring and all the other Christian fairytale nonsense is not having a church wedding? Have I entered the twilight zone?"

Tempted to retaliate regarding my mother's first, long term relationship since my father, I bit my tongue. I needed her help, and though I might be loath to admit it, I had missed my mother, warts and all.

"Freedom left a bad taste in both of our mouths," I said, "and I've been there, done that with the white wedding."

"Don't you want the chance for a big dress, tons of brides-maids, a deejay, four tiered cake, and all of that? I know I wasn't as supportive as I could have been when you and Baldy got married."

Shocked to see actual remorse from my mother, I was thankful my decision to hold my tongue earlier gave her a chance to let her guard down. I silently thanked God for this new chapter in our mother-daughter relationship.

"I had my shot at the dream wedding with Mitch. As far as I

knew, I did everything by the book, and it still ended in disaster. I want the dream *marriage*, not the dream wedding. I'm just thankful I can even consider remarriage at this point."

"I really do like him," my mother said, taking a sip of water, "and it's obvious he loves you, Taylor. As your mother, you don't know what it does to my heart to see that."

I held her gaze. "I know, Mom."

"This is nice, Taylor," my mother said, gesturing between the two of us. "I know I'm not the easiest person in the world to get along with sometimes."

I bit back a sarcastic comment fueled from a lifetime of hurt and resentment. At some point, I knew I would need to hash things out with my mother, but I felt a strong unction from the Holy Spirit to watch, wait, and let Him handle things at His own pace rather than mine. He reminded me of Bible verses regarding God's timing and that His purposes had more far reaching impact than just my own life.

"Have you guys set a date?" my mother asked.

"We're both leaning toward the fall. Ian's lease ends in September, so we've talked about listing the townhouse and buying something together after that."

"Are you sure you don't want to stay here?" my mother asked, her eyes flicking over my kitchen and family room. "Taylor, this is such a gorgeous home. Seems like a shame to give it up."

"What about you, Mom? You have that massive house in Winthrope, and you said the commute for Barry is hard since he lives in town. Why don't you compromise and buy my house since you seem to like it so much? Then, we both get a win."

My mother assessed my home like a realtor. "If you wanted to live out in Winthrope, I wouldn't mind doing a swap."

"Mom! You'd lose so much money. My house isn't worth

nearly as much as yours. Plus, your house is even bigger than the crazy mansion I bought with Mitch. We would never need that much space!"

"I assume you want to start a family, Taylor. You could do a lot worse for a starter home."

Touched and overwhelmed by mother's generosity, I surprised both of us by pulling her into an embrace. "I'm not saying no, but I need to talk it over with Ian and see what he thinks. I'm sure he would appreciate the extra tall ceilings you have, but I have no idea how we would clean and maintain that much square footage, Mom. We also need to afford the maintenance, utilities, and your HOA."

"Leave it to you to be practical," my mother said.

"Ian says it's one of the things he loves about me," I replied, flashing her a grin.

Ian's regard for my practicality suffered a big test when my mother took us on a tour of her palatial Winthrope home the following weekend. Like me, my mother had wanted to custom build her own home rather than live in someone else's memories or design taste. As the listing agent for this Triple J luxury community as well, she had negotiated down costs, adding bells and whistles by applying her commission toward the builder fees. My mother created breathtaking results from all of her hard work, though far more ostentatious than I preferred. Ian seemed positively starstruck.

"You okay?" I asked, looking up at him.

"My parents have a split level in Manchester," he said, referring to an outlying suburb south of the city. "I've only ever seen houses like this in magazines."

Frowning, I watched him ogle the fireplace in my mother's two-story family room. The intricate, stacked stone work lent it even greater grandeur. My personal weakness, the built-in bookcases, flanked the fireplace on either side. My mother had designed the home to impress and expertly used style to convey substance.

"I like the furniture," I said, running my hand against the back of her new sofa. "Did you replace the other set already?"

"Your brother needed furniture for his new apartment."

"New apartment?" I said in surprise.

"Gabriel said he felt cramped living with the other guys and wanted his own space. Truthfully, I think he wants to impress this new girl he's been seeing. He says he met her at your old church."

Ian and I both glanced over at my mother, genuinely curious.

"Her name is Guinevere or Genevieve, or some other pretentious name like that. Sounds semi-serious."

Ian's frown matched mine. My mother took note of the dour expressions on our faces. "Did I say something wrong? Taylor, I thought you'd be happy for your brother."

"I went out a few times with Genevieve," Ian confessed. "Didn't work out."

My mother glanced from me back to Ian. "Is, uh, that going to be a problem? I invited the two of them to dinner tonight."

"Mom!" I shrieked. "How could you?"

"How was I supposed to know Ian used to date your brother's girlfriend? I'm not a mind reader, Taylor Marie, and I thought you'd be happy to finally see your brother. I can't help it if you kids create your own soap operas."

Ian's staying hand on my arm kept me from retaliating against my mother's hypocrisy. Thankfully, it also cooled his fervent admiration for her home.

"It'll be fine," he said, referring to Genevieve. "We never even kissed, and I doubt she's hung up on me."

"But she's going to report everything back to Brian and

Chloe," I said, panic rising in my voice. "Believe me, Chloe will be all too happy to relay everything back to Mitch."

"Do you really think Chloe wants to encourage Mitch to get back in your life, Taylor? That means she'd have the competition back in her face too."

I sighed, not sure whether to trust my gut or Ian on this one. From the little Ian could see on FaceSpace, Chloe's gushing posts about Brian and Freedom had stopped rather suddenly. She occasionally posted pictures of the children, but things had gone curiously quiet.

"You guys okay over there?" my mother asked. "Do you want to see the upstairs?"

"I think I'm good, Mom. Even if we had twenty kids, I don't think we could ever fill up this much space. It reminds me of my townhouse in that respect. I have all of this amazing living space, but I only spend time in three rooms. Seems like kind of a waste."

Offended, she sniffed her nose in disdain. "It's not a waste to live with a little luxury, Taylor Marie. If you earn the money to do it, why not enjoy the fruits of your own labor? What seems like a waste to you reminds me of how much I sacrificed to get to where I am today."

Tempted to remind my mother that she sacrificed my childhood, I bit my tongue. It seemed wrong letting Sarah Meyers get away with believing her own lies, especially the ones where she willfully ignored how much she had hurt me.

I took a deep breath, memories from my thirtieth birthday resurfacing. More drunk than tipsy, Sarah Meyers asked a restaurant party room full of my friends and colleagues if anyone could help her daughter "begin her thirties with a bang."

The palpable shock, horror, and nightmarish cringe factor

left the room in complete silence. After an interminable pause, the buzz in the room slowly came back to life.

"I'm going to kill her," I said louder than I probably should have. "Brian, hold my drink, because I am seriously going to wrap my hands around that woman's neck and strangle the life out of her."

"Just let it go, Taylor," Chloe hissed, placing a hand on Brian's arm. "You know she's drunk and just wants attention."

"I'm not letting anything go!" I said angrily. I slammed my club soda down on a nearby table. "She publicly humiliated me, and she did it on purpose! I read my mother the riot act about bringing her twenty-eight-year-old boyfriend tonight, and she had to find a way to get back at me. I'm tired of biting my tongue. She was so out of line!"

"Just laugh it off," Chloe said. "We'll get the karaoke machine going, Taylor, and everyone will forget all about the stupid thing your mother said. You'll still get to be the center of attention, so no worries" she added with a smirk. "It's really not that big of a deal."

I looked over at Brian, his jaw clenched. He, in turn, watched my mother laugh obnoxiously with her boy toy *du jour*. My mother cackled about the phrase "with a bang," on an infuriating loop. To his credit, my brother looked absolutely mortified. Gabe slinked into a corner hoping no one noticed the obvious resemblance between him and Sarah Meyers.

Tears escaped from my eyes. The pain and impotent rage at my mother's antics combined with a room full of supposed friends that couldn't be bothered to speak up set me over the edge. In that moment, I felt painfully alone, even more so than being left to mourn the loss of my marriage and my baby all in one day.

"I'm going to say something," Brian finally said. "Taylor, this is your birthday celebration, and Sarah deliberately tried to ruin it."

"Brian!" Chloe exclaimed. "You'll just make things worse!"

"No," he said sternly. "I've watched Sarah do this to Taylor for years, and my brother just stood there like a spineless weasel. Taylor, you may not be my sister by marriage anymore, but you're my sister in Christ. If nobody else has the guts to stand up for you, then I'll do it. You don't deserve this, not after everything you've already been through."

"Brian!" Chloe shrilled, but to no avail. Her husband marched over to my mother and leveled her with both barrels. Chloe folded her arms over her chest about the same time my mother displayed her award worthy hysterics.

"Guess you got what you wanted for your birthday after all," Chloe said bitterly. "Congratulations, Taylor."

Confused by her words, I watched my former sister-in-law stalk away as Brian rejoined me.

"Thank you," I said, meeting the same sapphire blue eyes shared with his brother.

"My pleasure, Taylor."

My mother stormed from the room lamenting how embarrassed and humiliated she was. Chloe continued to sulk in the corner, and Brian largely ignored her. He spent most of the evening hovering like a big brother and making sure my new glass of club soda and lime stayed full. Conversely, my actual brother kept his distance. Ten minutes before Sarah Meyers destroyed his narrative, Gabe had been lecturing me about my "attitude toward Mom." Neither one of us was pleased that I had been right.

Blinking away that painful evening, Ian's large hand found mine and squeezed it gently. It was a comforting reminder that I wasn't alone anymore. "Time and season," he whispered.

Earlier that morning, he and I had discussed the pros and cons of swapping houses with my mother. After fifteen rounds, Ian finally suggested we stop talking and just ask the Lord what He wanted us to do.

Ian said he heard the phrase, "time and season," and I felt an immediate surge of peace from the Holy Spirit. Standing in my mother's living room, God reminded me of the famous poem in *Ecclesiastes*, specifically a time to tear down, and a time to build. God provided the answer to our housing dilemma before we left my mother's soaring, two-story family room.

CHAPTER 26

"I DON'T HAVE THE TIME TO TAKE ON ANOTHER NEW construction neighborhood, but I'll do what I can to help," my mother offered over dinner.

Gabe scowled across the table at me and Ian, Genevieve equally uncomfortable with the turn of events.

"Taylor, could you have made this any more awkward?" Gabe snapped. "You really had to go out with the same guy who dated Genevieve? Here comes my big bad sister, always making things more difficult for everyone."

"I seem to recall you urging me to go out with Ian," I said, tired of my twerpy brother and his demeaning comments.

"And as I seem to recall, you told me you weren't interested," he sneered. "Did you finally get desperate enough, or is it any qualified sperm donor these days?"

Ian's hands banged against the table at the same time my mother shouted my brother's name.

"That's enough!" Ian said through gritted teeth. "Gabe, if

you can't treat your sister with the respect she deserves, we can find somewhere else to eat."

"What respect?" my brother snarled. "Taylor gave Mom the silent treatment for more than a year, and now she suddenly acts like they're best friends again. Taylor doesn't care about Mom—just her money. When she needs Mom to sell her a house or help pay for something, Taylor always comes crawling back. Mom even said so!"

I stared daggers at Sarah Meyers. "Is that true?"

"Gabriel Alexander, you misunderstood me," my mother said, glancing nervously between me and my brother. "I told you I was more than happy to help your sister in her time of need. Sometimes, I don't know where you get these wild stories. Taylor's been rather nice to me lately, especially since she stopped living in the past and judging every mistake I've made."

I gripped Ian's hand under the table, too stunned to do much else. He squeezed back, looking at my mother with new eyes. He looked as furious as I felt. Just as Ian opened his mouth, my brother suddenly remembered his voice.

"Mom, have you gone completely unhinged?"

"What do you mean?" she asked innocently, placing a mani-cured hand on her heart.

Gabe now wore the look of confusion. "Mom, I have every-thing on text. I even read some of it to Genevieve on the way over here."

"I don't recall any unflattering messages about your sister," she said, turning wide eyes to me. "You know how much I love you, Taylor."

My mother's collagen plumped lips quivered, but Gabe cut her off. "Mom, you said Taylor met you for coffee because she needed help buying a house. You told me she and Ian only want to get married so they can have sex. What exactly did I misunderstand?"

All conversation ceased at our table and probably all surrounding tables within a twenty foot radius. Genevieve looked horrified. Ian looked irate. I just looked directly at Sarah Meyers, suddenly piecing things together.

Gabe persisted as he tried to make sense of our mother's machinations. "After everything you've said Taylor's done to you, Mom, I couldn't believe you invited her and Ian to dinner. You told me it was going to be a double date with just you and Barry, but then you sprang this on me at the last minute."

"She told us the same thing," Ian said, glaring at my mother. "This was after trying to convince us we needed to move into her house and start filling it up with grandchildren. We also suffered through inappropriate comments about our future sex life."

"You never even talked to Mitch, did you?" I said, accusing my mother. "You invented that entire story to make me drop my guard and look to you as an ally. You did it to manipulate me after the divorce, and you did it again in January, didn't you?"

"Taylor Marie, lower your voice," my mother hissed.

Undaunted, I said, "I should have known Mitch would never confide in you. I doubt he's even given me a second thought since the divorce."

"Clearly, there's been some kind of misunderstanding," my mother said through a forced smile.

"No wonder you had zero compassion when you told me about Mitch's son," I said angrily. "Was anything you said actually true? How could you make up a lie like that and then have the nerve to call my ex-husband a sociopath? Takes one to know one, right?"

Gabe looked frantically between the two of us. "Mom, what is she talking about?"

"I, um, may have embellished a little about seeing Mitch at the realtor convention," my mother said, squirming in her decolletage baring pant suit.

Gabe's brows furrowed in confusion. "What realtor convention? You told me you spotted Mitch on a weekend getaway with Barry in Vegas. You also told me you saw his son, his mistress, and that she's pregnant again. You never said anything about talking to Mitch."

Before she could answer, I said, "Because that's how Mom scared me into meeting with her in the first place. She said Mitch moved back to town and wants to reconcile. Are any of these lies starting to sound familiar, Mom?"

"Taylor, I didn't know what else to do!" she said in her practiced, martyr voice. "You stormed out of that church like you couldn't stand me, and then you ignored me for almost a year after that. I've only ever wanted what's best for you, but you constantly reject me just because I don't live some holy roller lifestyle."

My brother gaped at Sarah Meyers like a grotesque, Halloween exhibit. "Mom, you gave me and Genevieve this whole sob story about how Taylor was just using you, but the truth is that you were the one lying to everybody. Why would you do that?"

"I'm your mother!" she pleaded. "I love both of my children."

Gabe whipped out his cellphone. "Then explain these text messages, Mom! It's all right here!"

He read off a few lines of her texts, his summation proving less brutal and crass than my mother's actual words. Sarah Meyers had transformed herself into the innocent victim and me into some soulless nymphomaniac. I closed my eyes, took a deep breath, then reopened them. Genevieve and Ian both wore the same look of disgust while my brother seemed simultaneously crestfallen and livid.

"What else have you lied to me about?" Gabe demanded. "Has Taylor been right this whole time? Have you been selling me a bunch of lies about my own sister?"

"I just want my children to be happy," my mother said, her well-worn excuse even more pathetic in the face of her deception.

"Happy?" Gabe spat. "How could you deliberately turn your children against each other, Mom? Don't give me some story about wanting us to be happy when you've made both of us miserable with all of your self-serving lies!"

"Gabriel, I—"

"I'm not done," he said, cutting her off. "You talk so much about all of these *sacrifices* you've made for Taylor and me, but all I remember is Taylor being around while you were never home. Taylor made breakfast and dinner and helped me get ready for school. Taylor forged your signature on my report cards and permission slips because you always had an excuse why you forgot."

"You have no idea what it's like to be a single mother," she protested.

"Neither do you," I fired back. "You left me at home to do your job, Mom."

"I can't believe how ungrateful you two are!" she said indignantly. "My furniture is in both of your houses! My name is on your housing contracts as a co-signer. Don't you dare act like I did nothing for either of you!"

Ignoring her, Gabe turned to me and said, "Taylor, I'm sorry for everything. I didn't know they were lies, I swear, I didn't!"

"You knew what she was like, Gabe, and you chose to remain in denial. It was easier to attack me than face reality. You're not innocent in this either, little brother."

His expression was grim. "You're right. I've been condescending and judgmental, and I accused you of the same crime. I cut you off because I was mad at how you cut off Mom," his voice broke. "I just want you to know how sorry I am. For everything."

I nodded, never once thinking God would turn my mother's lies into real reconciliation with my baby brother.

"This is so wonderful," my mother cooed, wiping away fresh tears. "I'm so glad you two could work through your issues. I just want my children to be happy."

Surprising us all, Genevieve spoke up. "Is she serious, Gabe? I don't know if I would have believed it if I hadn't seen it with my own two eyes."

Following her cue, Ian threw down his napkin, put his hand under my elbow, and helped me to my feet. Gabe and Genevieve followed behind us, leaving my shell-shocked mother to sit alone at our table for six. Though I expected travailing cries of woe, my mother recovered quickly and hopped onto her cell phone. In a matter of seconds, all was forgotten. If my mother could pretend we didn't exist, she could pretend the entire episode never took place either. It was the Sarah Meyers way.

As we stood outside, Genevieve placed a hand on my arm to stop me. "I owe you a huge apology, Taylor," she said. "Chloe told me so many horrible things about you, and I believed them. She told me you invented reasons to be mad at your mother and secretly wanted Brian for yourself. Gabe had all of his stories from Sarah too, and it just seemed to make sense. From the bottom of my heart, I am so sorry! I totally misjudged you."

"Thank you," I said quietly, stunned by the details of her

confession and the continued weight of Chloe's personal vendetta against me.

"Ian, I'm glad things didn't work out between us," Genevieve said with a rueful grin, "and I think we both wound up with the right person."

Still mute, Ian nodded, acknowledging her statement.

"How could she do that, Taylor?" Gabe said, raking a hand through shaggy curls.

"Mom saw me and Ian together on Christmas day. I'm pretty sure she made up everything else to get back into my good graces."

Genevieve tsked and shook her head. "No offense, guys, but your mother is certifiable."

"Is there even a guy named Barry, or was that fictitious too?" I asked my brother.

"With Mom? Who knows?"

"Can we get out of here?" Ian finally said. "I'm going to need some time to process all of this."

"Yeah, we can meet up another day," Gabe said. Hesitating briefly, he wrapped me in a hug. My shoulders shook in sobs of both grief and relief as did my brother's. Whispering against my neck, he said, "I'm so sorry, Taylor."

After a few minutes, we pulled away, vowing to talk soon. Gabe fell into the awaiting arms of Genevieve who walked with him back to his car. I glanced at Ian, scared of what I might find.

"Please, say something," I begged. "If you don't want to marry me, I'll understand. I'm pretty sure my mother's issues are environmental not genetic, but being related to her would be a conscious choice on your part. For me, it's unavoidable."

My attempt at humor fell flat as I saw hurt in Ian's eyes. "I'm not Mitch or Kyle," he said.

"What do you mean?"

"Do you think I'm going to bail on you at the first sign of trouble, Taylor? I thought you knew me better than that. I told you my intentions from the beginning."

"Look, everybody always starts out with good intentions, Ian. All of the men in my life leave me. I have a track record of it. My father abandoned me. My brother abandoned me. My husband abandoned me. Kyle abandoned me. The common denominator in this equation is always me."

"Do you really think so little of me?" Ian asked.

"No," I replied, my vision blurring, "I think so little of *myself*. Why would everyone leave if I wasn't so worthless?"

"You're not worthless!" Ian said, cupping my face in his palms. "Taylor, I love you. I said I want to marry you, and I meant it. I talked to my leasing office, and they'll let me sublet the apartment. I didn't get a chance to tell you this earlier, but I have a coworker who needs a place to stay. He's being kicked out of his current rental and could move in by the beginning of June."

"What are you saying?" I drawled.

"I'm saying I have someone to cover my lease, and we can get married before summer."

"What?" I squeaked, scarcely believing my ears.

Ian produced a velvet box from his jeans pocket. Dropping down to one knee, he opened the box to reveal a solitaire, diamond ring with flowers carved into the yellow gold band. "Taylor, I know I haven't formally asked you yet, but I am now. Will you marry me?"

"Is this an antique?" I gasped, unable to help myself.

Ian laughed. "You have to say yes before I answer that."

"This has got to be the craziest day in existence," I murmured.

"That still doesn't sound like a yes. Also, my knee is starting to hurt."

Finally taller than Ian Horner, I looked down at his face and into bottomless brown eyes. "This will make for quite a story for the grandkids."

CHAPTER 27

"LET ME SEE IT AGAIN!" REBECCA SQUEALED, PULLING my ring finger toward her. Ted and Ian sat at the kitchen table, heads bent close together while Rebecca and I occupied the Margolin family room. Tabby Margolin toddled around the furniture dragging a blanket behind her.

"Did everything feel this crazy when you and Ted got married?" I asked, still getting used to the feel of a ring on my wedding finger again.

"It felt like the eye of a hurricane. As long as I didn't move too much, everything remained peaceful and calm. As soon as I started thinking about the details, I went into full-on panic mode."

"Mama," Tabby called, holding out her hands to be picked up.

Absolutely adorable with hazel eyes and short, dark curls, Tabby studied me as Rebecca pulled the little girl onto her lap.

"Can you believe this *sheyna punim?*" Rebecca said, showering her little girl with kisses on her plump cheeks.

"You're going to have to school me on all of this Yiddish, Rebecca."

"The joys of having Jewish grandparents and in-laws," she said with a smile. "When are you meeting your own in-laws, Taylor? Before or after the wedding?"

"Ian let his parents know he planned to propose, but I don't think he told them about getting married so soon. I know I should be scared out of my mind, but all I feel is peace."

Rebecca gave me a knowing smile. "And let the peace of God be your heart's decision maker," she quoted from *Colossians 3:15*.

"I was more nervous marrying Mitch even though we had the model, Christian youth group courtship. On paper, I knew more about Mitch than I do about Ian, but history proved I only knew what my ex-husband wanted me to believe. All of his premarital counseling answers were textbook perfect."

"Whereas Ian is just an open book," Rebecca said, glancing over into the kitchen. "Even when you weren't interested in him, you never doubted Ian's intentions. I don't think Ian knows how to be anything other than one hundred percent himself."

"One of the many things I love about him. I've had enough secrets and lies to last me a lifetime."

Rebecca rolled her eyes in commiseration. "Believe me, I'm right there with you, but eventually, all of the deception comes to light."

"Any change with the SBC case?" I asked.

Rebecca shook her head. "The investigation is still ongoing, but at least Pastor Sociopath is off the streets. Thank God, the judge denied him bail."

"What about dear, old Mom and Dad?" I said, referring to

the criminal charges against Rebecca's parents, also former pastors.

"My mother has to serve eighteen months because of the plea bargain, and my sister moved into their house. I'm guessing she agreed to maintain the place in exchange for free room and board. For whatever reason, my aunt likes to keep me in the loop about my family. Maybe she sees it as penance for all of the lies and abuse she helped my mother perpetrate."

"Has your aunt met Ted or Tabby?"

Rebecca shook her head. "She maintains her distance, so it's mostly just via text, which is fine with me anyway. It gives me time and space to heal. But enough about me," she said, brightening up and shifting Tabitha in her lap. "Tell me more about the wedding plans."

I grinned. "I'm supposed to meet Ian's parents next weekend, and we'll get married the following Friday. I remember what you told me about not going back to work the day after you have a shotgun wedding."

Rebecca groaned. "It was so awful! Miss Belle, God bless her, kept going on about our *married glow*."

"Oh, that's horrible!" I said with a laugh. "Funny to me, but probably not to you and Ted."

"Humiliating at the time, but at least we can joke about it now. I'm sure she and Phil will have plenty to say when we announce we're expecting baby number two."

"Phil did mention you and Ted trying to single handedly boost the human population."

Two pink spots appeared on Rebecca's cheeks. "I'm not surprised, yet I'm still shocked somehow."

I shrugged. "It's Phil."

"What's Phil?" Ted said, joining us along with Ian. Tabitha

happily crawled into her daddy's lap while Ian sat next to me on the adjoining loveseat.

Rebecca turned to face her husband. "Your CEO suggested that you and I want to repopulate the planet."

Ted rolled his eyes. "You know, there's this fine line between appropriate and inappropriate Phil Robbins likes to dance across."

"Is this the same guy who asked you about a bris?" Ian said to me.

If Ted had been drinking when Ian posed his question, his reaction would have caused a spit take. Rebecca and I laughed.

"Oh, did I forget to mention that?" Rebecca asked Ted.

Recovering quickly, Ted said, "I think Phil gets more wily with age. Maybe more senile. I guess it depends on your point of view."

"I look forward to meeting him," Ian said, grinning down at me. "He sounds like fun."

"That he is," Ted said. "I've known Phil my entire life. He actually attended my bris, and apparently, he's chomping at the bit to attend another one."

"We've got twelve more days before we find out about this one," Rebecca said, rubbing her belly.

"Any predictions?" I asked. "Does this pregnancy seem any different than Tabby's?"

At the mention of her name, Tabitha perked up. "Baby!" she declared before jumping down to locate a doll from her wooden toy chest near the front window.

"Take notes, my friends," Rebecca said, following her daughter with her eyes. "One second, you've got this gorgeous, grown up home, and the next, it's completely overrun with jumpers, kiddie gates, toys, diapers, and cereal crumbs."

"Can't wait!" I said, flashing a grin up at Ian.

He returned my smile with those disarming dimples of his. "So, we are setting up camp in your townhouse then?"

"For now, at least. Even if I sold my place tomorrow, we'd still need thirty days to close. We'd have to pack up everything, find a new place, move, etc. Being married is enough of a transition without tacking on any unnecessary stress."

"Amen!" both Margolins answered in unison.

The following work week sped by in anticipation of my first meeting with Nancy and Thomas Horner. Ian described his parents as pretty all-American, no notable heritage on display other than what one might expect of white, Anglo-Saxon protestants living in the Bible Belt. As I recalled Ian making mention of a guilt trip brunch on Christmas morning, I asked if his parents were anything like mine or Rebecca's in terms of emotional abuse. Ian shook his head saying it had more to do with "getting over that girl from church" and finally settling down.

"Are they going to hate me for not seeing what an amazing catch you are?" I asked while Ian wove through highway traffic down to Manchester.

"I'm not sure if they think you're real, Taylor."

"Do they know about Mitch?"

Ian shook his head. "My parents aren't so legalistic they'd look down on you for being divorced, especially under the circumstances, but I don't want them to judge you without getting to meet you first. Also, I need to warn you about something."

"I'm allergic to cat dander, so do they have a whole litter of kittens or something?"

"No, it's just something my mom mentioned during Christmas. Even though my dad prefers to take back roads, they were in a hurry and decided to hop on the interstate instead."

Dread welled up inside. "Dare I ask?"

Ian's mouth was grim. *"Sell it with Sarah* became a lengthy discussion on Christmas morning."

I closed my eyes and released a slow breath. "How does she manage to ruin my life even when she's not in it?"

Ian reached over to squeeze my hand. "You're nothing like your mother, and maybe it's better we're doing this quickly. My parents won't have any time to form wrong ideas about you based on her billboard."

"Are they really that judgmental?" I asked.

"Judgmental?" Ian repeated, eyebrows drawing together. "That's a little harsh considering how your mother sells her services."

I pulled my hand away from his. "Ian! You make my mother sound like a prostitute!"

My fiancé gave me a sidelong glance.

"I can't believe I'm even defending my mother right now, but this just crosses the line, Ian Horner!"

With a sharp swerve of the car, tires screeching to halt, Ian pulled the car over to the side of the road. Scared out of my mind, I put a hand over my racing heart.

"What were you thinking?" I yelled. "Are you trying to kill both of us?"

Ian studied me, his mouth a thin line.

"What?" I fumed. "Did you think the adorable little mouse doesn't have a temper? Ready to pull the ring off of my finger and tell me I'm exactly like my mother and a potential embarrassment to the holy Horner family?"

Slowly, he said, "Who are you, and what did you do with my fiancée?"

I yanked at the ring on my left hand, ready to throw it back in Ian's face. The blinding fury and resentment left me feeling like my head might legitimately detach from my neck.

"Knock it off," Ian said with more gravitas than I had ever heard from him. It caught me off guard, feeling like I had just received a scolding from my father. "What in the world is going on, Taylor?"

Sufficiently recovered, I spat, "You told me to hide the divorce and my family connections lest your parents judge me as a filthy streetwalker just like my mother!"

Ian clenched his jaw. "I did not use any of those words."

I rolled my eyes. "Don't try to argue over semantics, Ian. You haven't told your parents I've been married before. You didn't tell your parents the scandalous woman on the billboard is my mother. You all but assured me they're going to sit in self-righteous judgment as soon as they find out, so hey, let's just hush it all up and pretend, right? Obviously, you're ashamed of me, so why are we getting married? Oh, that's right. So you can lose your virginity to this fantasy version of me you've been holding onto for three years."

"You're out of line!" he yelled.

"How dare you!" I yelled back. "You just told me I'm unworthy of your family and my mother whores herself out to sell real estate."

"Taylor, are you even listening to yourself?" Ian said. "This is crazy!"

I pursed my lips. "Don't you even try that line with me, Ian! After six years of gaslighting from Mitchell Ross, I'm never falling for that accusation again."

Ian closed his eyes and took a deep breath. I could tell he was praying, and it dampened the fire of my own anger.

Eyes still closed, Ian said, "I'm sorry I lost my temper. I shouldn't have."

"Thank you," I responded tightly.

"What did I say to make you react like that?" he asked.

Incredulity gave way to apoplectic rage. "God, help me! Did I just agree to marry the most clueless man in existence?!"

Unmoved by my outburst, Ian said quietly, "I've never seen this side of you, Taylor."

"Ready to take the ring back?" I asked, my voice thick with sarcasm. "I'm damaged goods. Ask Kyle Goldstein. My temper is apparently why I'm sitting in this car with you instead of him."

"This was a bad idea," Ian said, turning the key in the engine.

"Marrying me? Of course it was! But hey, maybe there's a cute receptionist somewhere waiting to be the mother of your children."

Ian took a steadying breath. "What are you doing, Taylor?"

"I'm defending myself, what does it look like?" I snapped.

"No, you're pushing me away," he said, his eyes meeting mine. "I asked the Lord to show me what's really going on, and He said to listen to the message behind the words."

"You insulted me and my mother!" I said in frustration. "What's to understand, Ian?"

He looked at me patiently, my fortress of anger faltering as doubt crept in. "Taylor, you keep threatening to call off our engagement, but I hear fear underneath the anger."

"Fear?"

Seeing my defenses lowered, Ian said, "Do you think my parents' opinion of you or your mother makes one bit of difference to me? Why did you assume I'm going to agree with them and reject you too?"

My jaw opened and closed. "Isn't that what you said? You

insinuated that her billboards look like an advertisement for a female escort."

Ian's shoulders visibly relaxed, perhaps because my protective shield of anger lay limp in my hand. He looked at me like a man in love, and I began to wonder if maybe Ian was the crazy one in our relationship.

"Taylor, you really do love your mother, don't you?"

"Excuse me?"

"No matter what she's done to you, even lying to you and your brother and tricking you into reconciling with her, you still love Sarah. You're loyal to a fault. I made one comment about her billboard—a comment you've made countless times yourself —but because it was *me* saying it, you went ballistic."

I paused, stunned by the realization. "Why aren't you heading for the hills?"

"Because it speaks to the kind of person you are and how fiercely you'll protect your own. Taylor, I'm going to need it when we face my parents today. The passive aggressive criticism starts two seconds after I walk in the front door."

"Ian...I don't understand."

He took my hands in his. "Taylor, I was trying to explain where my parents are coming from, not that I agree with their point of view. I'm sorry I wasn't clearer about that. What I implied about your mother's billboard was wrong, not to mention horrible timing. I didn't realize how upset you were, and I'm sorry about that too."

Tears in my eyes, I searched Ian's face for any hint of a lie or manipulation. I found only remorse instead.

"I'm sorry I yelled at you," I said, convicted by my own behavior. "The things I said were so ugly. Please forgive me." A sob burst from my lips.

"You're forgiven," Ian said, releasing my hands so he could

cup my face. "If you would rather meet my parents after we go to the courthouse, I'm totally okay with that too."

"Are you scared of your parents, Ian? Am I going to find you cowering in the corner while I'm expected to go to battle? I've been there, and all it does is make the man look and feel emasculated. The wife looks like a shrew, and it just confirms whatever lies people spew about who wears the pants in the relationship."

"I assume this happened with Mitch."

"All the time."

"I'm not scared of my parents, Taylor. I just struggle finding the balance between honoring them and not letting them walk all over me. I don't need you to fight my battles. I just want to know you'll be by my side if we have to go to war."

CHAPTER 28

AFTER A FEW MORE APOLOGIES ON BOTH SIDES AND an ample amount of time spent praying together, we finally arrived at the Horner family home. I noted the yellow, vinyl siding, drive under garage, upper bedroom level on top, and cozy front porch leading to the main living portion of the house.

"You're doing it, aren't you?" Ian asked, referring to my penchant for creating listing flyers in my head.

I grinned. "Can't help it. It's a cute porch though. Just needs a swing or some rocking chairs to give it that old timey feel."

"That's what the salmon colored carpeting is for," he said, verbal sword in hand.

"Seriously?" I asked.

"Makes me want sushi every time I see it."

"Wild caught, though," I said, happy to hear the sound of my blade colliding against his. "I can't imagine what farmed salmon looks like in a carpet color."

Ian grimaced. "Can't be much worse than the textured wallpaper."

"Stop, already!" I laughed. "I promise I won't judge your parents or their home just because it's stuck in a time warp. I'm more concerned about potential, passive aggressive shenanigans. Kate said she's unavailable to help buffer, right?"

Ian shook his head. "She's got Fiona this weekend, and they had mother-daughter pedicures planned. I couldn't ask her to give that up."

I smiled up at him. "You are pretty amazing, Ian Horner, and I still feel badly about our fight in the car."

"You're *real*, Taylor, and I would rather you be honest than put on a mask and pretend. I can't stand how my parents smile to your face but slip in their snide little comments about everything."

"How do you want me to handle myself if they start in with that?"

"Follow my lead," Ian said, taking hold of my hand. "That's probably a strange feeling for you since Mitch left you to fend for yourself, but you can trust me, Taylor."

I nodded, thankful this man understood me, even the less than flattering parts. He knocked on the storm door, and we were greeted by a couple in their mid-sixties sporting hairstyles and clothes as dated as their home.

"I'm Thomas, and this is Nancy," Ian's father said, extending his hand toward me.

"Hi, I'm Taylor," I replied, shaking his hand first and then Nancy's.

"We almost thought you were a ghost Ian conjured up so we'd stop hounding him for grandchildren," Nancy said, attempting at humor.

Trying not to come across as awkward and forced as everything felt, I answered, "Thank you for having me over today."

"You guys are awfully late," Thomas said, glancing at his watch.

I looked to Ian, letting him decide the best way to answer his father's remark.

"We hit a little snag, but everything's been worked through," Ian hedged.

"She's not threatening to break up with you, is she?" Nancy asked with a chuckle. "You've never brought a girl home before, Ian, so I hope you don't screw this one up. The hands of time slow for no one." She gestured toward her graying hair. "We'd like to have more grandchildren before we've got a foot in the grave."

I watched Ian inhale and exhale a slow breath.

It was definitely going to be a long evening.

"So you don't like meatloaf?" Nancy said once we sat down to dinner. "Or rolls? Or mashed potatoes? Are you a vegan?" she asked, looking at the lonely green beans on my plate. "Maybe that's how you girls stay so skinny these days."

Ian coughed awkwardly. "Mom, I mentioned Taylor has food allergies. Several times."

Thomas looked mystified. "I think these so-called food allergies are nothing more than a bunch of hocus pocus. Your sister uses them to explain why Fiona gets so ill-tempered and defiant. What exactly do you eat, Taylor, other than rabbit food?"

"I eat most of what you do," I said.

Thomas scoffed, noting the lack of sustenance on my dinner plate.

"I can't dress it up with butter or milk, but I promise, I do eat. Kate told me about a gluten free pie crust recipe she found. It sounds amazing."

"Gluten free," Thomas said, blowing a raspberry. "Why

would you want to go through life not enjoying bread? Jesus is the bread of life. How do you take communion if you can't eat the body of our Lord and Savior?"

Prior to our arrival at his parents' home, Ian and I had worked out a hand code. One squeeze meant, "I'm doing okay." Two squeezes meant, "Help me." Three squeezes meant, "I'm about to lose it." Ian's three squeezes came in rapid succession, and I jumped to my feet, my dining room chair halting abruptly against the thick, orange carpeting.

Thomas and Nancy startled, as did Ian. I tried to come up with some semi-plausible excuse.

"Um, Nancy, do you mind if I check the ingredients on your ketchup bottle? Every company is different, so maybe there's no high fructose corn syrup in this one."

Ian's mother looked at me like an alien from the distant planet, Non GMO. Ian rose quickly, offering to help me locate something suitable to consume. Once inside the kitchen, he pulled me into his arms and rested his head on top of mine.

"I'm so sorry," came his muffled cry into my hair. "They assume everyone is just like them."

I looked up at Ian. "After the display two weeks ago with my mother, do you think I scare that easily? I can deal with idiotic quips about my food allergies. I've already heard the stupid communion jokes. Mitch used to deliberately moan and groan over bagels just to annoy me."

"I wish I'd stopped you from going out with that jerk twelve years ago," Ian said, his gaze intense.

The side of my mouth raised into a half smile. "Weren't you on your own date?"

"Doesn't mean I wouldn't go back in time if I could. It probably would have saved us both a lot of heartache, huh?"

I reached up a hand, loving the feel of Ian's beard growth.

Definitely a sucker for manly men, Ian encompassed traits I didn't know I wanted until God gift wrapped them for me on Christmas day.

"I love you," I said, "and I can't wait to marry you."

Ian laid his hand atop mine. "Stop looking at me like that, Taylor. I can't do anything about it until Friday."

I laughed, but I took his admonition to heart. Glancing around at dark brown cabinets and faux wood, laminate counters, the Horner kitchen felt as "old school" as the ketchup ingredients and anything else available to eat.

"Food allergies suck," I declared, my stomach rumbling in agreement. "I can't believe I used to eat so much of this stuff."

"Is this what you cooked for your brother?" Ian asked, looking over my shoulder at the name brands in the pantry I remembered all too well.

"Pretty much. My mother had one or two dishes she made, but dinner was usually on me."

"How can you claim you're not much of a chef when you've been cooking since you were eleven?"

I looked up at him. "Because everything I knew how to make came with easy instructions on the box. We never did anything from scratch. When I added food allergies to it, meals became overwhelming. Mitch complained about anything I tried to cook, so we either ate out, or I just made my own food. When he joined the gym and wanted to eat healthier, I thought he might finally come around, but he got into all of these weird protein shakes and boring chicken breasts. I have allergies, but I still enjoy flavor."

"What do you think about doing a cooking class with me? It would be something fun, and then you'll feel more empowered in the kitchen."

"You're sweet."

"Did you find anything?" Thomas called from the dining room. "Your food is getting cold, Ian, and I think a rabbit stole Taylor's dinner."

Ian groaned from behind me. "I tell myself they mean well, but I can only handle my parents in small doses."

Locating an overly ripe banana and a red apple on the counter, I figured it was better than nothing, and brought them with me back into the dining room.

Nancy looked at my plate in horror. "If she was just going to eat fruit and green beans, I wouldn't have bothered making all of this food."

"Back off, okay, Mom?" Ian said through clenched teeth. "I wish you took me seriously when I told you Taylor is allergic to a lot of things."

Thomas gave Ian and me a patronizing smirk. "Is this the pseudoscience you millennials read up on the internet, or did an actual, medical doctor give the diagnosis?"

I squeezed Ian's hand one time and replied, "I used to get horrible rashes and headaches, but I could never figure out what caused them. My mother suggested I go see an allergist since she was tired of watching me scratch at my hands until they bled."

"Until they bled?" Thomas said skeptically. Both parents glanced quickly at my smooth skin

"With sugar especially, I get something called dyshidrotic eczema. It's raised bumps, tiny little blisters, sort of like hives. They itch like you wouldn't believe, and if they bleed, they sting and can be incredibly painful. Gluten causes dry patches on my hands as well as headaches. Dairy, other than the occasional indulgence, results in inflammation in my low back and dry skin that eventually cracks and bleeds. It took a long time for my body to detox from all of that. Now, I can usually tell within thirty minutes if I've accidentally eaten something I shouldn't because it shows up on my hands."

"I've suddenly lost my appetite," Nancy said, pushing her plate away. "I've never heard of anything like this before. We certainly never had all of these allergies growing up."

Thomas looked at me with new eyes. "Have you always had these issues, Taylor?"

I shook my head. "No, I'm not sure when or how they developed. Growing up, I was home with my brother and cooked a lot of the same things you have in your pantry. I miss the convenience of it, if nothing else."

"Why wasn't your mother cooking?" Nancy asked.

"My parents divorced when I was eleven," I said. "My mother worked to support us, and I helped take care of my brother."

Thomas shook his head and tsked. "Doesn't anyone understand what 'til death do us part' means anymore? People just give up at the first sign of trouble. Hopefully, that won't be the case for the two of you," he said, gesturing toward my engagement ring. "Have you set a date?"

"Friday," Ian and I answered in unison.

"You mean you want to get married *on* a Friday?" Nancy choked, clearly thinking she misunderstood us.

"No, Mom. Five days from now," Ian said, taking hold of my hand, this time on top of the table.

"Taylor, are you in a family way?" Nancy whispered.

Easily, I replied, "No, Mrs. Horner, Ian and I have remained chaste this entire time."

"So what's the rush?" Thomas said. "What about premarital counseling? Ian's never been in a serious relationship before, and I doubt he knows the first thing about making a marriage work. Your sister certainly didn't give much of an effort to hers. This just screams of nothing but foolishness, Ian. You can't tell me you're going to ask Taylor to move into that tiny, little apartment you have in Hillcrest."

"We're moving into Taylor's townhouse just outside of Parkview," Ian said. "A guy from work is going to sublet my apartment. Once we get settled in, we'll figure out what we're going to do as a more permanent living situation."

"Taylor, you rent a townhouse?" Thomas asked incredulously. "In Parkview? Ian said you worked for a fancy company in the city. I didn't realize they paid college grads so well. To think, all these kids still live in their parents' basements complaining they can't find work. Way to show 'em!"

"Taylor owns the townhouse," Ian replied. "Her mother helped her purchase the home."

"Well, that makes more sense," Nancy said, apparently having regained her appetite as she shoveled in a mouthful of boxed mashed potatoes.

"My mom didn't pay for the townhouse," I said, correcting the misunderstanding. "She helped purchase some new furniture for it, but the townhouse came out of my own pocket."

"Ian, I didn't know you're marrying into money!" Thomas guffawed. He clapped his son on the back. "Good for you!"

Ian looked at me as if he wished for a hole in the ground large enough to sink into. I met his eyes questioningly, willing to rip off the bandage myself. I had no problem owning my past, even to these less than friendly people who might one day be called, "Grandma and Grandpa." Instead, Ian Horner kept his word and took the brunt of his parents' disbelief and outrage when he alleviated them of some very misguided notions regarding my age, my income, and my previous marital status.

Our fight on the way to Manchester paled in comparison to the fireworks ignited in the Horner household. It certainly explained why Ian didn't shrink away from my mother's melodramatic maelstroms. Nancy and Thomas Horner provided ample competition for Sarah Meyers.

CHAPTER 29

"CAN I TELL YOU AGAIN HOW SORRY I AM ABOUT Sunday?" Ian asked as we walked down the Parkview streets two days later.

"I appreciate you taking the week off of work to get everything packed and moved into my place, but I promise I'm fine. You have to know my mother broke me in a long time ago in terms of critical and overbearing parents."

"But the things my father said," Ian moaned. "I don't think I've ever been more embarrassed in my life. The accusations—"

"Were nothing I haven't already heard from Chloe," I said, interrupting him. "Ian, I told you I'm fine, and I meant it."

"What about everything you said in the car on the way down there? Why are you so calm now, Taylor?"

"I was upset with you, not your parents, Ian. I can handle Thomas and Nancy thinking whatever they want about me. I don't know them, and they only think they know the real me. Based on everything they've said, I'm not sure how much they're going to be a part of our lives anyway. You, however,

I'm planning to spend the rest of my life with, so if you shared their sentiments, we would definitely have some problems."

"They make it very easy to leave and cleave, don't they?" Ian said drolly.

I squeezed his hand in support. "I know it hurts, Ian. They're your parents. You love them, and you want their respect and support for our marriage. Nobody would fault you for that."

"I just don't get it," he said. "After all the years they beat me down for my hair, my job, my apartment, or how I was never going to meet anyone hiding behind the sound booth at church, it just feels like nothing is ever good enough. I bring home the woman of my dreams, and they're still criticizing me."

I looked up into Ian's soulful, dark eyes recognizing the same rejection I'd experienced from my mother. "Ian, it's their own insecurities. Frankly, your parents both seem miserable."

"I just don't understand what they want from me," he said, tormented. "They talk me up to everyone else, but to my face, all they do is rip me apart."

Tears filled my eyes. I knew the painful answer and hated being the one to deliver it. "Ian, if they don't keep moving the goalposts, they'd have no way to keep making you a slave for their approval."

"A slave?"

"Yes," I said. "They dangle that carrot of approval, and they expect you to jump. They've done the same thing to Kate and Fiona too. It's how your parents try to control all of your lives while pretending they're just looking out for your best interests. It's covert narcissism disguised as 'concern' for all of you. Talking you up to others just reinforces that sense of longing and creates confusion."

"Then why bother bragging about me if they think I'm so unworthy?" Ian asked.

"That's just it," I said. "They wouldn't brag about you to other people if you truly *were* unworthy. They just don't do it while you're around because then they can't take credit for your accomplishments on your behalf. This has very little to do with you and Kate and everything to do with your parents and their own issues."

Ian raised an eyebrow, still not totally convinced. "You got all that from just one evening with them?"

I shrugged. "I've been abused by people projecting their issues long enough. It's also easier to recognize when you're not emotionally tied to the people."

"What about Chloe?" Ian asked. "How did you miss the jealousy there?"

"Chloe came into my life just as everything fell apart with Mitch. The idea of her being jealous of anything in my upturned world made no sense."

"So, you think my parents are jealous of me?" Ian asked skeptically.

"I didn't say that. I said that they were insecure. From what I could tell with your parents, they have a very ordered and systematic way of doing things. Their version is the only 'right' way. I think the insecurity comes from a fear of being wrong or not in control of a situation. My mother acts like that, constantly trying to dictate what my values should look like. It's a way to establish dominance and authority over someone else. If they're the one setting the standards, then you'll always be dependent on them for approval. Essentially, they're setting themselves up as God in your life."

"For all of their faults, Taylor, my parents would never think of it that way. They're Christians. They'll be the first ones to tell you that Jesus is God, and they're not."

Countering his argument, I said, "If that's the case, why don't they give you the freedom to make your own choices and mistakes, Ian? I watched both of your parents cut into you mercilessly. With my mother, you get a full knife to the gut. Your parents seem content to saw at you with a dull butter knife."

"Well, that's morbid," Ian said, "and a horrible visual. Effective, but horrible."

"Sorry, sweetie. That's the picture that came to mind."

Before Ian could respond, a familiar face interrupted our conversation.

"Taylor? Is that you?" Julie Easton said, looking over my recently re-stylized pixie cut. "I barely recognized you!"

I squeezed Ian's hand two times.

When I didn't respond, Julie dropped the saccharine facade and said, "I guess you didn't stay heartbroken for too long." She eyed my hand held securely inside of Ian's, her eyes bulging at Grandma Horner's engagement ring.

Ian used his full height advantage to look down his nose at Julie. "As I'm sure you've noticed, I'm not Kyle Goldstein. I defend what's mine. Watch your tone with my fiancée," he warned.

Hello, Alpha Male!

"I see we've made an upgrade," Julie sneered. She eyed Ian with an appreciation that reminded me of that gangly legged receptionist who ruined my first marriage. I squeezed Ian's hand in desperation three times.

"I think it's time for lunch," Ian said, ignoring Julie and pulling me into the closest restaurant.

Unfortunately, we entered Los Bravos on a Tuesday afternoon.

Feeling like we'd stepped from the frying pan into the fire, Carlos greeted us. He immediately peppered me in Spanish about where I'd been all these months and did I know about my boyfriend and *la otra mujer*.

I could have gone the rest of my life without hearing the phrase "the other woman" regardless of the language spoken. I skidded to a halt as I spotted Kyle Goldstein sitting in a booth with food for two.

"Please, tell me that's not who I think it is," Ian said close to my ear, "because this looks like another one of those 'Dear Diary' moments."

I grimaced just as Kyle noticed the two of us at the hostess stand. I half expected him to cause a scene, but he snatched his phone off the table, a flurry of texting evidenced by his thumbs flying all over the screen.

One glance at Ian explained why, the death glare he levelled at my former beau certainly enough to wither an oak tree.

Fearing another public spectacle, I said, "I think we should just grab some Chick-A-Yum, and I'll bring you back to Culver to introduce you to Phil and Miss Belle. I've had all of the excitement I can handle for one day, Ian."

My fiancé nodded, not relinquishing his laser focus on Kyle until we exited the restaurant. As far as I could tell, Kyle's powder blue eyes never left his cell phone screen.

Feeling my phone buzz, I knew who was texting me before I even pulled it out of my pocket.

Nice job flaunting your new boyfriend. I guess you needed to announce you had no problem moving on. Is it hard to pepper spray a giant ninety feet taller than you?

Ian glanced over my shoulder and read the message. "He's baiting you, Taylor. You know that, right?"

I nodded. "How can he talk about flaunting my relationship when he did the exact same thing with MacKenzie?"

"What are you going to say back?" Ian asked.

I typed up a message and let Ian glance over it before I replied.

The new boyfriend is going to be my husband on Friday. I'm truly happy, Kyle, and I hope you will be too one day. God bless you.

I didn't expect to receive a response back from Kyle Goldstein, and I guessed correctly. Instead, I happily introduced Ian around the office. I grinned as Miss Belle fawned all over him, and Phil seemed too intimidated by Ian's height to make any teasing remarks. Lexie smiled knowingly at me as she shook Ian's hand. Her expression showed understanding about the "positive changes" in my life.

Ian and I were spared the potential catastrophe of his parents meeting the larger than life, billboard turned in-law since we invited none of them to our civil ceremony three days later. Gabe stood in place of my father, and the Margolins served as best man and matron of honor respectively. Tabby could not have been more adorable in her tutu dress, and she happily twirled for the slightest bit of applause or attention. Rebecca later whispered in my ear she would need matching outfits for her daughter and forthcoming little sister. I released an excited squeal as I embraced my friend.

"I pray God blesses you and Ian with the joy of being parents too," Rebecca said, squeezing my hands and looking into my tear-filled eyes. "You're a beautiful bride, Taylor Horner, and I know you will make an incredible wife and mother too."

"Thank you for everything," I whispered. I pulled her into another embrace, but Rebecca jolted a moment later.

"Did you feel that?" Rebecca asked, eyes wide. "That's the first time she's kicked me like that!"

I grinned. "Maybe it's confirmation?"

Rebecca's megawatt smile illuminated the entire room. "With the way your husband keeps looking at you in that purple dress, Taylor, I think you'll be well on your way soon enough."

"I told you I wanted to save it for a special occasion," I sing-songed.

"My father-in-law should be ready to take some pictures of you guys if he ever gets done with the impromptu photoshoot of his son and granddaughter."

I laughed as Ted's father, Steve Margolin, happily snapped photo after photo of Tabitha giggling while Ted threw her up in the air.

I felt Ian's presence before I saw him. "Do you think that will be us soon?" he asked. He glanced over to Ted and Tabby as Rebecca rejoined them.

"As long as we're still going with the not planning not preventing method," I replied, lacing my fingers into his.

Causing the hairs on my neck to stand on end, Ian said close to my ear, "How soon can we get out of here?"

I laughed and swatted his arm.

Ian stood back up to his full height and said, "I wasn't sure why you asked me to wear a purple tie today, but I'm definitely not complaining. I will take that purple work of art over some poofy, white dress any day. Taylor, you take my breath away."

I grinned up at him. "I told Rebecca I didn't want to wear this dress until I knew it was safe for you to see me in it."

"It's still not safe," he said, verbal sword in hand. The look in his dark eyes made my knees tremble.

"Keep it G-rated for the little one!" Steve Margolin teased, snapping photos of us. "The groom is looking at the bride like a Christmas present he can't wait to un—"

"We get it, Dad!" Ted interrupted with a look of apology. He whispered something to his father, and Steve pinked before his expression sobered. He resumed his duties as official wedding photographer without further incident.

Fiona, Ian's niece I had grown to love, hugged me with gusto. She then stepped aside when her mother wanted to do the same. I gave Kate a brief rundown of our horrific Sunday dinner with her parents, and she rolled her eyes. She promised her parents would come around eventually, especially if Ian and I gifted them with their first male grandchild.

Fiona seemed absolutely fascinated by the entire event. She wondered why Uncle Ian and Aunt Taylor didn't have a church wedding, why didn't Aunt Taylor wear a white dress, when was Mom going to get married again, and would she wear purple too? Kate took everything in stride, apparently used to being machine gunned with questions by her precocious daughter.

After enjoying a delicious, allergen free celebration at the Parkview Diner, we finally called it a night around eight o'clock. Ian and I drove back to my home as husband and wife, and Ian insisted upon carrying me over the threshold.

The nerves I had felt on my first wedding night were a distant memory to the hum of energy surging through me ten years later. The disparity between my past and my present filled my eyes with tears of gratitude. God took what had been shattered into unrecognizable nothingness and transformed it into something truly beautiful.

Two and a half months later, the Lord blessed Ian and I with the desire of both of our hearts. We also faced the daunting task of how to inform the new grandparents of our upcoming arrival.

CHAPTER 30

"Taylor," Ian called from outside of the bathroom. "You're going to be late for work."

Head still leaned over the toilet, I groaned. How was there anything left in my stomach?

I heard Ian's footsteps on the bathroom floor, and he crouched down beside me and pushed limp hair off of my forehead. "Are you sure it's normal to be this sick all the time? I'm really worried about you, Taylor. Do you need to see the OB?"

The intense nausea during my first pregnancy seemed like nothing compared to the all-out cookie tossing with my second. Eight weeks into my pregnancy, Ian and I just wanted to make it past the dreaded ten week mark. It was the same week five years earlier where I discovered that the precious little life inside of me no longer had a heartbeat.

"I know it looks bad," I said, "but it's actually a good thing. It means my body is doing what it's supposed to."

"Aren't there some women who never get nauseous?" Ian said. "I read something about that online the other day."

I raised a skeptical eyebrow at my husband. "Much like the Loch Ness Monster, I'm not sure those women have ever actually been sighted."

Ian grinned at me, though concern still showed in his eyes. "Does anybody in the office know?"

I shook my head then laid my hand on Ian's arm. Cautiously, I stood to my feet.

"Tell me what I can do," he said.

"Ginger tea in my lunch bag?" I asked.

"Check."

"Peppermint tea waiting for me downstairs?"

"Check."

"Green apples, fruit bars, and bland chicken in my lunch container?"

"Check."

Offering a brave smile, I said, "Then, I think we're all set."

"Do you want more of that bread Rebecca made? I have no idea how she turned your food allergies into actual bread, but at least we have the recipe to try for ourselves."

"Thank God for that woman," I said, stepping carefully into the closet to pull out a shapeless shift dress and some gladiator sandals.

Ian reached around me to pull down a polo shirt from his much higher closet shelf. "I'm sorry you can't eat eggs anymore."

I sighed. "If they didn't make me so nauseous, I'd try. God willing, once we get into the second trimester, all of the nausea should ease up. At least I hope so."

Already dressed for work, Ian planted a quick kiss on my cheek before hurrying downstairs to make breakfast for "my queen." He said he held no aspirations of me referring to him as "my king," only that he wanted me to know how much he loved and treasured me.

Miss Belle took note of the constant tea sipping occurring at my desk, but she refrained from commenting. Since Ian and I had gotten married, Deondre quit Culver, and Lexie thrived without him there. Though leery of trusting her, she acted both eager and scared to share whatever story kept her skittish at times. It seemed to sit just below the surface waiting for an excuse to be unleashed.

After eating half of my boring chicken lunch at my desk, I popped two magnesium malate supplement pills hoping to take the edge off my all-day morning sickness. I shoved a green apple in my purse in case I got hungry again and then decided to take a stroll around Parkview. Noting the day of the week, I walked right past Los Bravos and continued on my journey.

I eventually stopped into Vincenzo's coffee house for a respite from the heat and humidity as summer held on well into October. After procuring a bottle of water, I found a comfy spot to hang out. I pulled my legs up underneath me on the chair and read through a good portion of Rebecca's manuscript draft while I rehydrated.

Without warning, my mother sauntered into the coffee shop along with a man her own age. Taking a moment to study his features, nausea surged to my throat. I stared at a dead ringer for my father, but it seemed too impossible to believe. I remembered how much my parents despised each other toward the end of their marriage. The memories converged into overlayed sounds of screaming, fighting, and photo frames crashing against the walls after my father left.

Yet try as I might to deny it, there was no mistaking the dark brown eyes, heavy brows, and full lips I had memorized from family pictures before my mother trashed them all. Even with a silver beard and hair, I would recognize Jonathan Meyers anywhere. Keeping my face down, I did my best to eavesdrop on their conversation as they approached the counter.

"I wonder what Elaine will think," my mother said on a giggle.

"Since she's off vacationing with her personal trainer, probably not much," my father said dryly. "When do you plan to tell the kids my name isn't Barry?"

"Can I take your order?" the barista asked.

Not surprisingly, my mother ordered something complicated, non-fat, and highly expensive. My father ordered a black coffee. They sat at a small table about fifteen feet away from me, and I turned my body, lest my mother recognize me. My hair had grown considerably since Ian and I got married, but I knew my mother would take one look at me and guess correctly about the pregnancy.

More than anything, I wanted to find out how many more secrets my mother kept from me and my brother. I fired off a text to Ian, then a second to Gabe. My brother responded immediately, completely flabbergasted and asking for pictures. I wrote back saying I didn't think I could do it without being noticed. He barraged me with questions about how long our parents had been sneaking around. I wrote back telling him to stop asking so I could listen and find out.

"What's this all about, Sarah? Two years ago, you told me it was a matter of life and death with our daughter."

"Life and death?" I mouthed in question, not sure what hysteria my mother had invented.

My father continued, "I told you I would help any way I could, but the next thing I know, Taylor's apparently doing just fine. I finally see her after twenty years, but you tell me to stay put."

"Thank you for not approaching her on Christmas," my mother said. "I can't get information out of Gabe anymore, but I'm sure Taylor has to be married by now. She couldn't wait to hop in the sack with that hunky model she landed."

My mother's ability to project her own sins onto others never ceased to amaze or disgust me. I did my best to keep my raging hormones in check.

"Is he really a model?" my father asked.

My mother tsked. "Well, you know how I can be a little dramatic at times, Johnny. I think he works in computers or something. The first time I saw the guy, it looked like he had tumbleweed on top of his head. Apparently, our daughter cleaned him up."

"Well, at least she's happy, Sarah," my father said, "and you can hardly blame Taylor or Gabe after you completely botched things trying to tell them I'm back in your life."

"If you had been on time, *Barry*," she said, emphasizing his pseudonym, "they would have been too shocked to figure everything out. We would have finally been one big, happy family."

"Except you didn't invite *my* children to that happy reunion," he responded coolly.

"They're not your children, Johnny. They're Elaine's children."

"I practically raised them, Sarah. As far as I'm concerned, Lexie and Micah may as well be my own flesh and blood."

My blood ran cold. There was no way. Just no possible way.

Fumbling with my phone, I turned on the voice record app to capture my parents' clandestine meeting. Their conversation continued, and each lie exposed sent my world spiraling off its axis.

"You could have helped with your own children," my mother sniffed indignantly.

"You wouldn't let me, Sarah!" my father said, voice agitated. "First, you tell me you don't want a dime from me, just get out of your life. Then, you take and twist that to make me look like a lowlife who wants nothing to do with his own kids. Did Taylor and Gabriel ever receive the birthday cards I sent them?"

"Of course they did!" my mother snapped. "You got your thank you notes."

"In your handwriting," he said, voice hard. "I never wanted a divorce, Sarah. You did. I didn't plan on meeting and falling in love with Elaine a month after you kicked me out."

"Even if you didn't cheat with Elaine, it wasn't the first woman you slept with," my mother fired back.

"Only because you cheated first!" my father said angrily.

"Lower your voice, Johnny! Someone will hear you! Besides, that's all ancient history. I thought we were moving forward." Out of the corner of my eye, I watched my mother bat her lashes and reach across the table for his hand. "Come on, Johnny. This is the happiest we've ever been together, even before we got married."

"This is a lot more complicated than before we got married," my father said. "I want a chance to know my own children, Sarah. I'm beginning to wonder if that's even possible with all of the lies you've told."

"Look, we just call it a tragic misunderstanding, the kids get to see their parents happy together, and my children stop judging me for doing what's best for myself."

"What about what's best for *them*, Sarah?"

"Having a mother and father in their lives is what's best for them," my mother sniffed.

"Daddy?" a very familiar voice said from the front door of Vincenzo's, "I didn't know you'd be in Parkview today."

Stunned, I confirmed her identity as I stole a glance at my

father's stepdaughter with Elaine—technically my stepsister, and also technically nothing if my father's marriage to her mother was truly over. With my cell phone battery now running low, I typed as much as possible to Ian and then copied and pasted the message to my brother.

Ian called my phone desperate to make sure I was all right, but he didn't realize my ringtone would cause my mother, father, and step/non-sister to turn around and look behind them.

"Taylor?" Lexie said. "I didn't see you over there." She gestured toward Jonathan Meyers who looked as stunned as I did. "This is my dad, and this is his girlfriend—"

"My mother," I finished for her, glaring at the deceitful, manipulative blonde like the enemy she was.

"How much did you hear?" my mother said, not bothering with hysterics or lies.

"Everything," I said bitterly. "Just when I think you can't possibly stoop any lower, Sarah, you always manage to surprise me."

"What did you call me?" she gasped.

"As far as I'm concerned, I don't have a mother anymore. In fact, I'm not sure I ever did."

"See how quickly they forget all you've done for them," she said, hoping to save face with the man studying me like he might never see me again.

"Taylor, I…" Lexie's voice trailed off. "I had no idea."

I nodded at her. "Neither did I. It seems like our parents have a lot of explaining to do. Especially you," I said, finally turning to meet my father face-to-face.

Up close, I saw Jonathan Meyers was not a large man, maybe the same height as my mother, though slighter build. I recognized the shape of my own eyes and a larger version of my nose.

"You grew up beautifully," my father said, eyes boring into mine. "You look like a Meyers."

"Her eyes are muddy," my mother said, itching for blood, "and she's just as scrawny as you were thirty years ago, Johnny. Oh, and the temper on this one! Little Miss Holier-than-thou who married her fashion model just to get him in bed."

"It's hard to take anything you say seriously," I responded with icy coldness, "when you have a fourteen foot billboard making you look like the city's oldest streetwalker. What exactly *is* Sarah selling?"

Lexie looked back and forth between my mother and me as if caught in a crossfire. My father's expression seemed to be a mix of pain and admiration.

"What are you doing with her?" I said, gesturing toward my mother. "Why would you think anything has changed? And where have you been for the last two decades? Why didn't you try to find us or see us?"

My father visibly swallowed before answering. "Your mother and I had a verbal agreement that she didn't want any child support as long as I stayed out of her life. Little did I know, it was just a ploy to make me come crawling back to her. When it didn't work, she told the courts I failed to pay child support and had me thrown in jail. The judge revoked all visitation rights after a series of stories your mother made up making me look and sound like a raging alcoholic."

"Is this true?" I said, glaring at Sarah Meyers. "Did you force me to grow up and raise my own brother just so you could have your petty little vengeance against your ex-husband?"

"Oh, please," my mother said, rolling her eyes for my father's benefit.

My anger rose as did my voice. "Those woe is me, your

ANA WATERS

father abandoned us stories was all your own doing, Mom. You *stole* my childhood just to keep up some lie! You're sick!"

Sarah Meyers waved her hand as if swatting away a gnat. "What did I tell you, Johnny? Melodramatic and always inventing reasons to be mad at me. She tries to feed this poison to her brother too, you know. It takes a lot of work to undo all of the lies Taylor likes to spread. Keep that in mind when you talk to our son."

"You are certifiable," I yelled, clinging to my own sanity for dear life, "and I am not letting you anywhere near this baby!"

CHAPTER 31

"WHAT DID YOU JUST SAY?" MY FATHER ASKED, HIS eyes immediately searching my abdomen for telltale signs of pregnancy.

"I'm going to be a grandmother!" my mother gasped, china blue eyes immediately filling with tears. "Oh, Taylor, this is such wonderful news! Tell me what kind of a shower you want, and I'll start right now! I'm sure this baby will be just fine, especially since Ian treats you so much better than Baldy ever did."

Lexie's green eyes could not have been any wider. Although I never intended to share this much of my story with her, I no longer had any say in the matter. Moreover, our lives would be forever intertwined.

"Sarah, you need to get back on your meds," my father said, glancing between my mother and me. "I love you too much to let you destroy any chance of a relationship you have with our daughter. You need help. Professional help."

"Lithium makes my feet swell, and I have no energy when I take it," she whined.

"Wait, what am I missing here?" I said, eyeing my mother.

My father revealed years of irrational mood swings and narcissism in five simple words. "Your mother has bipolar disorder," he said. "Her psychiatrist also thinks she has histrionic personality disorder as well."

"*Your* psychiatrist," my mother corrected. "I feel just fine, thank you very much."

When my cell phone rang again, I turned my back on the lot of them to talk to my husband. I needed some sort of mooring to stay afloat in their sea of utter craziness.

"I'm in the twilight zone," I said low into the phone.

"Is he there now?" Ian asked.

"Yes. So is Lexie and my mother. If Kyle Goldstein walks in, I'm going to fall over."

"Just get out of there, okay? The stress isn't good for you or the baby."

"Speaking of that..."

"You told them," Ian said, somehow already knowing.

"I blurted it out."

He exhaled a heavy sigh. "Not how we planned, but I know you didn't expect to see your long lost father today either. Go back to the office, put everything out of your mind for now, and we'll discuss over dinner."

"Pho?" I asked.

"Works for me. I'll pick it up on my way home. I love you, and I have to go back to work."

"I love you too," I said, and I watched as my phone showed Ian disconnecting the call.

"I need to get back to the office," I announced while my parents went head to head in an argument.

Like a deer in headlights, Lexie jumped to her feet, grabbing my arm and practically pulling me out of the door.

"I won't say a word, I swear!" she exclaimed, glancing down at my belly.

"Well, you practically just announced it to everyone in Parkview," I hissed. I walked faster once I saw my father leap from his seat in the cafe window.

"Sorry," Lexie said. "I'm just in shock."

"You and me both," I replied. I slowed my gait as Lexie lagged behind.

"Thank you," she said, her hand touching her side in pain. "You're faster than you look."

"That's because I'm furious."

"My dad said he had two kids, but his ex-wife was crazy and got the state to keep him from seeing them. He talked about you all the time."

"You didn't clue into the fact that his daughter's name was Taylor and mine is too? That I look like a female version of my father?"

Lexie shook her head emphatically. "No, I swear! Your name was Taylor Ross, and Dad has been gray for as long as I can remember. Plus, your hair and eyes are lighter than his. Don't forget, I had MacKenzie and Julie telling me how awful you were, so it wasn't like I wanted to spend tons of time around you either."

I pulled Lexie to a stop. "What are you saying?"

She shrugged. "I don't know, Taylor. Things haven't been good between my parents for a long time. They got divorced last year, but I never expected Dad to start seeing anyone so soon. From the way he always talked about your mother, she was the last person I thought he'd be dating. I didn't find out her name until today. I think they got together some time last fall, but Dad didn't say much other than he found his soulmate."

"Soulmate?" I said mockingly. "Are you kidding? Did you see

the two of them in there? They're toxic for each other. How can my father possibly love her after everything she's done?"

"What does this make you and me?" Lexie asked, posing the question of the hour.

I shrugged. "The heck if I know. Did my father legally adopt you and your brother? Where does your last name come from because it's obviously not Meyers."

"My husband," Lexie answered, "although, I'm not sure for how much longer."

"Adultery?" I asked.

Lexie shook her head. "I'm infertile," she said quietly. "We've tried IVF three times, have gone crazy into debt, but I keep miscarrying. It's not something I really talk about," she sniffled, wiping her nose with her hand.

Compassion filled my heart. "I am so sorry, Lexie."

She offered a watery smile. "Blake and I are just really hurting financially, and we both wanted children so badly. I told him I was tired of trying, and I can't deal with the pain of another lost baby."

"What did he say?" I asked, all thoughts of our complicated parental situation forgotten.

"He doesn't want to adopt," she said, "so, we're at this impasse. We don't really talk to each other anymore. He thinks I'm being unreasonable even though he knows we can't afford another IVF treatment, and I think he's being unreasonable because he won't consider adoption."

"I lost a baby too," I said. "Not under the same circumstances as you, Lexie, but it was still traumatic. My ex-husband's mistress carried her baby full term, though." I braced myself, willing to take the leap and trust Lexie with information none but Ted Margolin and Miss Belle knew about at Culver.

Lexie's hand immediately went over her heart. "Oh my gosh, Taylor! That's awful!" Recalling the series of events bringing us into each other's lives, she said, "How long ago did all of this happen? You were already divorced when you dated Goldstein, weren't you?"

"Very much so. I lost my baby five-and-a-half years ago."

"Were you a teen bride, Taylor? You aren't older than me, are you? I'll be twenty-eight in November."

"I turned thirty-three last month," I said, "and you must have been seven years-old when my father married your mother."

Lexie nodded. "My birth father died of a heart attack. My brother was eight, and I was four. Jonathan Meyers is the only father I remember, and he is an amazing dad, Taylor. I hope you'll give him a chance and listen to his side of the story."

Her eyes implored mine, and I struggled with how to respond. Sighing wearily, I finally said, "I haven't seen or heard anything from Jonathan Meyers in two decades, Lexie. If everything he said in the coffee shop is true, it makes even less sense why my parents are together. My mother sabotaged him at every turn. I get that the heart may want what it wants, but something doesn't add up."

"Agreed. Then again, not much has made sense since my mom decided to leave my dad for her personal trainer. It seemed so out of character for her."

I shook my head in disgust. "I don't know if I am ever going to understand this boomer generation. I know I'm biased because of my mother and her slew of married boyfriends, but it's a level of selfishness beyond my capability to fathom."

Lexie grimaced. "I get it. Mom said she hadn't been happy with Dad for years and that he suddenly started acting weird.

They took a day trip somewhere south of Manchester, and he was never the same after that. She said Dad acted moody and withdrawn. I don't think she ever suspected him of cheating on her, only that he became a different person. Counseling didn't help."

"Why did your mother share all of this personal information with you? Didn't it mess up your relationship with your...our...father?"

Lexie shook her head. "Micah never wanted to listen to my mother, but Mom and I have always been close. Maybe she overshared, but it didn't change how much I love Dad. I just couldn't understand what was going on with the two of them."

"Sounds like something happened on their trip to trigger my father's change," I said.

"The only thing I found strange was when Dad told me his new girlfriend, Sarah, is the same one from the 'Sell it with Sarah' ads. Every time my mother drives by one of those billboards, she starts cussing up a storm. I've never understood the connection."

My eyes grew wide. "Are you saying my parents have been having an affair for the past nine years?"

"Nine years?" Lexie croaked.

"Regardless of what your mother said, Lexie, men act like my father did when they're thinking about cheating, when they're actually cheating, or when they're lying to you about their cheating and projecting all of their guilt onto you."

"But *nine* years?" she said, her eyes widening even farther than I previously thought possible.

"Nine years," I said emphatically, the disgust at both of my parents filling my throat. "I personally designed those billboards for my mother. I handled all of the marketing and collateral for the Sarah Meyers Team at StarRealty. Of course, I didn't know my mother would flaunt her silicone assets for the entire metro area, but she switched the photo behind my back after I submitted it to the sign company."

"My mom was always on the heavier side," Lexie said, her eyes drifting over her own frame. "She was never trendy or super into her looks, but it must have been right after the billboards went up that she started dieting and going to the gym. She bought herself a whole new wardrobe too."

"Do you think she was competing with old memories of my mother? I have no doubt she knew exactly who Sarah was, especially since they both had the same last name."

Lexie nodded, the pieces falling into place for her as well. "Dad got distant, and he and Mom argued all the time. At least that's what she told me. I was already away at school by then. When I graduated college, they were sleeping in separate bedrooms. Two years ago, she kept talking about her trainer, Richard. It was Richard this and Richard that, as if she worshiped the guy."

"Oh no," I said.

"Mom had a lot of money in savings because of the life insurance from my biological father, so she bankrolls her new life with Richard. Our mutual dad works as a land developer with Triple J Construction. I thought it was funny when I found out they're a client of Culver's."

My mouth went dry.

Triple J Construction built my townhome.

And my mother's home four years before that.

Feeling suddenly woozy, I faltered, and Lexie's panicked expression let me know it was no slight stumble.

"Are you all right?" she asked, holding out an arm to steady me. "It's really hot out here. Do you need some water?"

I nodded, withdrawing inside myself to seek respite from the pain and deception. I wondered if I would ever dare to roam the streets of Parkview again.

I didn't know how to explain everything to Phil, only that I needed to take some personal time away. My latest trainee, Poppy Levine, seemed to hit the ground running, and she proved to be a great fit for the all-encompassing marketing position. Though buried under three new proposals and a benefits guide, her eyes flicked up at me in concern before returning back to her dual computer monitors.

"Everything okay?" she asked, clicking on the mouse while she talked. "You haven't looked well for a few weeks."

"I'm a little off my game right now," I said. "My mother is determined to put the daytime soap operas to shame."

Poppy raised an eyebrow. "Yours too?"

I studied our newest Culver employee before answering. Poppy was in her mid-thirties with three, adorable kids pictured on her desk. Noticeably absent was their father.

"Is your mom a boomer?" I asked.

Poppy nodded in the affirmative. "She used to be very proud of the fact that she conceived my older brother at Woodstock if that tells you anything."

"Wow."

Poppy shrugged. "Just take care of yourself and that baby, okay? The associates will all be fine without you for a day, even two if you need it."

My gaze shot over to her in shock and terror. "How...?"

Poppy grinned at me. "My youngest daughter is four, and it doesn't feel like that long ago I survived on chamomile and peppermint tea too. Your secret is safe with me, Taylor. I haven't said anything, and I won't. Go home, enjoy some time with that gorgeous husband of yours, and let the mama drama sort itself out. You don't need that kind of added stress. Believe me."

And I did.

CHAPTER 32

I FELL INTO IAN'S ARMS THE SECOND HE WALKED IN our front door with dinner. Too anxious to eat, I relayed the entire story of my parents' marriage, divorce, and apparent reconciliation while filling in the details recently obtained from Lexie. We eventually migrated from the dining room table to the sofa as my story took longer than anticipated.

"I think I need a drink," Ian said, raking a hand through his overgrown hair, "and I don't even drink."

"I think you need a haircut," I said wryly.

"I'm glad you can crack jokes, Taylor. Your brother must have sent me a million texts after he couldn't get ahold of you. Are you sure you're feeling all right?"

"Low grade nausea as usual," I said. I retrieved my mug from a coffee table coaster and took a sip of peppermint tea.

"How did your parents take the news?" Ian asked, leaning back against the sofa and closing his eyes.

"My mother already asked about planning a baby shower, but we both know Sarah Meyers lives in her own reality. The only things she deigns to acknowledge in life are what make her feel good. Unless, of course, she can score some points with an old fashioned, woe is me tale. Then she'll happily relive her misery on a dime," I said with annoyance.

"How much of this is the personality disorder, how much is the chemical disorder, and how much is actually your mother?"

"I don't know if you can separate them, Ian. To my knowledge, I've never experienced my mother on medication. She spends most of her time high on life or looking for some other kind of high. She's always used her litany of men for that. Selling houses and being fawned all over by her clients also feeds into the grandiose fantasies she likes to maintain about herself."

Ian cracked one eye open. "Have you considered writing a book like Rebecca?"

"Seriously?"

"Yeah."

"I don't know, love. What am I going to do? Whine about my mother and my ex-husband for four hundred pages? Rebecca's story is about real abuse and trauma. Even just reading her manuscript, I stop and wonder what I'm complaining about. Thank God, I've never experienced the kind of suffering she did."

This time, both of Ian's soulful, dark eyes stared into mine. "Taylor, just because Rebecca's story sounds worse than yours on paper doesn't make your pain any less real or devastating than hers. Thank God, you were never abused or groomed by any of your former pastors, but you've got your own horror story, sweetheart."

"Horror story?" I asked. "Don't you think that's overstating things just a tad? I'll forgive you because you're biased, but I think you're exaggerating, love."

Ian sat up to his full height. "Taylor, how many of us youth group kids were promised a happily ever after if we just waited for the 'right one,' saved our virginity, and married another Christian?"

My patronizing smile became a thin line.

Ian continued, "How many people go into a Christian marriage just like you did, thinking that they checked off every box but then wake up to a total nightmare? How many of us heard a billion lectures on abstinence but were never taught how to make an actual marriage work? Taylor, I promise, you really do have a story to share. It might not be as dramatic as Rebecca's, but that doesn't make it less valuable or needed."

Tears slipped down my cheeks. Oh, how I wished that I'd seen past the mop on Ian Horner's head and married him three years earlier!

"Taylor, you've been shut down your entire life. You were told by your mother, your brother, and your ex-husband that your feelings didn't matter and you were crazy for how you felt. No, it's not some sociopath pastor molesting children, but how do you think somebody gets to the point where they can preach in a pulpit one second and then commit crimes an hour later? It starts small, and then it grows. Abuse is abuse, and your pain is real, Taylor. It's why you still beat yourself up for cutting your mother out of your life even though you know she's completely toxic for you."

I held up my hand, unable to emotionally process anymore. Ian pressed me tightly to his chest and held me while the watershed of emotion, exhaustion, and years of self-loathing burst forth. His eyebrows raised at my colorful language and occasional fisticuffs with my throw pillows, but he understood my need to release the pain. My husband didn't shrivel at the sight of raw emotion or rush me to finish. Instead, he let me empty myself of every tear before smiling tenderly at me when the cresting emotions subsided.

"Ready to eat?" he asked. He handed me a tissue to blow my nose.

I smiled back sheepishly. "Thank you."

"For what?"

"For listening. For not telling me to shut up. For not trying to fix everything."

Ian stood to his feet then pulled me alongside him. "I love you, Taylor Horner. I'm not everybody else who has hurt you or let you down. You don't deserve to be treated that way, and I made a lifelong promise to cherish and love you."

I reached up to caress the delightful scruff I begged Ian not to shave. "You were the fantasy man they sold us in youth group, Ian. After everything that happened with Mitch, I was convinced guys like you were about as real as the men in my movie queue."

"The kind who leave their smelly socks and shoes in the family room and then wait for you to trip over them?" he asked playfully.

I pulled a face.

"Or the ones who have to be reminded to empty out the coffee filter before it grows mold? What about the kind who forget to put the lid back on the gallon paint can for the nursery and then dry the whole thing out?"

I elbowed him good naturedly. "Yeah, Ian, you're a real monster. Don't forget how you left the toilet seat up yesterday either."

My husband grinned down at me. "See, not so perfect after all."

"Fine, fine," I said with a laugh. "Not perfect, but perfect for me. Happy now, Mr. Humility?"

"Almost," he said and leaned down to kiss me.

The sound of my grumbling stomach tore me away from Ian and his hypothetical kisses. I smiled down at my flat stomach while Ian insisted on bringing our cereal bowls turned pho service ware out into the family room.

"How many times have I forced you to eat pho?" I asked, slurping a noodle into my mouth.

He shrugged. "I don't mind, Taylor."

"But you're looking at thirty-two more weeks of this, so I want you to be honest."

"I can always order something else off the menu, Taylor. I'm just glad there's take-out you can eat without reacting to it."

"No kidding. I'm still trying to prop my eyelids open at work. I alternate between wanting to throw up and wanting to fall asleep at my computer."

"Have you told Phil?"

I shook my head. "Poppy figured it out, but not because I said anything. I think she'll be a good fit for Culver, especially after I'm gone." On a dramatic sigh, I added, "Once again, I'm following in the footsteps of Rebecca Margolin, marketing guru turned full time Mommy."

Ian dropped multiple jalapeño peppers into his bowl. "Are we definite on you staying home with the baby, Taylor? I want to be sure you won't go stir crazy being home all day with no adult conversation."

"Once we sell the townhouse, I'll feel a lot better about it, love. I just don't want you to feel emasculated because I'd be the one paying for our new home."

"Why would I feel emasculated? God gave you a beautiful home, and He's using it to bless us with a new house. I'm not going to turn my nose at an obvious win."

"See? Youth group dream guy," I sing-songed.

"Speaking of, what did you think of the church we visited last week?" Ian asked.

"It was fine right up until you slipped about being the former sound man at Freedom. That one lady wouldn't shut up about Chloe Ross and how wonderful she is."

"I'm impressed you held your tongue, Taylor."

"More like I totally panicked and froze. I don't understand how Chloe can do that church facade so well and then turn around and pull the manipulative horse manure she does behind my back."

Ian shrugged. "Some people are really good at putting on a show when they can get something from it. You saw how quickly my father changed his tune when he thought you came from money. It was disgusting."

"No different than my mother playing Saint Sarah for all of her clients but ignoring her two kids at home. Believe me, Ian, I get it."

He met my gaze and held it. "Taylor, I'm glad you released a lot of this garbage tonight. Do you think it would help to talk to a counselor?"

"Why? Are you already tired of my drama?" I asked only half-kiddingly.

My husband frowned. "I wish you would stop using that word, Taylor. It makes what you've been through sound petty and stupid, and we both know it isn't."

I sobered. "You're right, Ian. It's just hard admitting I've been through agony when I have the draft for Rebecca's manuscript sitting on my phone."

"And that's another thing," he said. He gently pulled my soup bowl away from me so he could hold my hands. "Stop comparing yourself to Rebecca. You know she's got her flaws and issues just like the rest of us."

"Ian, you have to read this," I said, picking up my phone and waving it at him. "Reading Rebecca's story made it even more real than the conversations we've had over the years. There are details she's never mentioned, things about her relationship with Ted I had no idea about."

Ian leveled those irresistible, brown eyes at me. "Stop, Taylor. You don't have to prove your worth to me or anybody else. Do you think God has some kind of a test in heaven, that unless your pain and suffering measure up on the Rebecca-meter, it doesn't count? What makes you think someone reading your story wouldn't feel the exact same way? That they wouldn't look at the story of Taylor Meyers-Ross-Horner and feel completely inadequate?"

"When you put that many last names on it, I sound like a soap opera diva," I teased, hoping to instill some humor.

Ian's grim expression remained. "The television shows crank up the drama, but I don't think anyone could invent a story as cruel as what Chloe said to you when you lost your baby, Taylor. What about the nightmare of Dr. Jekyll and Mr. Ross? My queen, it's okay to admit you were hurt and have a right to be angry. You act like you're unworthy to call yourself an abuse survivor because you weren't physically or sexually abused."

"There's no wiggle room here, is there?"

Ian shook his head. "Taylor, you have to stop denying the hell you've been through just because you think it doesn't compare to someone else's. From the outside looking in, what you've suffered is a nightmare. Even after the divorce, you were still being emotionally tortured at Freedom because that witch did everything in her power to hurt you."

"Witch?" I asked with a raised brow.

"That's the word God gave me a few weeks ago. I was praying specifically about your relationship with Chloe."

Stunned, my voice came out higher than normal. "Really? God actually said that?"

"It shocked me too," Ian said. "I heard myself ask God to break every curse that witch ever spoke over you. The words just flew out of my mouth."

"Wow," I murmured.

"I wouldn't ordinarily call a woman that, so I asked God if I was holding onto any anger or bitterness against Chloe."

"What did He say?" I asked.

"He reminded me that witchcraft is trying to manipulate or coerce a supernatural being into doing what we want."

"Okay," I drawled. "So, how does this apply to Chloe?"

"Chloe said your lack of faith sent your baby to heaven instead of the sovereign will of God. Do you see how demonic and twisted that is? Aside from deliberately shaming you for something you couldn't control, Chloe made a huge, arrogant assumption."

"How? Aren't we supposed to have faith to move mountains?" I asked.

Ian frowned. "Chloe's version of 'faith' means that saying the right prayers or believing the right things *requires* God to do what we want Him to. How is that different from a witch casting a spell or expecting a genie to grant us three wishes? We can have all the faith we want, Taylor, but the Bible is pretty clear that God's still the one in charge. What Chloe said to you was genuinely evil, and not just because of how insensitive it was."

I didn't want to open myself back up to the pain of that day or just how deeply Chloe's words cut to the very heart of me. Though I thought I had cried every tear in me, fresh ones moistened my eyes.

"Taylor, God says we have the power of life and death in our tongue, for blessings and curses. Are witches known for the blessings they pronounce or their curses? There was never anything holy in what that woman intended for you."

"Ever?" I asked weakly. "Even those rare moments of kindness from her? It was all just pettiness and spitefulness the entire time?"

"Do you really have to ask?" Ian said gently. "Chloe told you to go back to your mother because she didn't want you around. What Bible believing, woman of God actually says something like that? Where was the love or compassion, Taylor? Chloe just blew off your feelings because she wanted to remove your beautiful light in that church. If you think about all the accusations Chloe has ever made against you, you'll see she's just talking about herself."

Tempted to crack another joke, I refrained. I felt prompted by the Holy Spirit to grab onto the truth in Ian's words. "This is so hard," I said. "I don't want Chloe to be wrong. I would rather believe I made the mistake somehow."

"Taylor, I don't think anybody wants to believe another person—let alone a family member or Christian—maliciously intends to cause them pain. But Jesus said not everyone who comes to Him with works and wonders is truly one of His followers. Do you remember what He said about the sheep and the goats?"

Very familiar with that passage in *Matthew 7*, I replied, "Jesus said the ones who didn't take care of 'the least of these' didn't take care of Him. Even though they claimed to pray and prophesy and cast out demons in His Name, Jesus said he didn't know them at all."

"Christ said the world will know us by our love for one another," Ian said. "*1 John 4* says we can't love God and hate our brother. We can't intentionally mistreat other people and then call ourselves followers of Christ, let alone our brothers and sisters in the Lord."

"Does that mean Chloe's not really saved?" I asked.

Ian shrugged. "The fruit is rotten, and that's all we can go by. Only God knows for sure. I just want you to stop treating your broken arm like it's a papercut, Taylor. Your pain is real. You don't have to hide it, excuse it, or blame yourself anymore, my queen. Those whom the Son sets free are free indeed."

CHAPTER 33

FOUR WEEKS LATER, I SAT ON A BENCH OUTSIDE OF the office lightly humming and enjoying the fall weather. Our twelve week ultrasound went better than anticipated, and Baby Horner was active with a heartbeat exactly as it should be. Ian and I had stared in wonder at the tiny person on the screen, both of us eager to shower our child with all of the love and affection we had in us to give.

"You're glowing, and from the way you're rubbing your belly, I suppose congratulations are in order."

I met the powder blue gaze that no longer turned my insides into goo. "How are you doing, Kyle?"

He shrugged sadly. "The MacKenzie thing didn't last long. Not that they ever do."

"I hope you're not looking for sympathy."

"I'm not expecting any, if that's what you mean."

"Good."

"You married your perfect Christian guy, right? The one Rebecca wanted you to go out with?"

"What difference does it make to you, Kyle? We barely dated, and that feels like a lifetime ago."

"Maybe for you," he said longingly.

I rolled my eyes. "Cut the baloney, Goldstein."

Kyle's puppy dog expression transformed immediately into surprise and offense.

Irritated, I said, "Don't you ever get tired of playing the victim, Kyle? You stood there like a bump on a log while your sister publicly abused me. You even supplied the information to help her do it! Instead of acting clueless why things didn't work out between us, why don't you get a clue so you can be happy yourself?"

Kyle's mouth opened and shut.

More concerned about his potential future than if Kyle Goldstein liked me or not, I went for broke.

"That thing you find so irresistible about Rebecca and me is Jesus living inside of us. It's also what scared you to death. It kept you from pursuing anything outside of some fantasy with me that never quite touched your heart."

"You don't get to comment on my heart. Not anymore," he grit out. "Did you even cry a single tear over me, Taylor?"

Not about to fall back into that old trap, I said, "It's always about *you*, isn't it, Kyle? You're completely ignoring how you betrayed and abandoned me with your sister. That's why you and Jessica have this crazy, symbiotic relationship, and it has nothing to do with being twins. You boo-hoo and complain and blame the rest of the world for your problems instead of changing yourselves instead."

"I don't have to listen to this," he sniffed haughtily.

"I didn't ask you to come over here!" I shot back.

"All I did was say hello, Taylor. It was totally innocent."

"You came looking for a shoulder to cry on and to hear how

MacKenzie didn't deserve you. You wanted me to feel sorry for you because I'm happy and you're not."

"Thanks for rubbing it in, Taylor. Very Christ-like of you."

Ignoring his insult, I said, "You're unhappy because you act like you have no choice or responsibility for your decisions. You just play the clueless victim who can't figure out why the same things keep *mysteriously* happening to you. The worst part is that you use all of the self-pity to reel in the next, unsuspecting girlfriend who thinks she can help fix you if she just tries hard enough."

Kyle raised his jaw defensively. "I see you've been listening to the Culver gossip."

I stood up, meeting him square in the eyes. My determination was no less great than when I had threatened to pepper spray him in the parking garage. "Grow a backbone, Kyle, and stop pretending you're not responsible for the consequences of your own decisions. You can waste the rest of your life afraid of owning a mistake and actually changing, or you can experience the satisfaction of learning from your failures and conquering your fears. Anything less than that isn't really living. It's existing. And it's a waste of the life God gave you."

"You make it sound so easy."

I scoffed. "Hardly! It hurts. It's work. But it's worth it. You're only going to get back the effort you're willing to put in. That's true in any area of life."

"Are you truly happy, Taylor, or are you just telling yourself that because you've got the husband and the baby you've always wanted?"

Unflinching, I held his eyes. "I am truly happy, Kyle. I still have a long way to go, but I'm finally facing all of the pain and putting it to rest. I owe it to this little person," I said, glancing down at my belly, "and you owe it to yourself to get your act together and be worthy of the kind of woman you really want."

His protective armor of arrogance began to falter. "What is it about you Christians that makes you so frustrating and so fascinating all at the same time? Why aren't you preaching salvation or *Isaiah 53* at me? I can deal with all of that. You and Rebecca...you just cut to the heart of things."

"Jesus spoke to the real needs of people. Lepers wasting away because of their disease didn't need a Biblical dissertation. They needed a Savior who could heal them and would be willing to touch what society called 'unclean.' They wanted to be seen beyond their affliction. How could you *not* love a God willing to do that?"

With that familiar, inscrutable expression, he said, "I'll think about it."

Hearing my phone alarm buzz on the bench behind me, I quietly thanked God for the opportunity to share the Good News of Christ and hopefully bring Kyle the closure He needed. I felt his eyes follow me back inside of the Culver high rise, but I praised God that His plans far exceeded mine.

I bumped into Lexie in the lobby and sighed heavily when I realized we'd be sharing the elevator by ourselves. Not sure whether my father used Lexie as his convenient pawn or if she took it upon herself to push toward reconciliation, I quickly put those sentiments to bed. I had informed Lexie I wanted no part of a relationship where our father put her in the middle to do his dirty work. After a lifetime of triangulating and manipulation from my mother and brother, I refused to step into the same trap all over again.

"I, um, saw you talking to Goldstein," Lexie said quietly once we entered the elevator.

"And?"

Lexie hesitated, my no nonsense tone probably not conducive toward her line of questioning.

"What do you want to know?" I asked, annoyed. "Have I secretly been meeting with Kyle all along? Did we just happen to run into each other? Does my husband know I talked to him today? What's the burning gossip question for the Culver beehive?"

Lexie made a face. "You know, you can be really mean when you want to be, Taylor."

I glared at my adopted/step/non sister. "You're fishing for information that's none of your business, Lexie. Of course, I'm upset. Just because we have a father in common doesn't mean I trust you any more than I did when you let MacKenzie and Julie fill your head with all of their lies about me. If you have a question, then just ask me. If you're going to fish around hoping I'll spill my guts, then you obviously don't know me very well. I'm not trying to be mean. I'm just trying to protect myself and my marriage."

"If you're trying to protect your marriage, then why were you talking to your ex-boyfriend in the first place?" she asked with uncharacteristic moxie.

The elevator doors dinged open with fellow coworkers, and I pulled Lexie into a side hallway before I answered a question that didn't deserve an explanation.

"Kyle Goldstein may be a lot of things," I said, "but he's still a human being. God gave me an opportunity to share about Jesus, and I did. If someone sat there recording our conversation, I would have no problem with my husband or anybody else listening to what I said. I think my husband would actually be pretty proud of me."

Lexie's expression looked penitent, but her mouth remained sealed.

Irritated and eager for the conversation to come to an end, I said, "Is your curiosity satisfied now? Did you get all of the dirt you were hoping for? Do you have enough information to report back to Daddy Dearest, or were you waiting for something else?"

That finally got her mouth moving again. "You know, just because your mother screwed up your relationship with Jonathan Meyers doesn't mean you get to trash mine."

"Jonathan Meyers used and manipulated you in order to crawl back into my life, and I will call the situation exactly as I see it, Lexie. Did my father feed you some song and dance about how I would be jealous of you? That any anger you see is due to my own insecurities?"

From the look on her face, I could see that's exactly what he'd done. Perhaps my parents truly did deserve one another.

Sighing heavily, I said, "Lexie, has it ever occurred to you that my father is utilizing any underhanded method possible in order to get to me? That I might be angry on *your* behalf because he's just using you and has you convinced it's all for a noble cause? My mother has used my brother the same way my entire life. I'd recognize it anywhere."

"He's desperate!" Lexie pleaded. "Sarah took you and Gabe away from him for twenty years! I wasn't lying when I said Dad talked about you and your brother all the time. Can't you see he just wants a chance to know the children that were stolen from him?"

"Stolen?" I choked out. "What effort did Jonathan Meyers make outside of telling you his sob stories? Where was my father when I was raising my brother and going to middle school at the same time? I don't know what kind of father he was to you and your brother, Lexie, but I can only speak from the kind of father he was to me and mine. I don't know how much of what I overheard between my parents was real, but I don't trust either one of them to tell the truth. Frankly, neither should you."

"I just don't understand why you won't give him a chance," she persisted. "What would it hurt? Other than your pride anyway?"

The frustration at Lexie's obstinacy sent my blood pressure soaring. Overcome with a wave of dizziness, I put my hand against the wall to steady myself.

Our argument forgotten, Lexie said, "Taylor? Are you all right?"

Taking a few deep breaths, I finally met her eyes. "No, Lexie. I'm not all right. Nothing you say about Jonathan or Sarah Meyers will ever change my mind about them. All I see is the same manipulative shenanigans from both of them, and I won't discuss this with you anymore. It's not good for me or for my baby."

"I understand," she said tightly.

"Good. I'm going back to my office now. I'll have your proposal revisions done before EOB."

Lexie nodded. "Thanks. I'll tell Kelly we'll have the document ready for our meeting tomorrow morning."

I sent Ian a quick text but focused more on my altercation with Lexie than with Kyle. My husband reminded me that I also owed Phil Robbins a chat because my tiny body was already showing signs of a small bump.

Heart and mind heavy with conflicting thoughts, I ran a hand through my overgrown hair as I entered the office space shared with Poppy. "What do you think?" I asked her and gestured toward my shaggy mane. "Grow it out, or cut it off again?"

She shrugged. "You're the one who has to live with it, but I doubt you're really upset about your hair."

"Do you ever have those days where you wonder if you wound up in the loony bin, but the inmates keep insisting that you're the one who's crazy?"

"So you've met my ex-husband," she deadpanned.

I grinned, despite myself. "I was actually referring to Lexie."

Poppy nodded in understanding. "The older I get, the more I see it's pretty much just everybody."

"I'm not talking about run of the mill dysfunction here."

"Neither am I," she said. "Maybe I'm just getting cynical the closer I get to forty, but I haven't met anyone who doesn't have a horror story about their old nuclear family. It's when you start comparing notes with other people that you find out we all accept way too much as 'normal' behavior when we should be setting boundaries instead."

I studied my new coworker as the threads of silver in her curls attested to well-earned wisdom and complete comfortability in her own skin. Poppy typically wore just enough makeup to pass herself as "professional" without trying to bury herself under tons of cosmetics—not that she needed any. Whether she noticed it or not, I'd caught Joe Trautweig in our benefits department eyeing Poppy with a note of appreciation. I allowed myself a small smile at the thought of Poppy finding love after the disasters she'd shared about her own marriage.

"Taylor?" Poppy asked. "Did you hear a word I said?"

Her question returned me from my musings about Joe and the glances he stole across the break room when Poppy got her morning coffee. "Sorry. I was daydreaming a little. Bad habit."

"Pregnancy brain," she said with a grin. "Get used to it, kiddo. You'll be amazed at what months of sleep deprivation will do to a person."

"I guess I'll find out soon enough," I said, suddenly recalling

Ian's earlier request to email Phil. I drafted a quick message asking for a meeting.

Twenty minutes later, I read his response. *Do I even need to guess? I assume it's a gluten-free bun in the oven.*

I laughed out loud. Phil would forever be unapologetically Phil.

CHAPTER 34

EIGHT WEEKS LATER, I SAT WITH A SHELL SHOCKED Ian as we studied our baby's sonogram pictures in the waiting area of my OBGYN office. Our gender reveal appointment left us with more questions than before.

"What do you want to do?" Ian asked, running his hand over recently shorn hair.

"What do you mean?"

Ian met my gaze. "Well, Fiona already slipped with my parents about the pregnancy, and I can't even imagine what your mother or father will do when they find out the gender."

"Who says they're going to?" I asked. "Just because Gabe is now buddy-buddy with dear old Dad doesn't mean I'm touching that relationship with a ten foot pole."

"You set a boundary with your brother, Taylor, and he's honored it so far."

I rolled my eyes. "Only because he's got a brand new sister and brother instead of a cranky, hormonal basket case who can't stand the sight of Jonathan or Sarah Meyers."

"You're not a basket case," Ian growled. "That's my wife you're talking about."

I smiled despite my frustration with Gabe's perfidious change of heart. I felt like the odd man out all over again, now with two semi-siblings added to the mix.

"Does your CEO have the gift of prophecy?" Ian asked, his eyes glancing back over the printed sonogram photo in wonder.

"That part about leaving Culver and repopulating the earth or the one about being invited to a bris?" I asked.

"Are you really sure you want to do one, Taylor? You said you wanted nothing to do with your father, but having a Jewish ceremony seems to fly in the face of all of that."

"Are you opposed to having a bris?"

"Well, we're not planning to raise our son Jewish, are we?"

"The Margolins make it work somehow. Tabby will lay hands and pray for someone as easily as Rebecca, but she's also counting in Hebrew and loves the wooden Chanukah set I got for her birthday."

Ian paused before responding. "I guess I always thought of it as an either/or kind of thing. I've attended a few Messianic Jewish functions at Beth Shalom, but it was nothing like the holidays we've celebrated with the Margolins or Rebecca's grandparents."

I smiled. "I wonder if my own grandparents were anything like them."

"Lexie confirmed they passed away, right?"

I nodded. "She said her birth father wasn't Jewish and neither is her mother, but my father's parents adopted her and Micah as their own. I guess they thought Gabe and I were a lost cause."

I wiped away hasty tears from my eyes, surprised that rejection from people I couldn't remember still stung. Ian wrapped an arm around me and pulled me close. "We're going to do things differently, Taylor."

I looked into his dark brown eyes. "How, Ian? Aren't we just repeating the same cycle of broken relationships?"

My husband's hands found mine and squeezed them. "The difference is that your parents used you and your brother as pawns. Your mother withheld visitation as a way to punish your dad. Accessing the old court records proved what you overheard in the coffee shop. The problem is we don't know if anything your mother said to get sole custody was actually true. All we know is that she used them against your dad."

"I just don't get it, Ian. My father knows what my mother is like, but he jumped back into a relationship with her anyway. He can't possibly be that naïve or stupid, can he?"

"From what you've told me, it sounds like he blames your mother's selfishness on her disorders instead of her own choices."

I gestured for him to continue his thought.

"For the sake of argument, let's assume your mother is legitimately clueless. If she had any kind of a conscience, any part of her that truly cared about you or your brother, she would feel remorse for hurting you guys. Even if the behavior was on accident, she would at least feel bad about what she'd done. I don't see any of that with Sarah."

"Especially when she claims she just wants us to be happy," I added, thankful for Ian and the validation he provided. "Love, do you think there's any chance of reconciliation with your parents?"

My husband shrugged. "They'll play nice for now, especially since they're proud of passing on the family name. Beyond that, I expect more of the same. Kate used to cry about how my parents criticized her and Fiona about everything. She said they always acted like they knew better."

I frowned. "To be honest, it doesn't seem like that much has changed. Why does your sister feel comfortable with them babysitting Fiona if they made her so miserable?"

"Kate says they came to an understanding, but I think my folks just gave up and realized my sister was going to do what she wanted to do anyway. I wouldn't call my parents *abusive*, but they definitely put some of the 'funk' in dysfunctional."

I ran my hand through Ian's hair before he could do it himself. My husband smiled, then rested his forehead against mine. "Taylor, I don't know why I thought things would get easier after we got married. It seems more complicated now."

I chuckled softly. "Same issues, just more players involved. But you're not alone anymore, and neither am I. So for now, we go home, we pray, we figure out what we can, and the rest we trust God to show us."

Ian kissed me softly. "Sounds like a plan."

After a subdued car ride and several phone calls later, I found myself in a conundrum trying to find a *mohel* willing to circumcise our son. The common objection they gave was my mother not being Jewish. They claimed the Jewish line carried through the mother's mother, not the father. When I cited Ruth and Rahab as Biblical contradictions to their tradition, several of the rabbis laughed condescendingly about my ignorance of Judaism. I felt frustrated and helpless, unsure why I felt so strongly to circumcise my son according to Jewish law when none of the law keepers would help me fulfill the commandment.

"There's got to be at least one rabbi," Ian said, coming up behind me and looking over all of the crossed through names on my checklist. "Maybe one of the more liberal sects?"

I pouted. "It almost makes me wish the Margolins had a boy. At least they could try to call in a favor for me. As it is, Rebecca and little Eva are in the throes of another growth spurt. Rebecca said it finally lets up after the third month."

"Horse before the cart," Ian said with a wry smile. "We need to figure out what we're doing with the circumcision before we get to 'cluster feeding' and all of the other nursing lingo you've told me about."

I returned Ian's smile. "Fine, fine. Back to the bris."

"I know you're not going to renounce Jesus and fake a conversion just to get this done, Taylor, so how are we going to accomplish this?"

"Ian, I know nothing about my heritage, yet I read about these men and women in the Bible that half of me is related to by blood. I want to know more. I *need* to know more. I want to give our son a legacy bigger than the nominal religious upbringing I got from Sarah and Jonathan Meyers."

"What about there being neither Jew nor Greek in Christ?" Ian countered gently.

"You've read *Romans 11*," I said. "It talks about the cultivated and wild olive branches being grafted into a cultivated tree. Even though I know almost zero about Jewish anything, I know enough that circumcision is a sign of the covenant God made with Abraham and his descendants. Regardless of my absentee father, this is part of my bloodline."

"But we can do this in the hospital, Taylor. Dr. Donaldson already said he'd be happy to do the circumcision. He said we could read traditional Jewish prayers if we wanted to and that he's even had to play the part of a mohel for a Messianic couple who couldn't get a rabbi."

"But it's not the eighth day!" I said in frustration. "I want to do this right, Ian. Even if our son is technically one quarter

Jewish, he's still a Jew. If this was all just some religious song and dance, I would just say scrap it, but we both know it's not. I can't explain what God is stirring up in me right now, but I really feel this is from Him."

Ian sat down next to me and studied me. "What can I do to help, Taylor?"

"Pray with me," I said, touched by his concern rather than dismissing my feelings like Mitch would have. "Ever since I read *Genesis 17* a few weeks ago, the Holy Spirit has not let me go about this. Then the warfare ratcheted up with my brother and his wistful text messages about giving Lexie and Micah a chance. If that wasn't bad enough, we have Brian crawling out of the woodwork wanting to discuss the past."

The tender smile on Ian's face hardened. "I'd like to be there for that meeting, Taylor. Chloe's relationship status disappeared on FaceSpace, and now Brian suddenly wants to talk. It just looks bad. Really bad. I wish you would trust me on this."

"Ian, we're just meeting on the park bench outside of my office," I said, trying to reassure him. "It's a wide open place with plenty of witnesses. Anybody could see me or come up and interrupt."

"I still don't like it," he grumbled.

"Look at me," I said, gesturing toward my baby bump. "Clearly, I am very taken and happily married. Whatever is or isn't going on with Chloe is irrelevant. Maybe Brian wants to apologize for how he treated me or for how his wife abused me."

Ian raised his brows. "It's about time you stopped minimizing what she did to you."

I tucked the sides of my mouth into a slight smile. "It's still hard thinking of *abuse* as anything other than some kind of physical or sexual assault."

"Just because it doesn't leave a physical mark, doesn't mean it's not abuse," Ian said. "I've told you that, Rebecca's told you that, and now you've got a paid professional saying the same thing to you in counseling. Taylor, you don't wear the trauma on your body where people can see you've been hurt. Instead, all of the emotional abuse and gaslighting shows up in the warped belief that everything is always your own fault or imagination. The worst part is the people who twisted the Bible to shame for being upset, but they made excuses for the people abusing you."

"But Brian stood up for me," I said, more convinced his rejection resulted from Chloe and her lies.

"I think it's safe to say that Brian falls into the enabler category," Ian said. "I'm glad he stood up for you at least once, but what about the other times when his wife treated you like garbage? Or his brother did? Early midlife crisis, my—"

"I get it," I said, holding up a hand. "Please, don't get yourself worked up over this."

Ian looked outraged, but I knew it was on my behalf. "Brian tried to make you feel sorry for his brother, the monster. Why do you keep making excuses for it?"

I sighed wearily. "I'm getting there, Ian. I just don't see things as black and white as you do."

"You're walking into a trap, Taylor. I don't like that you're bringing our son with you."

I frowned. "Can we drop it for now? I never said I would meet with Brian, only that I would think about it. I don't mind if you're there, Ian. Since this obviously bothers you, maybe it's better that way."

My husband nodded emphatically. "Agreed."

Sighing, I said, "Now that we have that situation settled, can we get back to this list? I printed off a basic search of mohels, but maybe there's another search engine or online Jewish news-paper I could try."

Scanning down my list of Jewish circumcision practitioners, Ian said, "This one," and pointed to a name toward the bottom of the paper.

I glanced over. "What's so special about Rabbi Peretz? Do you know him?"

Ian shook his head. "Nope. But I asked God to show me which one, and this is where my eyes fell."

"Do you think he's going to bend protocol just for us?"

"God says we don't have because we don't ask. All he can say is 'no' and then we're no worse off than we were an hour ago."

I conceded the point. "Fair enough."

"And as far as Brian goes, I know you feel like you need closure on this."

I nodded, waiting for the "but" to follow.

"But," Ian said with a knowing smile, "I want you to be prepared for some kind of sob story. Brian knows you well enough to play on your sympathies and history together."

"I handled Kyle Goldstein just fine. Brian Ross should be a piece of cake."

"Don't underestimate a snake," Ian warned.

"A snake?" I said. "Brian is suddenly a snake?"

"Do you trust me, Taylor?"

"Of course, I trust you."

"Then trust me when I tell you Brian Ross is not the man you thought he was. Something changed about a year after you came to Freedom. I saw it in the extra sermons about tithing and serving in the congregation and the tension between him and Chloe. You'd never know it during the service or after, but

I've heard them go at it when they thought no one else was in the building."

"What about Declan and Kaley? They wouldn't argue in front of the kids like that, would they?"

"What did your parents do, Taylor?"

I scoffed. "Ian, you can't tell me you really think Chloe and Brian are anything like my parents. They're Christians, first of all, and they're in ministry, for second. You don't go into full time ministry if you're as selfish as my parents."

"Didn't Pastor Sociopath just receive multiple life sentences based on all of the child abuse counts against him? That man was in ministry a lot longer than your former in-laws."

"Ian, this is preposterous. Chloe is hardly a saint and neither is Brian, but are you really trying to compare them to that pedophile?"

"I'm just telling you to go in with your eyes open, expect anything, and don't let your guard down."

CHAPTER 35

"OH!" BRIAN SAID IN SURPRISE AS HE SAW ME approaching with Ian. His eyes traveled straight to my rounded belly. "Congratulations," he added, his eyes returning to my face.

"Thanks," Ian replied on my behalf. I saw my husband's look of determination that Brian would not exclude him from the conversation.

"How long ago did this happen?" Brian asked as we joined him on a bench near FBP. His sapphire eyes never left mine as they stared intently.

Ian answered first. "We were married last June and found out we were pregnant in mid-September." He tightened his arm around me, and I squeezed his hand in response. I hoped Ian might relax, but I could feel the tension radiating from him.

"Everything all right?" Brian asked, his eyes darting back and forth between us. "Ian, I'm picking up on some hostility, and I'm not really sure what I've done to deserve it."

Ian scowled. "Why did you want to meet with my wife?"

"First off, I had no idea you guys got married, let alone that Taylor is pregnant. Congratulations, by the way," he said, eyes shifting to me. "You have to know how happy I am for you."

I nodded, beginning to wonder if Brian's unease had to do with Ian's glare or the fact our meeting did not go as originally planned.

"Are you here to apologize to Taylor for the way you and Chloe blacklisted her from Freedom? For the way your wife slandered mine any time her back was turned? For the way she ambushed Taylor and conned Sarah into showing up at services so Taylor would leave?"

Brian's eyes widened with each accusation. He cleared his throat, obviously searching for an answer.

"Well?" I asked. "You can't pretend you didn't know, Brian. Chloe never hid her contempt for me. I imagine it was even worse behind closed doors."

"Chloe is not the easiest person to get along with," Brian admitted, "but she's still my wife, and I would appreciate you both speaking about her with some respect."

"Please, tell me where we spoke with any disrespect," Ian said angrily. "I stated facts, Brian, not a character assassination. I personally witnessed your wife do all of those things. Ask your former children's ministry director about the lies Chloe spread about Taylor."

"I can't say I was surprised when Genevieve left Freedom after she started dating your brother," Brian said to me with mild accusation.

My jaw fell open while Ian's grip on my hand strengthened. I squeezed one time as I began to see what I had been blind to before. Ian squeezed back, ready to let me go to battle.

"Brian, are you planning to take responsibility for anything?"

I asked. "Or at the very least, admit that your wife treated me horribly while you stood aside and did nothing?"

"I don't consider your thirtieth birthday party *nothing*," he said coolly.

"That was about my mother humiliating me, not Chloe. After your wife trivialized the entire fiasco, she sulked in the corner like a three year-old because you dared to defend me."

"Taylor, I didn't come here to talk to you about Chloe, and it saddens me to see how much bitterness and unforgiveness you hold against my wife. Chloe loves you. I don't understand how you could doubt that."

Feeling the lid on my temper beginning to rattle free, I squeezed Ian's hand twice, requesting back up.

"Spare us the self-righteous guilt trips," Ian said. "What do you want with my wife? What are these 'things from the past' you need to discuss with her?"

"It has to do with my brother."

"What about him?" Ian snarled.

Brian's eyes widened. "Maybe we should talk about some of your anger issues instead, Ian. I'm sure that can't be good for Taylor or your baby."

"Stop trying to manipulate us!" I snapped, glaring at my former brother-in-law. "I know what you're doing, and it's not going to work."

Brian pressed his lips together, anger sparkling in his eyes.

At his petulant silence, I continued, "Why did Chloe delete her relationship status on FaceSpace? Why did you want to meet with me alone after you blocked me for over a year? My husband thinks you have some sort of crush on me, and I know for a fact your wife felt that way."

"She said what?" Brian bellowed, his face reddening. "When did Chloe ever say something as ludicrous as that?"

"It was the first day I met Ian at Freedom. She accused me of trying to visit the sins of one Ross brother onto the other. She got upset when she found out the morning sickness advice you gave her actually came from me. Whatever you've told her about me has her seeing green with envy."

"Taylor, I have always looked at you like a sister. You know that!" Brian insisted.

"Then why am I here?" I asked, my eyes drilling into his. "You still haven't answered the question, and frankly, I'm beginning to wonder if Chloe isn't hiding behind a bush somewhere recording everything."

"She left me!" Brian wailed. "She took off and left the kids behind. Taylor, I hoped you might have some answers about why. I love my wife. I don't understand what happened!".

"Were you looking for Taylor to comfort you?" Ian asked. "For her to be that soft shoulder you could pour your soul into? You commiserate about Chloe, she opens up about your brother, and then you two find solace in each other's arms?"

Brian looked as though he'd been slapped. "Didn't you hear what I just said? My wife left me. My kids are going crazy without their mother there, and I'm in over my head."

"So you're looking for a babysitter?" I asked incredulously.

Brian averted his gaze. "You're practically their aunt, Taylor. I thought you'd want to help. The kids need some sort of stable female in their lives right now." His eyes came back up pleading with mine. "I know Chloe hasn't always been kind, but couldn't you help out a little? For the innocent kids involved?"

"Are you insane?" I cried, rising to my feet. "Are you seriously that selfish? That completely delusional?"

Brian's cajoling quickly gave way to offense. "I never thought my brother might actually be telling the truth about you, Taylor. You're giving your mother a real run for her money right now."

The feral growl in my ears did not start with my husband, but with me. I felt Ian's hand on my arm, restraining me from leaping at my former brother-in-law. Instead, Ian stood up next to me and pulled me behind him.

"This conversation is over," my husband said, using all six feet and four inches to his advantage. "I don't know what happened to the man I used to respect as my pastor or if you've always been this conniving, little weasel, but you will never talk to my wife that way again." Turning to me, Ian said, "Ready to go?"

Taking one last look at Brian and his self-pitying, stooped shouldered posture, I shook my head in disgust. "I can't believe I ever thought of you as a brother. What a joke! The real victims are Declan and Kaley, the two, innocent children who have such messed up, selfish monsters for parents."

"If you care so much about my kids, *Aunt Taylor*, why can't you help out so that Chloe and I can work on our marriage? Don't you want your niece and nephew to grow up with two parents? How can you abandon them when you just admitted they're the real victims in all of this? Do you want them to end up like you and your brother did?"

Ian growled. "Taylor, we're leaving. Now."

I squeezed his hand one time, and he looked into my eyes. "Ian, I can't leave yet."

"You don't owe him anything," he said low.

"No, I owe him *this*," I replied, my eyes flashing in anger. Ian took note with a smirk and extended his hand for me to unburden myself.

I stepped forward and kept my hand held firmly in my Ian's. "Do any of you insane Ross's understand that I am a real person and not some toaster oven that exists solely for your convenience? My purpose in life isn't making *your* lives easier. First, you tell me this conversation is about Mitch and then you launch into your woe is me story about Chloe. Which is it?" I demanded.

The haunted look on Brian's face surprised me. "Chloe didn't just leave me, Taylor. She left me for my brother. Mitch blew back in town and swept Chloe up with him. If you sit back down, I'll tell you everything."

Two hours later, Ian and I walked numbly through the mall. My mind feverishly tried to reconcile Brian's tale, my mother's story of her run-in with Mitch in Vegas, and the heart breaking devastation for all of the Ross cousins no matter whose story proved true.

"I don't think I've ever wanted to self-medicate with ice cream more in my life," I said, practically drooling over the gourmet ice cream vendor in the food court. "Can I pretend for just ten minutes that the sugar in the double chocolate, death by fudgy goodness won't leave me clawing at my hands in a half an hour? That I won't be doubled over wanting to hurl from the dairy or feel the instant throbbing in my low back?"

Ian raised an eyebrow and half a smile. "All that agony for just a little bit of chocolate?"

"It's been a rough day," I said. "Nothing makes sense anymore. I can't tell who's lying because nobody's stories add up. Everyone involved is trying to use or manipulate me somehow."

"Do you think there's any way to unravel all of it?" Ian asked, gesturing toward a small table. He pulled out a chair for me before he slumped down in the other with a weary sigh.

"You look as tired as I feel," I said.

"Taylor, I don't know how any of them keep track of so many lies. My head hurts just trying to piece it all together. Can you break it down one more time, please?"

I paused and tried to assemble as many of the puzzle pieces together as I could. "First, we have my mother's story about running into Mitch in Las Vegas. The original version was he wanted me back and his love child now resides with the grandparents. Version 2.0, courtesy of my brother, my mother was vacationing with 'Barry,' and she saw Mitch, his mistress, his love child, and another little one on the way."

"Version 3.0," Ian continued for me, "Mitch is shacked up somewhere with his brother's wife, we have no idea what happened to his child, and Chloe abandoned her own family. Taylor, I think you might just give Rebecca Margolin a run for her money."

I smirked and rolled my eyes. "None of this makes any sense, Ian. Chloe only ever mentioned Mitch when she told me to stop talking about him at church. She said people would associate his adultery with beloved Pastor Brian."

"A little too ironic, don't you think?"

I exhaled a heavy breath. "Why is any of this *my* drama to sort through?"

"It's not," Ian said, his dark eyes levelling mine. "Brian wants to rope you into his marital problems because he thinks he's entitled to do it. He's trying to use your compassion and empathy against you because of your history of abandonment with your own parents."

"You're right," I said, "and that's pretty sick using his own kids."

"I told you. He's a snake."

"Do you think he's lying?" I asked. "Do you think the need for childcare is real but only to help enable him to do something worse?"

"Well, it's not like we can ask Mrs. Ross what happened."

"I can try texting her," I said. "Unless Chloe's changed her cell number recently, I might be able to get through."

Ian raised an eyebrow. "Do you really think that's wise, Taylor? More than that, do you think Chloe will treat you any differently than she has the entire time you've known her? Don't let them drag you into their self-made misery. You don't need the stress, and frankly, all of their drama is none of our business."

"Mitch was my husband, Ian."

"Not anymore," he growled. "You are not responsible for him, your former in-laws, or the children involved, sad as it is."

"Declan and Kaley are so young, younger than Gabe and I were. I don't want to live with the guilt that their entire lives could be screwed up and I chose not to help."

Ian grabbed my hands from across the table. "Taylor, you are not Jesus. God hasn't asked you to be the savior of the world and take on everyone else's burdens as your own. The situation is a nightmare, but this isn't your problem to solve."

"How do we know God isn't asking us to help these innocent children?"

"Taylor, do you think Brian and Chloe will just hand their kids over for us to raise? I understand why you feel a burden for Declan and Kaley, but the answer is no."

"No?" I squeaked.

"No," Ian said more sternly. "We don't know the details of what's actually going on, and the responsibility for these children belongs to Brian and Chloe. If need be, the grandparents may have to get involved, but you were done with the Ross family when you signed those divorce papers four years ago."

I mulled over Ian's words, comforted that Chloe's parents, Ron and Deborah Jensen, were good people whose fault lay in pampering their only daughter.

"Why do I feel so selfish for not helping?" I asked.

"Because you're being manipulated," Ian said flatly. "Because you were trained to believe you need to be everyone's caretaker, and Brian knows it."

"But is it wrong in this case?" I asked as tears welled in my eyes. "Ian, the kids."

"Look, we don't know if God will use us to help in some other way, but we can't say He's asked us to do anything other than pray and seek His will. Your mother, your brother, and Brian have all blown off your feelings and shamed you for not bowing to their agenda, Taylor. I can't shake the feeling that we don't have the whole story, and I'm not willing to make a decision regarding Declan and Kaley until we've prayed about it together and start seeing the truth of what's actually going on. Who knows? Maybe Chloe will reach out to you."

I scoffed. "If she's shacked up with Mitch, the only thing she'd do is rub it in my face."

"Wouldn't it be something if Chloe was no more the villain in this story than you were?"

I gave Ian a sidelong glance. "Are you now saying there's a heart-wrenching excuse for all of the hurt Chloe's caused me? Do not start quoting me the 'hurting people hurt people' kumbaya nonsense. The last thing I need is to start throwing up again."

Ignoring my sarcasm, Ian replied, "You know I would never make excuses for someone hurting you, Taylor. Especially Chloe. You've seen me defend you enough times to know that."

I nodded. "You're right. I'm sorry."

"All I'm saying, my queen, is things may not always be what they appear to be on the surface."

CHAPTER 36

MY PREGNANCY PROGRESSED RATHER UNEVENTFULLY after that, and I thanked God for the quiet on all fronts. Returning the favor for her own baby shower, Rebecca, Miss Belle, and Poppy concocted the most adorable, boy-themed baby shower in existence. Poppy turned blue balloons into teddy bears complete with sharpie drawn faces, and Rebecca created cupcakes specific for my dietary issues.

"I know they're not that pretty," she said, gesturing toward the tower of mini vanilla cakes covered in chocolate ganache, "but they taste good. Ted and Tabby tried a few, and they're Margolin approved."

I grinned at my friend. "I don't know where you found these cupcake picks, but I love the blue bears. You will hear no complaints from me. I am so grateful for all of this. You have to know that."

Rebecca returned my smile with one of her own. "I know, I know. I just wanted them to be perfect for your shower. When you can't use confectioners' sugar or any sweetener besides maple syrup or honey, it feels like asking the laws of physics to reorder themselves. I need to play with my recipe."

"So, that icing recipe with dates didn't work?" I asked.

Rebecca shook her head. "I may try again next time, but Eva only started sleeping through the night a few weeks ago. My brain and body are still catching up from all of the exhaustion."

"Six months is a long time to be nursing every two hours, my friend. If you didn't already have my admiration, you have it now."

Mrs. Margolin promptly yawned. "Case in point," she said around a grin.

"Are we ready to celebrate?" Miss Belle asked, coming behind me and wrapping an arm around my shoulders. "I can't wait to hear all of the ladies ooh and ah over all the little man clothes you're gonna get."

Lexie surprised me by entering the break room with a medium sized gift bag and an envelope in distinctly masculine handwriting. She and I had barely spoken since our disagreement by the elevators months earlier.

"I hope you're not using my shower as a pretext to do your father's dirty work," I said curtly.

Lexie looked hurt. "I'm not surprised you'd think that, Taylor, but this isn't from our father. The gift is from me and Blake," she said, "and the envelope is from my brother, Micah. Even though you made it very clear you want nothing to do with us, we still consider you family. Gabe shared a lot of your story, and we understand that you've been hurt."

I steeled myself against the fury of my brother's betrayal. "Thank you for the gifts," I said through gritted teeth. "I have no idea what my brother said, but I can't help feeling like he violated my privacy."

Lexie surprised me by agreeing. "I get that, Taylor. I know it won't do much good hearing that your brother just wants to help, but that's where his heart is at. He and Dad hashed through a lot, and they're making peace with the past and starting a new relationship."

"If that's what Gabe wants, then I'm happy for him," I said in a clipped tone. I shifted my body toward the cupcake tower.

Taking the hint, she said, "I just want you to know that the gifts aren't a bribe or anything. We sincerely want the chance to get to know you, Taylor. I know we're not technically related anymore, but sometimes we get to make our own family."

"Time to do a word scramble!" Poppy announced to the party goers all enjoying their finger foods.

"I'm here if you want to talk," Lexie said quietly. She placed her gifts on the side table and exited the room.

"What was that about?" Rebecca said as she approached me. "Did she come to ruin your shower?"

"Not intentionally," I replied, wiping away a tear, "at least I hope not." Taking a deep breath and forcing a smile on my face, I resolved to enjoy the rest of Baby Horner's celebration. As predicted, there was plenty of oohing and aahing to be had, especially when I opened the layette purchased by my step/non sister. Rebecca watched me struggle and offered a sympathetic smile. When Ian came to pick me up along with all of our gifts, I finally let loose the tears I had kept at bay most of the afternoon.

"I don't care what she says," Ian said, bringing the last load of presents into our family room, "Lexie could have given that stuff to you privately instead of making you open it up in front of everyone. Even if it wasn't malicious, it was still thoughtless and selfish."

"And I look like a jerk for turning down a gift, right?"

Ian nodded in the affirmative. "How do we know your parents weren't involved in any of the gifts?"

"We don't," I said, "but if Johnathan Meyers was trying to get in my good graces, I don't think he'd do it going halfsies on a twenty dollar outfit. Then again, that's all speculation on my part."

"The gift card from Micah was nice," Ian said, depositing a boxed high chair in the kitchen. "If you don't feel comfortable taking it, I'm sure we can find someone who could use the store credit."

"Maybe Rebecca knows someone at the church they've been visiting," I said. "I'm glad the Margolins are looking again, but Rebecca says she feels like they're searching for something that may not exist. I asked if she and Ted had considered starting their own home group or Bible study."

"With a two year-old and a baby?" Ian asked. "That's a tall order, Taylor, and Ted is still a new believer. Rebecca has the training, but are they comfortable with Rebecca leading the group?"

I shrugged my shoulders before struggling to stand up from the couch.

Ian glanced over at me. "Are you feeling okay? I know you haven't been sleeping well the past few weeks. Are you sure you'll get even bigger than you already are?"

I pulled a face. "I'm going to assume you're not calling me fat."

My husband cocked a grin at me. "Well, it's not true anyway, but no, I'm not looking for an untimely demise. My sister called you 'all baby,' and you are, my queen. She also said you were a very cute pregnant lady."

I rolled my eyes. "I think it's written somewhere you can

only say kind and encouraging things to pregnant women, no matter how fat, bloated, or gross we feel."

Ian walked over to me and placed his hands gently on my shoulders. "You're beautiful, Taylor. You're even more beautiful carrying our son in your belly. If we can just agree on a name, that's all we have left to do."

"Other than meeting with Rabbi Peretz."

"At least he's willing to do the circumcision, Taylor. That was a huge answer to prayer."

I grimaced. "It would have been easier if he didn't know my father personally, but I suppose I can at least thank Jonathan Meyers for that favor. Some days, I wonder about talking to my father and getting to the bottom of what happened. If for nothing else, then for my own peace of mind. I can't help but be a little jealous of the relationship he has with my brother. Then, I wonder at the cost of welcoming Jonathan Meyers back into my life after all this time. I'm almost positive he had something to do with helping me get into this house. Part of me feels like it defiles my home, but another part is secretly grateful he found some way to take care of me. Does that make sense, love?"

Ian cupped the side of my face. "Perfect sense, my queen. I know you didn't pick these people to be your family, but they are. Did you ever confirm if your dad put Lexie up to talking to you a few months ago?"

I suddenly remembered exactly why I wanted no reconciliation with my father. "Oh, please! It was so obvious he came to her with his sob story to manipulate her. I've already dealt with that insanity with my mother and Gabe. I'm too old to fall for it again."

"Don't bite my head off for suggesting this," Ian said, eyeing me warily, "but is it possible you made an assumption about your father based on all of the emotional abuse from your mother?"

That gave me pause. "Do you think I should hear my father out?" I asked.

Instead of answering me, my husband reached for my hands to pray. He prayed for guidance from the Lord on what to do, for protection from any more deception, and for the truth to be revealed. Baby Horner joined us by kicking repeatedly, so much so, Ian chuckled softly.

"I think that's an amen from our son," Ian said, dark eyes glowing at me.

"If I decide to do this, I want you there, Ian. And Gabe too. Who knows what version of the truth Jonathan Meyers has already spun for my brother? I want both of you there as witnesses if things play out exactly like they did with my mother last year. At least I'd finally have the confirmation I need that going 'no contact' with all of these toxic grandparents was exactly the right decision for us and our son."

"The decision is still ours to make, Taylor, whether your brother agrees with it or not. This is our marriage and our family. Gabe...Lexie...my parents...your parents...none of them get to dictate what decisions we make. We will do what's best for us and our family, regardless of what they think."

"And they'll keep calling me selfish for doing it," I said bitterly.

"So what?" Ian said. "Let them think what they want. When our family members finally show respect and concern for your feelings instead of just demanding it for their own, then I might take their wishes into consideration. My job is to protect my wife—not cater to everyone else telling me how to 'handle' you or our marriage."

"Don't even get me started," I said angrily. "My brother who *loves* me thought that commiserating with you about how horrible I am would make you trust him. For a guy who always claims he doesn't want to get in the middle, Gabe sure has a funny way of showing it, doesn't he?"

"Tell me again why you want him there, Taylor. You're still furious."

"Why aren't you?" I demanded.

Ian raised a brow. "Because I told Gabe he was completely out of line and to never talk about my wife that way again. He apologized immediately."

"Yeah. To *you*," I said. "I'm still waiting for my own apology, Ian."

"Sweetheart, you're going to have to forgive him whether you ever get one or not, and don't look at me like that," he said, taking note of my readiness to breathe fire. "I didn't say sweep it under the rug or pretend it didn't happen. Gabe absolutely owes you an apology. I haven't forgotten, but we both know you're upset about a lot more than this one incident."

I pursed my lips. "I have every right to be."

Ian ran his hands up and down my arms soothingly. "You're the one who said you wanted your brother to be there, Taylor. If you go in looking daggers at him, he won't hear anything you have to say."

"Not that he listens to anything I have to say anyway," I said morosely. "Maybe it was a stupid idea. I don't need the stress right now. I'm not sure what I was thinking."

"Taylor, can you make peace with the idea you may never get the answers you're looking for? Can you trust God to bring everything to light when *He's* ready and not when you are?"

"What's wrong with wanting answers?" I said through tears of defeat. "Don't I deserve that much for all of the hell these people deliberately put me through? Don't I deserve some kind of justice for all of the ways I've been slandered and wrongfully accused?"

"Yes!" my husband said emphatically. "But we are about to welcome a healthy baby boy into our family. We're going to put an end to all of the dysfunction and abuse on both sides of our family and give our son a very different legacy. Taylor, if you want, I can even look into that job transfer my company offered to South Florida. It gets us out of here, and we can build a new life away from all of this mess."

"Tempting," I said. "But I heard the roaches fly down there."

Ian shrugged. "But you'd have the beach, warm weather year round, and they've even opened up Joey's Real Food in East Palm Bay."

"I can't run away from my problems, Ian. It's cowardly."

My husband frowned. "Living in constant fear and anxiety you're going to run into one of your family members is no way to live, Taylor."

"What about Kate and Fiona? What about the Margolins?"

"What about them?" Ian asked.

"Well, aren't you going to miss them?"

"You know, they do have these wonderful inventions called 'airplanes' and 'cars' that make it pretty easy to travel long distances," he said.

"I'll think about it."

CHAPTER 37

NOT ONLY DID I THINK ABOUT IT, BUT I PRAYED ABOUT Ian's suggestion that we relocate and start over. Given the price of housing in South Florida, any proceeds from the sale of my townhouse would go directly into the cost of securing a small home for ourselves rather than fretting over capital gains taxes if we stayed locally. Though too far along in my pregnancy to travel, Ian's company flew him down for a few days to their East Palm office to see how he liked the new terrain. He even sent me listings of a few available homes in the area, and the sticker shock reminded me this wasn't Hillcrest or Winthrope. As a joke, Ian sent me a selfie outside of the promised Joey's Real Food, reminding me I would still have some traces of "home" if we decided to move.

The more I fought the idea of moving and reprimanded myself for even considering it, the more I felt the Holy Spirit encouraging me to trust Him. Eschewing my tendency to go running to Rebecca for advice, I simply asked her to pray for direction.

The Margolins invited us to attend their annual Passover seder, and Rebecca promised to come up with allergen free alternatives to anything we ate. She wanted us to have recipes we could use should we decide to incorporate more of my Jewish heritage into our own family traditions.

"Do you think it's a sign from God?" Ian asked, helping me out of the car. I leaned heavily on his arm.

"What is?" I said, panting.

My husband glanced down at me in concern. "You all right?"

"Our son has his feet in my ribs, and he's running out of space."

"Are you sure you feel okay?"

I waved him off. "Just tired, Ian. It's all normal. I've been told the last month of pregnancy feels like the longest. Poppy said the pain of labor doesn't seem so bad when it means you can finally get your body back."

Ian chuckled. "I can't imagine."

"No. No, you can't. But we've got less than four weeks before my due date, and my last day at Culver is this Friday. I think I'm going to enjoy sitting around the house folding baby clothes and not thinking about RFPs or annual reports for a while."

"Do we have a decision about South Florida?" he asked, guiding me toward the front door of Ted's parents' home.

"I'm still thinking and praying about it."

"HR needs to know within the next week, so we have to give them an answer."

"Your wife is about to have a baby. I'm not moving to South Florida with a newborn, and there's no way I'm going to have the time or energy to pack up our house now or for the foreseeable future. It's not impossible, but I want to be realistic with how much transition we can handle. Can they give us a few more months to decide? Could you work remotely until moving is a more viable option? We'd still have to get my house ready to sell, put it on the market, and then hope there's a buyer."

Ian gave me a knowing smile. "Well, it sounds like we have our decision then."

Still unsure, I said, "I'm not trying to complain or make excuses, love. I just don't see how we could legitimately pull this off unless we had absolutely no other option."

My husband nodded and rang the doorbell.

Ted opened the door and welcomed Ian and me into the Margolin family mayhem. He shook hands with Ian and greeted me with an almost apologetic smile when I winced at the volume level of the house. I could barely hear above the din of children screaming, laughing, a little one crying, and intermittent admonitions from parents to their respective offspring.

"Taylor!" Rebecca called as she approached us with her megawatt smile. She gestured toward my hugely distended belly. "Look at you! You must be so ready to get that munchkin out of there."

I sighed and grinned. "It's definitely beginning to feel that way."

Greeting Ian with a side hug and a quick kiss on the cheek, Rebecca ushered us through the Margolin grandparents' entryway toward their dining room. The table was beautifully set with a second table extending into the adjoining living room.

"How can you possibly cook for this many people?" I asked close to Rebecca's ear.

"We all pitch in," she said. "Rose would take all of this on her own shoulders if we let her, so we make sure she doesn't."

"Are your grandparents coming?" I asked, looking around for Tabby and Lou Wasserman.

Rebecca shook her head. "My grandfather's recovering from a pretty serious bout of bronchitis, so Nana's playing nursemaid and shoveling matzah ball soup down his throat."

"That's a shame. I really enjoyed meeting them during Chanukah. Your grandmother is a riot."

Rebecca grinned wider and struck me with her beauty.

"What?" she said.

I waved her off. "Nothing. Where are your kiddos?"

Rebecca gestured beyond the dining room, and I surmised a family room or rec room provided the noise permeating throughout the house. She guided me into a small guest bedroom so we could talk for a few minutes in quiet.

"It's chaotic, but I wouldn't change a thing!" she said brightly.

"Really?"

Rebecca nodded. "Any get together at my parents' house always felt so cold, like visiting a museum. I know it gets loud, especially with my babies added to the mix, but this is the kind of family I always wished for growing up."

I smiled sadly. "I understand. My brother finally found his missing father figure, but I can't help feeling like he'll get his heart broken when he realizes Jonathan Meyers is no better than my mother."

"What about the non-siblings?" she asked.

I shrugged. "Lexie's convinced my father walks on water even though she knows he cheated on her mother with mine. I think she understands what happened intellectually, but she still has this rose tinted view of Jonathan Meyers. She'll rationalize anything he does so long as she doesn't have to take him off the pedestal."

Rebecca frowned. "Cognitive dissonance. I'm familiar with the predicament. My sister would rather blame Bud Riley for exposing the family secrets rather than admit the family secrets are what landed my parents in jail. Meanwhile, she's more than happy living it up in the Ivy Palace."

"Have you heard from your sister lately?"

Rebecca shook her head. "No, and I'm counting my blessings. I have no idea what's going on with my brother at all. Nobody's heard from him. We don't know if he's even dead or alive."

"That's sad."

My friend sighed heavily. "It is what it is. I've had to make peace with reality and trust God for the rest. I did finally meet up with my aunt a few days ago. I think time away from my mother helped her detox and see things more clearly. She apologized to me the entire time. I was pretty shocked."

"Wow."

"That's what my husband said. We have a tentative lunch scheduled with her after Passover. She said she wanted to meet her great nieces and regrets not having children or grandchildren."

"Sounds like God is doing some amazing things with your family."

"So, what about yours?" Rebecca asked. "Are you going to meet with your father?"

"Interestingly enough, I came up with another idea."

Rebecca raised an eyebrow. "Do tell."

"I have a meeting scheduled with Rabbi Peretz to discuss the bris. Obviously, we don't know when Baby Horner will arrive, but given how tiny I am, there's a good chance I won't make it to forty weeks. Rabbi Peretz says he knew my father, so I'm hoping he might have some information for me. He has no reason to lie that I'm aware of."

"So you'll see what he says, and then take it from there?" my friend asked astutely.

I nodded.

Poking his head in the door, Ian said, "Ted said I might find you two in here. They're ready to start the seder."

Rebecca glanced over to the digital, bedside clock. "A seder that actually starts on time? This night really *is* different from all others!"

At the puzzled look on our faces, Rebecca chuckled and said, "It'll make more sense in about ninety minutes."

Never having sat through a Passover meal before, I marveled at the ceremony and the obvious parallels to Jesus. Ted's mother, Rose, explained how the bread and wine normally taken for communion coincided with specific parts of the seder. The body of Christ represented by the *afikoman* matzah—the center of three matzah pieces—was broken, wrapped in white linen, hidden, and then found by a child. Once found, the hidden piece was then shared among the table as a type of "dessert." Noting the brown spots and holes poked inside of the store bought matzah as well as the gluten free version Rebecca had baked for me, I better understood the passage from *Isaiah 53:6* about God's suffering servant being bruised and pierced for our sins. It made sense why Jesus used the unleavened bread of matzah to illustrate his sinless sacrifice for all mankind.

Of the four cups of wine normally partaken during the meal, the communion cup was the cup of redemption, again, unmistakably pointing to the death and resurrection of Jesus. Steve and the other Margolin aunts and uncles shifted uncomfortably during Rose's explanation—even more so when Rebecca elaborated for me and Ian—but Ted beamed at his wife. He shifted baby Eva in his arms and offered Rebecca a small respite before the little one needed to nurse again.

Ian's eyes grew wider with each revelation and he looked at me in wonder.

"Now, do you understand why I want a bris?" I whispered close to his ear. "I know this might be rote tradition or ceremony for some people, but I see Jesus in all of it, love. I don't think we'll ever read about the Last Supper the same way again."

Ian met my gaze. "How did we go through life not knowing any of this? How did I come to faith not knowing the laws Jesus fulfilled?"

I smiled gently at my husband. "We're all sinners saved by grace, Ian. Knowing or practicing the Jewish traditions won't make us 'better' Christians, but it should make us even more in awe of God."

"I want this," he said fervently, looking to the table at large. "Taylor, I want to do Passover in our home. I want to learn about the other feasts. These are God's holidays, and we aren't celebrating any of them."

I cupped his face in my palms. "*Romans 11,* love. This is now part of your heritage too. We're all grafted into the same cultivated olive tree. It's there if you want it."

Ian nodded and briefly kissed my lips.

"No baby making at the table!" Steve playfully said.

All three of his grown children cringed while Rose slapped his arm.

"Is that where babies come from?" one of the young cousins asked her mother.

The uncomfortable pause was followed by a rapid succession of conversation that made for an unforgettable evening. By the end though, I found myself exhausted and eager to remove my elastic belly pants.

Sitting with Rabbi Peretz ten days later, I didn't mince words asking about my father. He shared what he knew with equal candor, shocking me with news that my mother underwent a formal Jewish conversion to marry my father. Even under rabbinic law, I was considered fully Jewish. More than that, he finally shed light on the demise of my parents' marriage.

"She had an affair with your son?" I asked, barely able to control my emotions.

Rabbi Peretz nodded grimly. "And we shunned Sarah for it."

"Then, why help her daughter all these years later? Don't you have an image to protect? After all, who wants to believe the rabbi's son is sowing illegitimate children around the synagogue and ruining marriages?" I said bitterly, throwing the rabbi's admission back in his face.

Rabbi Peretz looked appropriately aggrieved. "It was wrong, and my selfish denial caused both of your parents to turn their backs on Judaism. For years, I ignored Yossi's womanizing. I made allowances for his behavior even though I knew better. It's a regret I've had to live with for a very long time."

"I see," I said tightly, "but I want you to know that my mother turning her back on Judaism is what allowed me to become a Christian. I don't regret that decision."

"*Nu?* Then why are we sitting here talking about your son's circumcision, Taylor? Most rabbis would have walked out the door the second you mentioned Jesus. Obviously, there's something you want from me besides information about your parents."

The rabbi's blunt honesty brought a smile to my lips. "I may not fully understand what being Jewish is all about, but this is part of my heritage and my son's too. I will not give my child the same legacy my parents gave me."

Rabbi Peretz returned my smile with compassion. "If I can make amends and do some kind of *mitzvah* for the children of

Jonathan and Sarah Meyers, then may *Hashem* finally free me from the guilt weighing on me these past twenty-five years. Taylor, it's the least I can do for my part in the suffering caused to you and your brother"

"Then, I pray that God grants you the peace you need, Rabbi."

CHAPTER 38

"I'M SURPRISED YOU AGREED TO MEET WITH ME," MY father said as he glanced around my family room. "I'm even more surprised you invited me into your home."

"Did you help pay for it?" I asked. "Did my mother win this Triple J enclave because of her connection to you?"

My father shook his head. "No, I had nothing to do with this one. I helped your mother secure the community she lives in now, but she got the townhouses on her own. She did it totally for you, Taylor. Your mother loves you...in her own way."

"Why should I believe you?"

"You shouldn't, and you have no reason to," he answered matter-of-factly. "Your mother and I have been lying to everyone for a long time. I wouldn't expect you to believe anything I say, yet here I am."

"I met with Rabbi Peretz four days ago," I said. "He told me about Mom and Yossi."

My father's mouth hardened into a thin line. "What exactly did the good rabbi say about his beloved *boychik*?"

"He said he's been tormented by his sin for the past quarter of a century and wants to do right by me and my child."

My father looked visibly shocked.

"When was I ever going to find out Mom converted to Judaism? That Gabe and I both have Hebrew naming certificates buried in the *Temple Yisrael* archives?"

"Your mother said you became a Christian after we divorced. It seemed like a moot point."

"Why? Because you think it's impossible to be Jewish and believe in Jesus?"

"No," he said, "because your mother and I rejected religion when we saw the hypocrisy of these people. Yossi Peretz went out deflowering the daughters in the synagogue—including my wife—but they blamed your mother for the affair. They made Yossi look like the innocent lamb who didn't know any better. I'm sure your mother has told you how many of her boyfriends were regular churchgoers."

"Religious people being hypocrites doesn't excuse her own, willful choices," I said. "It makes you no better than Rabbi Peretz trying to shift the blame."

"I'm just explaining why your mother turned her back on religion," my father said tautly. "It's hardly the same thing."

"It doesn't change her disgusting behavior or rubbing it in my face. My mother has bragged about her sexual conquests since I was a teenager. She's slept with plenty of religious hypocrites and acts like she's making their marriages *easier* with her debauchery."

"Debauchery?" my father repeated mockingly. "I suppose this is the English Literature degree rearing its ugly head."

"Don't patronize me," I snapped. "You can pick at my words all you want, but it doesn't change my mother's behavior."

"Your mother isn't well, Taylor. She self-medicates with the oversexed behavior. She takes the bipolar meds, feels better, then believes she's cured. Once she stops the medication, she goes back to the manic behavior."

I crossed my arms on top of my belly. "Just because Sarah Meyers has a chemical disorder doesn't mean she's completely out of her mind. Can you honestly tell me none of this behavior results from my mother's narcissistic belief that the world revolves around her?"

"I understand you're hurt, Taylor, but she's still your mother."

I rolled my eyes. "She wasn't any kind of a mother, and we both know it. Even before the divorce, she pawned me and Gabe off on any babysitter she could find. Rabbi Peretz had quite a bit to say about the synagogue *bubbes* who watched me and Gabe so she could go out and engage in her affairs while you were at work."

"I wasn't aware of this," my father said quietly.

"Rabbi Peretz listed off several women who complained that Sarah Meyers never spent time with her own children but seemed to spend an awful lot of time with Yossi. People saw them around town while my mother lied and claimed she needed a sitter to run errands."

"Yossi convinced your mother she was being neglected by me because I worked so much in those early days," my father said. "Your mother wanted a certain lifestyle, but she didn't understand how much work it took to get it. I'll admit our marriage suffered because of the hours I kept."

"What about you? Rabbi Peretz mentioned you had your own synagogue bunny on the side."

My father shifted uncomfortably.

I repeated my question.

He still didn't answer.

I sighed wearily. "You can cut the act because I already know her name. Rabbi Peretz said it was such a relief not carrying everyone else's secrets anymore. If you were so busy working, how did you find time to cheat with Karen Farber?"

At the mention of her name, my father looked like he'd seen a ghost.

"Secrets have a way of eventually coming out," I continued, "and if you think it doesn't matter anymore because it happened thirty years ago, you're wrong."

"Your mother warned me how you hold onto grudges, Taylor. I should have listened. I don't even know why I came here," he said, rising from my sofa.

"You know exactly why you came here," I shot back. "You hoped to tickle my ears with tales of long suffering so that I'd forgive you for abandoning me and my brother. I'm sure my mother also informed you of every button and trigger to push in order to manipulate me. Let's not pretend your eagerness to meet with me had anything to do with telling the truth."

"You wouldn't believe me even if I tried," he accused.

"Well, why don't you try actually telling the truth?"

I sat down, hoping my father would follow suit. He returned to the couch with a dramatic sigh.

"When did Karen Farber enter the picture?" I asked.

"Only after I discovered your mother's affair with Yossi Peretz."

"None of your behavior makes sense. How could you divorce my mother, allow her to lie to me and Gabe and ruin any chance of a relationship with your own children, but then carry on an affair with her for the past nine years? You told Lexie that Sarah is your soulmate. Are you a glutton for punishment, or are you just that selfish and stupid?"

"Your mother and I have a connection," he offered weakly.

"What do the two of you have in common besides your toxic, sexual relationship? Sarah Meyers will always look out for Sarah Meyers first and foremost. If you think she won't discard you the second you stop allowing her to completely control your life, then you're in for a rude awakening. How could you leave Elaine, who by all accounts seemed to love you, whose kids adore you, to be with someone like my mother?"

"No matter what your mother's done, Taylor, she'll always be the one for me," my father said. "I loved Elaine —I swear to you I did—but nobody could ever compare to Sarah. I couldn't handle Elaine's jealousy anymore. She never understood our connection."

I closed my eyes to grieve for the lives impacted by the obscene selfishness of my parents.

Breaking through my thoughts, my father said, "You can't fault me for loving your mother, Taylor. If anything, I thought you'd be happy we could be a real family again."

"Happy?" I choked. "What about Elaine and her children? Should they be happy that you lied to them and used them like a temporary band aid? Elaine had every reason to suspect you were still attached to my mother. It's exactly how things turned out!"

My father puffed out his chest. "Once again, you're jumping to conclusions, Taylor. Elaine didn't like how much I talked about you and Gabe. Your mother didn't factor into any of this until ten years into the marriage. Elaine also wanted a father for her own children. She said fate brought me a son and daughter to replace the ones that were stolen from me."

"Stolen?" I repeated in disbelief. "I think you mean the kids you didn't even bother fighting for."

"Go read the court records," my father said tersely. "Your mother made me look like a monster. Back in those days, fathers had almost zero rights. A mother had to be a serial killer before they'd give full custody to the father."

"I've read through the records, and you contested nothing," I said angrily. "I was forced to grow up and do Sarah's job as a mother because you didn't do your job as a father. She used you as her perpetual excuse because we had no other means of support."

"I sent checks, Taylor. Your mother scribbled 'we don't need your blood money' on them and sent them back. After the fifth or sixth one, I got the message. I tried sending birthday cards to you and your brother, but your mother made sure you never saw them."

"If all of that is true, then explain this magical connection you claim to have with my Sarah Meyers. She sabotaged your marriage. She sabotaged your relationship with your biological children. Yet, you somehow find yourself back in her clutches as if the past never happened. Do you have some sort of personality disorder too?"

"It's complicated."

"No, it isn't," I said. "It's simple. If you really cared about me and Gabe, you would be livid over what my mother put us through. You would be furious about how she slandered you, neglected us, and then used you as the convenient scapegoat. How could you play father of the year with Lexie and Micah but ignore your own flesh and blood?"

My father sniffed indignantly. "Stop living in the past, Taylor. Your mother and I have moved on from all of that ancient history, and you should too. I thought you Christians were all about love and forgiveness."

"Insulting me doesn't change any of that ancient history," I said coolly. "I want to know how you can be in a relationship with someone who has no problem ruining the lives of whoever gets in her way. I want to know how you can blame your poor, second wife for your own inability to let go of the past. I want to know how you can have the audacity to paint yourself as the victim of Elaine's jealousy when she had every right to feel it."

My father clenched his jaw and sat in petulant silence.

Not finished with him, I added, "Your so-called 'connection' with my mother is a sick, codependent relationship where you validate each other's lies so neither of you has to face the reality of what you've done."

"You don't have much of an opinion of me, do you?" my father said with self-pity. "I suppose I can blame your mother for that, but it seems like you've already made up your mind."

"Dad," I said, using that title as a last ditch effort to reach him, "this is the part where you start telling the truth and taking responsibility for your behavior."

"I've already told you everything!" he said, throwing his arms up in exasperation. "What more do you want from me, Taylor Marie? You may think your mother and I did something wrong because of your narrow, right wing view of things, but what about honoring your mother and father?" he accused.

At that oft quoted line from the Sarah Meyers manipulation playbook, I finally had the closure I needed. My heart cut off the final string of hope that Jonathan Meyers would be any different than my mother. Truly, these two were cut from the same narcissistic cloth.

"Though my father and mother forsake me, the Lord will lift me up," I quoted from *Psalm 27:10*.

"Forsake you?" my father said incredulously. "I'm sitting right here, Taylor. If you would just give me and your mother a chance instead of judging us based on the past, you would see how much we love you."

I shook my head. "I don't think either of you understand

what that word means. Love isn't turning a blind eye to someone else's sin. Love isn't abandoning your children because you can't keep your lust in your pants. Love isn't committing revenge adultery to get back at your spouse for cheating on you. What you call 'love' is what I call selfishness, and I want no part of it."

My father rose to his feet and looked me up and down dismissively. "I hope you experience the pain of having a child reject you the same way you've done to me and your mother. Maybe then, you'll realize the suffering you've caused your own parents and actually feel sorry for the things you've done, Taylor Marie."

Not missing a beat, I said, "You can take your curses and send them straight back to the pit of hell where they came from. How dare you speak that garbage over me or my child! Your other children will find out every disgusting word you've said."

"They'll never believe you," my father sneered, dark eyes glittering angrily. "They'll just see the bitter, unforgiving—"

"Lies that you've said about my sister?" Gabe interrupted, entering from the office located just off of my family room.

"Gabriel?" my father gaped. "How much did you hear?"

"All of it," Lexie said, joining Gabe along with her brother, Micah, trailing behind her.

I gestured to the baby monitor sitting on my end table. "My siblings agreed to humor me and listen to our conversation. I told them if I was wrong, I would be more than happy to eat crow and make an effort to welcome you into my life. Thank God, they were also willing to listen and see if I'd been right about you all along. Having Rabbi Peretz vouch for me went a long way in convincing them."

"How could you do that to Mom?" Micah said, nearly as tall as my own husband. "She loved you, Dad, and you broke her heart! Mom was jealous because you talked about Sarah just as much as you talked about Taylor or Gabe. How can you pretend we didn't hear you bellyaching about 'Sarah this' and 'Sarah that'? You couldn't talk about your other kids without blasting their mother."

Cornered, my father's eyes darted from kid to kid, hoping for a crack in the armor of anger encasing all four of us.

"I can't believe your husband puts up with this kind of behavior," my father finally said, his eyes returning to me. "I feel sorry for my grandson already."

Ian emerged from the office, the last one to reveal his presence to Jonathan Meyers. He walked directly to my father and knocked him unconscious.

CHAPTER 39

A WEEK BEFORE MY DUE DATE, MY WATER BROKE.
Twenty-four hours and a lot of epidural later, I held my firstborn
son in my arms. I stared at him and cooed, my heart never
knowing such love.

"He's perfect," I whispered to Ian with our heads bowed
close together.

The labor and delivery nurse snapped a few photos of us
then quietly cleaned up the room. When she removed the blood
pressure cuff from my arm, I sighed in relief.

"I've got bruises, don't I?" I said. "Nobody ever warns you
that epidural pain relief means having that stupid thing squeeze
your arm every fifteen minutes."

Ian chuckled. "If you didn't have such low blood pressure,
the cuff wouldn't keep attacking you."

"Talking about your parents helped," I said. "Amazing how
the possibility of Thomas and Nancy Horner actually attending
the bris managed to spike it right back up."

"When do you want to talk about it?" Ian asked, standing up to pack our belongings onto a rolling cart.

"Does it have to be now? Oh, Ian! Look at him! He's holding my finger!"

My husband grinned, his height making it easy to see as he deposited my overnight suitcase onto the cart. "That's a healthy grip our boy has."

"Not to mention when he wants milk," I groaned. "The nurse said they'll send a lactation consultant tomorrow night to show me what to do. Rebecca sent a text and told me she'll be over in the morning to show me first."

Ian laughed. "She's a great friend. I know you're going to miss her."

"We can talk about the move later. I just want to enjoy every second with this boy before the adrenaline wears off and I pass out from exhaustion."

Picking up my Bible and hospital water cup from the tray table, Ian said, "God's timing is something else, isn't it?"

I grinned, still bent over our precious boy and savoring the silky feel of his skin against my fingers. "Daddy's office is letting him wait three months before we have to move, yes they are," I cooed.

"The HR manager in the Florida office gave me the name of her realtor. I'm guessing you want me to handle it since you're going to be busy with Mr. Growth Spurt."

Laying my darling boy over my heart so I could stroke his back and focus more of my attention on my husband, I said, "Pick the three you like best, love, and I'll use my real estate brain after that. I'm curious what kind of house you'd choose for us."

"Apparently, they all have pools, at least the area I'm thinking of."

I smiled sleepily. "Just find one with a kiddie gate already installed around it."

"Are you ready to go from condo life to mowing your own yard and maintaining a pool, Taylor? No more HOA to cover all of the house repairs? Hurricane season? Mutant animals? Crazy snowbird drivers who think they're still in New York?"

I laughed. "I won't be the one cleaning the pool, mowing the yard, or disposing of insect and reptilian wildlife that dare to encroach on our property."

"Still have your sword I see," Ian said with a smile. He finished with the last of our belongings and sat down on the edge of the hospital bed next to me. "We start a brand new adventure today, my queen."

"That we do," I said. I reached out to squeeze Ian's hand. "Do you really think your parents were serious about moving to Florida just to see their grandson? Didn't that bother Kate or Fiona?"

Fatigue set in, and Ian's head flopped forward before he could answer.

"Go lie down, love," I said, gesturing toward the window seat that doubled as an expectant father's couch. "You need to rest."

"What about you?" he said, bending over to kiss the top of my head. He gazed lovingly at our son, and tears wet my eyes. I silently thanked God for giving my child the father I'd never had. I thanked Him that even the pain could be used as a reminder to savor all of the blessings in my life.

I cupped Ian's cheek and pulled his face down for a kiss. "I love you. I never thought I could be as happy as I am right now."

My husband bestowed me with the most beautiful smile I'd

ever seen. It was a smile I later realized he'd also passed down
to our son.

The following week blurred by in between snatches of sleep
and prep work for our son's bris. Rebecca recruited the services
of her mother-in-law and grandmother as well as Ian's sister.
Rebecca's grandmother, Tabby, chirped happily in the kitchen
while I nursed in the family room.

"So, you won't tell us the baby's name until tomorrow?"
Kate asked for the hundredth time.

"No, and stop bugging me," I said, sticking out my tongue.
"You'll wake up the baby."

From the kitchen, Rose Margolin said to Rebecca, "I can't
believe you're making your own mayonnaise for this egg salad.
Looks like that stick blender we got you for Chanukah has been
put to good use."

"When you've got two babies two and under, there's a lot of
Food Network going on," her daughter-in-law replied with a grin.

Rose pulled a face. "Rebecca, you've had those cooking
shows on long before the kids were born. We both know you
love to reinvent food."

Jumping into the conversation, Tabby looked up from a
skillet of sauteed onions and said, "Taylor, did you get those
naming certificates for you and your brother from the synagogue? Did they tell you your Hebrew names?"

I burped my sleepy son on my shoulder. *"Talyah Miriam* is
what the certificate says."

"Pretty," Rose and Rebecca said at the same time.

"Did it include your parents' names on there?" Tabby asked
as she turned off the burner.

"It does," I said, "but I don't want the connection to Sarah
or Jonathan Meyers anymore."

"It's a miracle you got your father to admit to anything," Rebecca said. She scooped her homemade mayo into a plastic container. "Even smarter that you used the baby monitor to feed everything into the next room."

"Well, I didn't wear a police wire, but it definitely had elements of crime drama to it," I said, referring to Rebecca's own experience catching a confession. "I'm just thankful I can put all of it behind me."

"What about the former sister-in-law?" Rose asked as she walked to the family room and sank onto the leather sofa across from me. "These are nice. I don't think I'm getting up."

"What about my mock chopped liver?" Tabby called from the kitchen. "Rose Margolin, how can you abandon an old woman in her hour of need?"

"Nobody would ever believe that you're helpless, Nana," Rebecca said, planting a kiss on her grandmother's cheek. "We can switch out the attachment on my stick blender to make your chopped liver."

"I'm not sure how it will taste with sunflower seeds instead of walnuts, but you said she's got allergies," Tabby said, pointing toward me.

Rose exchanged a quick glance with me and laughed silently. "She means well," she mouthed.

I smiled back. "It's fine. I can't tell you how grateful I am for all of this."

"After what you've been through, *bubbeleh*, you deserve it!" Tabby said. "It's so nice to see young people doing things the right way. I don't know where we went wrong with your parents' generation, Rebecca darling, but at least Eleanor has finally seen the light."

I noticed the quick tears in Rebecca's eyes. "It's been a long road, Nana, but I'm glad some good came out of what my parents have done."

Tabby gave Rebecca a side hug. "They never deserved you, bubbeleh, but I know you and Ted will do a much better job with your girls than we did with ours."

"Thanks," my friend whispered back.

Clearing her throat, Kate said, "So...back to the former in-laws?"

I nodded, acknowledging her request. "Whatever issues Brian and Chloe had appear to be resolved—if we can believe FaceSpace. Of course, it's Brian posting all of this gushy, love nonsense. Chloe still has me blocked, so I have no idea what's going on. Either way, it's not any of my business."

"What's all this *mishigas*?" Tabby asked, gesturing between me and her granddaughter. "Rebecca said there's been some trouble with your former sister-in-law, but she never gave me any details."

"A few months back, my ex brother-in-law tried to con me into babysitting his kids. Brian said his wife ran off with his brother, aka my former, philandering husband. He acted like I owed him free childcare."

Tabby tsked, "Why would you owe him anything? Who did they use for babysitting all of the other times?"

"Exactly," I said, "which is why I told him no way."

"Is it possible he was telling the truth?" Kate asked, finishing with the last of her fruit salad chopping and joining Rose on the sofa.

I shifted my son in my arms and enjoyed the heavenly aroma of newborn baby. "At this point, it really doesn't matter. I'm just glad we're moving away from all of the Ross and Meyers family drama and starting over in a new place. It's a new beginning for us and the baby, and I'll be glad to leave my past behind."

"Except we're all still here," Kate pouted. "The least you could do is let me hold my nameless nephew before you move seven hundred miles away."

I rolled my eyes good naturedly and smiled. "Fine, fine. Go see Auntie Kate," I said to my son while Kate eagerly hopped off the couch to hold the baby.

"Oh, he looks just like Ian," she cooed, studying his features. "You're going to be so handsome, aren't you, my sweet boy?"

I stretched my back in the recliner and savored a few seconds with empty arms. Standing and stretching again, I took the opportunity to run to the bathroom and close the door without fearing something terrible would happen to my son in the one hundred and eighty seconds spent away from his side.

When I returned, Rebecca and Tabby stood in front of my refrigerator counting out all of the main dishes and side dishes for the bris the following day. My darling son lay fast asleep in his aunt's arms, and Rose dozed lightly on the sofa.

"Taylor, do you need anything else for tomorrow?" Rebecca called.

"Food wise or ceremony wise?" I asked, approaching her and Tabby in the kitchen.

"Do you have a *kiddush* cup for the wine?" she asked.

"She can borrow one of ours," Rose said, eyes still closed. "Steve and I have more than enough."

"What about the pillow cover?" Tabby said to me. "Did you find one of those, or are you borrowing from Rose and Steve?"

I grinned. "I found this gorgeous pillow cover online two months ago. The embroidery is stunning."

"*Nu*, so what are we waiting for? Go get it!" Tabby said imperiously.

Rebecca chuckled at her feisty grandmother. "Easy there, Nana. Taylor just had a baby. Besides, we can see it tomorrow."

"Did you get the Mandelwitz?" Tabby fired next. "You know I do prefer a good chianti, but I'm sure little baby what's-his-name will like that kosher sugar water they have the gall to *wine*."

Exchanging a laugh with Rebecca, I said, "That's passive aggressive with a sense of humor."

Tabby shrugged her shoulders. "What? It was worth a shot even though Taylor holds secrets better than Fort Knox. You hang onto someone like this, bubbeleh," she said to Rebecca. "Such a shame she's moving away to the promised land."

"Nana, she's not moving to Israel," Rebecca said, confused.

"It was a joke, darling. Lighten up. It was the dream of every New Yorker I knew back in the fifties to make it down to Miami. Of course, your grandfather and I didn't make it further than Cordele, but it is what it is."

"Sharp as a tack," I mouthed to my friend.

Rebecca nodded and grinned. "Are we forgetting anything else, Nana?"

"Why are you asking me? I had two girls. Go ask your husband's mother before she falls into a coma on the sofa over there."

"I'm tired, not deaf," Rose quipped.

"Just making sure," Nana said with a mischievous twinkle in her dark eyes.

"Taylor, do you still need a kiddush cup," Rose asked, "or are you going to use a regular wine glass?"

"Rabbi Peretz said he could bring one, but we'd love to borrow one of yours."

"Consider it done. What are you dressing the baby in?"

"Rabbi Peretz says to put him in a nightgown so it's easier

to cover his legs when he finishes the circumcision. I found this super cute outfit at the baby store. Comes with a hat." I held it up for everyone to see.

Rebecca and Kate cooed at the same time.

Rose was ready with her next question. "Are you doing the shtick with Elijah's chair?"

"We're using the recliner for that," I said.

"I assume Ted and Rebecca are performing the role of *sandekim*," Rose said.

"Is there a cheat sheet for all of the Jewish lingo?" Katie called from behind the back of the couch. "I'm glad the rest of you know what you're talking about, because I am totally lost."

"The *sandek* is someone given a special place of honor during the bris," Rose explained. "They help carry the baby from the mother and father to the mohel and back again. It's mostly just ceremonial. In some cases, they put the pillow on the sandek's lap and circumcise the baby."

"Which Ted is *not* doing," Rebecca said quickly.

"Rabbi Peretz said he has a special table and pillow for the baby," I said. "We'll have it set up by the fireplace, but we'll start the processional from the foyer. Kate, your parents were actually very excited about the whole thing and wanted a chance to carry the baby on the pillow."

I heard my sister-in-law choke on her own spit from the other side of the room. "Are you sure we're talking about Thomas and Nancy Horner here? They're about as multicultural as a loaf of white bread."

"Apparently, they're very impressed I'm one of God's chosen people," I said, quoting my mother-in-law from our reconciliation three days earlier.

"Well, wonders never cease," Kate deadpanned. "White bread indeed."

CHAPTER 40

THE FOLLOWING DAY, OUR SMALL GATHERING OF friends and family positioned themselves in different parts of the house as we began the circumcision ceremony. Thomas and Nancy looked genuinely happy and very proud of their son. Kate said she bore no ill will toward her brother and was elated their parents finally began treating Ian with the respect he deserved.

My own brother and his fiancée, Genevieve, stood a few feet in front of my in-laws ready to take the pillow and carry our son into the awaiting arms of Kate. From there, Kate gently passed the pillow to me. My heart burst with joy and something else I couldn't quite define as I brought my son the rest of the way into the family room. I placed him on our recliner doubling as Elijah's Seat.

Rabbi Peretz beamed at me, his long prayer shawl tucked around his sides with some sort of special brace. Loudly, he proclaimed, "Happy is the man You choose and bring near to dwell in Your courtyards; we will be satiated with the goodness of Your House, Your Holy Temple."

Deep in my gut, I felt a connection to something much larger, as if my tiny family of three had stepped into the weight and history of God's covenant made with Abraham four thousand years earlier. This was no rote ceremony for me, my husband, or our son. Though Ian and I both knew our salvation came from Jesus and not from our observance of holidays or ceremonies, we also felt the presence of the Holy Spirit so strongly over the entire bris. More than we could even understand, we had become a part of a worldwide community of faith stretching across history.

Looking green, Ted Margolin offered a tremulous smile as he picked up the pillow and brought it to Ian. I chuckled inwardly at the thought of Culver's Mighty Margolin scared of anything, but he seemed genuinely petrified by the entire circumcision process. It certainly seemed God's mercy that he and Rebecca were blessed with two beautiful girls.

Once Ted handed our son off to his father, Ian's chest puffed with pride and joy at our precious boy. I glanced over and saw Thomas with his arm around Nancy, both of them transfixed by the Jewish ceremony. Rebecca came up beside me and put her arm around me.

"How are you holding up, Mama?" she whispered.

"Ask me again, after he cries," I whispered back, my nerves on pins and needles.

After chanting the prayer in Hebrew, Rabbi Peretz said, "Blessed are You, Lord our God, King of the universe, Who has sanctified us with His commandments and commanded us concerning circumcision."

At this point, the ceremony became a blur because the sound of my son's wails tore my heart out. I counted down the seconds until he was back in my arms. Rebecca later told me my boy barely cried as Rabbi Peretz offered several, generous droplets of Mandelwitz to help ease his pain.

"Today we give this boy the name *Eitan Shmu'el,* Ethan Samuel," Rabbi Peretz announced to the room, and then he continued with further blessings. My chest ached at the sound of my son's cry, more than ready to nurse him and comfort both of us.

"Open your eyes, Taylor," Ian said, walking toward me with our precious Ethan. Donning a smaller prayer shawl loaned to us from Rabbi Peretz, Ian recited the blessing for the wine in both Hebrew and English, impressing the room with his pronunciation and commitment to this rite of passage.

Although I had earlier volunteered to chant the prayer of God's blessing over our family for bringing us to this happy season, I sat glued to the recliner. I was too shell shocked to do much more than nod when Rabbi Peretz offered to say it for me instead.

I stared down at my son, eager to escape the room and the noise. I simply wanted a few quiet moments with my boy after all of the nerves and emotion of the bris ceremony. Ian wrapped his *tallit* around Ethan and I as Rabbi Peretz pronounced God's blessing for the families of Israel.

"*Yivarekh'kha Adonai vayishmerekha. Ya'er Adonai panav eleikha v'khunekkah. Yissa Adonai panav eleikha v'yasem lecha shalom.* May the Lord bless you and keep you. May He make His face shine upon you and be gracious unto you. May He lift up His countenance upon you, and give you peace," Rabbi Peretz said, a smile clear in his voice. "*Mazel tov* on this wonderful day, and congratulations to Ian and Taylor, the grandparents, and all of the friends and family gathered together."

"Can we eat now?" Fiona asked her mother.

With Ethan secure in my arms, I dashed upstairs to his

nursery and allowed the commotion of our downstairs attendees to become white noise.

"No wonder Zipporah was so mad at Moses for making her circumcise their son," I said to Ethan as he eagerly latched on to nurse. I stroked his soft skin, tears falling from my cheeks.

Following a gentle rap at the door, Ian poked his head inside. "You okay, Taylor?"

I shook my head. "Ian, I'm glad we did this, but I don't know if my heart could survive another one. Did you watch the actual circumcision?"

My husband grinned. "I thought it was pretty cool actually. Ted, not so much."

I chuckled softly, and my shaking chest roused Ethan from his milk coma. He deepened his latch and began to nurse again in earnest.

"Are you coming back downstairs, or do you want me to bring you some food up here? You need to eat, Taylor."

"Just give me a few more minutes with the baby. I know he's going to sleep for a while, but I'm not ready to face everyone yet."

Ian walked over and planted a kiss on my forehead and then Ethan's. "We did it, Taylor. Next step is the move."

I sighed. "From one thing to the next."

"I thought you loved the excitement," Ian said jokingly.

"I've had my fill," I replied, my voice lowered as Ethan had fallen back asleep. Gently, I released his latch and propped him on my shoulder for a burp.

Ian simply stared at both of us in wonder. "This is the dream," he said, dark eyes full of love for both of us.

"Yes it is," I whispered.

Standing up, I walked silently to our bedroom and deposited

Ethan safely into his bassinet. Checking the baby monitor to make sure it was on, I left our bedroom door ajar.

"He'll be okay, won't he?" I asked Ian.

"Between the Mandelwitz and the milk, I think he'll be taking a nice, long nap for us."

I released the heavy breath sitting in my lungs and then leaned forward to rest my head against Ian's chest. He stroked my back in small circles, the two of us enjoying a private moment before we descended back into the melee of congratulations, pictures, and Steve Margolin good naturedly teasing his son.

"If you and Rebecca try for a third, you better hope it's another girl!" he guffawed. "Ted, the look on your face was priceless!"

"Slow down, Grandpa!" Rebecca said, scooping up a bite of egg salad. "We just gave you a second granddaughter in less than two years. Mom and Dad need a break too."

"And we already have Asher and Riley," Rose added for moral support. "Oh, Rebecca! This egg salad is fabulous! You really outdid yourself!"

My friend's megawatt smile appeared, and I felt a tinge of sadness. I realized how much I would miss Rebecca and her family and how much her story had helped shape mine. If not for the pep talks, the challenging words, the arm extended down to pull me out of an emotional ditch, I may have missed the blessing of my husband and son. I would have spent the rest of my life not really living at all.

And to give credit where it was due, I couldn't ignore the impact of Kyle Goldstein in my life. God had placed a soft spot in my heart for him, and I sat dumbfounded when I received a text message from Kyle several weeks following the bris.

"What did he want?" Ian asked

Looking up from my long neglected guitar, I replied, "He wants to talk to you, love. He said he has some questions, and he thought you might be able to help."

"Your ex-boyfriend wants *my* help?"

"Apparently."

"Well, what did you say?"

"I told him I would talk to you and ask. So, I'm talking to you and asking," I said with a tiny grin on my face. I strummed an old favorite on the guitar, humming along.

Ian crossed his arms over his chest and looked at me like the most beautiful creature he'd ever seen. "It's even better than it was the first time I heard you sing that song."

"Hardly. I can't go full voice unless I want to wake up our son."

"Are you ever going to just accept a compliment for what it is, Taylor? I don't say these things just to boost your ego. I meant what I said."

"So, you're telling me that sleep deprived, bags under the eyes, belly pooched Taylor Horner sings better than that hot young thing in her mary-jane platform heels and twenty pounds of eye makeup?" I teased.

"How much longer until Dr. Donaldson says I can make love to my wife again?" Ian asked, his eyes staring intently into mine

I blushed as Ian's direct approach left me in no doubt of his sincerity.

"Well?" he prompted, wiggling his eyebrows just to make me laugh.

"Assuming everything is as it should be, you've got two weeks left, cowboy."

Ian placed a dramatic hand over his heart and groaned. "Torture! Pure torture!"

"You're incorrigible, Ian Joseph Horner! Now, if you will excuse me, I have some callouses to put back on my fingers."

Despite the packing, downsizing, and holes patched in the walls to prepare my townhome for resale, I made time to play my guitar daily, even if just for five or ten minutes. Rebecca warned me that life after children totally upended any previous reality, and my guitar felt like a connection to my past long before Ian, Mitch, and the rigorous journey God had used to refine me. Expressing my love for God through music and song brought those reminders that my Father in heaven had not forgotten about me.

A week before our move to South Florida, Ian finally agreed to meet with Kyle. Knowing we would be out of the state a mere seven days later meant that even if Kyle hatched some ridiculous plot to sabotage my marriage, badmouth me, or somehow woo me back, he would be unsuccessful on all fronts. When Ian came home, he looked bewildered and elated.

"Where's Ethan?" Ian said as he greeted me with a kiss hello.

I muted the television. "Our Little Man has been nursing like a wild beast. I finally got him to sleep about an hour ago. Hopefully, he'll be out until midnight."

Ian nodded. "If you're too tired to talk, we can discuss this in the morning."

"Love, you look like Moses coming down the mountain with two tablets in your hand. Tell me what's going on."

"I had no idea how this night would go," my husband began. "We've both prayed about it, and I knew God had my back no matter what stunt Kyle might try."

"So, what happened?" I said.

"I heard about your last conversation with Kyle from his perspective. Taylor, you really shook him up. He said he started

EX NIHILO357

reading his prayer book, talking to God, and looking for answers."

"Did you lead him to Christ?" I said with bated breath.

"I didn't need to," Ian said, breaking into a full grin.

"What do you mean?"

"Before I go on, I want to let you know I asked Kyle if I could share his story with you or if he wanted to keep it just between the two of us."

"Oh," I said, the flame of my excitement dimming considerably. "Well, that was very thoughtful of you, love. What was his answer?"

"That guy is hard to read. I don't think he's still hung up on you, Taylor, but he needs more time to heal."

"I'm not following."

"Kyle said how much he regrets everything and you deserved better than what he was willing to give. He said he was happy for both of us but sad for himself."

I paused to consider all of Ian's words. "So if he's happy for us, why is he sad?"

"He's mad at himself for what his pride and selfishness cost him. He told me not to let you go."

I smiled sadly. "Well, that was sweet."

"I told Kyle he had nothing to worry about on that front. You are the woman of my dreams, and we established early on that I am not an idiot."

My smile widened. "No, love, you are not an idiot."

"So, to circle back to the original purpose of the meeting, Kyle said he ran into Mitch and Chloe."

My mouth fell open. "Excuse me? What does this have to do with Kyle praying and looking for God? And what do you mean he saw them?"

"Apparently, Brian wasn't lying when he said Chloe left him."

"But for Mitch?" I asked, my voice coming out like a high pitched squeak. "I don't get it. How would Kyle even know who they are? He's never met either of them."

"Kyle admitted to cyber stalking some of the important people in your life during one of his lower points. He looked up Mitch, Brian, Chloe, and me on FaceSpace. He recognized them as soon as he saw them."

"Where was this?" I said. "I had no idea Mitch was even in town."

"Where does any excitement happen with Kyle Goldstein?"

I smacked my forehead. "How does Carlos even stand all of the drama at Los Bravos anymore? They should turn it into a *telenovela*. Did Kyle confront them?"

Ian shook his head. "That's where the story gets even better."

I raised an eyebrow.

"Kyle didn't initially confront Chloe and Mitch. Instead, God confronted *him*. Even though Kyle said he wanted to punch both of them for how they'd betrayed you, God showed Kyle his own betrayal of you. He also said God confronted him about all the ways he had behaved like Mitch to other women."

"So, he didn't punch Mitch?"

"No. Instead, he got down on his knees in the middle of Los Bravos and gave his life to the Lord. He said he got up off the floor, walked directly to Chloe and Mitch, called them both by name, and told them to repent and go home to their spouses. They were so stunned, they looked like they'd seen a ghost."

"Wow," I breathed. "That's incredible. Did they listen?"

Ian shrugged. "I guess we'll find out soon enough. In the meantime, Kyle asked if I could recommend some reading materials or if I knew of a church that might be more knowledgeable about Jewish traditions. Taylor, he's totally on fire for Jesus, but he's just as passionate about really understanding what it means to be a Jew."

Tears pricked my eyes as I remembered my conversation with Kyle Goldstein in that very same living room over a year earlier. The words spoken had not fallen on barren soil. God had used the ugly from my life to deliver Kyle from the ugly in his own. I thanked God for the purpose Kyle Goldstein had served and for the path that led me toward my fashion model husband masquerading as a web developer.

"What are you thinking, Taylor?" Ian asked. "I told Kyle I'd ask if you knew of anything. Of course, the first person that came to mind seemed too ridiculous to mention, so I bit my tongue."

I burst into a fit of joyous laughter. Ian's declaration served as confirmation of what the Holy Spirit spoke to my own heart. God's sense of humor never ceased to amaze me.

"I guess I'll text Ted in the morning," Ian said with a grin. "At least the Margolins won't be short on excitement once we're gone."

"Oh, my love," I said cupping my husband's scruffy face in my palms, "they're going to turn this city upside down for Jesus. And it's going to be glorious!"

EPILOGUE

IAN FLEW DOWN TWICE TO MEET WITH THE REALTOR in East Palm Bay and look for houses. He videoed himself walking through our top choice so I could experience the home vicariously. I laughed at Ian's colorful commentary poking fun at the way I would probably use my realtor lingo to describe the house.

"And would you look at this wall-to-wall tile flooring?" he said with panache, "absolutely perfect for a mom who's tired of scrubbing baby boy rain showers out of the carpet."

I paused his video in a fit of hysterics, certain I might have woken up Ethan. Checking to ensure my baby remained asleep, I continued the video.

"Here you have your wide open living area," Ian prattled on, the laughter of our realtor clear in the background. "You could throw a fabulous, first birthday party, host a seder big enough for all of South Florida, or simply cozy up and enjoy the sunset beyond your wall of sliding glass doors."

Moving from the renovated kitchen to the screened patio, Ian began to hum some sort of offkey fanfare as the camera view traveled out to the swimming pool with a small hot tub attached to it. I oohed and aahed appropriately, a swimming pool being the one luxury feature my mother's palace did not possess. I could already imagine a tableau of our son making cannonball dives into the pool, Ian grilling outside, and me picking fruit from the citrus trees visible in the backyard.

Turning the camera to selfie mode, I beheld my husband's handsome face. "Taylor Marie Horner, I hope you've enjoyed this virtual tour of our potential future home. The place looks even better in person, by the way. Text me after you've seen the video and let me know what you think."

"Did you see that?" our realtor asked from off camera.

Laughing and praising God, Ian switched the camera back to standard mode, and the last image on Ian's home tour featured not one, but two rainbows in the sky.

"Taylor," Ian sing-songed into the camera, "I think this is our sign. Speaking of, tell me when you're ready to sign the paperwork. Anthony can get everything ready online."

When the video finally stopped with an image of double rainbows frozen on my phone, I glanced up toward heaven. Thankful beyond words for all that God had done for me, I sang the song that had once served as my milestone marker with Mitchell Ross. I'd since reclaimed the song as my own. When I shared photos of our future home with my brother and the Margolins, they all agreed God was great indeed.

Ian, Ethan, and I settled into our new tropical environment fairly easily. We closed on my townhouse on a Wednesday and then drove to Florida to close on our new home that Friday. A few walks with Ethan in the stroller brought me in contact with some wonderful neighbors. Another young mom lived a few doors down with a two and four year-old, and two sets of empty nesters flanked us on either side.

True to their word, Thomas and Nancy relocated down to Florida six months after we moved. They insisted they'd always dreamt of retiring further south and finally had a reason. They purchased a small condo overlooking a golf course, and Thomas took great delight in naming all of the professional golfers he saw from the comfort of his screened patio.

God used those rough, early months of my marriage to work on my in-laws, especially when they ran to Kate with their tales of victimhood during my pregnancy. Uncharacteristic for easy-going Kate Horner, she finally let her parents have it. She later recounted how she had never intended to share so much, but she was glad she'd told her parents the unfiltered truth. To their credit, my in-laws apologized to her and Fiona and promised to do better.

Not long after my own confrontation with my father, Thomas called Ian to apologize. The two of them spent several hours on the phone hashing through the past. Although hesitant to believe their change of heart wasn't due to the impending arrival of their grandson, Ian insisted it was real. When they visited me in the hospital following Ethan's birth, I saw the differences in both Thomas and Nancy. It provided much needed comfort as Jonathan and Sarah Meyers did their level best to create chaos once the bris happened without them.

Seated at our patio table while Ethan happily jumped in his bouncer, Nancy and I peeled pink grapefruits recently plucked from our backyard tree. Ian and Thomas stood by the poolside grill engaged in conversation and outdoor burger cookery.

"This is the life, hmm?" Nancy said.

"Growing produce in my yard or seeing father and son getting along?"

Nancy's smile grew. "All of it. I wish your parents knew how much they're missing. That little Ethan could charm a snake."

"Let's hope he doesn't try. I nearly fainted when I saw one swimming in our pool last week."

Nancy shuddered involuntarily. "Well, nevermind then. Have you heard anything about that home group Ted and Rebecca started? What about that Jewish friend of yours who came to Christ? Was he able to sort through whatever bad blood he has with the Margolins?"

I grinned. "I think everyone has made peace with the past. Rebecca said Kyle brought a girl to their Bible study, and it looks pretty serious. For his sake, I hope this is the one."

"Well, that's nice. And your brother is getting married soon, isn't he?"

"Next month. We'll be flying up for the wedding. Jonathan and Sarah Meyers have not been invited, but I'm bracing myself in case they try to crash the wedding."

"Burgers are done!" Ian called. My husband opened the patio door, and his father stepped in front holding a heaping platter. My son fussed from his jumper, hungry and eager to be held.

I pulled Ethan into my arms while Nancy began assembling dinner plates for everyone. Thomas set the burgers down while Ian sat down next to me.

"Thomas, Taylor was just telling me about her brother's wedding," Nancy said, handing me enough food to share with Ethan. "For everyone's sake, I hope her mother behaves."

I laughed and shrugged. "With Sarah Meyers, who knows? For right now, though, I'm going to let tomorrow worry about itself. My plate has more than enough for today," I said, glancing down at two hamburgers, watermelon, and homemade potato salad.

"Amen," my husband said.

From my overflowing plate, our son snatched a fistful of hamburger and shoved it in his mouth. I had more than enough happiness to share.

ACKNOWLEDGMENTS

To all of the amazing authors I have met and become friends with on Instagram. You ladies are incredible. Thank you for the honest feedback, encouragement, and friendship. Thank you for loving my books as much as I love all of yours!

Hannah Linder for once again creating a gorgeous cover and helping to take the muddle in my head and transforming it into real life.

My precious Amy for walking with me through fire, holding my hand, praying with me, and encouraging me to my very soul. You have truly been God's instrument of peace.

Irina, Kellie, and Kacie who made surviving COVID and two rounds of quarantine an example of God's love in action. You're all angels.

Mike and Kasea, thank you for the love, the encouragement, the Ulta care packages, and for just being awesome. Mahalo!

Mom and Ted, I'm so happy you two are so happy. You both deserve it.

Tuna Michele, thank you for letting me use your cappuccino maker, have a safe place to write and relax, and occasionally letting me win a round of backgammon.

My beautiful babies who have survived the unspeakable, continue to grow and thrive, and daily remind me of God's love. I could not be more proud of the three of you.

My Lord and Savior who has left me in no doubt of his faithfulness, His power, His victory, or just how much He loves me.

COMING 2022

BOOK 3 IN THE BEAUTY FOR ASHES SERIES:
TIKKUN OLAM: RESTORING WHAT
WAS LOST

Poppy Berman gave her heart to Jared Levine at sixteen years-
old, but twenty years later, Jared crushes her dreams and their
marriage with the mention of just one name. More than two
years after their separation, Jared swoops back in spouting new
religious beliefs and says he wants his family back. At the same
time, the pale green eyes of Joe Trautweig urge Poppy toward a
future free from Jared. Poppy has always used medieval fiction
and its tales of courtly love as an escape from real life, but she
finds herself as the heroine in her own story of romance,
intrigue, betrayal, and redemption. Either man Poppy chooses
brings her toward a holy book she's never understood, and it
challenges her own beliefs about God. Ultimately, Poppy must
decide if repairing what's been broken (*tikkun olam*) means
restoring the past or creating something brand new.

EXCERPT FROM TIKKUN OLAM: RESTORING WHAT WAS LOST

"I THOUGHT JARED LOST HIS MIND WHEN HE TOLD ME he didn't love me. When he told me he never really loved me," I said, unburdening myself to my coffee shop buddy.

"Brutal," she gasped. "And your husband just woke up one day and decided all of this?"

"That's how he tried to sell it anyway. Like he had some magical epiphany." Shaking my head ruefully, I said, "Two strangers bond in line over coffee flavors a month ago, and now I'm telling you my whole life story."

My new friend shrugged. "Sometimes you meet people but feel like you've known them forever. My rabbi growing up called that *beshert*. Two people destined to meet."

"So, you're religious?" I asked, though hardly much of a practicing Jew myself.

She shook her head vehemently and laughed. "Pretty sure they would have taken me out and stoned me by now."

I grinned back at her. "I can relate."

"So what happened?" she asked, eager to hear the rest.

"My ex tried blaming our failing marriage on me. Eventually, he confessed to cheating on me with my best friend from high school. He wanted a sugar mama, not a wife, and he found that with her. They broke up last March, and then he suddenly found Jesus. Now, he says he wants me back and acts like I'm just supposed to forget everything that happened."

Multiple emotions crossed my friend's face while a steaming cup of *Vincenzo's* coffee sat motionless in her hand.

"Am I oversharing?" I asked. Her honey brown eyes that ordinarily expressed warmth and humor showed wariness instead. "I don't think you've even told me your name yet, and here I am spilling my guts. Maybe they put truth serum in the flavor shots."

"Not oversharing," my friend said after a lengthy pause. "It, um, just hits close to home."

I raised an eyebrow. "Did you have someone cheat on you too?"

She took a sip before answering. "Let's just say I've been on both sides of the cheating spectrum."

"Have you ever been married?" I asked with my usual candor.

My coffee buddy surprised me when tears filled her pretty eyes. "Almost."

"Ah," I said in slow understanding. "Didn't work out?"

"Yeah, you could say that," she said. As another customer entered behind us and placed his order, my nameless friend startled violently. Excusing herself, she barreled out the front door.

"What was that about?" I murmured above the rim of my cinnamon latte. Taking a sip, I checked the wall clock. Ten more minutes before another work day began at Culver, Incorporated.

"Poppy?"

Surprised that I missed the telltale sound of jangling keys and squeaky loafers, I glanced up at Culver's top, east coast producer, Ted Margolin.

"I didn't realize you'd started coming to Vincenzo's too," he said.

"You can thank your wife for turning me into a regular here. The last time we met up for brunch, Rebecca told me I had no idea what I was missing." I lifted up my cup in salute. "She wasn't kidding. The grounds at home are great, but I love the old world Italy feel of this place."

Ted's expression seemed as pained as my coffee buddy's when a silver car sped away in the parking lot. "I thought that was her."

"Who?" I said.

Ignoring my question, Ted continued, "I saw you guys talking through the window, but her back was to me. That's definitely her, though."

"Who?" I repeated.

"Jessica Goldstein."

Realization dawned as I pieced together Rebecca Margolin's description along with that of my former coworker, Taylor Horner. Knowing both Rebecca's and Taylor's stories firsthand, I marveled at not recognizing Jessica sooner.

"How do you know her?" Ted asked, pulling me from my thoughts.

"I don't," I said. "Jessica and I struck up a conversation about a month ago in line, but we never exchanged names. She's just a familiar face when I scrape together some extra nickels for Vincenzo's."

"Extra nickels, huh? Do I need to talk to Phil about properly compensating our marketing department again?"

I shook my head. "Your wife has already threatened to get

me a Vincenzo's gift card because she knows anything else I would just spend on my kids. I have three little mouths to feed and clothe. They take priority over Mommy's fancy bean water."

I expected a grin from the father of two toddler girls himself, but Ted frowned. "My wife isn't a gossip, Poppy, but she did share a few details about your current situation. Have you and your children settled in okay?"

I grimaced, not liking the idea of anyone at work knowing about my personal life. Strangers seemed safer somehow. Then again, Jessica Goldstein was only a stranger because we'd never been formally introduced.

"Sorry, Poppy," Ted said. "I didn't mean to violate any confidence shared between you and Rebecca."

I exhaled a slow sigh. "She's your wife. I get it. I do appreciate the concern, and yes, we've adjusted to living in my parents' basement. We've been there for over two years."

As the entry bell jangled against the glass door of Vincenzo's, I saw another coworker of mine enter the small coffee shop. Joe Trautweig stopped short and smiled at both of us.

"Private party, or can I join too?" he asked, winking at me.

I found myself involuntarily blushing at an attractive, single man showing me a shred of attention. And I felt ashamed, knowing I had a broken marriage and three, devastated children at home. Clearing my throat, I said, "That's okay, Joe. I need to get to my desk anyway. Ted has bestowed the marketing department with yet another Request for Proposal."

"I think the letters 'RFP' might be the most hated letters in all of commercial insurance," Joe said, giving me a conspiratorial grin.

I swallowed down a lump of panic and turned my full attention to Ted. "Gentlemen, I'll see you back at the office."

Snatching my worn coat and shoulder bag, I attempted a hasty exit. Instead, I heard a laughing Joe call my name.

"You forgot your coffee," he said, extending the cup to me.

Taking it from him, our fingers brushed. I felt awareness along every nerve ending from the brief encounter. Meeting Joe's pale green eyes, I knew immediately I was playing with fire. As old as I felt with a tweenager and two other children in elementary school, I had not forgotten the sensation of physical attraction.

"Thanks," I mouthed, feeling my accelerated heartbeat down to my toes.

"See you in the office, Poppy," Joe said. He made my name sound like something beautiful rather than the result of former hippies naming their only daughter after an opioid producing plant.

Against my better judgment, I ventured a closer look into pale eyes studying me as if truly seeing me for the first time. I circumvented any further conversation with a curt nod and a hasty retreat.

OTHER WORKS BY ANA WATERS

BEAUTY FOR ASHES SERIES
Book 1: Tabula Rasa: Writing a New Story

CPSIA information can be obtained
at www.ICGtesting.com
Printed in the USA
LVHW051456180122
708822LV00013B/1014